MW01116144

NATIVE FATE

BOOK 10 ZEB HANKS MYSTERY SERIES

MARK REPS

This book is a work of fiction. Names and characters are products of the author's imagination. Any similarities between the good people of southeastern Arizona and tribal members of the San Carlos Indian Reservation are purely coincidental.

NATIVE FATE

ISBN: 9798603654560 paperback

ALSO BY MARK REPS

ZEB HANKS MYSTERY SERIES

NATIVE BLOOD

HOLES IN THE SKY

ADIÓS ÁNGEL

NATIVE JUSTICE

NATIVE BONES

NATIVE WARRIOR

NATIVE EARTH

NATIVE DESTINY

NATIVE TROUBLE

NATIVE FATE

NATIVE ROOTS (PREQUEL NOVELLA)

THE ZEB HANKS MYSTERY SERIES 1-3

AUDIOBOOKS

NATIVE BLOOD

HOLES IN THE SKY

ADIÓS ÁNGEL

OTHER BOOKS

HEARTLAND HEROES

BUTTERFLY (WITH PUI CHOMNAK)

ACKNOWLEDGMENTS

A chance encounter with the Sheriff of Graham County some thirty year ago planted the seeds for this series. I want to thank him. Kathy, my wife, was with me then and with me now. I thank her for help and encouragement. When I was reading this book aloud to my grandson, Max Jensen, he offered up a couple of creative hooks that helped me bring it across home plate. Thanks, Dude. I must also mention all the constant readers without whom I would only be writing for myself. Thank you.

1

CORPUS DELICTI

Chindi had required but a single kill shot to complete her mission. She then cleaned the gun, stuck it in her pocket and left the building. She tossed the alcohol wipes and her gloves into the burning barrel, waiting only for the surety that the flames devoured the evidence. Chindi got in her car and headed northwest to a remote landing strip where a plane was waiting to take her home. Her heart was lustful for gold and power. Such was the payoff for her deed.

Two men in white coats lifted what remained of the Sheriff of Graham County's body from the aluminum gurney. Taking extreme care not to spill as much as a single drop of blood, they placed the body on a large sheet of thick plastic. Without a word passing between them they pushed the cart to the side and began wrapping the body tightly in it. They completed the task by securing the plastic shut with duct tape.

With the aid of Dr. Steinman they spent another hour removing every iota of evidence concerning the procedure that had just taken place. The three men scoured the room from top to bottom one final time making certain no confirmation of their actions was left behind.

Dr. Steinman spoke. "We're done here. You know what to do."

The men nodded in unison. One man opened the door, left it ajar and stepped outside into the desert air. The veil of darkness was creeping in quietly from every direction. The desert was at that special time of day when all was hushed. In an area as remote and unpopulated as Cochise it was highly unlikely anyone would see them. Still, caution was the most valuable currency. Glancing in all directions, the man waited until he was certain there were no witnesses to what would happen next. He reached into his pocket, took out his car keys, pointed them and with the press of a button popped open the trunk of the Lincoln Town car. Retracing his steps, the man re-entered the building.

"We're good to go."

The second white-coated man stood near the head of the dead sheriff's body. The first man bent down to grab the plastic sheet at the foot end. Together they hoisted the body, exited the building through the open door and walked directly to the trunk of the car. A second piece of plastic covered the bottom of the trunk. On the edge of the plastic was an anchor and a pair of heavy metal chains. They laid the body down on top of the plastic and closed the trunk. Behind them Dr. Steinman shut the door to the building, locked it, grabbing the door handle one more time. Certain that it was sealed he walked to his car as if it were just any old day. A moment later he was heading down a dusty road in a westerly direction. In an hour and a quarter, driving at precisely the speed limit, he would be safely home with this incident but another foggy memory in a long line of illicit deeds.

Seconds later the men in the Lincoln Town car were headed toward their destination. It would take them one hour to get to Safford. Based on three nighttime trial rehearsal runs, in roughly eighty minutes they would have climbed the road up Mount Graham to Riggs Lake. They had been instructed to pull into the trailer park just across from the Mount Graham Market. Once there, they would stop in front of lot six and flick their headlights twice. An unknown accomplice living in the trailer would turn his outside light on and off to acknowledge the situation.

The signal would set in motion a phone call to an inmate at the

Federal Correctional Institution just two miles down the road. The imprisoned computer hacker would then set a timer for seventy minutes. When that time had passed, the men in the Lincoln would be at the edge of the parking lot for Riggs Lake. The hacker inmate had one job, shut down for two hours the motion activated sensors that ran all the video cameras in and around Riggs Lake.

Two hours would give the men enough time, with an extra forty-minute window of room for error, to remove the sheriff's body from the trunk, tie a heavy anchor around his waist and engird each arm with thick metal chains. An inflatable rubber safety boat had been pre-set for them at the eastern edge of the Riggs Lake campground. Rowing to the deepest part of the 11-acre lake would take no more than six or seven minutes once the body was loaded into the boat.

L oading and dumping the body went smoothly. A glance at their synchronized watches let them know they still had seventy-three minutes to get the inflatable boat off the lake. Once ashore they took out their knives and sliced large holes into the inflatable boat. They rolled up the deflated raft, placed it in an oversized baggie and tossed it in the trunk of the Lincoln Town car. Then, as instructed, they headed down the winding mountain road with their lights off. When they passed the two-mile marker, they turned their lights back on.

When the promise of a new day would begin, both men would be sleeping restfully, richer for the work they had just done.

2

TOWN TALK

The Safford City Hall tower clock chimed eleven times, signaling the owner of the Town Talk Café that the breakfast rush and morning coffee breaks were officially over. Maxine Miller, owner of the café, scurried about in preparation for the lunch crowd which would start wandering through the door in roughly thirty minutes.

In the back of the otherwise empty café late breakfast arrivals, Jimmy Song Bird and Jake Dablo, slid into their usual booth. An instant later Maxine poured the blackest of black coffee, collected from the bottom remains of the café's three Bunn-O-Matic pots, into cups with their names marked on them.

"You're a darling, young woman," said Song Bird, placing an ancient healing hand on what he perceived to be an aching back.

Maxine returned the compliment with a quick but brief smile, silently mouthed a thank you, spun around and hustled back to work. When she was out of earshot, Jake turned toward Song Bird and spoke softly with a hint of mystery in his tone.

"Heard the news?"

"I didn't see any smoke signals rising with the awakening dawn."

Jake's only reaction to Song Bird's witty response was to gently blow into the hot cup of brew he gripped in his craggy hands. The small ripple of waves his breath created reminded him of a trick common to 1940s noir films. The ploy involved reading tea leaves and prophesying a person's fate. Song Bird silently cast his gaze on his friend of some six decades. Fate floated in the balance that stood between their close friendship and eternity.

Jake remained mesmerized by the ripples on the surface of his black, muddy coffee. He spoke to Song Bird without shifting his gaze from the cup.

"I heard on the morning news that Senator Russell has some health issues," said Jake. "Serious ones."

Song Bird listened, waiting a long time before giving a seemingly incongruous response.

"A highly skilled and quite beautiful female Chinese doctor came to me years ago. She wanted to study me."

Jake glanced up from his coffee. These long-time friends often shared stories never manifest in a linear fashion. Jake knew Song Bird's story would be told in a manner unique to the old Indian medicine man.

"Study you?"

Jake's words were frankly incredulous.

"Was she beautiful?"

"She was as beautiful as a baby's smile."

Jake rapped his knuckles twice on the table.

"Continue, please, my friend."

"She wanted to know exactly what an Indian medicine man does."

"How long ago was this?" asked Jake.

"Decades. I was young and inexperienced. I was still wet behind the ears at that point in my life."

Jake reached over and ran a finger behind Song Bird's extraordinarily large, old man, Apache ear.

"They still are. Wet that is."

"One is always a babe in the woods when it comes to knowledge," responded Song Bird. "Learning is an eternal task."

"Amen."

"The beautiful young Chinese doctor and I agreed to exchange knowledge. I explained the healing power of smoke to her. In return, she taught me about how the organs of the body are directly related to human emotions. I remember her telling me that a man with a cold heart will have illnesses in his organs that could kill him," said Song Bird.

Jake discretely rubbed his chin, circled his tongue around the inside of his mouth, clicked it twice against the roof of his mouth and placed his hand over his heart.

"The news did say Senator Russell suffered from many diseases of the heart," said Jake.

"But he is old. Old men rarely have strong hearts. I believe the reporter may have been simply guessing."

"Fake news?"

"Lazy reporting," replied Song Bird.

Jake and Song Bird sat quietly pondering the potential fate of Senator Russell, a man they considered to be somewhat of a nemesis to them and an extremely dangerous adversary of Zeb Hanks, former sheriff.

The back door of the café flew open and was slammed shut immediately by a gust of wind. Jake and Song Bird lifted their eyes from the table to see Rambler Braing standing next to them. The former Tribal Police Chief was quite literally panting with what appeared to be a peculiar, breathless exhilaration. He slid in the booth next to Song Bird. He was sweating and smelled of nervousness.

"Did you hear?"

"About Senator Russell's health?" asked Song Bird. "That is old news at this table."

"No. Hell, no. I could give a rip if that dirty, old bastard is dead or alive. Actually, I might prefer it if Usen disguised as Shoz-Dijiji were to snatch him up and carry his mortal dust away on the wind."

Rambler paused, took a moment to catch his breath, and, in the process, changed the odd look that covered every inch of his face. His breath reeked with a strange, stale dampness.

Jake had never heard of Shoz-Dijiji. He assumed Rambler was referring to the devil. Song Bird knew the literal translation of the Shoz-Dijiji. Its English interpretation was 'the black bear that lived in the mountains'. Song Bird found the reference intriguing.

The old men's contemplative thoughts moved much slower than Rambler's tongue. The younger man blurted out his obvious question.

"What do they say is going on with Senator Russell? And who are the 'they' that is talking about him?"

"Bum ticker," said Jake, glancing at Song Bird. Song Bird then paused before adding one more word. "Maybe."

"The 'they' who are talking about him are the TV talking heads."

Rambler wasted no time in ripping back into Senator Russell.

"Big fucking deal. I guess the only thing that might surprise me is that a man who has no heart would have any heart problems."

"Ironic would be a good word for that," said Jake.

"So, what do you have to tell us that's so hell fire important that it's stealing your breath and making it reek of dank mustiness?" asked Song Bird.

Rambler checked the smell of his own breath by placing a flat hand in front of his face and blowing into it. He shrugged his shoulders before offering up an explanation to his friends.

"Garlic, onions and road kill stew."

Rambler got up and poured himself a cup of cold, dark coffee.

"Fair enough," said Jake. "The news?"

Rambler slid in closer to his friends, once again checking his breath.

"Oh, yeah, the news. Sheriff Black Bear is dead."

The news caught Song Bird and Jake totally off guard. The news of Black Bear's death was as strange as hearing of a jegos blowing in January. This time it was Jake's and Song Bird's breaths that had been stolen.

"Do you mean dead as in D-E-A-D, dead?" asked Jake.

"Is there another kind of dead?" asked Rambler.

Jake shook his head from side to side.

"Then, that's exactly what I mean. They found his body by acci-dent late yesterday afternoon."

"Found his body?" asked Song Bird.

"Where did they find Black Bear's body?" asked Jake.

"In Riggs Lake," replied Rambler.

"Who found it?" asked Jake.

Their conversation was interrupted by the sirens of two Safford Fire Department trucks blaring down Main Street.

"Probably another grease fire at Tiny's Leaping Frog Café," said Rambler.

Jake reached into his back pocket and pulled out a Whistler analog portable police scanner. He fiddled with the settings for about ten seconds before he got the information he was after.

"Fire at 16592 Quail Run Road," said Jake.

"That address rings a bell," said Rambler.

"It ought to," said Song Bird. "That's Black Bear's house."

Oddly, not one of the men found it the least bit surprising. Both had been around enough fires to know that the Arizona sunshine beating through a stray piece of glass onto paper or dry grass could easily cause a fire to flare-up. It had been a week since Black Bear's house had burned to the ground. That seemed like a proper amount of time for everything to dry out and create a latent secondary fire. Without saying a word about the possible fire, they returned to their conversation at exactly the spot they had left it.

"Some federal guys. Environmental types. They found Black Bear's body."

"What do you mean, environmental types? Eco-freaks? Save the nasty, destructive, red squirrel types? Or just old farts who are hanging onto memories of their hippie dippie days in the 60's?"

Jake was only half-joking when he mentioned the Mount Graham red squirrel, an endangered species found in the Pinaleño Mountains of which Mount Graham was the keystone. The red squirrel had destroyed the wiring of many buildings on the Mount as well as chewing into the electrical systems of cars, trucks and RVs in the area. Since they were considered an endangered species by the feds, you could not trap or shoot them. Jake considered them a species with more enemies than friends. Song Bird, knowing the Mount was the natural home of the red squirrel carried a more relaxed attitude regarding the damage they did.

"No, none of those. The real federal government. The EPA," explained Rambler. "Regular working guys...and gals."

Jake and Song Bird chuckled at the political correctness of the younger man. Liberal multicultural sensitivity was sweeping the country, even the far reaches of Graham County. It appeared to Jake and Song Bird that the liberal body politic had grabbed a toehold in Rambler. They shrugged it off as a sign of the times. Like much they had witnessed in their lives this too would either become the new normal or disappear in the sands of time.

"What the hell is the EPA doing up there if it doesn't have to do with the red squirrel?" asked Jake.

"Damned if I know, but I heard straight from Alma Greenbough's lips," said Rambler. "She's the one who takes food up to Geronimo Star in the Night. Alma said Geronimo Star in the Night told her that the federal government brought in a couple of truckloads of heavy equipment with some fancy gear. He figured they were checking on the ecological condition of Riggs Lake."

"Did Alma say how my old friend Geronimo Star in the Night is doing?" asked Song Bird.

The men all knew Geronimo Star in the Night as a traditional Apache healer who performed sweat lodge ceremonies on Mount Graham. The ancient healer had his lodge tucked away in a place the Apaches considered to be sacred and holy. It was the place where Apaches could commune directly with Usen, the Creator of all things. It was known by The First People as the Holes in the Sky. Geronimo Star in the Night not only directed the sacrosanct ceremonies on Mount Graham but was known for having the somewhat unique gift of clairvoyance through time.

"Alma says he's doing pretty good for a man who is over 110 years old."

Song Bird chuckled. He knew full well that Geronimo Star in the Night was not a day over 106, but he loved to prank people about his age.

"The EPA must have too damn much money left in their annual budget if they're spending it on anything remotely linked to the Rez," asserted Song Bird.

"Probably doing a fish count in Riggs Lake," suggested Jake.

"Alma Greenbough talked to some of the female EPA workers. One of them is her cousin. They told her a senatorial subcommittee headed by Senator Russell was responsible for getting the work done up there. They were happy because they were getting paid overtime wages."

The mere mention of Senator Russell, whom they had been discussing only moments earlier, brought Song Bird and Jake back to full attention. Something, likely something devious, was in the air. They silently recounted every word they had just heard. The stony silence was eventually broken by a confused Rambler.

"What? What are you guys thinking about so intently? Let me inside the circle."

It was a reasonable request. Song Bird eventually broke the solemnity with a simple but obvious question.

"Are you going to call Zeb? You should let him know about Black Bear's death?"

Jake, head tilted downward, pondered the question.

"He's still in Paris on his honeymoon. I really hate to disturb him."

"He is going to want to know," replied Song Bird. "After all that passed between the two of them, I think Zeb is not going to want to be the last one to hear about this."

Jake smirked. "I don't think Zeb bears any ill will toward Black Bear, the sheriff. But I don't think he'll miss Black Bear, the man. I suppose Zeb should know...eventually."

"Call him."

Song Bird's reiteration sounded like a command rather than a suggestion.

"Helen will call him. She'll let him know," suggested Jake.

"Maybe she will. Maybe she will choose not to bother him. Helen respects the sanctity of marriage. Plus, she is a romantic. I would suppose that she views the honeymoon as part of the entire process of wedded bliss."

Jake once again became quiet as he dove into the memory bank of his own life. Eventually he directed a question at Song Bird.

"Did you want to be interrupted on your honeymoon?" asked Jake.

"I didn't even have a phone back then. In fact, there was no phone service on the Rez back in those days," replied Song Bird.

"Times are different," said Jake. "People feel like they need to know things right away. Sometimes I think the 24/7 news around the clock business creates little more than universal anxiety, fear and depression."

Song Bird pulled a cellphone from his pants pocket. With his long, spotlessly clean and deeply ridged fingernails, he pulled a few stray pieces of lint off the face of the mobile phone. He placed the cellphone on the Formica tabletop and slid it across the table. It came to a halt directly in front of Jake.

"Back then I didn't even own a phone. Now, I can call anywhere in the world on a phone that isn't even connected to a wall," said Song Bird. "Nothing stays the same."

"But your first car was a horse, too," said Jake. "Wasn't it?"

Song Bird smiled. Jake stared peculiarly at Song Bird, wondering why Song Bird would have international calling on his cellphone. Song Bird implicitly understood Jake's expression.

"I've been there."

"Where?"

"Paris...France."

Jake's eyes turned back to the phone.

"Then what time is it in Paris?" asked Jake.

"Probably about seven or eight in the evening."

Song Bird's instant response took Jake by surprise.

"Zeb and Echo are probably eating supper," said Jake. "I heard everyone eats late in France. Me, I eat when I'm hungry."

"Maybe he and Echo are strolling along the Champs-Elysées," suggested Song Bird. "If I was on my honeymoon in Paris, that is one of the things I would be doing."

"You say you've been to France?" asked Jake.

"Once. It was nice, but the French people acted strangely around me because I am what the French referred to as an *Indien Américain*."

"As opposed to what?" asked Jake.

Song Bird put a dab of red, hot sauce on his thumb and proceeded to rub it on the middle of his forehead. "Dot, not feather, as the kids say," replied Song Bird. "I am feather, not dot."

Jake laughed out loud as he watched the hot sauce run down the bridge of Song Bird's nose. When Song Bird's eyes began to water, the old medicine man laughed along with his friend. Being the butt of one's own joke and playing the part of the fool was a testament to the closeness of their friendship.

"What do you mean they acted strangely around you?" asked Jake.

"I had on some traditional Indian clothes. I was speaking at a convention of The International Tribes. There were tribes from all seven continents. I must admit that being part of the global tribal chain was pretty cool."

"When was this?" asked Jake.

"1973."

"How'd you get asked to go and speak? Why'd they ask you?" asked Rambler.

"Who knows?" Song Bird shrugged his shoulders. "Honestly, I don't really remember. It was a strange time when the Indian was being worshiped by culture vultures from around the globe."

Jake grunted with a fair amount of disinterest.

"What the hell was Paris like?" asked Rambler.

"Good, strong coffee, but it came in little, tiny cups." Song Bird held his finger and thumb about an inch apart.

"As potent as the Apache brew you cook up?"

Song Bird rolled his eyes.

"No. Do not be foolish. But the coffee was not all that bad."

"Anything besides the coffee that sticks out in your memory?" asked Jake.

"I guess I remember the Catacombs and the Notre Dame Cathedral most of all."

"Bummer about the recent Notre Dame Cathedral fire," said Rambler.

Jake and Song Bird nodded in assent.

"A building almost nine hundred years old, what a shame to see it burn." added Jake.

"I've seen pictures of the catacombs...all those skulls," said Jake.

"Six million of them. I think I saw them all," replied Song Bird, shaking his head. "It made my heart feel empty. Treating the dead with such a lack of respect is disgraceful. I remember thinking at the time that the French were barbarians. But I also thought that if they were barbarians, they would have made better warriors."

"Speaking of dead bodies. Where is Black Bear's body now?" asked Jake.

"The morgue. I figured that was where it would be taken so I stopped by and talked with Doc. Saw the body, too."

Jake fiddled with Song Bird's cellphone. Song Bird gently grabbed Jake's wrist.

"Call him."

"What do I have to dial to reach France?" asked Jake.

"01133 plus Zeb's number will get you to him."

Jake punched in the number. Rambler and Song Bird watched silently.

3

PARIS

Zeb and Echo let their eyes drift across the River Seine toward the Eiffel Tower. As Zeb's eyes took in the landscape, Echo magically pulled a bottle of Pinot Noir she had hidden in the bottom of their picnic basket under some cloth napkins. She proudly displayed it for Zeb's approval.

"It's from the Burgundy region in the eastern part of central France."

In the little picnic basket Echo had prepared, there was also a small package of cheese. She deftly extracted a cutting knife from her pocket and sliced them each a small wedge.

"This is Cantal. It is an uncooked, pressed cheese from the Auvergne mountains."

Zeb eyed the cheese with pretend suspicion.

"Looks like cheddar to me."

Echo pecked Zeb on the cheek. *"Je t'aime."*

Zeb knew Echo was telling him that she loved him. He butchered his attempt to repeat the phrase. That he tried so hard and stumbled over fairly simple words brought joy to Echo's face.

"It still looks like cheddar cheese to me."

"You're ever the connoisseur."

Zeb grinned as only a man of passion involved with a new experience is able.

"You can take the sheriff out of Arizona, but you can't take Arizona out of the sheriff," said Echo.

Zeb was on a roll and he knew it. The chambers of his heart were bursting at the seams with joy. He tasted the Cantal, mimicking the man at the cheese shop, acting as though he was sampling a fine wine.

"*Merci, mon chéri*. How do you say, lovely?"

"*Charmant*," replied Echo.

Zeb's echoed response was nothing short of blissful.

"*Charmant. Charmant. Charmant. Charmant!*"

Zeb, who had rarely crossed over the lines of Graham County, gazed up at the Eiffel Tower with the same admiration he felt for Mount Graham. He implicitly understood the greatness of both wonders. Lying back, he pointed toward the tower.

"How tall is that dang thing?"

"It's 3224, or, 1063 feet tall and it contains two and a half million rivets." answered Echo.

"That's a fact that I'll etch into my memory for all time and eternity."

"You'd better remember it. Otherwise, I'll begin to think you're taking me for granted," replied Echo.

"*Au contraire, mon amie.*"

Echo feigned fainting and dropped her head onto Zeb's lap.

"You're such a sweetheart for trying so hard with your French."

Echo laughed freely as she snuggled in tightly against her husband. She wanted to breathe in the moment, to inhale and become part of Zeb's very essence. Life simply could be no better than it was at this exact second.

With her parents having come along on the trip to watch their twins, this was the first moment since Elan and Onawa had been born that Echo felt totally free from responsibility. Her heart pulsated joyfully. All was well with the world. Her children were healthy. She was imminently comfortable in becoming the Knowledge Keeper of all the People. She felt that soon she would be able to share more of that sacred knowledge with Zeb. But, most of all, at this moment she was more deeply in love with Zeb than her imagination had ever allowed her to believe was even possible. As her eyes glanced toward the cloudless, blue sky, Zeb's cellphone ringtone cut like a knife through her joyously beating heart.

Zeb had placed his phone next to the open bottle of wine. He glanced down.

"That's odd."

Echo assumed it was her parents wanting to tell her about the next fantastic achievement the twins had accomplished. Something like crawling and turning over completely in a single move. They were so proud of their grandchildren that it almost embarrassed Echo.

"What's odd?"

"It's Song Bird."

"Normally, I would say don't answer," said Echo. "Especially right now. But if Song Bird is calling you, it has to be important."

Zeb let it ring four times. A tiny voice in the back of his head told him not to answer. Echo reached over, picked up the phone, pressed the accept button and slipped the phone into Zeb's palm. Her eyes were commanding him to do the right thing. Her practicality stunned him. Zeb greeted his old friend with a hint of sarcasm.

"Song Bird, I didn't expect to hear from you on my honeymoon."

The voice coming through the speaker startled him somewhat.

"Zeb, this is Jake."

"Jake, I really didn't expect to hear from you, especially on Song Bird's phone. What's up?"

"You busy?"

"I'm on my honeymoon."

"I know."

"Echo and I are having our first few hours of peace and quiet since the twins were born. Wouldn't say I'm busy, but I am enjoying myself."

"Okay. I getcha. I'll be brief."

"What is it?"

From thousands of miles away, Zeb could make out only a few words of a conversation that consisted of three men talking over one another. He instantly recognized Song Bird and Rambler as the other men. He envisioned them sitting at the Town Talk. The one thing that struck him the most was the sound of astonishment in Rambler's voice.

"Jake. Jake??"

"Yeah, Zeb?"

"Did I just hear what I thought I heard?"

"What do you think you heard?" Jake's response was typical Jake.

"I heard someone say Sheriff Black Bear is dead. Did I hear that right?"

"Yup. You heard right."

As direct as the response was, it didn't quite register in Zeb's mind because it came from out of left field.

"What the hell happened? What's going on?"

"Don't exactly know. Here, I'll let you talk with Rambler. He just now brought the news to Song Bird and me. You know about as much as we do."

As the phone was being handed between the men, Zeb quickly whispered to Echo that he had just heard that Black Bear was dead. The look on her face was hardly one of pity for the deceased sheriff. In fact, she appeared unfazed by the news. Echo had seen much death up close and personal. She had even held death in her arms as she shared the final breath of a dying soldier. The end of life was no stranger to Echo Skysong.

"Zeb, that you?"

"Yeah, it is. Now what's this I hear about Sheriff Black Bear?"

Rambler, having already allowed the news of Black Bear's demise to sink into his consciousness, had a few questions of his own before replying to Zeb's question.

"What's Paris like?" asked Rambler. "Always wanted to go there. I always thought the Folies Bergère would be quite the experience."

"We can discuss my trip later. Now, what's this about Black Bear?"

"He left here a little over a week ago, the day before you left, if I recall right. I'm not one hundred percent certain on the timing. Might've been the same day you left."

Jake interrupted Rambler. Zeb could not make out what they were saying. Rambler handed the phone over to Jake.

"Like Rambler said, this all started almost exactly when you left Graham County, Arizona, USA, for Paris, France. Black Bear said he was taking some vacation time. At least that's what he told Helen and Helen shared that information with me a few days back. According to Kate, he left Helen a phone message saying he was taking a couple of weeks off."

"Did he say where he was going?" asked Zeb.

"According to the message he left Helen, and she said she saved the message on the answering machine, Black Bear said he was headed down to the Sea of Cortez. He said he was going to scratch deep-sea fishing for striped marlin off his bucket list."

"Nothing wrong with a man taking a vacation," said Zeb.

"There's nothing at all wrong with a hard-working sheriff kicking back a little and enjoying life," said Jake.

Jake's words rolled off his tongue with more than a whit of cynicism. Song Bird, Rambler and Jake shared some words that Zeb couldn't quite make out. Evidently, it had to do with the ability for all of them to be in on the conversation.

"I'm putting you on speaker," announced Jake.

"Good idea. Can you all hear me okay?"

Yup."

"Go on."

"But that isn't all there is to it," continued Jake.

"Enlighten me, Jake. No sense beating around the bush."

"Well, actually there's a couple of more things. For one, in addition to leaving the phone message for Helen, Black Bear left a note on Kate's desk with some specific instructions regarding a few things that are currently on the docket."

"Okay. That makes sense. That's the right thing to do. I'm glad to hear he was being professional in his duties. I'm assuming you got this information from Helen."

"I did. It makes sense and it is the right thing to do. But he ended the note by telling Kate that she might end up in charge of the sheriff's office very soon. He also asked her in the note to keep that information under her hat for the time being."

"Did he say why?"

"He implied, at least this is how Kate interpreted it, that he was considering retiring and spending the rest of his days fishing," said Jake. "He mentioned a foretelling dream that he was paying attention to."

"A dream?"

"That's what he said. Sounds like a premonition to me, but you'll have to talk to Kate if you want more than that."

"Did Kate keep the note Black Bear left for her?"

"Yes, of course she did."

"Is it in Black Bear's handwriting?" asked Zeb.

"Good question for which I don't have an answer," replied Jake. "Remember, I'm retired now. I don't have my finger on the pulse like I used to. I rather enjoy being a man of leisure."

"I just thought that your usual level of curiosity might have had you asking Kate," said Zeb.

Jake realized he had been lazy about the whole thing.

"I should have. My bad. Then again, you know damn good and well that Black Bear was not high on my list of those I consider to be one of the good guys. It's a nasty to thing to say about the recently deceased, but actually I'm just fine with the fact that he's no longer walking around upright."

"Obviously you're not the only one who felt that way," replied Zeb.

"And," Jake continued, "I had no idea about any of this until right now. The fact that he was thinking about retiring this early into his term is just as surprising to me as it is to you. We both know this job is no piece of cake, but I thought he'd have the cojones to hang in there at least for one full term. That, too, makes him a real piece of work in my book."

Zeb was stunned.

"Retiring? That's bullshit. Hell, he hasn't even been on the job a year yet."

"I know. But here's the real kicker. He wasn't down ol' Mexico way."

"Where was he?" asked Zeb.

"My guess is he never so much as crossed the county line."

"Yeah? What do you mean?"

"Seems the EPA was getting complaints about pollution in the lake..."

"Lake? What are you talking about? What's a lake got to do with Black Bear's death?"

"Riggs Lake."

"Really? Riggs Lake? What's it got to do with Black Bear's death?" asked Zeb.

"I'll let Rambler speak. He seems to know more than either me or Song Bird about that part of the story."

"Zeb? This is Rambler."

"Go on," said Zeb. "Tell me what you know."

"The EPA recently hauled in some fancy equipment. They trucked it all thirty-five miles up Mount Graham to Riggs Lake. They had to shut down one side of the road for the better part of half a day. A few birder tourists were really mad about it."

This time it was Song Bird who did the interrupting. He purposefully said it loud enough that he could be certain Zeb could hear it.

"The big boys in Washington must have too much money left in their budget if they're spending it on anything remotely linked to the Rez," said Song Bird.

"Song Bird, you know the land up by Riggs Lake is both Rez and federally owned," interjected Zeb.

"We all know that," added Rambler. "The land around Riggs Lake is co-jointly owned by individual tribal members, the tribe itself, as well as the federal government."

"If that's the case, they probably had two sources of money, tribal and Department of Interior. Anyway, among other things that they were up to, they were using grappling hooks to clear the lake bottom of natural and manmade debris."

"Who ordered the dredging? Do you know?" asked Zeb.

"The Feds."

"No, I mean specifically."

Zeb heard Jake, Song Bird and Rambler talking amongst themselves. They quickly concluded that since it was a bureaucratic decision they might never know.

"You hear that?" asked Rambler.

"I did and I agree."

"Guess what they dragged up?" asked Rambler.

"Er, let me take a wild stab at this one. Black Bear's body?"

"Bingo. You might also be interested in hearing he was wearing an anchor necklace and iron bracelets."

Zeb thought that was a pretty shitty way to go, even for an asshole like Black Bear, especially if they tossed him in while he was still alive. He also considered the anchor and bracelets might just be somebody's way of sending a message.

"Where'd you get all your information?"

"Got some from Alma. She wasn't fifteen feet away from the body and she talked to a bunch of the feds who were figuring things out. I also figured they brought the body down for Doc to have a look at. I stopped by the morgue and had a chat with Doc and a look at the body."

Zeb knew environmentalists were not crime scene experts and that Alma was old and could likely have gotten things confused. But Rambler might have learned something from Doc.

"What can you tell me from your visit with Doc?"

"Fish ate up Black Bear's eyes right down to the sockets. Both of 'em."

Zeb blinked and shook his head. Fish eating the eyeballs out of a head was an easily imagined and quite brutal image.

"Anything other than that?"

"He took a single shot, probably execution style, from a low caliber gun, likely a .22 to the base of the skull."

"I take it the wound size told you it was small caliber?"

"The entry wound fit the specs of a .22. Anything larger would have blasted a large hole in his head. And, there was no exit wound."

"Do you have a theory on that?"

"Likely the shooter used .22 shorts. The firing pin was probably off center because there wasn't enough power behind it to push the bullet through the skull."

"Makes sense. What else? Anything?"

"That's all we've got at the moment. Wait a second. Alma Greenbough overheard one other thing. It's probably nothing," said Rambler.

"The new sheriff might have to hire Alma. She's better than any of you guys at gathering information," said Zeb.

"She got all that information because one of the feds working up there was her gossipy cousin," replied Rambler.

"What else have you learned?" asked Zeb.

"The body was pretty damaged from being in the water. His body was shirtless according to Alma. The skin was discolored from what I saw at Doc's."

"Just being in the water for a few days would distort the skin," said Zeb.

"Alma also thought she noticed a hole in his stomach area. Like I said, she was pretty close to the body. Doc had the body covered except for the head and I didn't ask about the stomach area."

"Yeah. Go on."

"Alma also overheard the EPA guys say it looked like the fish ate up his insides. I would guess that to mean he was belly stabbed and gutted. The fish might have chewed up his insides too. Or, now that I hear myself say that, he might have been laying on the side of the lake before he got tossed in and some critters probably made a meal out of his internal organs. They might have chewed through the soft spots in his belly. Kind of gruesome when you think about it."

"It's nature's way," added Song Bird.

"I should've gotten more information from Doc, but he was busy with a dozen things. I told him I'd be back."

None of the men faulted Rambler, as he was no long tribal police chief and lacked any real authority to ask questions.

A dozen thoughts about how all that might have happened zipped through Zeb's brain. Black Bear could have been tortured, gutted and then thrown in the water. Whatever fish living in the mountain lake nibbled away at his innards. A cartoonish image of fish swimming in and out of a dead body came to his mind. Zeb agreed with the possibility that he could have been left out in the open overnight and anything from coyotes to bears might have feasted on him. He may even have been gutted as an act of torture or retribution by the men or women who killed him. The possibilities were at once both natural or manmade and seemingly endless.

"Oh, there was one other thing. His body was laying on the ground on a sheet of plastic. Alma didn't know if the EPA folks put the plastic sheet down or if he was wrapped in it when they found him."

Zeb made mental notes of everything he heard.

"I hope he wasn't alive when his insides got eaten," said Zeb.

"That would be bad," said Rambler.

"It really would. I guess we can only hope that the bullet to his brain killed him," said Zeb.

"Lots of people live through a head wound, especially if it's from a small caliber weapon," said Rambler. "I've seen it myself."

"It could also be that Alma let her imagination run a little wild when she saw the body and overheard things. She could have misheard. The truth would be better found out by talking to someone from the EPA who was actually at the site."

"True. True. You're right, Zeb," said Rambler. "I'm assuming you want to be kept in the loop in case I do find something out?"

Zeb glanced over at Echo. Her keen ears had not missed a single word. If she was going to remind him that he was no longer sheriff, she would have already done so. The look on her face told him what he already knew. She wanted to know, probably just as badly as he did, the who, what, when and why of Black Bear's death.

"Yes. Please keep me looped in. Thanks."

"Hold on, Jake wants to say something."

"Zeb?"

"Yup?'

"You think we should get Shelly involved?" asked Jake.

Zeb's mind ground to a halt when Jake used the word 'we'. Jake was officially retired. Zeb was no longer Sheriff of Graham County. Rambler was gainfully unemployed. Once again, Zeb looked over at Echo. His wife merely nodded her head up and down. Zeb was in. Echo was one hundred percent okay with it. If anyone could be of significant assistance when it came to breaching the federal wall of information, it would be Shelly.

"Hell, yes. That is, if you want to get to the bottom of things in a hurry."

"I do."

"But...but you're retired, Jake."

"Yup, I am."

"Then, what...?"

"Enjoy the rest of your honeymoon," exclaimed Jake.

Jake cut the phone call off without answering Zeb's question. Zeb replied to an empty phone line.

"Yeah, right."

4

BLACK BEAR'S AUTOPSY

A crowded autopsy room at the Safford Regional Hospital was a rare event. In the past it had been specifically prohibited by Doc Yackley. Today was the exception to his unwritten rule.

Newly appointed San Carlos Tribal Police Chief Goseyun Burries, the first woman ever to hold the job, practically stood on top of Doc Yackley. Doc, a little testy at working with a crowd around him, expanded his elbows to give himself more room. In the process he jabbed Chief Burries in the ribs and mumbled under his breath, "Back off." His actions were followed by an empty apology. On his left was Deputy Kate Steele Diamond, currently acting as temporary Sheriff of Graham County. The job fell into her lap based on her length of time as a Deputy Sheriff. She knew from experience and just plain decency not to crowd the doctor. Doc had called her to the autopsy as a counterbalance when he found out there was no way he could prohibit Chief Burries from being in attendance.

Doc's long-standing orderlies, Pee-Wee and Duke, always at his beck and call, were standing, military guard fashion, next to the autopsy instruments. They had prepared the body, table and room

exactly as Doc had taught them. They were as put off at Chief Burries'
actions as Doc was. This was their turf, not hers.

Pee-Wee, Doc's assistant, placed a clipboard in front of Doc and
handed him a sterilized pen. Doc looked around, doublechecking
everything in sight and signed off on the routine check list which was
headlined by the name and title of the man he was examining,
Sawyer Black Bear, Sheriff, Graham County, Arizona.

With the minutiae out of the way, it was now legal for him to
proceed. In truth his actions were all a bit of show for the lawmen
as well as a sign of his distrust of Chief Burries. Doc knew she
would be lurking over his shoulder, looking for any little thing that
did not follow legal procedures and might be viewed as improper
protocol. It was also necessary just in case Black Bear's family hired
some hot shot, big city lawyer to stick his nose into the case. Doc
wanted to make certain no one could tear apart the details of his
work.

"I need a little breathing room," groused Doc.

Kate promptly took one step back and another to the side.
Goseyun, frozen in place, held her ground. Doc repeated his easily
understood instructions. This time Goseyun shuffled her feet but
maintained the same closeness to the autopsy physician. Doc, with
his elbow extended upwards, turned swiftly just missing Goseyun's
nose and mumbled something under his breath about manners that
made Pee Wee and Duke chuckle.

"Pee-Wee, I could use a little more A/C. Handle that would you?"

The orderly, intimately familiar with Doc's desires, walked to the
wall control and pressed the temperature button to cool the room.
The quiet hum of an air conditioning unit kicked in. Doc stepped
back from the body of Sheriff Sawyer Black Bear and made a stern
announcement.

"All visitors must now take a chair until I have completed my
examination."

Doc's frustration rose when Goseyun remained stationed at his
elbow. Sterilized scalpel in hand, he turned to the tribal police chief.

"Is your hearing sufficient?" he asked.

"It's normal," she replied. "I just had my annual physical at the Reservation clinic."

Doc drew his face so close to hers that their noses practically touched. He slowly drew the scalpel into the narrow space between their faces. When the dangerously sharp blade was directly between their proboscides, the old but steady handed doctor abruptly thrust the sharp end of the blade toward the chairs that lined the edge of the room.

"I was giving you an order," he said, "not making a suggestion."

With a bemused smirk, Goseyun slowly stepped backward toward the chairs. Pee-Wee, standing behind her, extended his leg and foot to trip her. Quite discreetly, Doc Yackley shook his head and, at the last second, Pee-Wee pulled his leg away. An accidental, on purpose collision was avoided in the name of professionalism.

"Pee-Wee."

"Yes, Doctor Yackley?"

"Tell Kaye in human resources that I requested you get a dollar an hour raise. She can contact me if she has any questions."

Everyone, save Chief Burries, had seen what happened. The mood lightened as the room temperature began its descent to a more comfortable 60 degrees. Doc Yackley began his autopsy with an external visual examination of the body. He dictated a few things that sounded like mumbo-jumbo to the medically uneducated. After a thorough visual body exam, he turned his head slightly in Duke's direction.

"Let's get some X-rays."

"Routine views?" asked Duke.

"Yes. Jane is the X-ray tech on duty. She'll know what I need. Get a blood draw done while you're down there."

The blood had previously been drawn and the X-rays already taken, but Doc's aging prostate was irritating him, and he knew Chief Burries wanted everything done on her time frame. This was a simple way to slow down the process and put a bee in her bonnet.

Duke and Pee-Wee rolled Black Bear out of the room and down the hall to the X-ray room. Doc retreated to a bathroom and fitfully emptied his bladder. Fifteen minutes later Doc's aides returned with the gurney and the body. Doc thought about the rumor he had heard that the hospital was going to buy a portable X-ray unit. Under normal circumstances it would be welcomed and a time saver. By the time Pee-Wee and Duke returned, a new set of digital films were already up on Doc's computer. The assistants brought with them two sets of discs, a habit of Doc's from the pre-digital days.

"Any issues with the blood draw?" asked Doc.

"No, Doctor Yackley," replied Pee-Wee.

Doc glanced over at the already filled gray top tubes marked 'femoral blood' and 'heart blood.' He noted a red top tube labeled 'vitreous' and five conical tubes pre-labeled 'gastric', 'liver', 'brain', 'bile' and 'urine'.

"X-rays turn out?" asked Doc.

"Yes, sir."

Doc already knew a couple of secrets from the X-rays. One, even though there appeared to be a tiny, fragmented exit wound, the bullet was still embedded in Black Bear's brain. Two, Black Bear had a small, two by three-inch metal plate in the back of his head in the right occipital lobe. The bullet had deflected off the metal plate, then partially pierced the skull bone making it look like there was a very small exit wound. At that point the bullet lodged itself in the brain near the third ventricle. Ironically, the third ventricle functioned to protect the brain from trauma and injury.

"Good. Let's get down to business," said Doc, turning to Duke.

"Scalpel."

Doc opened his hand. An instant later Duke placed the required instrument in the seasoned autopsy veteran's hand. From rib cutter to forceps to enterotome to skull key and many other tools of the trade in-between, Doc spent the next several hours checking internal organs with his eyes and hands before beginning the process of removing the necessary histological samples from Black Bear's body. The entire time he purposefully kept his body in a position that obstructed Chief Goseyun's prying eyes from his work. Ultimately, when he asked for the Hagedorn needle, Duke knew it was his time to sew the cadaver shut. Final closure of a cadaver was his specialty. He was both good at it and enjoyed owning such an unusual skill set.

As Duke did his job, Chief Goseyun Burries rose from her chair and moved close to Doc Yackley. Doc responded by holding his bloodied gloved hand near her mouth.

"Yes?"

The tone of Doc's voice did nothing at all to hide his disdain for the Chief.

"You're done, right?" asked Burries.

"I'm done if we don't need to look at the eyes and head."

Doc rested a scalpel half-way into the empty eye socket.

"However, I'm guessing you're curious about what I might find here," said Doc, directing Burries attention to Black Bear's eyeless head.

Chief Burries reluctantly sat back down in her chair. Doc did a thorough exam of the head, skull and eye sockets. When the old master completed his work, he spoke but a single word.

"Finito."

Chief Burries quickly stood and followed Doc to the cleanup station. When she accidentally bumped his elbow, Doc gave her a glare so severe that even the tenacious tribal police chief quickly backed off. Kate remained a respectful distance away from Doc. Both women waited until Doc had scrubbed up and dried himself off before Chief Burries once again opened her yap.

"Doctor Yackley, tell me exactly what you found."

Ol' Doc Yackley, not one to take orders from anyone and already perturbed by the inexperienced and poorly mannered Tribal Police Chief, was in no mood for questions he either could not or would not answer.

"Sawyer Black Bear is deceased," replied Doc.

Chief Burries sighed loudly and with obvious contempt. Her reaction to his absurd statement did not sit well with him.

"Yes?" he replied. "Do you disagree with my opinion?"

"No, er, it's just that I thought maybe you had some idea of the cause of death," said Chief Burries.

"Wasn't drowning. That much I can tell you," said Doc.

"Torture?" queried Chief Burries.

"Yes, there exists the possibility that torture was involved," mumbled Doc. "The disfigurement would indicate that."

"The wound at the base of his skull? Was that the cause of his death?"

"That is a distinct possibility. At this time, I would say that declaring the skull wound to be the exact or even primary cause of death is premature."

Technically Doc wasn't lying. The bullet may or may not have been the cause of death. He did not yet know. And, there was no need to explain the fact that he had found a bullet in Black Bear's brain to Chief Burries. In fact, he left the .22 bullet right where he found it, near the third ventricle between the cerebral hemispheres of Black Bear's brain. In the back of his mind he was formulating a plan. When or if the bullet became relevant, he would, or he might, tell Chief Burries. Until then, things were still up in the air. For all Doc knew, Black Bear could have been poisoned before he was shot. The toxicology tests were not even close to being completed. Plus, he had no way of knowing whether Chief Burries had played a hand in Black Bear's death. There was absolutely no reason to show all his cards at this time.

"Do you have any idea what the cause of death was?" asked Kate.

"I have a few," replied Doc. "Nothing definitive."

"Mind telling me what you're thinking?"

"You'll have to wait, just like everyone else, including myself."

Kate nodded. She knew Doc well enough to see he was holding back something.

"When will that happen?" asked Chief Burries.

"When I get my reports back," snapped Doc.

"Any idea when that might happen?" asked Burries.

"Yes."

Burries' face turned a deep shade of red as her anger melded into scorn.

"Mind sharing that information?"

Doc was clearly annoyed by the new tribal police chief and his actions made that more obvious by the second.

"No."

"And?"

Chief Burries' impatience continued to rise precipitously. Doc was having a little fun with her and she knew it. It was unprofessional on his part, but she had been a royal pain in the patootie.

"And what?" asked Doc.

"And when might you get your reports back?"

"Some in twenty-four hours. Others will take up to a week."

"I'm interested in the ones that will give me the cause of death."

"I think those are the ones that are of interest to all of us," replied Doc.

"When will you get those?" asked Burries, squeezing her fists tightly shut.

Chief Burries was becoming downright brusque. An intense Mexican stand-off was rapidly brewing between the aggressive young Apache police chief and the old, methodical white medical examiner. Neither were about to back down, not even so much as an inch. Doc Yackley politely handed her his professional card.

"Oh, I'd say a week. Yes, one week. Please feel free to call me in seven days. If I don't answer, leave a message and I'll get back to you as soon as I can."

"That's the best you can do?" asked Chief Burries.

Doc, having taken off his gloves and washed his hands, grabbed a sterile, unused scalpel. He moved with intention toward Burries. When he was once again face to face with her, he elevated the sterile scalpel and began, with great nonchalance, cleaning his already spotlessly clean fingernails. What he had discovered in doing the autopsy was, at this point, no business of hers. In time it would be. But at this moment he and he alone owned the knowledge of his results. Should Tribal Chief Burries get her hands on the information Doc had just discovered, it would be highly unlikely the case would ever get solved. It might even lead to more death. Worst case scenario would be that she would gain enough information to refute the possibility of her being a suspect.

"That is the best I can do for you."

Doc Yackley raised the flat, unsharpened end of the scalpel and dragged it across his own jugular vein. In the next instant he flipped the sharp end of the scalpel outward and directed it toward Burries jugular vein.

Burries appeared unfazed by his thinly veiled threat and sidled in closer to the old country doctor. Obviously, she had been confronted with a sharp object more than once in her life. Plus, her actions were making Doc's blood uncomfortably hot. It took years of experience to hold him back from saying or doing what was on his mind. He succeeded in holding his tongue on this occasion.

"I believe you're done here, Chief Burries. Most certainly, you are."

Doc nodded to Pee-Wee and Duke. Ever loyal to their boss, the tough young interns gently but firmly escorted Chief Burries out the door of the autopsy room. Once outside, in the hallway and away from the others, she grabbed them by their collars and pushed them away, hard. Her words to them were stern and threatening.

"Don't fuck with me ever again. If either of you so much as step foot on the Rez, Doc may be doing his next autopsy on one or both of you little bastards."

Pee-Wee and Duke were young, tough and street smart. Doc had pulled them out of the gutter and made their lives better. Their loyalties to him and all that he did were fierce. No pissant broad with a San Carlos tribal sheriff's badge was going to intimidate them.

Back in the office, Doc Yackley had already forgotten about his confrontation and was on a phone call with Dr. Nitis Zata, good friend, White Mountain Apache and head pathologist at the state medical school in Tucson.

Outside, as Tribal Police Chief Goseyun Burries strode toward her pickup, she pulled a wicked-looking switchblade from her pocket, running the tip of the hardened steel blade across the five-thousand-dollar paint job Doc had recently given his favorite passion. She barely broke stride as she jammed the tip of the blade down to the metal from the passenger's side back bumper to the front corner on Doc's pride and joy, a 1973 candy apple red Cadillac Sedan Deville convertible. She proudly gloated to herself.

"Now that's some upscale keying, if you ask me."

To top it off, as she reached the front wheel well, Burries stopped, bent over and jammed the entire blade through the side wall of the custom made, five-hundred-dollar tire. So certain was Chief Burries of her actions she did not even bother to check and see if anyone was watching. Satisfied, she once again had words with herself.

"You racist, sexist, old, white motherfucker, you don't have a clue as to who you're dealing with."

5

OLD SCHOOL CHUMS

Doc Yackley took a seat at his desk. The old man's rear end had eroded a perfect indentation in the shape of his aging and somewhat flabby buttocks into the chair. Pulling out an ancient leather-bound address book from the bottom right drawer of his desk, Doc flipped to the last page with the letter Z. There was but a single entry—Zata, Dr. Nitis aka 'Zits'. The work phone number was fading. The cellphone number looked to have been added within the last decade. The address had not changed in over thirty years. Merely looking at his old friend's name brought a grin to Doc Yackley's face and unleased a storybook of memories from the deepest corners of his brain. Doc peered over the top of his bifocals and read the phone number aloud. Tapping the digits into his cellphone, he whispered each number, moving his lips as he pressed its key. The phone rang five times before his old medical school comrade answered.

"Doctor Zata."

"Zits, that you? Jesus, you sound like an old man."

"Jimbo Yackley. Eat my shorts and bite my crank, you farting old dog."

Nitis Zata, probably the only person on the planet who called

Doc by his med school moniker, Jimbo, was glad to hear from his old pal.

"Damn, but it's good to hear your voice," said Doc Yackley.

"What the hell are you calling me about? Somebody die? You dyin'? Jesus, I hope you're not on the way out the door. We may be old, but we shouldn't be dead yet."

"Yes, as a matter of fact, someone did die. But I'm still on the green side of life," replied Doc Yackley. "On the other hand, we're all dying, are we not?"

"That we are, ash, that we are. But I'm glad to hear that you're still sucking in a fresh supply of air."

Doc Yackley searched his mind. It quickly came to him that ash was the western Apache word for friend. His old pal was still sharp as a proverbial tack.

"Fourteen breaths a minute and not one single irregular heart-beat, in case you're taking notes."

"Regular as monsoon rain," said Zits. "Healthy as a horse, albeit an old one that has a fairly decent view of the glue factory on his horizon."

"Livin' the good life, I take it?" replied Doc Yackley.

Zits had enough of the small talk. Life might be short, and the road may be long, but this call meant there was work to do. Zits' cognizance of time and the foolishness of wasting it was always dancing around in his frontal cortex.

"This dead man you're calling me about. Was he a friend of yours?"

"I knew him."

"And did you play any part in his demise?"

Like always Dr. Zata's tongue was quick and wit dry. His mannerisms were also direct.

"His passing, at least to the best of my knowledge, had nothing to do with me."

"Was he murdered?"

"If I had to render an opinion, I'd say yes."

"Hmm. You have an opinion. It must be important," said Zata.

Doc Yackley responded by addressing his former school pal by his own once upon a time moniker.

"Zits, why do you surmise that it must be important?"

"When was the last time you made a social call to me?" asked Zits.

"Good point."

"Mmm-hmm."

"Zits, I need your expertise," said Doc.

"Who was it that bit the dust?"

"Local sheriff. A guy by the name of Sawyer Black Bear."

"From the sound of his name, he's not a local San Carlos Apache. I know for certain he's not a White Mountain Apache either."

"Lakota," replied Doc Yackley. "Lakota, not a Nakota or a Dakota, from South Dakota. At least that's how he tells his story, or should I say told his story. Hard to know if any word that came out of his mouth had truth attached to it."

The little Dakota rhyme scheme brought a chuckle. Zits knew he had to be on his game to keep up with Jimbo.

"I take it you doubt his story about being a true Lakota."

"He's half-White. The other half is up for question. Claimed Lakota heritage, but he looks Navajo to me, but I'm no expert."

"You're right. You're not an expert in such matters. What the hell is he doing in this neck of the woods?"

"Fishing."

"Fishing? For what? Sand bass?"

"He moved here, sort of in the middle of his career, to spend time fishing in the Sea of Cortez…"

"…or so the story goes," interrupted Zits.

"You read my mind."

"Sounds like you think the fishing tale is just that," said Zits. "A bit of the old cock-and-bull."

"I do smell something that doesn't have the fresh scent of veracity clinging to it. The fishing thing never made much sense to me. I know for a fact he spent a whole lot more time bird-dogging and bullshitting than he ever did fishing."

"I take it that since he's no longer among the living you want some help figuring out what really happened?"

"Like I said, I got a dead body, a whole lot of questions and not nearly enough answers."

"Make it easy on an old-timer. Can you give me the most obvious information?"

"For starters, he was found wearing heavy weights around his neck, feet and wrists when they dredged him up from the bottom of Riggs Lake," explained Doc. Whoever dumped his body wrapped it in plastic."

One thought jumped to Zits' mind. Since the body was wrapped in plastic someone was trying to eliminate the likelihood of a blood trail. A body wrapped in cloth, or even a rug, could leak blood onto a floor, the trunk of a car or the back of a pickup truck.

"Long story short, the person who gave us our original information told us that the body was laying on plastic immediately after it was pulled out of Riggs Lake."

"Riggs Lake? That's the place you took me fishing, up on Mount Graham, way back when."

"One and the same," replied Doc Yackley.

"I take it you're calling me because the cause of death didn't match the findings of a drowning victim?"

"You're as sharp as a marble, maybe even more astute than the first day we put our first scalpels into that old lady cadaver in dissection lab," replied Doc.

"Ira Blount from Bend, Oregon," said Zits. "I remember her well. As a dead woman, she taught me a ton more than many of my living professors. For that I am eternally grateful. God rest her soul and the disease plagued body that she grew into."

"Good memory, Zits. Her name had escaped my mind. Boy, does that take me back."

"Ditto, but let's bring ourselves back into the present moment. Do you have any theories about what happened to the dead man making laps around your prefrontal cortex?" asked Zits.

"Sheriff Black Bear beat out a long-standing incumbent in a hotly contested political race using outside money," said Doc. "Things got down and dirty during last election season, at least for a rural county like ours."

"He beat out your pal, Sheriff Zeb Hanks, right?"

"Right."

"I remember reading about it in the paper. Hell, as I remember, it even made the regional news."

"It was a huge upset. Tucson papers covered it big time," said Doc Yackley.

"CNN even sent a stringer out to cover it."

"Because the winner was a Native American. That's big news on that station."

"Right. Well, we all have our biases, don't we?"

"We most certainly do," replied Doc Yackley.

"You think your pal Sheriff Zeb Hanks might have a hand in this?"

"Zeb? He's got a dark side, but this isn't is style. I wouldn't rule him out entirely, but he wouldn't be on my top ten list either."

"You're certain of that?"

"I am. I personally delivered him into this vale of tears. Eight pounds and eight ounces when his mother's womb gave him over to my receiving hands. I've known him all his life and been his doctor since day one. Besides, he was on his honeymoon in Paris when this occurred."

"Got somebody else in mind as the possible killer?"

"No one in particular jumps out at me. At least not off the top of my noggin."

Maybe his death is about money?" queried Zata.

"Could be. We all know money don't sing, dance or walk, but people kill for it every day."

"We might have a professional hit on our hands. Is that what you're thinking?"

"Maybe...Probably."

"Is it a maybe or a probably.'

"It's a probably...maybe."

"I'd guess from the sounds of it, that's one of the primary questions you want looked into?"

"It is."

"Power? Is it about power?" asked Zits.

"Isn't all of politics about power to some degree or another."

"Okay. Ya' got me on that one. Keep going. Time is marching ever onward and with each breath we take, we've got just a little less time to spend on this planet."

"For sure something weird happened," said Doc Yackley.

"I take it you found something on the autopsy that doesn't fit into what you would consider normal protocol?"

"Yup. You got that right."

"Don't keep me in suspense. What'd you find?"

"Fairly high possibility of bodily torture based on disfigurement."

"Was he disfigured before or after death?" asked Zits.

"That's one of the reasons I'm calling you. I suspect after, but I don't know how certain things occur and..."

Doc Yackley paused for a very long thirty seconds before Doctor Zata interjected.

"And? What?"

"This is the odd part that I can't quite figure exactly. The dead sheriff's eyes, kidneys and his heart were professionally removed."

"That could be a big payoff day for an organ harvester," replied Zata.

"It could be. The thought crossed my mind, if ever so briefly. We don't get that kind of thing around these parts."

"Just sayin'," replied Zits.

"And I'm just sayin' that kind of thing has never happened around here. At least as far as I know."

"There's always the first time for everything."

"Be that as it may, and we should take it under consideration, the location of the body is odd, too."

"Location of the body? Riggs Lake is what you said, right?"

"Yes, sir. And like you remembered it's up near the top of Mount Graham."

"Do you believe the location of Sheriff Black Bear's body plays into this?" asked Zata.

"The whole top of the Mount is a political hot potato," said Doc.

"How so?"

"Years, hell, decades ago, the federal government used their right of eminent domain to confiscate a lot of el primo Apache land. The acreage the feds took is religiously historic to many of the San Carlos Apache clans. The Apache Nation and the United States government have been in and out of court for the same number of decades trying to straighten it out. It's not been a pretty battle. Some of the land around Riggs Lake is still owned by Apache families and the tribe itself. For approximately three-quarters of a mile in each direction the land is marked as private property. Most everything else is owned by an international corporation called AIMGO," explained Doc Yackley.

"That's the telescope conglomerate, isn't it?"

"It is."

"Let me guess. The land owned by the Apaches is marked private and has no trespassing signs everywhere," stated Zits. "The Apache landowners don't want anyone messing with what little remains in their hands for both personal and religious purposes?"

"Yes, sir. You nailed it. The tribe has helped out the landowners with its privacy issues by surrounding the lake with motion-activated video cameras," stated Yackley. "No one gets on or off the lake without being captured on video at least a dozen times."

"Sounds complexly thought out."

"It was."

"Was anyone caught on the video feed, say, dumping a body into the lake?"

"Now that's the funny part. There's a two-hour time frame, about a week or so back, when all the cameras were mysteriously shut off," explained Doc Yackley.

"Who told you that?"

"Acting Sheriff Kate Steele Diamond slipped me that bit of information in passing."

"Hmm. I'd guess you're thinking it was no coincidence that the video cameras were down?" asked Zata.

"No, hell no," replied Doc. "It was no coincidence."

"You know that for a fact, or are you playing Sheer Luck Holmes again?"

Both men rip-snorted with laughter. Back in their school days, they had become known as Sheer Luck Holmes and What's Up, Doc? because of their attempted crime-solving reputation created by using the pathology lab. The nicknames stuck partly because of their twisted senses of humor. Mostly it was the gratitude from the Tucson Police Department related to their amateur sleuthing abilities that caused them to carry the nicknames forward. But it was also a matter of their successes, of which they were unabashedly proud, that allowed them to so easily revert to youthful ways.

"You might say that old Sheer Luck has risen from a long restful repose," replied Doc.

"Looks like the old team is going to be back in action."

Though they were on the phone and one hundred miles separated, the doctors slapped an invisible high-five between them.

"Hope you're as good as you used to be," said Doc Yackley.

"I'm older, but wiser," replied Zata. "Can't say beyond a shadow of a doubt that older and wiser equates to being any better."

"Ditto, especially on the older part," added Doc.

The men shared a chuckle that was both boyish and mournfully real.

"For starters, we need to think outside the box," said Zata.

"I've already prepped some pretty decent tissue samples for you. My intern, Duke, is on his way over there as we speak."

"Is he bringing tissue samples or the whole body?" asked Zata.

"The whole shebang, including a hard disc of the digital X-rays and some blood for your lab to test."

"Good."

"I'm going to need the body back fairly quickly."

"Why? What's the rush? Don't you want the job done right?"

"Like I already told you, the body was found on what is arguably, although not necessarily legally, Rez property. The Tribal Police Chief, a radical dogcatcher turned police chief, doesn't much care for me. Hell, to tell you the truth, she hates my guts. I'm operating under the assumption she is going to want the body in her possession, STAT. Not only does she, per tribal law, have the right to the body, but she's got a big ol' hard-on for me personally."

"You always did have your ways with the girls."

"Piss off, mate," replied Doc.

Zata chuckled. "I'll put it at the head of my list of things that I need to do for old friends."

"Muchas gracias," replied Doc.

"Speaking of old friends, are you still driving that '73 Caddy of yours?"

"Yes, hell yes. Runs like it came off the assembly line yesterday. Not as much as a single scratch on my pride and joy. Just had a custom paint job and new rims and wheels put on it."

"Interested in selling it?" asked Zata.

"What's your soul worth these days?" asked Doc.

"We're both getting old, Jimbo. Our souls are about ready to glow like gold in heavenly sunshine or turn to dust from the heat of furnace fires in hell."

"I'm hoping for the best, Zits," replied Doc Yackley. "For both you and me."

"I'll give you a call when I've got something, anything. Expect to hear from me in a week or so," replied the head of the Pathology Department at the Tucson Medical School.

When Doc Yackley started to say goodbye, his old chum interrupted him.

"You're certain, just between you and me, that Sheriff Hanks didn't have anything to do with this?"

Doc Yackley looked around his office, checking that his office door was completely shut and making absolutely certain no one was listening in on him.

"How certain can a person be of anything these days?"

6

ZEB AND ECHO RETURN

The sixteen-hour Air France flight from Paris Roissy-Charles de Gaulle airport to Phoenix International went smoothly. A flight attendant, who was the mother of twins herself, bumped Zeb, Echo and the babies up to first class. In a second kind gesture, she moved Echo's parents, who were exhausted from having taken care of Elan and Onawa for much of the two weeks in Paris, to business class. The flight attendant's husband, coincidentally, was a sheriff. His turf was Gallagher County, Utah. Echo could tell by the shape of her head and the placement of her eyes the airline hostess was genetically part-Ute Indian. When Zeb was getting off the plane in Phoenix, he took the few hundred dollars-worth of euros he had in his pocket and tried to give them to her. She politely declined.

"Did you ever take a tip for doing the right thing in your line of work, Sheriff Hanks?"

"It's Zeb, ma'am, and it's ex-sheriff," replied Zeb. "I used to take free tea whenever it was offered up. Maybe a donut here and there."

The flight attendant smiled, gently rubbed the heads of the eight-month-old twins and wished the family well. Picking up their luggage and clearing customs went more smoothly than expected. Zeb felt good to be back home and have his feet firmly planted on American soil. For the first time, he had a tiny glimpse into how Echo must have felt when she returned from war. Just being in America lifted an unseen weight off his shoulders.

As they loaded Elan and Onawa into their new Toyota Sienna minivan, Zeb's first non-American branded vehicle, Echo's dad slipped off into the Land of Nod. Her mother entered dreamland shortly thereafter. Echo had changed the kids' diapers and was feeding them as Zeb headed south toward Safford. Zeb gently caressed Echo's shoulder.

"It was a great trip, wasn't it, honey?" said Zeb.

"A trip of a lifetime," replied Echo. "I couldn't have done it, wouldn't have wanted to do it, with anyone else but you. Especially with kids in tow."

"Your parents were a great help," said Zeb. "We owe them."

"It was a bucket list thing for them," said Echo. "You paid for the trip and almost all of their expenses. That's quite enough. Don't make a big deal out of it or they'll be embarrassed."

Zeb nodded. He already had a gift in mind for them. They loved getting massaged at Kachina Springs Spa and Baths followed by dinner at the El Coronado restaurant. The combination would likely mean as much to them as the trip to Paris, especially since they could share their experiences with friends. Zeb would set up a private dinner party at the El Coronado. It would mean the world to them.

As they passed by the supermax federal prison at Florence Junction, Zeb's phone rang. It was Helen.

"Welcome home. Where are you? How did Elan and Onawa hold up? Did Echo's parents have fun? How was the trip for you honeymooners? Is Paris as beautiful as it looks in the pictures? How was the food? Are Parisians nice people or are they snobby like they show in movies?"

Zeb pressed the Bluetooth button on the steering wheel to put the phone on speaker. He wanted to share Helen's excitement with Echo.

"Elan and Onawa are sleeping. They did beautifully. Not that they will remember any of it. Echo's parents are also knocked out so we will be talking quietly," said Zeb.

Throughout the conversation Helen kept her voice to an excited whisper.

"What was the very best part of the trip?"

Echo, knowing Helen's penchant for confectionaries, quickly replied.

"Parisian bakeries have the finest sweets on the planet. They are to die for."

Helen did not hide her decadence at the thought of Parisian sweets.

"Heavenly days. My oh my. Lordy. I can only imagine."

Zeb and Echo turned to each other and smiled, giggling softly and delightfully at Helen's anticipated response.

"You won't need to let your imagination fly too far," said Echo. "We brought you back a dozen of your favorites."

"Oh, Echo. Oh, Zeb. You shouldn't have. Echo, I'll bet just about anything that you were the one who thought of me."

Not that Zeb would have forgotten something special for his auntie, but indeed it was Echo who had thought of the sweet treats as a special present for Helen.

The trio talked about the trip to Paris from Florence Junction all the way south to the northern edge of the San Carlos Reservation before Helen brought up the real reason for her call.

"A special election is going to be held in seven days," said Helen.

"Seven days? Isn't that kind of quick?" asked Zeb.

"The city council made the decision."

"Right," said Zeb. "Is one of the council member's family going to run for sheriff?"

"Don't get paranoid on me, Zeb. It's just with so many unsolved crimes and the drug problem along with the hordes of south and central Americans, Africans, Asians and Lord knows who else sneaking across the border and through the county, something has to be done right away. Then there's the mules trafficking child prostitutes in larger than ever numbers. There are real issues that need immediate attention. We can't solve any of these issues without strong and trusted local leadership right now."

Helen was urgently breathless by the time she got out what she had to say.

"I guess you're right," said Zeb.

"Helen's absolutely right," added Echo.

"Zeb, you need to get your paperwork in. You have two days to get it done. I've already filled out most of it for you."

"Um, er, I haven't made a final decision on that yet. Life has been so good and..."

Echo interrupted Zeb by gently placing her hand over his mouth.

"Thank you, Helen. That is so kind of you. Sometimes Zeb isn't so great at showing his gratitude. So, I'll say thank you for him. I assure you he is most grateful. He'll stop by and sign the papers tomorrow morning. He'll be there early. I'll make certain he gets them to the county clerk's office on time."

"Behind every good man is a woman who keeps him from back-sliding," said Helen. "I'm afraid my nephew would be a mighty sinner without you, and likely not be good at decision making."

Echo smiled at the code talk. She had secretly called Helen from Paris the day they heard about Black Bear's murder. She made the call to check with Helen about when a special election might be held.

Echo was acutely aware she and the kids were the only reason Zeb was hesitant to regain his old job. Echo knew the blood in her husband's veins ran thick with the desire to see that the law was properly served in Graham County, Arizona. From her point of view, there was literally no reason for him not to run again.

In Black Bear's short tenure, he had solved none of the crimes left behind in Zeb's wake. It was rumored that not only had the crimes gone unresolved, but Black Bear had mucked up the works something terrible. In certain corners of gossip, the word was that his hands weren't necessarily clean when it came to the slowness of clearing up the backlog of crime in Graham County.

However, with numerous new businesses, the increased railroad freightage carrying goods from Mexico and the expansion of several copper mines, the flames of prosperity in Graham County were being fanned like never before. With the almighty dollar speaking as loudly as it naturally did, locals were willing to look the other way until something directly affected them. During Black Bear's term in office, things had not become so troublesome as to create an increase in county-wide crime anxiety.

Along with the new wealth Safford was experiencing, crime was proportionately on the rise. Two gangs, the Bouncy Baby Boys and the Djangos, both out of Tucson, had essentially divided the county. Drug usage was purportedly increasing dramatically. Two new treatment clinics were already overflowing with patients due to significant increases in fentanyl, heroin and meth usage. Seven deaths from ODs, three in the county and four on the Rez, had occurred in the last six months. The Rez had hired two more deputies and three more full-time social workers. Dropout rates at the new All-County Regional High School were at record levels. Thefts and petty crimes were up nearly fifty percent. Graham County was on the precipice of becoming a very troubled place. However, since the crimes affected mostly the underclass, people intentionally looked the other way.

With the boom-bust nature of the mining business and all the noise the President was making about more complex border enforcement including thirty miles of a local wall and tariffs on Mexican goods, the inevitability of a local recession was more of a question of when, not if.

Echo placed her soft hand on Zeb's arm and gently caressed him. She knew it was his fate to run for and once again become Sheriff of Graham County. It was not simply the right thing for him to do, but the only thing. It was also the best thing for the citizens of Graham County. As the Knowledge Keeper of all the People, Echo understood destiny, not only her own but that of Zeb. Most of all, she knew the future was already written in the stars above and in the ancient, earthly hieroglyphs and petroglyphs of the Galiuro mountains. Such was her power as one who had been innately blessed with nearly divine powers. She silently vowed to use her skills to help all the people of the Rez and Graham County.

Zeb inhaled so heavily his chest heaved upwards. His exhalation was a soft, long sigh. When his eyes met Echo's, a future lifetime of ongoing trust passed between them. Echo whispered to him softly, but firmly.

"Zeb. Run for sheriff. Graham County needs you. It's your duty to figure out who killed Black Bear. To help others is the destiny you were born into. I stand by your side."

Zeb swelled with pride at Echo's pronounced acknowledgment of his fate and her desire to be with him through thick and thin. Echo had been thinking about little else since he had heard of Black Bear's death. There was no doubt the providence of it all had given birth in his mind. But everything was much more complex than that. He needed to know the whole truth about Black Bear's death. His heart had long told him that without the entire truth all else was a lie.

On one hand, Zeb knew that Black Bear was despicably underhanded, and there was a reasonably good chance that his death was related to his own actions. On the other hand, Zeb knew the power of true justice. The killer of Black Bear, regardless of the dead sheriff's nefarious ways, must be found and brought to justice. The murder of a county sheriff, if left unsolved, would leave the entire county on edge and its people feeling wholly unprotected. Plus, the mere concept of a lawman's death going unanswered practically begged for a criminal insurgency.

Zeb looked in the rearview mirror at his twins. Both of his children were being true to the nature of their given names. Elan, whose name in Apache translated to friendly, was sound asleep, but smiling. Onawa, or girl wide awake in Apache, sat quietly, eyes wide open, babbling away while taking in everything an eight-month-old child is capable of, which Zeb was slowly beginning to understand as everything, or at least far more than an eight-month old is normally given credit for.

What would the future for them look like if the law in Graham County was not strong and solid? Would one of those two little rascals, whom he had given his heart to, follow in his footsteps and become part of the law? Or, would trouble and violence drive them away from the town they would come to know as home?

7

ZEB HANKS FOR SHERIFF

The morning after returning to Safford, Zeb dropped by his former office. Helen stepped out from behind her desk, hugged him firmly, kissed him on the cheek, held him at arms-length and looked him straight in the eye. She then drew him close and hugged him a second time while planting a kiss on his other cheek. Without saying a word, she handed him the election forms, turned him around, placed her hands on his back and gently pushed him out the office door. Wordlessly, she pointed a single finger in the direction of the county clerk's office. Zeb looked at Helen, smiled sweetly, and with a spring in his step headed exactly where he had been directed. Five minutes later, Zeb Hanks, candidate for Sheriff of Graham County, walked back through the Sheriff's Office door.

"Looks like you filled them out okay," said Zeb. "All I had to do was give them my John Hancock. Thank you, Helen. There is really no way I can repay you for your everlasting support."

Helen's eyes glistened as a solitary tear pooled in each eye.

"Don't get all sappy on me, young man. You can repay me by being a good father, husband, sheriff, son and nephew. Now it's time to get to work."

She lightly dabbed at the tears with a Kleenex.

"What exactly do you mean by that?" asked Zeb.

"Jake kept a bunch of your old 'Zeb Hanks for Sheriff' signs. He's stopping by in a few minutes. The two of you are going to make the rounds and pound them into the ground. It's called marketing 101."

"Are you my campaign manager now, Auntie Helen?"

Helen Nazelrod stood squarely with her hands on her hips. Zeb recognized her no-nonsense look. Her response was one hundred percent Nazelrod.

"As a matter of fact, I am," she replied. "Whether you like it or not."

"Self-appointed?" asked Zeb.

"Indeed," said Helen. "And since you have no job, are not currently Sheriff of Graham County and have four mouths to feed, you had best listen closely to what I tell you to do."

A horn honked. Zeb glanced out the window. It was Jake. Zeb took a quick look back at Helen who had neither moved a muscle nor changed the seriousness of the expression on her face. The hands on the hips as well as the fact that her feet seemed glued to the floor exactly where she was standing was a clue for Zeb to act accordingly.

"Gotta run."

"Well then, don't just stand there like a bump on a log, get a move on," said Helen, shooing him with a flick of the wrist. "Election day is quite literally just around the corner."

Zeb stopped at the door, turned and directed his words at Helen.

"Thank you."

Helen beamed radiantly.

"It's so good to have you home."

For the first time since Zeb's defeat by Black Bear in the recent election, a sense of normality was returning to Helen's job, maybe even to her life. Her heart was teeming with hope, love and the belief that good things do really happen to good people. Once again, Zeb thanked her.

"You can thank me properly by bringing Echo, Elan and Onawa

over for dinner soon and letting me see some pictures of your trip to France."

"We can do that," replied Zeb.

Helen responded wistfully.

"I have always wanted to go to Paris. Maybe someday I'll get there. Maybe when I retire? Who knows?"

"Helen, if I win the election, you are going to stay around and keep us all in line, aren't you?" asked Zeb.

Helen rolled her eyes, shook her head and tsked twice, loudly.

"Do you think for one minute this place could run itself without me? My retirement can wait. It's not going anywhere soon. I am fulfilling my fate and my God-designed destiny by being here with you and your staff. I cannot imagine it being any other way."

Zeb's heart beat with delight. He was fired up to get back in the business of being the top law enforcement officer in Graham County. He double-timed it to Jake's truck. Jake reached across the seat and pushed open the passenger door. Zeb's mentor and former deputy was grinning like the cat who just ate the canary.

"Hey, cowboy. Ça va?"

"Oui, ca va," replied Zeb. "Parlez-vous Francais?"

"Nope. Not hardly a dang lick of it," said Jake. "I was just practicing so I could ask how you were doin'."

"Mighty nice of you, Jake."

"Good trip?"

"Great trip."

"Those Froggie women as good looking as they say?" asked Jake with a twinkle in his eyes.

"I was with the best-looking woman in the country. I can't say as I spent any time ogling the locals," replied Zeb.

Zeb high-fived his former mentor. They both laughed the way men do who were damn glad to see each other. Zeb felt as though he had been gone from Safford for much longer than he had, and it seemed an eternity since he had been sheriff.

"If I win this election, are you coming back to work for me?" asked Zeb.

"Work with you?" said Jake. "Isn't that what you meant to say?"

"That is precisely what I meant to say," replied Zeb. "Slip of the tongue. Sorry."

"You know I'm too set in my ways to work for anybody. But I am sure damn well experienced enough to kick up dust alongside the likes of you."

"I didn't fall off the turnip truck yesterday," said Zeb, laughing. "I know exactly where you stand and what you stand for."

"As long as working with you doesn't screw up my social security check," replied Jake. "I'm in."

"Helen already clued me in on that particular subject," said Zeb. "She told me you can put your social security check on hold until you're seventy and a half. That way it won't have any negative effect on you financially. And, you'll get an automatic eight percent bump in your social security for every year you wait to take your check."

"Why you sneaky rascal," said Jake. "I'm aware that I've got to take social security when I'm seventy and a half. Just coincidentally, that'll run me right up to the end of your term."

"That make you feel old?" asked Zeb.

"Nah. Age is an issue of mind over matter. If you don't mind, it doesn't matter."

"Good line. You think of that one all by yourself?" asked Zeb.

"Stole it from Mark Twain," replied Jake. "One of my favorite writers ever since I read Huckleberry Finn back in Mrs. Blakeslee's sixth grade class."

"That's what I'd call a righteous kind of thievery. But seriously, do you ever feel old?"

"Outside of the occasional ache, pain or shortness of breath from all those damn years of being a two-pack a day Marlboro man, I feel damn good. I did once, though. Feel old, that is."

Zeb was fairly certain he knew what Jake was referring to, but he kept his lip mostly zipped, wanting to hear it directly from his mentor's lips.

"When was that?"

"When I think back on the seven years that I was living my life through the bottom of a whiskey bottle. That kind of slow death makes a man feel old as mountain dirt. Fuck it. The way I feel now, I imagine I can probably last just about as long as you can."

"I got two little ones to raise," said Zeb. "I gotta work a whole lot longer than you do."

"You are blessed, Zeb. You are truly blessed. Don't you ever let that thought slip from your noggin."

Zeb tipped his hat up and wiped a touch of sweat from his brow.

"I am only beginning to realize just how blessed I am and how much responsibility a family is."

"Okay, then. Let's get to work. You can count your blessings along the way."

Zeb and Jake made the rounds, pounding one hundred-fifty signs in the hard, dry desert dirt before stopping to take a break.

When the time was right, Zeb reached into his billfold and removed a folded piece of paper. Without saying a word, he handed it to Jake. Zeb had found the note upon his return from Paris. Before this moment he had neither discussed it nor shown it to anyone, not even Echo.

"You're the first person to see this," said Zeb.

Jake put the note in his lap. He pulled his glasses from his pocket, wrapped them snugly around his ears and, using his middle finger, adjusted them on the tip of his nose. He pointed to the words, dragging a craggy, bent pointer finger over them one at a time. He read the note, word for word, including the exclamation points.

DO NOT RUN FOR SHERIFF! THINK ABOUT ELAN AND ONAWA!

The threat was written in blood red ink.

"Where the hell did this come from?" asked Jake.

"Someone somehow got it into my house, through the back door, I think, when I was away. This note ended up in the middle of the room next to the kitchen table. They also left this behind."

Zeb showed him a picture of Carmelita just after her death. The sword Zeb had ended her life with was still stuck through her body, pinning her down. The image reeked of death.

"Think someone broke into your house and put it there?" asked Jake.

"I don't know for sure. There were no signs of forced entry. At least none that I saw, and I took a damn close look."

Jake leaned in and garnered a second, closer look at the note. He thought about the kind of effect the threatening words must be having on Zeb's psyche. Being threatened was just part of the job. But threatening family was strictly off limits. Threatening children meant a psychopath had likely written the note. The apparent ease with which someone obviously broke into Zeb's house without leaving any clues of how they entered was troublesome.

"Anything missing?"

"I checked. I don't think so. But maybe..."

"But maybe what?"

"I recently was cleaning an old .22 pistol. I had it on my workbench in the garage, last I remember. I was about to start cleaning it when I got called to the office. I was in a hurry, so I put it away on one of the shelves in the garage cabinets. I assume it's still there. I put it behind some stuff so no one would accidentally come across it. To tell you the truth, I'd forgotten about that until just now."

"Check on it when you get home. I wouldn't want someone like that walking around with one of your weapons," said Jake. "Even if it's just a .22."

"Right. I'll check on it first thing when I get home."

Both men paused as the same thought entered their heads. Black Bear had been shot with a .22 caliber gun. Since Zeb only now had remembered the possibility that one of his own .22s was potentially missing, there was no direct reason to think his gun had been stolen and used in the murder. Yet, the thought festered in his mind.

"I'm going to assume that we're dealing with a psychopath," said Jake. "Or an A-number one asshole."

"If I get a vote on it, I'm going with asshole," replied Zeb.

"Trouble is, you don't get a say in the matter," said Jake. "It is what it is."

Jake's weather-beaten fingers once again touched lightly on the paper. The paper was embossed with a myriad of barely visible semi-hidden images. To Jake, they looked almost medieval, like mythical monsters. He was only able to make out their shapes due to gold flecks that outlined some of the illustrations. He angled the note so the sunlight could pass through the thin paper, which Jake assumed was vellum.

"Red ink. That's sort of odd, wouldn't you say?" asked Jake.

"It is, but red ink isn't much of a clue to go on," replied Zeb.

"I think the paper is vellum."

Zeb touched it softly. He wasn't familiar enough with vellum to know one way or the other.

"How do you know that?"

"My once upon a time wife used to buy it for fancy invitations or when she wanted to make an impression on someone. It's made from calfskin. It used to be expensive because it used to be handmade. Now you can buy it at your local Wal-Mart."

"Hmm," replied Zeb. "If you can get it at Wal-Mart, odds are it is going to be tough to track down where it came from."

"Any chance in hell you recognized the handwriting, er, I mean, printing?" asked Jake.

"Nope. It's neat enough. And there are two exclamation points. It may not mean anything, but it seems to me that women use exclamation points more than men do."

"The printing is neat and legible. No smears either. Therefore, we can assume and be fairly certain that whoever wrote it used a good quality pen. A good quality pen is a reasonable indicator of education or status."

"From little clues, big cases grow," said Zeb.

"Which says perhaps, but only perhaps, whoever wrote it is not a complete imbecile," said Jake. "They may be a psychopath, but they aren't a buffoon."

"No, we're apparently not dealing with an idiot. Not a complete idiot, anyway. Red ink, decent printing on vellum paper, exclamation points and possibly a new pen. That's still not much of start on figuring out who had the guts to walk right up my back-porch steps and possibly enter my house."

"It sure as hell isn't much to go on, but we've started cases with less information than this."

"Like I said, it really gets under my craw that whoever did this had the audacity to feel comfortable enough to simply walk up on my back porch. For all they knew, I could have had security cameras covering every inch of my property."

"My guess is that they knew you didn't have a security set-up," replied Jake.

"Yeah. Could be. You're probably right on that account. It would take a lot of balls to sneak into my place if you knew I had camera security."

"They know the names of your kids," added Jake.

Zeb felt dry heat rising in his ever-tightening body. Bad thoughts entered his mind. If anyone hurt his children, or Echo, he would not hesitate for one single second to kill them with his bare hands. His voice became a growl.

"How dare they mention my children!"

"The fact that whoever it was knew you didn't have security cameras tells us it's likely somebody who lives locally. They probably read Elan and Onawa's names in the paper when you and Echo did the birth announcement."

Zeb's heart fired hot with anger. Revenge rose up rapidly.

Jake knew the inner workings of Zeb's mind. He had mentored him since his childhood. Jake could see, could feel, the hatred emanating from Zeb's heart.

"Why haven't you told Echo about this?" asked Jake.

"I'm waiting for the right moment," replied Zeb.

"And when is that going to magically appear?"

"Soon."

"Soon?"

"Soon enough."

Jake pulled out his phone and turned on the magnifying glass app. He held the note under the dashboard where it was darker.

"You look over these images that are imprinted into the paper?"

"Yup. I sure as hell did."

"They mean anything to you?"

"Nope. Can't say as they mean a damn thing. They look like those gargoyles we saw at the top corners of the Notre Dame Cathedral in Paris."

Jake continued to study the images. He could make neither heads nor tails of them.

"Maybe they're just random images embossed into the paper. The yellowish-golden color of the paper makes it hard to see the design precisely. The gold speckles also seem odd."

Zeb answered with a disinterested, "Yeah." Jake eyeballed his partner closely. He could see Zeb's mind was drifting elsewhere.

"You've got a faraway look in your eye, young man. It looks like a dangerous one," said Jake. "What's going through your head?"

Jake's words seemed to temporarily snap Zeb back into the present moment.

Zeb held out his hand.

"Give me the note."

Jake handed him back the piece of paper. Zeb pulled out his phone and turned on the lighted magnifying glass application. He shined the magnifying glass on the paper, pulled a pen from his pocket and pointed the tip at a small, embossed icon.

"This one," replied Zeb.

Jake adjusted his glasses and moved his head toward the paper.

"It looks a little bit like a dragon with curved tail," said Jake. "Embossing on light gold colored paper makes for decent camouflage."

Zeb nodded in agreement, shrugged his shoulders. Then, one by one, using the tip of his pen he moved across the paper from symbol to symbol.

"These all look like abstract art to me," said Zeb.

"Abstract art?"

"Yeah. We visited the Louvre one day. Echo has an interest in art."

"And I'll bet you saw a lot of abstract art?"

"We did, as a matter of fact."

"It's no wonder that's how you're interpreting the embossing on the letter then. Abstract art gets stuck in your head," said Jake.

"And you would know that because?"

"Because I'm not totally without a cultural background," said Jake.

Both men chuckled. The drawings in comic books, *Mad* magazines and comic art in old *Playboy* magazines were about the extent of their artistic background.

"After a while all museum paintings blend into one," said Zeb. "But I did enjoy the Louvre for about an hour, especially seeing the Mona Lisa."

"Is she actually smiling in the real painting?" asked Jake.

"Not if you ask me. She looks befuddled."

Zeb's response to Jake's comment lightened the mood.

"The symbols on this note don't look anything like the Mona Lisa at all."

"Nope," replied Zeb. "They sure don't."

"But just what the hell does a golden dragon with a curved tail have to do with anything?" posed Jake.

"Why would someone send me an anonymous threatening note on paper with barely discernible images of what appears to be a dragon with a curly tail embossed into it?" asked Zeb.

"Probably some whack job trying to get you to think about something other than what you should be thinking about," said Jake.

Jake tapped a gnarly finger against Zeb's temple.

"They're trying to mess with your head when you should be thinking," continued Jake.

"What is it that you think I should be thinking about?" asked Zeb.

"Getting elected Sheriff of Graham County. Right now that should be in the forefront of your mind."

Jake was uncharacteristically stern.

"Right, but this note is linked to that," replied Zeb.

"That's one thing we're both sure of," said Jake.

"I'm not much of a conspiracy guy…"

"If that sentence doesn't have 'but' as the next word, I'll admit to being a monkey's uncle," said Jake.

Zeb responded very slowly.

"...but someone is sending me a message. And for some reason it feels like it's coming from the other side of the grave."

"What the hell are you talking about? Do you think Black Bear did this?" asked Jake.

"No, but I think whoever killed him wants me and possibly my family dead. This note is more than a warning shot fired across my bow."

"Do you think it's a warning shot meant to send you a specific message?"

Jake paused and looked at himself in the mirror, then at Zeb.

"Jesus, listen to me. Listen to us. We sound like a couple of conspiracy nut jobs."

"Yeah," replied Zeb. "Maybe we do. Maybe we are."

Zeb's response had Jake doing a doubletake. Zeb had never been the kind of sheriff that acted confused at the onset of a case. But now was not the time to mention Zeb's uncharacteristic reaction. If Zeb was going to properly protect his family, one thing had to happen. He needed to have the power of authority to get things done. In short, he needed, above all else, to win the election. If he lost the election, he would end up acting outside the law. That would be dangerous and likely cause him a great deal of trouble. This was Zeb's last chance. If he lost his bid for county sheriff, not only were he and his family going to be in significant danger, but his political career would wind up in the toilet. The stakes involved in winning back his job as Sheriff of Graham County were just multiplied by a factor of ten.

"Let's get back to work pounding these signs in. We should take one out by the Mount Graham Market. Grumpy Halvorson is a big backer of yours," said Jake. "And just about everyone out that way votes."

"You're right. Let's get a move on. We're burning daylight."

Jake waited until they were almost finished posting the election signs before asking Zeb about Black Bear. He did it without as much as mentioning Black Bear's name, but Zeb knew who Jake was talking about.

"You glad he's dead?"

"Nah, not really," replied Zeb. "I'd like to have caught Black Bear, that son of a bitch, red-handed, doing whatever it was that he was doing."

"He definitely got in bed with the wrong crowd," said Jake.

"Maybe, then again, maybe not. Maybe it was his fate."

"Death is the ultimate fate we all face," added Jake.

Zeb tipped his cowboy hat up and stared off into space. That truth was inarguable.

8

AUTOPSY: SAWYER BLACK BEAR

When Doc Yackley's phone rang, he was intensely studying an X-ray of a compound fracture of the right tibia of a heavy-set elderly woman who fell while getting off the toilet and got stuck between the commode and the wall. Doc's assistant, Pee-Wee, seeing Doc was engrossed in his work, answered the phone on his bosses' desk.

"Doc Yackley's office. What can I help you with?"

"Jimbo around?"

"Sorry, you must have the wrong number. This is Doctor Yackley's office. There's no Jimbo here," replied Pee-Wee.

Overhearing the conversation, Doc silently signaled Pee-Wee with a nod of the head to bring him the phone. He didn't feel the need to explain his age-old nickname to a young whelp like Pee-Wee. Besides, he knew exactly what the phone call was about.

"Zits, what've you got?"

"I just sent my preliminary autopsy report on Sheriff Sawyer Black Bear to your computer. Open it up."

"Give me a minute."

Doc walked to his old desktop computer and opened the email

from Zscalpeldoc@gmail.com. He set his phone down and read the report thoroughly.

"Jesus," said Doc. "I was 100% right."

"You were," replied Zits. "But I think you would have had the skill set to figure that out back when we were in school."

"Still, I'd never seen it in real life before. But, you're right. There's really nothing else it could have been."

"Righto."

"What do you make of it? Have you seen it before?"

"A corpse with illegally harvested organs?" asked Zata. "I've personally seen it twice. His kidneys, his heart and…"

"…and it wasn't the fish that ate his eyes, then was it?"

"Nope, I should say not. The eye removal was a clean cut. Highly professional. But fish actually do eat out the eyes of submerged human body as cleanly as surgeon's scalpel can remove them. Sometimes they even do a better job. In this case, the fish put a clean edge on the prior incisions."

"Yeah. Anyone who has seen a body that's been freshly pulled out of water knows that fish are exacting in their work."

"Right. Also, a single, clean shot with a small caliber gun to the base of the skull was the killing weapon. A .22 short shell was used."

"What does that tell you?" asked Doc.

"Mos' def' professionals did the work."

"Mos' def'? What the hell kind of jive talk is that?"

"Street lingo for most definitely. I picked it up from watching reruns of *The Wire* on Netflix."

"Aren't you the hep cat?" asked Doc Yackley.

"Barely street legal and probably not even close to being up to date with today's lingo."

"Like always, you are too cool for school."

"But hep cat is right out of the swing era of Satchmo Armstrong. In this day and age, I believe the proper vernacular would be to say someone was chill."

The old men dated themselves in more ways than one. However, they were keen on their work and living on the cutting edge of pathology was what really mattered to them. Keeping up on all things medical while maintaining some sort of societal relevancy meant a lot to their egos.

"Like I was saying, most definitely highly trained and experienced professionals were involved. The detective in me is pondering the thought that the organs were taken because someone didn't want to wait in line for a legitimate donor," explained Zits.

"The Grim Reaper may have been knocking a little too loudly and a little too suddenly."

"At a well-connected, rich man's door."

"Even if time was of the essence, don't you find it a bit odd that the target would be a county sheriff? A sheriff is a high-profile personality. His death would naturally provoke significantly more questions than if the victim was just a regular citizen."

"Personally, were I in search of replacement organs for this old bag of bones, I would go after someone with a much lower profile. But I'm not in that sort of business. I don't even pretend to know how an organ harvester's mind works," said Zata.

"Maybe I have a theory," said Doc Yackley.

"Do tell."

"Maybe someone picked Black Bear because his blood type, crossmatch and tissue type all matched the person or persons who were getting the organs?"

"Whoa! While that makes perfect sense, it takes this to a whole different level," said Zata.

"Yes, indeed it does."

"It means that someone with access to Black Bear's medical records would have to have been involved."

"I suppose it's easy enough for the right person to steal information from his medical doctor's clinic," said Doc Yackley. "Or his or her computer."

"Or, someone. Wait one second. How long has Black Bear been working for Graham County?"

"Less than three years," replied Doc Yackley.

"Who hired him?" asked Zata.

"Zeb, I imagine. Just a second. But when I think about it, Helen is probably the one who did the actual hiring."

"Does, did, she get along with him?" asked Zata.

"Yes, at first. Not so much lately. I know for a fact she didn't trust him. She had a problem with his ethics."

"Enough to have him put away for good?"

"Helen? No way. She's a true lamb of God," said Doc. "I can say with almost one hundred percent certainty that a thought like that is very unlikely to enter into her way of thinking."

"Sometimes those who appear to be the meekest among us are the most horrific killers," replied Zits. "Maybe the meek inherit the earth one organ at a time?"

"I just can't imagine Helen would even allow such a thought to cross her mind. Or, for that matter, have it done," said Doc.

"I'm just saying. Don't rule anyone out."

Zits' words sounded strangely ominous.

"Sounds like you're including me in that group," stated Doc.

Doc's attempt to rebuff him was met with an even odder response.

"You possess the skill required to do such an act," said Dr. Zata.

"Balderdash," replied Doc. "All bullshit aside, what exactly are you thinking, Zits?"

"I'm thinking that perhaps you're right. Maybe Black Bear was murdered very specifically because of his blood and tissue types," said Zits.

"Then you agree with my theory? You think somebody planned that far ahead?" asked Doc. "You believe the poachers were seeking out someone with a certain blood type, etcetera, that matched what they needed?"

"Just a thought to add to the mix," said Zits. "Does Helen have any loved ones who need an organ transplant?" asked Zits.

"Not that I've heard of," replied Doc. "But, like I said, I'm certain Helen is not the person who did this."

"Keep an open mind and keep your eyes wide open. Nothing should be ruled out," said Zits. "When it comes to family, people cross lines they wouldn't ordinarily even go near."

Doc paused, thinking. He was no detective, but he knew better than to shut his mind off to any possibility when family need was involved.

"I suppose it is not outside the realm of possibility that Helen is involved, but I really, really doubt it. Illegal organ harvesting is a mean and vicious business. It would be just so out of character for Helen to be involved. In fact, I was only today reading some of the recent literature on illegal organ harvesting."

"Upgrade my cranial data base," said Zata.

"For starters, most organs are illegally harvested in China, Africa and the Middle East. It's also a viable business in Mexico and India."

"Mexico?"

"Yes, our friendly neighbor to the south has a growing business in organ harvesting."

"Hmm. Proximity adds a little twist to all of this."

"Putting that to the side, let's just say that if you are a wealthy Chinese businessman, a member of the Saudi Royal Family perhaps, hell, any royal family for that matter, maybe a connected cartel member and you need a heart or some other vital organ, you'd have one STAT."

"I believe that to be true. After all, money makes the world go 'round."

"And absolute power corrupts absolutely."

"Listen to us, regular old philosophers. Emphasis on old."

"There are also broker-friendly hospitals in the larger U.S. cities. There's no shortage of American surgeons who are willing, for a significant fee, to do an illegal transplant."

"What kind of money does an illicit surgeon charge for transplanting a stolen organ? asked Zata.

"Organs sell for one to two-hundred grand a pop. Double that when you include the surgeon and hospital fees."

Doc heard his old pal whistle on the other end of the line.

"Yup, it's definitely the big leagues when it comes to the amount of cash involved," continued Doc.

"As we both know, if an organ is harvested, it has to have a continual flow of blood and oxygen right up to the moment of harvest," said Zata. "Once harvested, a kidney can last thirty to forty-eight hours and a heart lasts roughly six hours outside the body."

"Inferring that someone has to know what they're doing and have the proper equipment, set-up and storage equipment."

"Precisely."

"Hold on one sec," said Doc. "Let me pull up a website I was checking out. Yup, here it is."

"Whatcha got?"

"It agrees with what you said. A typical kidney can last in proper cold storage for roughly thirty hours according to one website. Another site says twenty-four to forty-eight hours."

"Makes sense," said Zits, "that different places would have slightly varying findings."

"And get this. You probably already figured some of this out, but kidneys from brain-dead donors are generally of superior quality because they aren't exposed to warm ischemia..."

"...the time between the heart stopping and the kidney being cooled."

"Figured you knew that."

"It all makes perfect sense to me," replied Zits.

"Also, the longer a kidney is outside the donor's body, the more likely complications are to occur, even under the best of circumstances," said Doc.

"Well that explains a lot," said Zits.

"Do tell," said Doc.

"I should have had it figured from the first time I saw Black Bear's body."

"The gunshot wound to the head, right?" asked Doc.

"Yes. Jesus we are dealing with top end professionals. They shot Black Bear in the head, making him brain dead, but may have also kept him artificially alive to ensure the viability of his kidneys and eyes," said Zits.

"Jesus, whoever did this, knew exactly what they were doing," said Doc. "They've been trained for this type of killing and probably done it before. Not to mention the equipment they had to have."

"Amen," replied Zits. "This thing was orchestrated like *La Campanella* by Franz Liszt."

"Whoa, just one second, my old friend. What the hell does that mean?" asked Doc.

"*La Campanella*, by Liszt, is generally considered..."

"*La Campanella* translates as, hmm?"

"Think about it," said Zits. "You're a smart fellow."

"I've got it. The little bell. Right?"

"*Igennel*," replied Zits.

"Which means?"

"You are correct."

"Lucky guess," said Doc.

"The piece of music is an etude. It is a demonically fearsome display of power when played correctly. It is also considered to be almost perfectly choreographed and wickedly virtuosic. It's full of surprises."

"As are you, but how does this relate to our situation?" asked Doc.

"It tells us someone went way, way out of their way, choreographed, to coin a phrase, to make sure this was done impeccably. We are dealing with big time operators here," said Zits.

"Which means a lot of money was involved," said Doc. "And that whoever is involved is highly connected."

"As much as money being an issue, these types of people are pathologically dangerous. Even knowing what little we do at this time, we could absolutely be in serious peril if someone figured out that we know what we suspect we know," said Zits.

"Someone spared no expense in jumping the line," said Doc.

"Time must have been of the absolute essence," said Zits.

"Which is a fairly positive indicator the Grim Reaper had already placed his grip on someone and that certain someone had all the information, including crossmatch, blood type and tissue match on Black Bear well in advance," said Doc.

Dead silence hung over the doctors like a black cloud about to burst into a violent storm. Neither being fools, Doctors Yackley and Zata knew precisely the level of danger they could be putting them-selves in. The idea of danger somehow brought out the youth in them. Doc Yackley broke the deafening stillness.

"Are you ready to do some serious amateur sleuthing?" asked Doc.

"You bet I am."

The old team of Doc Yackley and Doc Zata, Jimbo and Zits, AKA Sheer Luck and What's Up Doc? was back in business. It was just like old times. It was medical school side money all over again. Only this time they weren't young bucks, they were old stags. This time they weren't doing it for tuition money. And this time huge danger lurked in every possible corner. What did they have to lose besides every-thing? The hunt was on and the blood winds were howling.

9

SHERIFF ZEB HANKS IS BACK IN BUSINESS

The special election was little more than a runaway train. Victory was inevitable for Zeb as no one chose to run against him. His prior shortcomings apparently had either been forgiven, forgotten or just plain set aside. Zeb received so many apologies that it became downright embarrassing at the Town Talk when four or five people would approach him, heads hung low, and confess how they had made a bad choice in voting for Black Bear. As far as Zeb was concerned, it was all water washed down a gully. Right now, there was a mountain of work to be done, and it involved the death of Sheriff Black Bear and anything that might be linked to his bizarre demise. Oddly enough, the rumor mill regarding the circumstances surrounding his death had been somehow minimized.

Jake, as promised, came out of retirement to be Zeb's right-hand man. Deputies Kate Steele Diamond and Clarissa Kerkhoff were his right and left-hand women. Helen remained perpetually Helen. Shelly was a rising star. She was eager, thorough and apparently in the police business for the long haul. In fact, she had never quit looking for the criminals or crime syndicate that helped shove Zeb out of office. Leads were numerous, for the most part erroneous, never truly solid and invariably led to dead ends.

Shelly's hope was that the death of Sheriff Black Bear would lure some rats out from their hiding places. Death, she knew, often carried opportunity on its back. People would move quickly to remove themselves from any potentially illicit ties to the dead man. Others would try to step in and create a spot for themselves in the criminal activities that most certainly would continue. When that happened, mistakes would eventually occur. So far, only a few small things were triggering any kind of insight and none of them provided hard evidence.

A Monday morning meeting with everyone in Zeb's office felt like old times, positive old times. The only new face in the crowd was that of former Tribal Police Chief Rambler Braing. Zeb, knowing Rambler still had solid Rez contacts, had hired him on temporarily as a consultant. Zeb opened the meeting with a blunt but familiar credo.

"Let's get right to work."

The gathered team nodded and mumbled some positive affirmations. Each and every team member knew without a doubt they were on the same page and desired the same end result.

"We've got a backlog of crimes to clean up," said Zeb.

Everyone was acutely aware that the faux school shooting, the robbery at Swig's, the rubber knife stabbings of Constantina and Apolonia at the Care Center as well as the incident involving the discoloration of the city water were still open cases. All of those criminal acts needed at least some sort of resolution. The voters had voted Zeb out because of those situations. Zeb was certain they had voted him back in believing he might give people enough answers to these issues so that they felt less fearful.

But the elephant in the room was the murder of Zeb's predecessor, the late Sheriff Sawyer Black Bear. When Zeb asked if anyone had new information, Shelly addressed the staff.

"Shappa Hówakȟaŋyaŋ, Black Bear's mother, has been in touch with me."

"Why did she contact you?" asked Zeb.

"My name was in Black Bear's little black book. If you remember, very early on, he and I went on a couple of dates."

Zeb had pushed that bit of information out of his mind. Shelly was not prone to making bad choices, but dating Black Bear was hardly a good one. He didn't want one bad decision on Shelly's part to taint his impression of her ability to maximize her performance in the investigation into Black Bear's death.

"Oh, right," said Zeb. "Forgive me if I don't keep track of your social life."

His words broke any potential tension.

"From my conversations with Shappa, I think Black Bear felt a whole lot more for me than I did for him. At least that's how it came across from her."

"Love is funny that way."

Kate spoke from experience. She had been involved with a few men before marrying Josh Diamond. Among them was the late San Carlos Tribal Chairman, Eskadi Black Robes, who loved her far more deeply than she had loved him.

"What exactly did Shappa want?" asked Zeb.

"She wanted information about her son. In fact, she was quite direct about it."

"What sort of information was she looking for?"

Shelly, though never one to gossip, had a mouthful to say.

"Shappa thinks Black Bear made some enemies because he was Lakota. She's a very politically minded person. Her thoughts are black and white. From talking with her, I would say that beyond a shadow of a doubt there were no gray areas with her when it came to her son. She figured I knew who might have something against him not only because I once dated him, but because she knew I worked for Graham County. I hate to say it, but, from the sounds of it, she doesn't trust other Native Americans any more than she trusts Whites, Blacks or the United States government. I get the feeling she doesn't trust anyone. I doubt she even trusted her own son."

"It sounds like Shappa wanted to know if you had any idea or inside information on who might have wanted to kill him, or have him killed and why, I presume?" asked Zeb.

"Exactly. She was being a good mother, a thoughtful one, at least in her words. I can't say for certain that she carries revenge in her heart. But I did get an uneasy feeling, an almost dangerous vibe, when I was talking to her. I got the distinct feeling she could talk out of either side of her mouth without so much as having to think. But that was just my impression from our conversation. I can't back my words with any sort of proof...yet."

"It would be nice if we knew exactly what Shappa's motivation is," added Jake. "I mean if she has a force driving her other than the death of her son."

"She's smart, powerful, clever and quite possibly deceptive," added Shelly. "Remember she has history going all the way back to the creation of AILM, the American Indian Liberation Movement. She has been arrested numerous times for political activities. And don't forget her close links to Senator Russell. There are even rumors of her having an affair with him. Her estranged husband is a retired federal agent who has a cross-border business and government contracts that allow him a significant amount of freedom when it comes to all things regarding the Mexico-U.S. border. She's no inno-cent little lamb, that's for sure. In fact, she has been booted from most of the political organizations she has ever been affiliated with, including AILM."

"What kind of information did you give her?"

"I made certain not to tell her anything she didn't already have prior knowledge of," replied Shelly.

"You're certain of that?" asked Zeb.

"I could tell she was digging, digging hard and deep. I kept my guard up. I can assure you that I gave nothing away," replied Shelly.

That was a statement Zeb knew would hold up in court. It would be a cold day in hell before someone was sharp enough to pull the wool over Shelly's eyes. If Shelly was suspicious of Shappa, that was reason enough for Zeb to keep his guard up when it came to Black Bear's mother.

"Does anyone have a gut feeling Shappa was involved in her son's death?" asked Zeb.

The room became wholly uncomfortable as Zeb watched his

team racking their brains as each concentrated their attention on the possibility of filicide, the act of a parent killing their own child. The mere thought of it left a foul and bitter taste in everyone's mouths.

"Let's not rule it out. Shappa having Black Bear killed is not high on my list, but it's on the list," said Zeb. "Shelly, can you possibly dig around and find out if someone close to Shappa needs a transplant?"

"I can do that," replied Shelly.

"I'll contact the Sheriff of Oglala Lakota County, that's part of the Pine Ridge Reservation and where Shappa lives," said Zeb. "He might know something."

Jake grabbed the coffee pot and refilled everyone's cups. He poured some hot water in Zeb's cup and dropped a new tea bag next to it. Zeb gave them a few minutes to mull over what he had suggested. He, of all people, with two infant children, was horrified by the possibility of a mother killing her own child. Jake, who had lost his granddaughter to an act of violence, seemed lost in thought. Clarissa, who had killed her own brother in the line of duty, stared straight ahead. Zeb brought them all back into the present moment.

"Have all of you read Doctor Zata's pathology report Doc Yackley asked for?"

They all nodded. For the most part each of them had it memorized.

"Thoughts? Anyone? Jake?"

"He sure as hell died violently."

Jake held an imaginary gun to the base of his own skull. The dramatic re-enactment was especially brutal since Black Bear's photo was hanging on the wall just behind him. The others watched in silence.

"The shot to the back of the head makes it seem professional," continued Jake. "I have to believe, whoever did this, it wasn't their first kill shot."

"Therefore, in your opinion, Black Bear was killed by a professional assassin?" asked Zeb.

Jake blinked his eyes as he nodded. Everyone else had pretty much come to the same conclusion. So had Zeb. Therefore, his questions were by and large rhetorical.

"If it was a professional hit, our pool of suspects is vastly narrower. But, at the same time, it makes it more difficult to lay our hands on a specific person," said Zeb.

"Dumping his body in Riggs Lake with an anchor around his neck and his wrists shackled was a bit over the top," said Rambler. "I think whoever did it wanted to make it look like an Indian-on-Indian crime."

"The body mutilation makes it look like a crime of passion. Everyone knows he fooled around with married women," said Kate. "But if his organs were harvested for money, well, that's another issue altogether, isn't it?" added Kate.

"Meaning what exactly?" asked Jake.

Kate gulped ever so slightly. She did not really want to say it aloud, but she did.

"If it had been a crime of sexual retribution, wouldn't the killer have removed his sex organs?"

Zeb and Jake appeared squeamish at the thought of castration and penectomy. The women in the room remained stoic.

"Burning his house to the ground," added Clarissa. "Makes me think someone was destroying evidence they assumed he was holding."

"It's yet another way to make it look like Indian-on-Indian crime. Burning down the house of an enemy is as Native American as apple pie is American," said Rambler. "It is Lakota tradition to burn down the house of a dead man."

Potential complications were multiplying rapidly.

"I still have to believe Black Bear was connected to the wrong people. In this case, the wrong people could very well be the same people who helped him win the election," said Shelly. "He might have double-crossed them."

"If you play with fire, you're bound to get burned," said Kate.

"If you dance with the devil, Satan sidles in and gets a grip on your soul," added Clarissa.

"Experience has taught me that when people with power are betrayed, they'll stab you in the back and hurt you more than you hurt them," said Jake. "A lot more."

"Helen? What are your thoughts on the matter?" asked Zeb. "Anything?"

Helen cleared her throat. She looked at the floor and glanced around the room before speaking. Zeb knew her well enough to know that if she was about to speak ill of the recently dead sheriff, it would weigh heavily on her conscience. He was more than a little surprised by what actually came out of her mouth.

"Sheriff Sawyer Black Bear was a sneaky, pardon my French, varmint, even when he didn't have to be. A man like that can't ever be trusted. Since you asked, I truly believe he was hiding from himself. I think he was ashamed of whoever he really was and whatever he was doing. In the end it finally caught up with him in a very bad way. There was something wrong with him, something that had probably been wrong with him from the get-go."

Zeb's eyes widened as he nodded his head and looked around the room. He was surprised by Helen, impressed by his team, proud to be back at work and wholly resolved to get to the bottom of everything, especially Black Bear's murder. He was never more certain than at this moment that all the recent bad things that happened in Graham County were either directly or indirectly linked to Black Bear.

"It's good to see we have no shortage of theories," said Zeb. "For now, I'd like everyone to keep the information from Doctor Zata's autopsy report in-house. Got it? Hold that card close to your vests."

Everyone understood the need for confidentiality regarding the coroner's report. If its information got out, panic could ensue, and that would be a bad start to Zeb's new term as sheriff. Graham County, as large as it was in terms of area and as small as it was in terms of population, could be a veritable rumor mill.

The newly re-elected Sheriff of Graham County idly rapped his fingers on his desk and glanced up at Mount Graham. Sunlight reflected off the international telescopes. The red-tailed hawks were circling in pairs. The Pinaleño Mountains, so named because of the high density of pine trees, were lushly green. He was at home and back at work. It all felt so right. Zeb felt confident that things would work out for the best when it came to solving the murder of his predecessor.

"Here's where we start," said Zeb.

The gathered Graham County Sheriff's team shifted into high gear, getting down to serious business mode. They were all anxious to get back to work with Zeb and for Zeb. The fiery and fresh air in the room juxtaposed the dark and dour crime they needed to solve.

"We're operating under the assumption that we've covered everything regarding the petty crimes that led to Black Bear defeating me in the election last year. The little man inside of me tells me we missed something, maybe even something obvious. We start by revisiting those crimes. We have to look at them with fresh eyes. That is our first task at hand. When we're certain we've seen them with crisp clarity, we focus on either integrating those crimes with the death of Black Bear or removing them from the possibility of being involved with it."

"I take it you're certain there's a relationship between some of the prior crimes and Black Bear's death?" asked Jake.

Zeb directly faced them all. He wanted to be certain everyone could see his facial expressions clearly.

"As sure of it as I can be sure of anything at this point," said Zeb. "I'm as sure as I am that you..." Zeb nodded to Jake. "...and Song Bird are responsible for me becoming the man I am when the two of you saw to it that I ended up with this hat."

Shelly, a relative newcomer to the crew, did not know the entire story behind Zeb's hat. She glanced at Jake. The look on his face was all telling, but all telling of what she was uncertain.

"How can you be so certain of the relationship between Black Bear's demise and the other crimes?" asked Shelly.

"When I was in Paris, I had an epiphany. Truth be told, I didn't recognize the epiphany until I was on the plane coming back home. I was thinking, daydreaming if you will, about the six million skulls in the catacombs of underground Paris."

What he didn't tell them was that Echo, as the Knowledge Keeper of all the People, had been teaching him small things. Among other things was how to see what wasn't there and how to remember what seemed forgotten. The information she shared expanded his thinking exponentially. However, most of what she taught him was to be kept only between the two of them. And none of it was the protected wisdom of the Knowledge Keeper.

"I realized in retrospect that being surrounded by so much death brought every fiber of my being to life. Like I said, it was so vivid at the time that I didn't even realize what was going on with me. I only knew that I had a revelation that opened up a part of me to a new way of thinking. Staring out over the Atlantic Ocean on the way back, I realized what had been revealed to me down there in those dank catacombs. Everything that has happened in Graham County is a conspiracy. Black Bear's death is just a piece of a much larger plot."

"Jeez, Zeb, that all sounds kind of out there. You know what I'm saying?" asked Jake.

"Echo has taught me to pay attention to the silent voice of Death. She taught me that every day we walk over the bones of our ancestors that are right beneath our feet. We never even give it a second thought. We should. It would make us stand back and count our blessings as well as bring us into the present moment."

Simultaneous with Zeb's words, a strange, twisting/tightening/pressurized sensation struck Jake in the chest. Pain shot down his left arm. His left shoulder ached. A heaviness in his chest caused him to break into a cold sweat. He felt nauseous and weak as he felt his heart's erratic rhythm. He tried to shake it off as nothing, but he could not. Jake felt his heart rate increase. He gasped for air. For some reason, Zeb's description of the six million skulls he had seen in the sewers of Paris popped into his head. He grabbed his left arm.

"Are you okay?" asked Shelly.

Jake hesitated for a long moment before gathering his words. The look in his eyes was ancient and childlike at the same time. As quickly as his symptoms had flared, they calmed to almost nothing. His response was typical Jake.

"Too much coffee for breakfast. I've got some indigestion. I slept poorly last night. I'm fine."

Shelly, Helen, Clarissa and Kate all kept an eye on Jake. Rambler thought little of Jake's complaints. Jake was a rock of a man. He knew many men of Jake's age. They all had transient pains. He would be fine. Zeb had the same kind of icky feelings Jake was describing back in the day when he was a heavy coffee drinker. He carried on as though everything about Jake was more or less normal.

"Today each of us is going to take one hour and talk to the victims of the crimes that got me booted out of office. Leave no stone unturned. Try to get at least one tidbit of new information from everyone. I'll talk to Swig, Clarissa you've got Maxon Mazie at the water utility. Jake, you head on over to the Desert Rose to talk to Constantina and Apolonia, and, Kate, head out to the school. Shelly, see if you can get anything more out of Black Bear's mother."

"And what about Black Bear?" asked Jake, still lightly gripping a less acutely painful arm.

"We, all of us in this room, are going to put our heads together on that one. I want you all to know and understand that there is no bad blood lingering from the last election or from the bullshit Black Bear pulled. I hold nothing against him personally. The whole thing was just politics at its worst. Our job now is to solve his murder."

Zeb's team knew Zeb better than he knew himself. His words carried the wind of a hollow ring. They all were acutely aware that Zeb had a burning disgust for Black Bear and all that he stood for. Yet they knew Zeb would follow through with anything and everything that would help him resolve the murder of Sheriff Sawyer Black Bear.

ANSWERS/NO ANSWERS/RING A DING DOO

The overhead doorbell jingled out the sheriff's arrival. Zeb reached up and stopped the clanger by grabbing it in his right hand. Swig was leaning on the counter near the cash register drinking a diet Doctor Pepper. He barely glanced up as Zeb strode through the door. Swig's only movement was a quick uptick of his eyes.

"10-2-4," said Swig.

Zeb responded with a blank stare. This time Swig tipped his head forward and glanced over the top of his glasses, which hung snugly on the lower bridge of his nose.

"10-2-4," Swig held up the bottle he was drinking from and pointed to the motto emblazoned on its front. "It's Doctor Pepper's motto. I love the stuff. Now they've got twenty-three flavors. Tried 'em all. Been drinkin' it for years. Drink it when I don't have any Diet Coke around."

"Haven't had one since I was a young whippersnapper," said Zeb. "Fond memories of it, though."

His words prompted Swig into motion. He ambled side to side with an open stance that resembled a long-time horse rider toward the back of the store. He reached into an old-fashioned, water-filled soda pop cooler, took out a bottle and clicked the cap off with the ancient machine's built in opener. After wiping the bottle dry with a reasonably clean towel, he swayed as he strutted back to the front counter. He handed the opened bottle of ice-cold Dr. Pepper to the sheriff with an expression of great anticipation. Zeb took a deep swig.

"Hmm, not bad. Only a little different than my memory serves."

"That's because it's sarsaparilla, Doctor Pepper style. New on the market since you were a young man. Thought you might like it."

"I do. In fact, I'd have to say I love it. Thanks."

"Ten four. Whaddaya need, Sheriff?"

"The robbery that happened here back when I was Sheriff..."

"Yer Sheriff agin, ain't ya?"

"Yes, but I mean before now."

"You talkin' about the Obama and Nixon caper?"

Zeb was glad he didn't have to go into any further explanation as a conversation regarding that situation with Swig could take all day.

"Yup. One and the same."

"I got nothin' more to say about that little incident."

"Nothing?"

"Already popped my cherry on that one. Time hasn't improved what little bits of ancient memory that floats around the inside my noggin."

Swig set down his empty Doctor Pepper next to the cash register, reached into his pocket and pulled out his Red Man chewing tobacco. Biting down slowly and firmly, as not to dislodge his false choppers, Swig wriggled off a plug of the chaw. Zeb's mind meandered back to the time he and his older brother tried chewing tobacco. Zeb recalled puking his guts out and being sick for nearly an entire week from the experience.

"I was just wanting to go over things one more time," said Zeb.

Swig glanced around the empty store. Zeb assumed Swig wanted to make sure they were alone. The Vietnam war veteran kept his voice at barely above a whisper as he spoke to Zeb. His hushed tone made the sheriff consider perhaps Swig was a bit paranoid.

"Sure. What do you want to know?"

"Those two men..."

"Nixon and Obama?" Swig hawked a chigger into the old spittoon he kept near the register. It reverberated flatly in the empty, lidless pot. "Didn't vote for neither of 'em. Didn't vote for you the other day, neither."

"Either," said Zeb.

"It's neither," replied Swig. "English grammar is the only class I ever got anything other than a D or outright flunk. How do you think I got such an easy trip to the Nam jungle?" Swig stared off into the distance and veritably sang a remembered refrain. "Either, neither, neither, nor, just remember to shut the kitchen door."

Zeb chuckled not only at the sing-song manner in which Swig called out a familiar refrain, but that his teacher had taught him that even though either and neither were only one letter different from each other they had opposite meanings. Zeb laughed out loud recalling a prior conversation about how Swig had never voted, ever.

"Right. Didn't vote again, huh?"

"Didn't say that."

"You voted?" asked Zeb.

"Nope."

"What the...?"

"Just yankin' yer chain, Sheriff Zeb."

"Well, Swig, you got me for your sheriff, regardless of the fact you didn't cast a vote in my direction."

Swig chortled. "The only thing you got goin' for you is that fisher-gal. What's her name agin?"

"Shelly," replied Zeb.

"That's right, Shelly."

"Don't b.s. me Swig, you remember her name."

Swig's cheeks warmed to a ruddy shade of purplish-red. Even his nose plumped up more than usual.

"Are you taking her fishing?" asked Zeb.

Swig's forehead began to sweat. He barely understood his own emotions. After all, he was old enough to be Shelly's grandfather.

"Uh, yeah, I am. We got a date all set."

"You've got a couple of years on her, Swig."

The proprietor hawked another gob of expectorate into the spittoon. As it struck the copper side of the spit catcher, an echo zinged through the otherwise deadly quiet store.

"Ain't that kind of a date. It's fishing."

Zeb could tell Swig was embarrassed.

"Good for you teaching the young folks about bass fishing. It's becoming a lost art."

"Enough of the b.s. What do you want to know, Zeb?"

"Close your eyes…"

"You gonna hypnotize me or something?"

"Kind of, but not really."

"You ain't gonna make me squawk like a chicken, are you?" asked Swig.

"No. Just pay attention and keep quiet. Okay?"

Zeb was using an old-fashioned memory recall trick that Echo had recently taught him. It was a Knowledge Keeper method of withdrawing something seemingly forgotten from a person's bank of memories.

"No. Just close your eyes and think back to the day of the robbery."

Swig did as Zeb suggested. To keep the sheriff honest, he peeked out from one eye just to see what Zeb was up to. Zeb had not moved an inch, so Swig shut his eye.

"Attempted robbery. I got all my money back. I even found some loose change out in the street. I actually came out ahead on the deal. Found me enough spare change, a buck plus a little more, to get me a cup of joe over at the Town Talk."

"I've never seen you set foot into the Town Talk," said Zeb.

"Didn't say I had," replied Swig.

Zeb rolled his eyes and shook his head. Having a straight-line conversation with Swig was about as likely as being able to lick the back side of your elbow.

"Okay. Let's get back to the day of the attempted robbery. Think about what you saw."

Swig's eyes jumped open.

"Damn. Well, what the Sam Hill do you know? I just remembered something. Shee-it. Pretty good trick you pulled on me, Zeb."

"What do you remember, Swig?"

"When Obama was tossing the money up in the air, that's when I was sneaking a peek at them through my front window, the glove on his left hand came off. He put it right back on. But when it was off, I saw that he had a ring on his pinky finger. I saw it because it glistened in the sun. Ain't that something? I forgot all about that 'til just right now. Having me shut my eyes is a pretty dang good memory trick. Think I'll use it myself sometime."

Zeb watched as Swig temporarily left his present moment and drifted off into his imagination. Zeb imagined Swig was pondering on how he might use the little memory trick. A cough brought Swig back to the job at hand.

"Sorry, Sheriff, I was driftin' away. Old man's disease, or pleasure, depending on your point of view and the situation."

"I could see you were a long distance off. That's fine. Can you tell me anything more about the ring?" asked Zeb.

"Yes. Yes. The ring." Swig shut his eyes softly. "That's what's really weird. It was daytime and it was bright like a cloudless late summer Arizona afternoon outside. Maybe it was a trick of the mind, maybe it was just the conditions, but his ring glistened so strongly in the sunshine that I could see it like it was only ten feet away. It was like it was lit up or something."

Swig quit talking for a moment, opened his eyes and fired a loogy into the spittoon. When he looked up at Zeb, Swig had the look of a man who had just had a realization about himself that he did not necessarily care for. He scratched his balding head with the middle finger of his hand before he spoke.

"Now, how the hell could I forget that?"

"What exactly did you see? As precisely as possible can you tell me what you saw?" asked Zeb.

Swig grabbed a pen and one of his business cards that sat next to the register.

"It looked like this."

Swig scrawled a childlike image of a winged dragon with a curly tail. In the background were the sun and its gleaming rays.

"You could see all of that from the distance you were away?"

Swig shrugged his shoulders. This time he spit into the spittoon from between his two front teeth.

"Like I said, probably a trick of the mind. Who knows? All I know is that I could see it plain as I can see you or a camouflaged Cong back in the day."

"You're sure of that?"

"What'd I just say? It glistened like sunshine, too," said Swig.

Zeb figured the ring, because of the glinting sun, was almost certainly made of metal, probably gold or polished silver. Zeb stared at the drawing briefly before taking Swig's art work and slipping it into his shirt pocket.

"I don't see how that can help you," said Swig.

"It might not, but, then again, it just might. It's a long shot. Anything and everything helps," replied Zeb. "Remember anything else?"

Swig swept his head from side to side.

"Nope. Damn lucky I remember that. Not that it'll do you any good."

Zeb tipped his hat and walked out the door. He walked across the street to his office and called Clarissa. She was efficient with her work. He was certain her conversation with Maxon Mazie at the utility had been completed. As she answered her phone, Clarissa just happened to be walking through the back door of the sheriff's office. She entered Zeb's office, still on the phone with him. They both smiled at the inadvertent coincidence.

"Get anything from Max Mazie?"

"We reviewed the enhanced video footage that Shelly sent them," said Clarissa.

"Find anything?" asked Zeb.

"Here is what I got."

Clarissa laid a picture downloaded from Max Mazie's computer. It was a picture of a hand turning the security camera away from the mainline control valve.

"Looks like this person has a bend in his little finger," said Clarissa.

"Or they're wearing a big pinkie ring," said Zeb.

Clarissa placed the downloaded image directly in front of Zeb, on his desk. She grabbed a pen and drew a circle around what might be either an arthritic finger or a large pinkie ring.

"Take this over to Shelly." Zeb re-circled the area on the pinkie finger Clarissa was referring to. "See if Shelly can further enhance it."

"What are you looking for, Sheriff Hanks?"

Zeb showed her the almost cartoonish image on the card Swig had drawn.

"I just want to see if she can enhance the image," replied Zeb. "I'd like to know if we can determine if it's arthritis, a bent finger or a ring."

"What about the ring?"

Jake tossed out his question as he strutted into Zeb's office.

"I'll tell you after you tell me what you learned from Constantina and Apolonia," said Zeb.

"Constantina and Apolonia send their best to the both of you."

"That's sweet," said Clarissa.

"They were pretty sharp today," said Jake. "Both of them seemed as clear as any of us."

"That's not necessarily saying much," said Zeb.

It was clear to Clarissa and Jake that he was joking. But, Helen, listening through the partially open door, heard it otherwise. Her tone was a scolding one as she spoke directly to the sheriff.

"Zeb Hanks, you will be old one day, that is, if God blesses you with a long life. Mind your manners when it comes to speaking poorly of the elderly."

"Yes, Helen, you are right. I apologize. I hope you realize I was only joking."

"Alzheimer's disease is no joke. Neither are the troubles one bears when they age. I suggest you never forget that, or you'll end up a forgotten and lonely old man."

Helen's voice was stern enough to make Zeb, Jake and Clarissa snap to attention. Zeb pointed to the door. Jake slipped over and quietly closed it. Helen could be heard harrumphing from her desk.

"What've you got, Jake? Anything?"

"Maybe, probably not, but both gals remembered something they had forgotten earlier. Why they remembered it now, I can't say, and neither could they. Both claimed it popped into their heads when they were watching an old Sherlock Holmes movie starring Basil Rathbone."

"Yes? And what popped into their heads?" asked Zeb.

"Apparently, even though her memory isn't so great, Constantina can remember lines an actor says from a movie, especially if she's seen it a few times before. Apolonia agrees with everything Constantina says, so I don't know if her word is good or she just is an agreeable sort."

"What did they see or hear?" asked Clarissa.

"Like I said, they were watching a movie, *The Hound of the Baskervilles*. There's a part in the movie when Holmes notes the odd shape of Watson's little finger."

"Odd shape?" asked Zeb.

"Yes, Holmes describes Watson's finger as being as bent as a shepherd's crook."

"And that all adds up to what, exactly?" asked Zeb.

"It was then Constantina said she remembered the man who stood by her bed and whispered in her ear not to worry because she wasn't hurt and wasn't really bleeding."

"I remember that part of her statement," said Clarissa.

Zeb nodded in agreement. "Go on."

"Constantina remembers the man holding his gloved hand so close to her that she could smell it."

"I remember that part of her statement as well," interjected Zeb. "Many people can't stand the odor of latex."

"But more than smell," continued Jake, "she said she saw the little finger of his hand. It was crooked, just like Watson's finger. Then when I walk in here you two are talking about a finger. Funny coincidence isn't..."

Jake stopped in mid-sentence as he witnessed the exchanged glance between Clarissa and Zeb.

"What? What is that look all about?" asked Jake.

Zeb quickly explained the close-up shot of the pinkie finger from the camera image Max Mazie at the utility company had given them along with the little finger ring on the Obama mask wearer in the robbery at Swig's.

"Strange," said Jake. "But in and of itself it doesn't mean anything, other than it may possibly link the crimes since everyone who was violated seems to have noticed the pinkie finger ring. It merely tells us the same person was possibly, maybe even likely, involved. That's something we have all sort of expected anyway. But, in reality, it doesn't prove anything beyond a reasonable doubt."

"It's something, and something is better than nothing," said Zeb.

"Yeah, and that plus a buck and a quarter will get you a cup of coffee at the Town Talk."

"When was the last time you paid for a cup of joe at the Town Talk?"

"I was just making a point," said Zeb.

It was clear Jake needed something more, something bigger. At that moment Kate rapped on the door of Zeb's office. Jake, with a movement of his hand, signaled her in.

"You all look very serious," said Kate. "What's up?"

Simultaneously, Zeb, Jake and Clarissa held up their pinkie fingers. Kate's eyes widened. She reached into her pocket and pulled out a small evidence bag. Carefully, she laid it on Zeb's desk. Zeb, Jake and Clarissa leaned forward. Inside the bag was a ring.

"The school janitor found this recently in the floor air conditioning grate. It probably came off the criminal's hand when they were setting up the crime scene."

All heads tipped toward the gold ring and the dragon with a bent tail design.

11

DOCTORS YACKLEY AND ZATA

D oc Yackley's cellphone sang out *Not Fade Away*, the Rolling Stones version. Doc and Zits had seen the Stones in 1978 at the Tucson Convention Center. Pee-Wee had set his phone up so Doc could identify certain callers. *Not Fade Away* indicated the call was from his school chum and pathologist, Dr. Nitis 'Zits' Zata. Doc pressed the answer circle.

"Zits."

"Jimbo."

"What'd you find out?"

Doc Yackley was of course referring to the final autopsy results the pathologist had obtained on Sheriff Black Bear. The final report confirmed what Zata's preliminary report had suggested and added the results which had taken time to complete.

"I just now sent a report to your computer. Open it up. Let's go over this line by line."

Doc did as Zits suggested. In a moment the autopsy report was open. He jumped to the bottom and Doctor Zata's summary of findings.

"Black Bear had cancer?"

"Jimbo, you should have some respect for my work and not read ahead."

"Too late for that," replied Doc Yackley.

"He had cancer in his bones, in at least one kidney, adrenal glands, brain, liver and lungs," said Zits.

"Jesus H. Kee-rist on a crutch. If his organs were harvested for resale, someone just bought themselves a death sentence from a cancerous kidney."

"You got that right," replied Zits.

"I shouldn't say it serves them right..."

Doc Yackley's old medical school chum completed the sentence.

"But, in a manner of speaking, it does, doesn't it?"

"Zits, what was your mind thinking? I mean what led you to discover kidney cancer in a cadaver that didn't have any kidneys?"

"My first hint came when we emptied his bladder."

Doc Yackley snapped his fingers.

"You found blood," said Doc.

"I did. Ergo, I checked for anemia, increased liver enzymes and blood calcium levels," replied Zits. "Simple deductive reasoning."

"And you found increased liver enzymes, anemia and increased blood calcium?"

"Good call. I guess you didn't sleep through every class in med school."

"The interesting ones kept me awake," said Doc Yackley. "But that's old news. Let me guess what you did next."

"Give it your best shot."

"You did a bone scan?"

"Yessiree, Jimbo, I did. I found cancerous cells in the femur and tibia"

"And, therefore, your next step was to..."

"To progress forward with a full-body MRI. That's when I found tumors and tumor cells in the lungs, brain and liver."

"I see you graded the cancer cells T4M1."

"I gave it that grade because I also found tumors in both of the adrenal glands, adrenal glands that were obviously left behind."

"That's odd. But, as you remember, I did note that in my initial autopsy report."

"You did. Nice job. Well done and all that kind of tommy rot."

"Just tooting my own horn."

"You needn't do that with me."

"Right."

"I found that leaving the adrenal glands behind was rather undisciplined," said Dr. Zata. "I mean, really? Leaving the adrenal glands behind? A rookie mistake from what we have assumed to be experts."

"True, true," said Doc Yackley.

"But it is to our advantage, and I can say with almost one hundred percent certainty that the tumor in the adrenal glands migrated there from the kidneys. Leaving the adrenal glands behind, especially since they were malignant, is like leaving bread crumbs for a pigeon."

"In the right hands it is a trail of clues that are totally obvious," said Doc.

"In our hands it's not only a trail of clues, it's damn near a roadmap from a Rand McNally atlas."

"Everyone uses a phone app these days," said Doc Yackley.

"That's because no one pays attention to where they're going. Just one more sign of a society in decay," said Dr. Zata.

"Maybe, but ranting and raving about it won't help us figure out what we need to know," said Doc.

"I guess you're right," replied Zits. "Back to business."

Doc Yackley chuckled. Zits was a wild man with strong opinions, but he always knew that work came first.

"Whoever was organ shopping must not have had adrenal glands on their list," said Doc Yackley.

The dark humor caused both men to snicker. They spoke the next four words in unison.

"Gallows humor. Knock wood."

This time they laughed aloud. Forty years had passed since medical school graduation, but the link between them had remained unchanged and rock solid.

"At least they left behind a damning clue."

Jimbo and Zits were back at it. A modern-day Watson and Holmes carried the memory of their youth in the medical school pathology lab into the literal present.

"Was Black Bear seeing you for cancer by any chance?"

"No.

"Some other illnesses?"

"He did his doctoring over in Tucson. He saw a guy that got his medical degree from some obscure, unlicensed med school in rural Mexico. I remember his name. Doctor Stanislaus Steinman."

"I don't know him personally. However, I do know him by reputation," said Zits. "He is reportedly a bit of a quack. He's a pill pusher. He primarily runs a chain of pain clinics and hands out Oxycontin and fentanyl like they're candy. Rumor has it he works for the local mafia, and his patients are Mexican cartel bigwigs and their minions. Once again, I've heard via the grapevine that he is frequently called on for midnight surgeries when someone takes a stray bullet and wants to stay off the police or hospital radar. Rumor also has it that he has removed organs for illegal transplants, but all I have is an unfounded rumor of that from a single source. Therefore, I consider it not to be real evidence."

"Does the rumor mill suggest he does the implantation surgeries as well?" asked Doc Yackley.

"Not based on what I've heard. I would sort of suspect that level of skill is out of his league. But, if he removes organs, he definitely could be in cahoots with the surgeon who puts them into a new body."

"Since he had all of Black Bear's vital information, he could have easily offered his organs up for the right price," said Doc Yackley.

"So much for the Hippocratic oath," added Zits.

"His adherence to our sacred oath, I suspect, was always somewhat lacking, especially when it comes to the part that says we must do the most good and the least harm."

The old doctors' conversation went silent. Both knew their findings had to be shared with Zeb. Whatever was going on had suddenly moved out of their league. Sighs of disappointment dribbled through the airwaves. Neither wanted to mess with the mafia, the cartel, some billionaire or whomever was behind this. They were old men, too old to be seeking the kind of trouble that could take away what remained of their time on this planet.

"Could be some cartel big shot or some mafioso needed an organ, and Doctor Steinman was their go-to guy," said Zits. "In which case…"

"In which case I think it's time to hand what we know over to the sheriff's department," said Doc Yackley.

"I'm afraid so," replied Zits.

"Besides, Zeb is going to want that bullet you pulled from Black Bear's brain," said Doc.

"It's sitting right here on my desk. It's a .22 caliber short. It banged up against that metal plate Black Bear had in his occipital lobe."

"Any solid theories on what happened that caused him to have a metal plate in his skull?" asked Doc.

"No, but the material is stainless steel."

"Which means what?" asked Doc.

"It means there is a highly significant chance it was implanted in the 1980s when Black Bear was a kid. Or, it could also mean the Rez didn't have the best care available, and they were using older-type materials. If that was the case, the implant could have been done at a later date," said Zits.

"Got it."

"No matter how you look at it, the bullet put a pretty good dent in the metal implant before it danced around some and ended up near the third ventricle," said Zits.

"I found that ironic," said Doc. "I mean that it landed in the in the part of the brain that directs morality."

"Perhaps more aptly it could be called poetic justice. Justice sometimes finds its own end."

"Probably more often than we know," replied Zits.

"Listen to us. There we go again."

"Philosophizing like we might actually know something."

The old docs enjoyed a good chuckle at their own expense.

"Holmes and Watson are going to have to wait for another time," said Doc Yackley.

"I'll send an official copy of the final autopsy report and lab findings, along with a personal note, to Sheriff Hanks' office."

"Thanks," said Doc Yackley. "Appreciate it."

An odd silence ensued. Each man was obviously swimming deeply through their own pool of thoughts.

"Are you thinking what I'm thinking?" asked Doctor Zata.

"I might be."

"What are you thinking, Jimbo?"

"I'm thinking that if the mafia, the cartel or some other organized entity is behind this, I'm suspecting they purposefully sent a cancerous kidney to someone they wanted dead."

"Damn near a perfect crime. Wouldn't you say?" asked Doc Yackley.

"Damn near perfect enough," said Zits. "But not picture-perfect when Holmes and Watson are back in the game."

"We've got to keep our information on the down low."

"Just between us is where this theory lives and dies," replied Zits.

"Maybe I should tell Zeb our theory," said Doc Yackley.

"I don't know. He might think we're nuts. We've got no proof of any scheme like the one we're talking about."

"He already thinks I stick my nose into too many crimes," said Doc Yackley. "Still, I think I should tell him that whoever is going to get those cancerous organs is going to be in trouble."

"You don't think he can figure that much out?"

"I do, but I'd feel better if I said something," said Doc Yackley.

"How about this? You emphasize that you'd hate to see the organs transplanted into anyone because of the potential harm they could do. That would leave us to do our sleuthing around without any interference from anyone."

"And keep us off the radar."

"Right."

"Deal," said Doc Yackley. "No one needs to know what we are up to. If we can help, we will. If we find nothing out, then so be it. No one will suspect we are up to anything."

"Jolly good, old bean."

Doc Yackley replied with his best imitation of a British accent.

"Quite right. Quite right."

"And the bullet?"

"Well, that's where being a good sheriff comes into play. We can only tell him what we know to be factual."

"Watson and Holmes, Holmes and Watson. By Jove, they've still got it," said Zits.

As Doc Yackley ended the phone call, the vigor of youth flowed through his veins with the velocity of the phantom punch Muhammad Ali threw at Sonny Liston in their 1965 championship rematch.

12
SHAPPA HÓWAKȞANYAŊ

K ate was sitting at her desk doing paperwork when her cell phone buzzed. Glancing down, she didn't immediately recognize the number, but the 605-area code rang a bell. A quick sweep of her mind told her it was likely Shappa Hówakȟanyaŋ. Kate pressed the answer button. The person on the other end spoke before Kate could utter a single word.

"Sheriff Kate, this is Shappa Hówakȟanyaŋ."

"Hello," replied Kate. "I thought we might be hearing from you."

"I'm coming to town to pick up my son's body. I'd like to meet with you."

Though a call from Shappa to the Sheriff's Office was anticipated, the request to meet with Kate was a bit of a bolt out of the blue.

"When are you coming to Safford?"

"I've got a flight out of Rapid City tomorrow. I'll arrive in Phoenix in the early afternoon. I'm renting a vehicle and driving to Safford. MapQuest routes it at 165 miles, roughly two and half hours. I'd like to meet with you around five p.m., if that works for you."

Kate hesitated. She was no longer the temporary Sheriff of Graham County. Her immediate thought was to let Zeb in on what Shappa was planning.

Black Bear's body was in Tucson. The exhaustive autopsy had been completed only days earlier and the body was being stored in a cooler at the pathology lab at the Tucson Medical School. Kate had no idea who had final say, or, for that matter, the exact chain of custody over control of Black Bear's body.

"How are you planning on transporting the, er, Black Bear's body?" asked Kate.

"I rented an oversized van. A friend of mind in Tucson built me a crate for transportation purposes. It will fit in the back of the van. I'll pack his body in dry ice."

Shappa's plan sounded dubious, at best, and possibly unlawful.

"Dry ice?"

"I've done it before," said Shappa. "It works fine."

Kate was taken aback by Shappa's admission that this was the kind of task she had previously been involved with. The slowness of her response to Shappa's request juxtaposed Shappa's firm words.

"I want to take my son on one last drive."

Shappa's words and wishes were becoming curiouser and curiouser.

"One last drive?"

"Yes. You heard me correctly. One last drive. When Black Bear was a boy, we spent countless hours riding around together in a van on the Rez and the upper Midwest in general. I was doing a lot of political work, talking to people, handing out information, organizing groups, getting people involved in the free health care clinics and informing them of their personal rights as indigenous people. It was one of the missions the Creator had bestowed upon me. Black Bear rode along with me. You might say he was my co-pilot. He was just an innocent adolescent, but he was wise beyond his years. During that time, in those days, we talked about anything and everything under the sun. We became as close as a mother and a son can possibly become."

Kate could feel Shappa's motherly love through her words. She could also clearly sense the hurt Shappa was carrying in her heart.

Yet something about the way Shappa spoke, something Kate couldn't quite put her finger on, didn't have the ring of absolute truth.

"I plan on driving Black Bear's body back to South Dakota. There I can do the proper Lakota ceremonial rites."

"A Lakota ceremony. For his funeral."

"Yes. We Lakota, our cultural heritage, takes the end of a person's life very seriously."

Kate's interest was piqued. She sensed a genuine softening in Shappa.

"I've never been to a Lakota end of life ceremony," said Kate. "What happens at one?"

Kate was surprised by her own bluntness. But she had been professionally close to Black Bear, and they had shared confidentialities. She felt as though she had the right to ask such a question.

"It's nice of you to ask. It's not a complicated process. We, my sisters, Black Bear's grandmothers and I, will wrap Black Bear in his finest traditional Lakota clothes. I have his ceremonial clothes here. I have already laid them out and they have been blessed by a medicine man. We will use those as they have been prepared for exactly this moment since the day he performed his Sun Dance. He had a small house on the Pine Ridge. We've already burned that to the ground. I suspect that whoever killed him burned his house down there already."

"The house being burned to the ground. That's why you think it was a Native American that killed him?" asked Kate.

"Yes. It only makes sense that another Lakota did the killing. There is also a distinct possibility that someone who knows the ways of the Lakota murdered my son."

Because Zeb had suggested Black Bear may have been involved with various nefarious types, Kate had previously assumed Black Bear's house had been burned to the ground in retribution or to hide evidence. The additional information Shappa was providing might prove valuable. Kate made a note about the recent arson at Black Bear's Safford residence as well as the purposeful burning down of his house on the Pine Ridge Rez. The arson investigators could probably do more with the information than she could.

"I understand," said Kate.

"I am going to offer his earthly body to the next world with a scaffold burial," said Shappa.

"Which is what?" asked Kate.

"The men will build a scaffold. We, Black Bear's family and three Lakota medicine men, will burn his body to ashes. I will light the fire that will make it all happen. It is my duty as his mother to return him to dust. The scaffold will be built very high up in the air. The elevated platform will encourage the journey of his spirit into the sky and to the Creator."

Kate could see it all in her head. Somehow, it made perfect sense. The process would indeed complete the cycle of life for Sawyer Black Bear. She thought back upon their conversations and how he had talked of the future. It felt strange to think that he would soon become ashes. Shappa's voice snapped her back to reality.

"I would very much like it if you would empty his locker and desk at the sheriff's office. Those items will be sent with him to the next world," explained Shappa.

"I will need to get permission from Sheriff Hanks," said Kate.

"I thought you were acting as Sheriff of Graham County?" asked Shappa.

"We just held an election. Sheriff Hanks won. No one ran against him," said Kate.

"Why didn't you oppose him on the ballot?" asked Shappa.

Before Kate could formulate her answer, Shappa had more to say on the subject.

"It's about time a woman ran that place. In fact, it is far past the time when a woman should be Sheriff of Graham County."

"A time will come when there will be a woman sheriff here," said Kate. "But, for now, I am choosing not to run for sheriff because my husband and I are raising a family. In fact, I just found out I may be pregnant."

"Congratulations."

"Thank you."

"May you be as proud of your children as I was, as I am, of Black Bear."

"I will love my children and teach them the best that I can," replied Kate.

As quickly as she spoke of love of children, Shappa turned back to the business at hand.

"It is a dangerous time to be seated behind the sheriff's desk in Graham County. Perhaps another time will be more suitable for you."

Kate was uncertain as to exactly what Shappa was referring to. When she pursued the subject, Shappa quickly changed it.

"I am certain that a time will come when you can run and win the office of Sheriff in Graham County."

"Yes. That day will arrive," replied Kate. "A woman sheriff is almost an inevitability at some point soon."

"With all that's going on, now is not the right time for you," said Shappa. "Especially for someone like you who already has one child and possibly another on the way. It might be a bad time not only for you, but for your husband and children."

Her words, when spoken a second time, including Josh and Alexis in the mix, sounded as much like a warning as anything.

"A mother should never have to live longer than her child. It is out of the natural order of things, but it happens. It happens far more often to minorities than it does to Whites. It is a reality I have seen too many times. It is also a reality I accept."

Shappa's dire words carried a fierceness in them. Kate shivered as her gut instinct told her Shappa's words were indeed a warning. Kate needed to change the subject. She felt that Shappa's mind, in its grief, was definitely winding its way toward dark places. It may have been only her interpretation of Shappa's words, but Kate felt as though she needed to steer Shappa toward light and away from potential vast darkness.

"It seems that statistics would bear that out," said Kate.

"Trust me. They do," replied Shappa.

"But things can and do change for the better," said Kate.

Kate realized she had not asked Shappa how she was doing. The sternness in Shappa's voice had given her pause. Because Kate needed to move Shappa away from the bad place she was headed, she asked the most basic of questions.

"How are you doing, Shappa?"

Black Bear's mother sighed heavily. Her voice cracked as she exhaled. A distinct but peculiar kind of stress hung on every word.

"I have done everything I know how to do. I have sung. I have cried. I have wailed. I pegged my hair with an oak branch. I cut off the tip of my second finger, the index finger, as Black Bear was my second child."

Kate waited in silence for further explanation. Not only the excision of the fingertip but the fact that Shappa had another child brought up questions in her mind. Shappa understood the pause. She could tell that Kate was unfamiliar with the reasoning behind her act of self-mutilation. As well, she guessed that Black Bear had not mentioned his sibling to Kate.

"It is an old tradition that is rarely followed these days. I felt as though I would be a hypocrite if I didn't follow the most difficult of the traditional ways for my son. I have spent a lifetime trying to educate young Indians in the ways of the wise ones who have carried our traditions since time began. I truly believe that since I went as far as cutting off the tip of my finger, the young tribal members are listening to me more closely. It was a small sacrifice to make for my son and for the tribe."

"I understand tradition," said Kate. "I am sorry you had to follow this one."

"Thank you, my dear woman," replied Shappa.

Shappa's tone triggered two other questions.

"Would it be okay if Sheriff Hanks is here tomorrow when you arrive in Safford?"

"Yes," replied Shappa. "It is yet another circle that must be closed. I know that Zeb and Black Bear did not see eye to eye. I am aware of the conflict that raged between them. There is no sense for my son to carry that with him on his journey to the afterlife."

"Thank you," replied Kate. "I'll talk with him."

"Philámayayapi," said Shappa.

Kate did not speak Lakota but easily understood that Shappa was thanking her.

"You had another question for me?" asked Shappa.

Kate, much younger and far less experienced in life than Shappa, felt a bit foolish asking the second question. Shappa's response was even more confusing.

"Are you going to be okay?"

Before she spoke, Shappa laughed. Her laughter was out of harmony with not only the situation, but with the purpose of laughter itself. Her actions and words aroused a strange apprehension in Kate's heart and mind. It was a suspicion she could not put her finger directly on.

"Although things are not in the natural order, they are exactly as they should be."

13

ECHO AND SHELLY

The security system built into Shelly's computer spotted Echo's truck parked at the end of the driveway. It began to sing out the old Porter Wagoner song, *Company's Coming,* a full minute before Echo pressed the security gate call button.

"Echo, I wasn't expecting you. Please come in."

"Just a heads up. I'm not alone," said Echo. "I've got the kids."

"Come through the gate and up to the house. I'll buzz open the front door. Let yourself in. I've got a couple of quick things to do to make certain the house is one hundred percent kid-proofed."

Shelly could hear Echo's happy laughter as she buzzed open the security gate to her mini mansion. When she arrived near the front door, Shelly bounded down through the front entry, offering a hand with Onawa and Elan. Echo handed Onawa to Shelly. Onawa cooed. Shelly tickled her cheek. Both laughed.

"I think she likes me," said Shelly.

"She does, but don't let it go to your head. She likes everybody. My mother says I was the same way," explained Echo. "If I could only get her to find the same joy in sleeping."

"I might have an answer for you," said Shelly.

The women with babies in arms walked through to Shelly's office.

The sleek and ultra-modern house opened into a room built in the classic style of an early 1900s east coast mansion library. The blend of past and present was architecturally stunning. Somehow it all seemed to work perfectly.

"Like it?" asked Shelly.

"You've got a decorator's touch and a keen eye for blending the past and the future."

Shelly laughed. Echo continued to admire the room.

"And yet I firmly believe that I live in the present. The entire project was created by suggestions I input into a computer program that aids in room design."

"Cool."

"Over here," said Shelly.

At her computer she entered a few keystrokes, and, like magic, computer synthesized sounds filled the room.

"It's from a company called Nature's Heartbeat," said Shelly.

By the end of the first stanza, the already sleeping Elan began to snore. Within a minute Onawa was sound asleep.

"I'll buy one," said Echo. "Heck, I'll take a half-dozen of them and share them with friends."

Shelly opened her hand. In the palm was a thumb drive that was marked 'Sleep, Little Ones, Sleep'. Echo immediately snatched it away with the speed and dexterity of a magician's hand.

"You could make a million dollars on this. You should write up a business plan and go on *Shark Tank*. Every new mother in the world would buy one or two or three of these and then buy some for their friends."

The excitement in Echo's voice was only found in a sleep-deprived new mother who has at last found hope for an ailment brought on by love.

"Let me get you a glass of wine while those little ones are asleep."

"I'm nursing."

"Of course. A non-alcoholic wine or beer?" asked Shelly.

"Some herbal tea would nice," replied Echo. "Something relaxing."

"Here, check this one out. I saw it on-line and decided there might come a time when you might use it."

Shelly handed Echo a box that read 'Earth Mama Angel Baby Milkmaid Nursing Tea'.

Echo read the front of the box, turned it ninety degrees and scoured the ingredients. It was perfectly healthy and something she was looking for without even knowing it.

"Shelly, you are so sweet and so perceptive."

"And you are an overtired mother," replied Shelly.

"Sometimes I think mothering twins can be more tiring than combat," said Echo.

"But the outcome is better," added Shelly.

"It most certainly is."

Shelly made tea. The women sat down in a small room just off the kitchen that was private and perfect for nursing. A few cups of tea and after a bit of small talk, Echo got down to the real reason for her visit.

"I need your help," said Echo.

"Anything," replied Shelly. "All you have to do is ask."

"It's about Zeb."

Echo and Shelly had been friends but not particularly close ones. Shelly was more than a bit surprised that Echo would come to her for help regarding something as personal as her husband.

"Yes? If I can help you, I'll be glad to."

"It's touchy."

"Sure."

Shelly took a sip of wine and tuned her always heightened senses into Echo's words and body language.

"I trust you. Zeb speaks so highly of your skills. I've seen what kind of work you do. Most of all, my gut tells me to trust you. To top it off, you carry the mark of one who can be trusted."

Echo pointed to a constellation of tiny moles on Shelly's neck. Shelly's curiosity rose instantly.

"Recent knowledge has taught me to read physical signs on a

woman's body that have spiritual meanings. You carry the signs of trust, love and friendship," said Echo.

Shelly walked to a mirror and took a look. For the first time in her life, she noticed an amazing array of tiny dotted moles on her neck. They were so small as to be almost imperceptible to even the most discernable eye. She rubbed her hand across them. They emitted a light buzz of electricity.

"These are as good a reason as any to trust me," said Shelly. "I guess."

"I don't want to be dishonest. And, I truly don't want to withhold anything from Zeb. That being said, I would like to keep this between us. Just you and me," said Echo, gently wagging a finger between them.

"Does it have anything to do with cases the sheriff's department is currently working on?" asked Shelly.

"I can't say for certain one way or the other," replied Echo.

"Can't say or don't know?"

"Can't say," replied Echo.

"That's a most peculiar answer coming from you. Tell me more."

"If I tell you, I have to trust you won't discuss this with Zeb until I give you the okay. I hate to be so obtuse about what I need to discuss, but I am sort of boxed into a corner myself."

"Are you and Zeb doing all right? I mean, I've never had kids and new twins certainly seem like they would be a lot of work. So much work that it might leave little time for the marriage."

"We're good, great actually, in the marriage department. It's something else entirely," explained Echo.

"And...?"

"I need you to promise me that this stays strictly between the two of us."

Shelly's mind danced through a dozen potential scenarios. What on earth could Echo need to keep from Zeb? What was it that she could not share with her husband? There had to be underlying trouble. Echo was as strong and as competent a woman as she knew. The thought also crossed Shelly's mind as to why Echo was choosing her as a confidante. Shelly did her best to get a read on Echo. Echo's face was replete with both stoicism and concern. Shelly cleared her throat.

"I can do as you ask if and only if it doesn't interfere with any ongoing investigation Zeb or anyone in the sheriff's department is doing."

"What if I put it this way?" This time Echo was the one clearing her throat. "What I am about to share with you doesn't have any bearing on any case anyone at the sheriff's office is currently investigating. However, in the future, someone might be looking into what I am about to share with you."

Shelly gazed into Echo's eyes, looked over at the sleeping babies, then returned her eyes to their mother. Echo's face showed no significant signs of stress or fatigue. A thought passed through her mind of how combat trained Echo's mind and body must be. Shelly felt a tinge of envy.

"Okay. Whatever it is, it'll be just between us girls," said Shelly.

"This is going to sound weird."

"Ha! In my line of work, nothing sounds weird," laughed Shelly.

"Okay. I'm just going to come right out and say it."

Echo sighed heavily. Both Elan and Onawa cooed in their sleep.

"Zeb carries hatred in his heart for Senator Russell."

"That's no secret," interrupted Shelly. "Everyone at the office is well aware of that fact."

"But he might have one very legitimate reason for having such strong emotions toward Senator Russell," said Echo.

Shelly moved in closer to Echo on the oversized couch. She couldn't help but notice the slightest hint of a sweat bead on Echo's ever so slightly quivering upper lip. It was the first sign of strain that showed on her face. Shelly reached out and held Echo's hand. Her hand was vibrating with the subtle energy that accompanies well-controlled stress.

"Zeb's mother had an affair with Senator Russell for about six months."

"When was this?" asked Shelly.

"It began approximately one year before Zeb was born."

As she spoke, Echo watched the expression on Shelly's face turn from interest to concern.

Like a steel tipped projectile aimed for the double bullseye on a dartboard, Shelly slammed the target.

"You have reasons to believe Zeb is the illegitimate son of Senator Russell, don't you?"

Echo's silence spoke volumes. Shelly re-asked essentially the same question in another way.

"You don't think Zeb believes he is Senator Russell's son, do you?"

"I don't know what he thinks. It's the first time ever I feel as though a subject has been taboo between us," said Echo. "I don't even know how to bring it up to Zeb."

"That's too bad," replied Shelly. "However, it is completely understandable, considering the history between the two men."

"But wait, there's more, a lot more," said Echo.

Shelly, already stunned by the news, wondered what else there could be. Did Zeb have some half-siblings in Safford? Had Zeb known this big secret for his entire life? What else could there be?

"There's also a rumor floating around that Zeb will one day be inheriting Senator Russell's property."

"His ranch just outside of town or his condo in Phoenix?" asked Shelly.

"All of it according to my source," replied Echo. "As well as a townhouse in D.C."

"Mind sharing your source regarding the property Zeb might inherit?"

"Helen."

"Helen? How would she know?"

Spontaneously Echo and Shelly burst into laughter. If anyone was privy to any bit of gossip, it would be Helen.

"She heard it through the grapevine. In this case the grapevine was Cheryl Blackstrom, the Registrar of Deeds for Graham County. According to Helen, some aide from an attorney's office in D.C. contacted the county registrar's office. They needed technical details regarding Senator Russell's property. They wanted to add a name to the ownership of the properties."

"Zeb's, I take it?"

"Precisely," replied Echo. "I just happened to be dropping by the sheriff's office when Cheryl stopped by to tell Helen all about it. I heard just the tail end of the conversation. When I asked Helen what was going on, she only very sheepishly shared the information with me."

"Sheepishly? That's not like Helen," said Shelly. "She's usually leading the charge when it comes to gossip."

"I got the weird impression that the secret of Senator Russell being Zeb's biological father was something she has always known about," said Echo.

A thunderbolt struck Echo and Shelly at that exact moment. Of course Helen knew. Helen and Zeb's mother were sisters. If Zeb's mom confided in anyone, it would have been Helen.

The two women sat in silence. Echo drank her tea. Shelly sipped on a glass of white wine. Both knew there was no simple way of dealing with this. Zeb and Senator Russell's long-time feud and the secrets they knew about each other would only be further complicated by Zeb knowing Senator Russell was possibly his father. Then, there was the issue of how Zeb dealt with his feelings toward his mother regarding this truly delicate matter. Several times Echo and Shelly began to speak, but each time it ended up in a sigh. The problem at hand was deep and wide and potentially emotionally brutal.

"I assume Zeb has no idea that Senator Russell might be his biological father?"

"No," said Echo. "As far as I know, he doesn't have even the slightest hint that Russell could be his father."

"I also take it Zeb doesn't know about his name being added to the property," said Shelly.

"I only found out yesterday," said Echo. "And that was by accident. I don't even know that Helen told me the exact truth or if she shared only part of the facts."

"Did Helen ask you to be discreet?"

"She asked that I give her a few days to decide what to say, whom to talk to, etcetera, etcetera. It's all in the early stages of discovery and all very complex."

"You can't really expect Helen to say anything. After all, she and Zeb's mother are sisters," said Shelly.

"And from what Zeb tells me, they are very close," said Echo.

"I'm sure Helen is protecting her sister. It's the natural thing to do."

"Of course she is. What choice does she have?"

"It's not Helen's job to tell Zeb," said Shelly.

"No, of course it's not," replied Echo.

"I guess that leaves you, Echo, as the bearer of strange and very disconcerting news," said Shelly.

"It does. I haven't found the right moment to talk to him yet. I don't know what I'm going to say when I do. I don't feel as though I have all the facts. However, I don't want to sit on this information for very much longer either. I know there was great disharmony between Zeb and the man who raised him as his father. But if he finds out that Senator Russell is his biological father, his actual flesh and blood, he might go ballistic. He carries such rage within that I have no idea how he might react should he find out."

Shelly nodded, sipped her wine and sank back into the oversized cushions. Zeb's seething storm of ire was well-known, rarely spoken of and, for the most part, considered to be just part of his complex personality by those who knew him best.

"When is it better not to know something, something that might be harmful to your very being?" posed Shelly.

"That's just it. Zeb is rock solid in almost everything in his life, except his history with his father. If he finds out his mother had an affair with Senator Russell, it might destroy his relationship with her, to say nothing of what it will do to him or her," said Echo. "Yet, I feel like I have to tell him."

"I'm guessing you're concerned about the personal explosion that might rise up inside of Zeb over this situation?" asked Shelly.

"I am horribly concerned about it."

"I can only imagine the basketful of emotions you are feeling. They must feel like an onerous burden."

"To tell you the truth, Shelly, I haven't felt like this inside since the night before heading into my first combat mission."

Shelly could see what she imagined to be a PTSD-like reaction rising in Echo's eyes.

"There's an awful lot to ponder. I'd have to say in this case, timing will be critical."

"Please help me out here, Shelly. What is the proper time to tell someone they have been lied to for decades by their mother about their father?"

Onawa and Elan awoke from their naps and began mewling and crying. Echo spun into mommy mode just as the text tone on Shelly's cellphone sounded. It was Zeb, he needed her ASAP.

"Echo, I hate to run out on you, but Zeb needs my skill set. He says it's an emergency. This is a terrible time to have to go. I am so sorry."

"Go. Go. I understand how duty works," said Echo. "Can we talk later? Tomorrow, maybe?"

"Of course. I'll help you figure this out. Can you live with the pressure of it one more day?"

"I can."

"Stay around as long as you like. The front door will automatically lock behind you when you leave, so try not to forget anything."

As Echo headed down the road, her children safely buckled in their car seats, she couldn't help but wonder how or even if this could be straightened out without an immense amount of pain and suffering. She was built and trained to protect, not only her children but her husband as well.

Echo drove past their house, out of Safford and headed to the Galiuro Mountains. Lugging two children in her Twingaroo Twin Baby Carrier, Onawa in front, Elan on her back, she made her way to the secret place of the Knowledge Keeper. She laid the children on a blanket and began to pray to the Creator for guidance.

Almost instantly a rainbow bridge appeared in the sky. It was a particularly peculiar sight given that it was the middle of a sunny day. Echo recognized the message she had just received from the Creator. The meaning was clear. She must find the passage between heaven and earth. She bowed her head to the ground, rested her forehead on Mother Earth and listened. The spirit of Knowledge was guiding her, speaking to her. Black Bear had died at Riggs Lake, atop Mount Graham, near the sacred place where the Apaches believed heaven and earth met. Echo was certain she needed to help Zeb solve the murder of Black Bear. She also knew she could only do it with Shelly's help. She lit a small bundle of sage, thanking the Creator for guidance.

Echo knew the only place she could safely give Zeb the news about Senator Russell being his biological father was where heaven and earth became one. She knew it as one of the safest and holiest places on earth.

Echo looked upon her pure and happy children as they played with each other and dirtied their hands in the sandy earth. Tears fell from her eyes as she considered what might run through Zeb's mind when he found out the truth about his biological father. Yet, she knew she had to tell him. The truth was the only thing that could bring freedom to his soul.

She shuddered as she considered how Zeb might feel towards his mother when he found out she had an affair with a man he had grown to hate. She also understood that Zeb would immediately go into denial that his mother was capable of such an act. Echo presumed Zeb's fallback position could easily be that Senator Russell had raped his mother. That kind of thinking would shatter him as he would think of himself as the end product of a heinous act. If his mind went in that direction, Echo had little doubt Zeb would kill Senator Russell. Given that set of circumstances, from what she had seen in war and learned as the Knowledge Keeper, such an action could be considered justifiable. Even so, it was the wrong thing to do. Echo in no way wanted such an act hanging over the head of the father of her children.

Echo's mind tumbled through a world of questions. How would Zeb approach his mother when he found out the truth? How would his mother react to Zeb knowing the truth? Had Helen known all along what the situation was? Had she never verbalized it to Zeb in order to protect everyone involved?

Most importantly, Echo loved Zeb with a depth that knew no boundaries. She needed to use every bit of power she had to see that the situation was resolved without Zeb being killed, killing someone or ending up in prison. She would continue talking to Shelly, the smartest woman she knew. Her hope was that Shelly would help her shed some clear light on everything.

While Elan and Onawa cooed, played in the sand, grabbed at sunlight, bugs and air, Echo lit a fresh bundle of sage and continued praying to Usen for guidance, guidance that she would most certainly need.

14

SHAPPA HÓWAKȞANYAN AND TOM SAWYER

A powerful updraft of air turbulence rattled Shappa's flight and touched off her nerves as the plane was struck by Rocky Mountain updrafts. Shappa immediately knew it was an omen from Mother Nature. Natural disturbances were often the Creator's way of warning a person or many people of what they might be getting themselves into. Her knowledge of global warming only added to the confirmation of her belief system. In her mind the Creator was not happy with the current manner in which the human beings were treating Mother Earth. Even a fool could see that. Shappa knew who she liked to blame, the White power brokers who were driven by greed, money and the need for control. Their spirits had long ago separated their innate connection with the Creator.

Shappa's political beliefs supplanted religious convictions when it came to the death of her son. She had long ago concluded that much of modern western religion was little more than superstition aimed at keeping the unenlightened in a state of fear. However, the tingle that shot through her body when the plane abruptly dropped one thousand feet brought with it the complex array of emotions she carried in her heart regarding Black Bear. Shappa knew she had just felt the power of the Creator up close and first-hand. What she believed through direct knowledge now became her Truth. Old Indian super-stitions, her prior experiences and traditional understanding of Wakan Tanka, the Great Spirit, was of secondary importance. The taut tingle in her torso when the plane dipped in mid-air had instantly created enhanced awareness and the distinct aura of a supernatural warning. The circumstance led her to understand that her own death could be close, very close. Shappa was kidding herself as she allowed for the false belief that she was prepared for death and did not fear the end of this life on Mother Earth. Little was further from the truth.

Sheriff Sawyer Black Bear's father, Tom Sawyer, was busy managing his contract work linked to the upper echelons of the old Mexican cartels who were tied to the most prominent govern-ment officials in Mexico. He was dealing with them for the U.S. federal government in Monterrey, Mexico when word of his son's death reached him.

His business, CO-INTEL-PRO, saw to it that federal requirements for goods made in Mexico met U.S. standards. Through a federal contract directed to his company by Senator Russell, he controlled almost everything that crossed the Arizona border between the U.S. and Mexico, in both directions.

Tom and Shappa had had very little interaction over the prior several decades. Both, however kept in constant contact with their only mutual child, Sawyer Black Bear. Both also opted to keep their individual complex relations with their son secret from one another.

Tom Sawyer kept an especially clandestine pact with his son that Shappa was unaware of. The surreptitious contract was not a father-son thing. The pact was one of those things that superseded the importance of life and death. The concord between father and son was not only dark, it was potentially life-threateningly dangerous to both men. The arrangement was so dangerous that it may have pitted them against one another had certain circumstances arisen. Once their covert agreement had been made there was no turning back. It was sealed with blood and it was final. Also, the accordance was never spoken of again once it was made.

Tom promised to meet Shappa in Safford and help her drive their son's body back to the Rez in South Dakota. He also agreed to partake in the traditional Lakota burial ceremony to the extent that someone who was not full-blooded Lakota was allowed. When they had recently talked about picking up Black Bear's body in Safford, Shappa had urged Tom to be on time. His tardiness had been a longstanding issue between them.

The truth was that she did not want to face Sheriff Hanks alone. She feared that he could read her facial expressions. Tom had sworn to be prompt.

Tom and Shappa had originally met during the 1973 Wounded Knee incident on the Pine Ridge Reservation in South Dakota. At the time Tom was an up and coming FBI agent. He was under orders to infiltrate the Lakota leadership and cause disruption within the AILM movement. He was one quarter Native Lakota by blood, so he fit in better than most federal agents. At the time Shappa questioned neither his love nor his loyalty, but she kept a close eye on what he was allowed to hear, see and have firsthand knowledge of.

Shappa had been a founder and feminist leader of the then recently founded and rapidly growing American Indian Liberation Movement. She was driven by a firm and hopeful idealism that things could change for all Indian Nations, not only in the United States but internationally. She was well aware that interactions with someone from within a government agency, especially the FBI, could lead to information that might help the political movement to which she was so highly dedicated. That specific motivation was part of the reason she gravitated towards Tom.

Their love ran as hot and as unbounded as the politics of the Wounded Knee incident. Their mutual passion for all things in love and war was the spark that produced Sawyer Black Bear during these tumultuous times. The marriage quickly fizzled out as playing for teams that hailed from different sides of the fence often led to diffi-cult circumstances. It was far too common for political and legal situations to arise that led to conflict and confrontation between the couple. Yet, through it all, they managed to remain reasonably civil to each other. Because of Black Bear, they never got around to formalizing divorce proceedings. However, Shappa had raised Black Bear and an older child mostly on her own. Black Bear's half-sister died tragically in a car accident on the Rez as a teenager.

Ultimately, through both fate and business, both Shappa and Tom ended up clutched within the nasty grasp of Senator Russell. Each had something they desperately wanted that only could be given to them via Russell's power within the federal government. In turn, Senator Russell was an expert at using people to his advantage, even when they knew and suspected his end game, which both Tom and Shappa did.

Tom, through his federal contracts, had more than a few shady dealings with the Senator. Both he and Senator Russell considered it merely part of doing business. Shappa, who spearheaded Native American programs that always needed the type of funding that could be obtained only at the federal level, found herself in bed, literally and figuratively with Senator Russell whenever she needed cash or legislation moved through the upper house of Congress. Politics, power, corruption and need made for curious relationships among the willing, the needy and the powerbrokers.

As Tom Sawyer neared the Mexican border, his phone buzzed silently. It was Shappa.

"Where are you?"

"On my way."

"No, I mean where are you, exactly?"

"Naco."

"Which side of the border?"

"Mexican."

"Good. I want you to bring me something back."

"Fine. What do you need?"

"There's no way your phone is tapped, is there?"

"Not one in a million. I change the SIM card twice a day."

When Shappa explained what she wanted, her one-time life partner exhaled heavily.

"You're sure that's what you want?" he asked.

"I don't see any other way to keep one of us from going down hard if we don't do this," said Shappa.

Tom was hesitant. He knew all too well how the long arm of the federal government reached into places where no one else could possibly get. After all, he was part of the highly toxic and often nasty business that occurred on the border between the U.S. and Mexico. Getting what Shappa wanted was not an issue, nor was getting it across the border. But fluoroantimonic acid, the strongest acid in the world, was ten quadrillion times stronger than sulphuric acid. The compound could eat through metal and glass, melt a man's skin and bones and still be hungry for more. Extraordinary measures were required in its transportation. Off the top of his head Tom knew he needed to get Teflon containers which were resistant to its corrosive effects. If fluoroantimonic acid interacted with water, the reaction was as violent as five-thousand-pound bomb at close range.

Tom knew Shappa never hesitated when it came to sticking her nose directly under the corner of a tent full of trouble. He knew full well that whatever it was that Shappa wanted to destroy, the act of destruction would be a final one. He did not want to know what Shappa's endgame was. That was her business. The amount she was asking for was small in quantity. He assumed her intention was the destruction of a human body. He wanted to keep his awareness to a minimum because knowledge, in this circumstance, could be as dangerous as the chemical itself.

A spinning top of thoughts whizzed through the former FBI agent's head. What was Shappa's end game? Was the Sheriff of Graham County the target? Who else would die? When would they die? Tom smelled an onion like odor emitting from his armpit. The stench was the tell of his stress reaction. Even though he felt mostly calm in his body, Tom could not help but feel the ominous danger which was lurking nearby and turning its evil eye toward him.

15

A DARK TRUTH DEEPLY HIDDEN

The Safford City Hall bell tower clock reverberated five times. The zero-humidity air made its crisp and clear peal carry miles into the surrounding desert. Zeb eyed Main Street up and down from the steps of the sheriff's office building. What he saw had him pondering human nature and habit. The 9-5 shops locked their doors in tune with the bell tower. The foot traffic to the local restaurants picked up precisely as the fifth chime sang out. It felt as though the workday had let out one final exhalation and brought with it, relaxation. He also knew it as the time of day when criminals opened their eyes.

As Zeb pondered life in general, Shappa Hówakȟaŋyaŋ pulled in front of his office. He knew the time to be exactly five p.m. Kate exited the building and joined Zeb when she noticed Shappa's blue, over-sized cargo van pulling into the parking lot. Jointly, they walked down the front steps to greet her.

Shappa first extended her hand to shake hands with Kate. Kate noticed a hint of masculinity in her grip. Zeb reached out for a hand-clasp. Shappa grasped his hand hard enough to make him cringe. He took it as a sign that she was letting him know she was not to be trifled with.

Both Zeb and Kate noticed the tip of Shappa's trigger finger was missing midway through the nailbed. Zeb eyed a small line of irregular stitches at the fingertip. Her grip and firm coarseness bought to mind the hands of local cotton farmers. The look in Shappa's eyes and her manner of dress, however, did not remind him of someone who worked with her hands for a living.

"Let's go inside," offered Zeb.

Shappa glanced at the sheriff's building with disquieting consternation. She had decades of first-hand experience in dealing with county, state and federal officers. Her encounters with officers of the law had led to more than a few nights as a guest in one of their jail cells. Such buildings brought to the forefront of her mind the extreme level of inequity in the power structure between the Indian Nations and their long-time, historical oppressors. She shook off the sickening feeling of ill will and pointedly directed a question at Zeb.

"May I see my son's office?"

Before Zeb had a chance to answer, Shappa reaffirmed what she believed was her right.

"I'm certain that is a wish you will grant me. It would likely be illegal if you did not allow the next of kin to have one last look at her son's workplace things."

He knew Shappa's legal threat held no weight, but he felt it was the right thing to do and felt comfortable letting her see Black Bear's office.

"Of course," replied Zeb. "Not a problem."

As they headed up the steps, Shappa suddenly stopped and pointed out to the vehicle lot.

"Which one did Black Bear drive?"

"He drove the Sheriff's official vehicle when he was sheriff. When he was a deputy, he drove all of the other ones at one time or another. Mostly he liked Squad Six," replied Kate. "It's an older vehicle, lots of miles on it. Let's say it is broken in and your son felt very comfortable driving it. In fact, he was about the only one who ever sat behind it's wheel in the past few years."

"Mind if I sit in the sheriff's vehicle first and Squad Six after that?"

The request had Zeb and Kate exchanging a quick, curious glance. Was Shappa seeking Black Bear's growing spiritual vibration or a dose of his fading human emanation which undoubtedly lingered?

Zeb handed Shappa the keys to the sheriff's truck.

"Kate, do you have the keys to Squad Six?"

"I'll run in and get them," replied Kate. "Be right back."

Kate hustled into the sheriff's office as Shappa opened the door to the official sheriff's truck and climbed in. Placing her hands at ten and two, she glanced into the rearview and adjusted the sideview mirrors before glancing through the front windshield. She reached forward and brushed the tip of her injured finger against a spot on the glass that had been chipped by a stone.

"Don't you fix the windshields on your vehicles?" asked Shappa.

"Early John's Window Replacement is scheduled to fix it next Friday."

Shappa put the key into the ignition. She turned to Zeb who was standing next to the door of the truck and barked a quick command.

"Get in."

"I'm sorry, but you're not authorized to be behind the wheel of an official county vehicle," said Zeb. "I don't want there to be an issue with the insurance company should we get into an accident."

Shappa turned her neck. Staring directly into Zeb's eyes, she wordlessly expressed deep disdain.

"My son is dead...murdered. I merely want to see if I can pick up any of his living ambience. Is that not okay with you, Sheriff Hanks? Is that something you would deny his mother?"

Zeb, from his many talks with Echo, suspected he knew exactly what Shappa was hoping to find. She was seeking one final thread from her son's life, a thread that might go a long way toward reducing her pain. Zeb opened the passenger door, slipped into the seat, moved it back to fit his large frame and snapped on his seatbelt. Shappa turned the key in the ignition, backed up and headed down the street. Kate watched it all from the steps of the sheriff's office.

Shappa drove for about a mile in silence before turning to Zeb and bringing up a hard question.

"Who killed my son?"

"I don't know. Yet."

"But you will find out?" asked Shappa. "Won't you?"

"Yes, ma'am. I most certainly will."

Zeb's answer did little to impress Shappa.

"I don't much care for you, Sheriff Hanks. I have reason to believe you had a hand in the killing of my son. In fact, I'm working on proving just that."

An acerbic tone laced Shappa's words.

"Why would I kill your son, ma'am?"

"He's an Indian for one thing."

Zeb's first thought was that he was married to a full-blood Apache.

"I'm not prejudiced against Indians, ma'am."

"Ceding any kind of power to Indians, especially legal authority, is a step in the wrong direction in the eyes of the White man. Giving primary legal authority to an Indian is a truly dangerous thing in every White man's eyes."

"He won the election," replied Zeb. "I didn't give any power to him. The people of Graham County did, and they are mostly White people."

Shappa, apparently dissatisfied with Zeb's response, merely mumbled inaudibly under her breath. The action rubbed Zeb in exactly the same wrong way that Black Bear did. He sensed with Black Bear the fruit had not fallen far from the tree.

"Besides, what reason could I possibly have for killing Black Bear?"

Shappa responded to Zeb's answer with a hard glare and a snarl in her voice.

"You resented him, Zeb Hanks. And in your heart, you know exactly what that is about."

Zeb hesitated. Confusion swept through his mind. He had no idea what Shappa was talking about. He studied her for a brief second and then asked a question whose answer might inextricably change his life forever.

"Why would you believe I resented your son enough to kill him, Shappa?"

"Because of your father."

Zeb's head began to spin to the point of feelings nauseous. He knew that some kind of truth had just pounded him in the gut. The only problem was he had no idea which truth Shappa was talking about. Black Bear had not moved to town until decades after his father was killed in prison. As he was about to ask Shappa to explain herself, she pulled into the sheriff's parking spot. She jumped out of the car and left Zeb with little more than his stunned imagination and a whole lot of questions.

Zeb watched Shappa get into her oversized cargo van. She didn't so much as look back. Zeb took off his hat and ran his fingers through his thick black mane of hair. His spinning mind revved in neutral as he stepped out of the vehicle, turned and headed to his office. As he slowly turned, his mind dropped into gear and went from neutral to high speed. Lost in a field of thoughts, he nearly ran into Kate. She grabbed Zeb by the arm to prevent herself from falling to the ground as he spun to avoid her. Reflexively, Zeb grabbed onto Kate's arm.

"Jesus. Sorry, Kate. My mind was elsewhere. It feels as though it is about to drive off a cliff."

"Don't worry about it. I'm fine. But what is going on? I watched the two of you take off, come back and then saw her take off. What's that all about?"

"She thinks I killed Black Bear."

Zeb expected Kate to have a completely stunned look on her face upon hearing the accusation. Oddly, she didn't.

"Did she say why she thinks you killed him?" asked Kate.

"She said it had to do with my father," replied Zeb.

"What'd she mean by that? Neither she nor Black Bear could have known your father. Did she explain it any further?"

"No, hell, no," replied Zeb. "Hell...no."

Zeb took a step toward the office, still in a daze.

"Zeb?"

"Yup?"

"Did you kill Black Bear?"

The question was bold and to the point. Kate needed to hear the answer directly from Zeb.

"I didn't," said Zeb. "But I can't say he didn't have it coming."

Kate didn't like what she was hearing. Kate did not agree with Zeb. No man deserved to die the way Black Bear had. She paused before giving Zeb some bad new she had for him.

"Doc Yackley called."

"Yes?"

"His cohort, Dr. Zata, wants to do a couple of rare and unusual autopsy tests on Black Bear's body. They won't be ready to release the body to Shappa and Tom for a few hours. He wants you there in order to make everything official when he hands over the body."

"When will Dr. Zata be ready to release the body?" asked Zeb.

"First thing tomorrow morning," replied Kate.

Zeb felt the muscles in the back of his neck contract as a powerful headache rolled up the back of his head into his temples. Shappa was the last person Zeb wanted to interact with. He most definitely did not want to be the one to give her unwanted, unexpected news. But he had no choice. He opened his cellphone and called Shappa. When he explained it would be morning before she could get her son's body and be on her way, she went ballistic. When he reminded her that she forgot to go through Black Bear's personal belongings at the office, a storm of hellfire came racing through the phone.

In the end, after a fair amount of squabbling, it was agreed that Shappa and Tom would stop by first thing in the morning to go through Black Bear's belongings. After that, they would pick up his body and head north. Zeb half expected Shappa would come to the office with murder on her mind. His murder.

16

SEEKING TRUTH

Echo arrived at Shelly's estate promptly at ten a.m. Echo's mother had kindly stopped by to watch the twins. Shelly was waiting with Milking Mother's Tea and some healthy treats. Small talk was brief. Neither woman was the kind that wasted time. Far more serious matters were at hand.

"I have some genuine concerns..."

In very untypical fashion, Echo sighed and hesitated before continuing. Shelly's assumed it was very difficult for Echo to share her version of the truth.

"...regarding Zeb."

Shelly focused intently on Echo. Present time consciousness was an absolute necessity if she were going to help her friend. Shelly once again wondered why Echo had chosen her as the confidante with whom to confess her fears. She also pondered what good she could do for Echo concerning the issues at hand. She knew little of what was on Echo's mind other than Zeb's mother possibly having an affair ages ago with Senator Russell. Outside of the obvious issue of Senator Russell being Zeb's biological father, a rather large and important issue, Shelly pondered a myriad of other related issues. Had Senator Russell had an ongoing relationship with Zeb's mother? Had Russell raped Zeb's mother? What kind of thoughts went through Zeb's mother's head every time she looked at her son? Did she see Senator Russell in Zeb's eyes? Did she see Zeb in Senator Russell's eyes? Did she see Senator Russell in her grandchildren? The complexity of it all, when mixed with the rage that Zeb carried within him, created the possibility of some very bad outcomes.

In their previous conversation, Echo had mentioned, in am offhanded, yet poignant manner, that timing was everything. It seemed obvious Echo wanted to share this knowledge about Zeb's mother with her husband. As to Echo's concerns regarding Zeb, Shelly was of two minds when it came to what Echo should do. Either tell Zeb her suspicions or leave it alone for the time being. What to do was exactly that straightforward in her mind. The important thing was to not get caught in a bear trap that was waiting to be sprung. To that end, she spoke.

"Regarding Zeb."

"Yes?"

"Do you believe that he is not man enough to face whatever it is you are going to tell him?" asked Shelly.

"Yes and no."

The women exploded with laughter. A slight bit of the tension that had been hanging between them was released. Both realized how masculine and ambivalent it was to answer, 'yes and no'. A sudden but deep bonding moment occurred. Two women together, women who needed each other's help and insights, were far stronger than one woman by herself. Both knew it. Both believed it wholeheartedly. Both were willing to move forward with that in mind.

"Like a point we discussed the other day, when is it better not to know something, something that might be harmful to your very essence?" asked Shelly.

"And when is it better to know the full and complete reality of a situation, even though the truth may be hurtful?" added Echo.

Echo sipped her tea. She thought of her twins, Zeb's twins. How might this hidden truth affect them? Was she being selfish and self-serving if she chose to speak to Zeb about what she knew and what she suspected about his mother and Senator Russell's relationship?

"I feel like I have to tell him everything I know and suspect about his mother and Senator Russell. It feels like anything less than being completely open with him about the knowledge I have would be like lying to him," said Echo. "It pains me to think that I am not being completely honest with him."

Shelly assumed Echo was being true to her words and reacted bluntly,

"Then tell him."

"Er…"

Acutely aware of Echo's hesitancy, Shelly added an important addendum.

"But bear in mind that the truth has the potential to destroy him."

Both women knew Zeb's mother had been the guiding light in his life. Despite all that Song Bird and Jake had done for him, she had been the primary factor in the formulation of who he was. And, no matter how you looked at it, the man everyone assumed to be Zeb's biological father had also played a major role in defining Zeb's character and belief system. Echo sighed heavily with the weight of it all.

"I don't want to destroy his relationship with his mother. However, I feel like I have to tell him."

"Why?" asked Shelly. "Why do you feel it is so important to tell him?"

Echo knew that although Shelly meant well with her question, she was coming from the point of view of an unmarried woman.

"If I don't tell him what I know, my life, his life and our children's lives will have a falsehood attached to them. I don't know if I could live with that lie."

"If you can't live with this, well, that makes it sound like it is more about you than it is about him," said Shelly.

Echo sat back. Maybe she was being self-serving. Maybe she was stepping into a minefield that would be best simply avoided.

"Echo, what will change if you tell Zeb the truth?" asked Shelly.

"If I don't tell him, I'll feel like I've lied to him," replied Echo.

Shelly's response was direct and to the point. Echo had only heard this kind of directness before from her commanding field officer in Afghanistan. She appreciated the straightforwardness Shelly was presenting. However, the actual words took her by surprise. This was a side of Shelly she had never witnessed. The bluntness with which Shelly offered her opinion was reassuring to Echo. Her words confirmed to Echo she had chosen the right person to confide in.

"Again, that's about you, not him. What will change for Zeb if you tell him?"

Echo allowed herself extra time to think. Both women felt completely comfortable in quietude. Shelly waited patiently until Echo eventually broke the silence.

"For one thing, the children would have a better idea of their health history," said Echo.

"That is what I would call a weak response," replied Shelly. "Healthwise, testing can be done regarding just about everything coming down the pike at them these days. What are you going to prepare for if you find something out? If something is bad in Senator Russell's health history, something that can be inherited, there are many other ways you can discover those issues."

"Family history is important," added Echo.

"Really? Do you want your lovely children to know they have Senator Russell's evil blood flowing through their veins? Do you want them to know they carry his genetic traits and all the potential that goes with that?"

"Maybe I need to think on this differently," said Echo. "But, then again, maybe I just need to let Zeb know that I know."

"Once again, that's really only about you, is it not?" asked Shelly.

"Sometimes what goes on in my life as a sheriff's wife in Graham County makes what I went through in the Afghan war seem uncomplicated," said Echo.

"That's life, isn't it?" said Shelly. "Sometimes, especially in situations that are not cut and dried, rules are made up on the spot. Those rules are dependent upon the circumstances surrounding the situation. Why don't you just let it play out for a while and see what happens? Is there any reason that Zeb needs to know this information immediately?"

Echo's mind wandered as she pondered the information that had been presented. Her response was reflexive.

"I guess not. However, when Zeb and I discuss it, and he becomes aware that I held back what I know, what will he think of me?"

This time Shelly did not need to remind Echo that she was thinking more of herself than Zeb.

"Once again, and maybe legitimately so, your concerns are centered on you. That isn't necessarily a bad thing, but you need to look at it more globally."

Shelly's advice was solid, but it was also a touch unsettling since the outcome could not be known. Even though nothing was resolved, Echo felt some sense of ease for the first time in a while. Shelly was correct. Truly nothing had to be done immediately. Patience was a virtue too easily overlooked. Time seemed, at least for the moment, to be on her side. As the Knowledge Keeper, she knew that contextually and historically speaking everything would unfold exactly as it was intended to. Hopefully, with that in mind, everything would be all right. Time would be the teller of the tale.

"There is one more thing I need to talk with you about," said Echo.

"I've still got my ears on. Have at it," replied Shelly.

"I have some genuine concerns regarding Zeb."

"That is very understandable, considering the circumstances," said Shelly.

"We both know Zeb very well."

"I think I can say with certainty that you know him significantly better than I do," said Shelly.

"In many ways I do," said Echo. "But in other ways, since you have worked with him professionally and very closely, you may understand his thinking in a different manner than I do. It's like when I served in Afghanistan. I knew the members of my unit far better than I have ever known my own family. Situational circumstance often leads to a deeper understanding of someone than does everyday life."

"That can be a true statement," replied Shelly. "I get the sense that something very specific is on your mind."

"You're correct. I do have something explicit on my mind. And, I must say, I am a little bit uncomfortable talking about it with anyone, even you."

"I promise what passes between us will be held in the strictest of confidence," said Shelly.

"I'll try to be direct," said Echo.

"I think I already know what you're concerns might be," said Shelly. "My suspicion is that you are concerned about Zeb's reaction when he finds out that Senator Russell may be his father. I understand that concern."

"As disconcerting as that might be, I am equally as concerned about how Zeb's mother may react. As you know she is elderly. What you may not know is that her health is not the best. I am truly uncertain as to whether Zeb will blame her, Senator Russell or the man whom he believed was his father for what happened. God only knows, but he may even blame himself."

"Tell me your greatest fear?" asked Shelly.

Echo gulped before answering.

"That Zeb will kill Senator Russell. That in his anger and confusion he may possibly even torture him in the process."

"You know Zeb better than I do. Is your fear a reality or a manifestation of your own fear?"

"I truly believe that Zeb has it in him to kill and even brutalize Senator Russell if he believes that Russell raped his mother. And, I have great concern that is how Zeb will frame it in his mind. He can be thorough and thoughtful, but he can also wildly jump to emotional conclusions when it comes to certain issues. One person who really can set him off is Senator Russell."

What no one knew, what Echo and Shelly couldn't possibly have knowledge of, was that circumstances were about to emerge that would shed a guiding light on Echo's problem.

17

BLACK BEAR'S BODY AND BELONGINGS

As had been agreed upon under great duress the previous evening, Kate and Zeb would meet Shappa and Tom at the sheriff's office before regular office hours. After giving what remained of Black Bear's personal effects to the grieving parents, Zeb and Kate would take them to the morgue where the body had been brought to Safford in the wee morning hours from Tucson. There Shappa and Tom would pick up the body of their only child. Kate was waiting at the office when Zeb arrived.

"Thanks for coming in early," said Zeb.

"Not a problem. I talked with Shappa last night," replied Kate.

"Good," replied Zeb. "I've had it up to here with her."

Zeb slid a finger across his throat.

"Then you know she's a strong, determined woman," said Kate.

"She's angry, that's for certain," replied Zeb. "If she were a bull, I'd be the matador's cape."

"She's angry, confused, bitter, political and much, much more than that," replied Kate.

"Do you know something about her that I don't?" asked Zeb.

"Not yet, but I'm going to dig in and figure out exactly what's motivating her. I suspect there are secrets about her that are telling and dangerous."

"Be careful. You may be jumping head first into a rattlesnake pit."

"Sometimes you need to dance with the devil to figure out what her next move is," replied Kate.

"Keep me apprised," said Zeb.

"Roger that."

"Oh, and good luck."

Kate tipped her hat while nodding her head. She was clearly mimicking one of Zeb's habitual behaviors. He returned the gesture with a warm smile. He understood the gesticulation was a matter of respect as well as an indicator that they were close enough to tease each other.

"How do you see our interaction with Shappa and Tom going down this morning?" asked Zeb.

"I can't say for certain. I think Shappa truly wants to dine on a pound of your flesh. Very likely a pound of your corpus would only begin to satisfy her blood lust for you."

Zeb's eyes widened. He knew Shappa carried revenge in her heart and soul. He also knew her history and that she was capable of violence. While not choosing to be totally naïve, he hoped that a night's sleep may have quelled the fire that was fulminating inside every cell of her body.

"I talked with Echo about just that thing this morning," replied Zeb. "She warned me to keep calm if Shappa confronted me. She believes that my mere presence can trigger her. Echo also believes Shappa is easily set off by my actions, no matter what they are."

"I agree with Echo. I must also confess the vibe I get is that Shappa carries the honed point of a highly sharpened blade aimed directly at your heart at all times," said Kate.

"I can't say I get what you'd call a good vibe from her either," said Zeb.

Kate looked at Zeb. Both laughed. Good vibrations were highly unlikely to be present when the four of them met.

"Let's play it out and see what happens," continued Zeb.

"What else can we do?"

Kate chambered a shell in her weapon. Zeb did the same. Kate pointed to the street in front of the sheriff's office.

"Look who's here."

Zeb glanced up at the clock in the bell tower.

"Right on time.

"Nice of them to be punctual."

Outside the sheriff's office, a blue cargo van pulled up and parked in the tow away zone. Out stepped Shappa and Tom. It felt like the set-up for an old western showdown at sun-up. The situation made Zeb feel ill at ease. The rising sun was in his eyes. Kate kept a clear view on Shappa and Tom as she whispered in Zeb's direction out of the side of her mouth.

"They don't appear to be armed."

"Relax," said Zeb. "Relax. They just want his things. I'm fully prepared to hand them over, but I don't doubt for one second they are packing heat and prepared to use it."

"Hell of a way to start a day," said Kate.

"It's the nature of the beast known as Shappa Hówakȟaŋyaŋ," said Zeb.

"To think my other career option was teaching kindergarten," said Kate.

"Your day would likely be starting differently than this. That's for sure," replied Zeb.

"Maybe. Kindergarteners aren't what they used to be."

They both emitted a small snicker. Zeb eyeballed Kate's loaded weapon. She was ready for business.

Shappa and Tom moved with a strange combination of heaviness, confidence and anger as they strode up the sidewalk to the front door of the Graham County Sheriff's Office.

Anxiety shot through Kate as Black Bear's parents each yanked open their respective sides of the sheriff's office entrance door. Zeb felt calm, centered. He knew he was built for this kind of situation. He also had a strong sense that this would not be his day to die. As Zeb tipped his hat to Black Bear's parents, he sensed no danger imminent in the air. He found himself letting go of the confrontation of the prior night.

"Shappa."

The tone of her response was akin to the snarl of a cornered wildcat.

"Zeb."

"You must be Tom Sawyer?" said Zeb.

The men shook hands. Sawyer's hands were gentle, soft to the touch.

"And you must be Sheriff Hanks?"

Zeb nodded and introduced Kate.

"I'd like to make this brief. We need to be on our way," said Shappa.

"Follow me," said Kate. "I'll take you to Black Bear's office."

Shappa and Tom followed Kate down the hall past Zeb's office, which clearly read Sheriff of Graham County. Two doors beyond Zeb's office was a smaller, less well-furnished office that had the name Sheriff Sawyer Black Bear hand painted on the door.

"Black Bear used this office since the day he originally started working here. He never took over the office space reserved for the duly elected sheriff."

"Why?" asked Tom.

"His choice," replied Kate. "He said he didn't care for the view."

Zeb nodded, confirming Kate's words.

"Typical," snorted Shappa.

Tom put his hand on Shappa's shoulder. It was clearly his attempt to keep her as calm as possible.

"Has anything been moved?" asked Shappa. "Maybe I should put it this way. What have you moved and what have you removed of Black Bear's personal belongings?"

"Helen and I went through his desk," said Kate. "We removed only Graham County property. We put everything else in those boxes."

Kate pointed to four medium-sized boxes that stood in the corner of the dead sheriff's office.

"Four boxes? That's everything?" asked Shappa.

"It is," replied Kate. "As you probably know, your son was a bare bones kind of man."

This time Tom nodded.

"You didn't remove anything that personally belonged to him, did you?" asked Shappa.

Kate's reply was firm.

"No, ma'am, we did not. That is not our policy."

"We would like to have the room to ourselves for a moment." said Shappa.

"Not a problem," replied Zeb.

Kate and Zeb departed Black Bear's former office. Zeb pulled the door shut tightly behind them. Fifteen minutes later Tom opened the door. Without saying a single word, Shappa and Tom carried the four boxes of Black Bear's earthly property to the rented cargo van. When Zeb offered Shappa a hand with the boxes she was carrying, she quickly pulled them away from his open hands.

"Did you find everything in order?" asked Zeb.

"Yes, sir," replied Tom.

"We found what we came for," added Shappa.

"Something in particular?" asked Zeb.

Zeb's question was met with a cold stare from Shappa. Tom interjected.

"Sometimes what isn't there is as important as what is."

"The morgue?" inquired Shappa coldly.

"You can follow me. I'll have to officially sign the body over to you," replied Zeb.

"Why?" snapped Shappa. "Who do you think you are? My son's body is not yours to give or take."

"I'm following standard protocol," replied Zeb.

"White man's protocol?" reverberated Shappa. "Doesn't mean a damn thing to me."

"Arizona state law," answered Zeb. "I can cite the statute if you want."

Tom stepped between Zeb and Shappa.

"Never mind. It's all good. We'll follow you."

The drive to the hospital morgue took less than five minutes. Doc Yackley was waiting for them. At his side was a man neither Zeb nor Kate recognized. Zeb shook Doc's hand and tipped his head almost imperceptibly toward the other man.

"Zeb meet Doctor Zata of the University of Arizona. His signature is on the official autopsy. Shappa, Tom, my condolences. I knew your son. I wasn't his doctor, but I knew him. Doctor Zata acted as the primary coroner for your son. He is an expert pathologist. If you have any questions, he will be glad to answer them."

"Would you mind going over the findings with us?" asked Tom.

Doctor Zata had delivered the official autopsy results to family members a hundred times. This was the first time organ harvesting was involved. He eyed the parents of Black Bear. Speeding through his brain was what to tell them in terms of what was most important. He got right to it.

"Your son was murdered."

Doc Yackley's cellphone buzzed quietly. He stepped to the back of the room, quietly took the call and excused himself.

"How was his life taken from him?" asked Shappa.

"Please have a seat," replied Doctor Zata.

He pointed to a pair of chairs that sat in front of a large wooden desk.

18

KACHINA RUMOR MILL

odaway and Lolotea Skysong rose early, as they always did.
Not only lifelong military careers but the aging process did
the same to them as it does to all, steals a slice from the
restful side of slumber.

However, today with something special at hand, they rose extra
early of their own accord. They had scheduled 2-hour massages and
mineral baths at the Kachina Springs Spa. This was a special gift
from Echo and Zeb for traveling with them to Paris and tending to
Elan and Onawa when Echo and Zeb took in the sights of a strange
and foreign land.

After rising early, they jointly made the bed, did their morning
exercise routine and ate breakfast together. Bodaway cooked as he
always did and, together, they ended with another daily ritual, their
morning prayers to Usen. These days their prayers were mostly for
their only direct descendants, the young children of Echo and Zeb.
Bodaway and Lolotea believed in prayer as it had worked well for
them. Praying for no harm to come had gotten them and their military teams through multiple trials of combat. Now Elan and Onawa
were first on their list of prayers.

This morning Lolotea took the wheel and drove them to Safford.

Bodaway and Lolotea Skysong arrived at Kachina Spa precisely at five minutes to ten. Out of habit and simultaneously, they checked their Luminox 8880 Series Black Ops watches. When they entered the spa, they were greeted by the sound of rushing water splashing against ceramic tiles. The owner of the mineral baths, Henrietta Schmill and her daughter, Lana, were busy preparing the freshly cleaned tubs by filling them with hot mineral water.

Henrietta caught them out of the corner of her eye as they entered the spa. She slipped in behind her desk to take care of business.

"Do you have the gift certificate?"

Lolotea reached into her purse and handed the neatly tri-folded certificate to the owner. Henrietta quickly ran her eyes over the certificate.

"Of course. Of course. I remember now. Echo got you two the Gold Cadillac treatments."

Bodaway and Lolotea looked at each other. They had no idea what Henrietta meant.

"You've been here before, lots of times," said Lana.

"Yes, we have," said Lolotea.

"I see here that you usually just come in a couple of times a year for a bath and a massage."

"Yes, ma'am, that's correct."

They usually treated each other to a massage and spa for each other's respective birthday. The other annual event was related to the day of their discharge from the United States Marine Corps.

"Well today you're getting the WORKS."

"The WORKS? What does that mean?" asked Bodaway.

Lana pointed to a handwritten sign thumbtacked to the wall just behind her. She spoke it verbatim without giving it as much as a glance. Neither Bodaway nor Lolotea had paid any attention to the sign before. They considered the high-end expensive treatment to be excessive. However, this was a gift and the cost of no consequence.

"A ten-minute soak followed by a seventy-five-minute full body massage, a second ten-minute soak, a sweat wrap treatment, a twenty-minute foot reflexology, a sage smudge that Song Bird taught us and you can wrap it up with one last soak for as long as you want to stay in the tub," explained Lana. "It takes roughly two and one-half hours from start to finish."

A broadly smiling Bodaway rubbed his hands together in delight and stretched his aging, but still muscularly toned body.

"Sounds like the cat's pajamas to me, but I'll probably be all shriveled up by the time you're done with me."

Lolotea nudged her husband with a pointy elbow. She didn't want the ladies to think her husband was referring to his private parts.

"One tub or two?" asked Henrietta.

"We'll share a tub," said Lolotea.

Bodaway winked at the masseuses.

"We always do."

Lana handed them each a towel and a large plastic glass of water with a straw. She pointed toward a door that had the number 1 brightly hand-painted on it.

"That one. I'll give a shout in about ten minutes. Wrap up in the towel when you get out of the tub. We'll massage you in the same room if that's what you want?"

"That's what we want," insisted Lolotea.

Twelve minutes later they were stretched out on the massage tables. Henrietta and Lana wasted no time in beginning the process of increasing the circulation, toning the muscle tissue and rubbing out the aches and pains of their late-middle-aged customers.

"Bodaway, it's time to eliminate your toxins and clean up your liver, kidneys and lymph glands," said Henrietta.

"He can use it," said Lolotea. "He made a big batch of Captain Apache wine last season and he seems to be running an ongoing testing mission. That old man of mine can get pretty toxic from his home brew."

Bodaway grinned proudly. In his humble opinion he created the best homemade wine in the tri-county wine area, even when compared with the local professional vineyards.

The women laughed heartily at Bodaway's expense. He took it all in good nature.

The first half hour of massaging was done in silence, save the occasional grunt and groan from Bodaway, with soothing, relaxing, new age music in the background. After a while the masseuses felt the need to chat.

"How are those grandbabies doing?" asked Henrietta.

"Beautifully," replied Lolotea. "Just beautifully. They are heaven sent."

"We watch them whenever we can," said Bodaway.

"Always keep a loving eye on them," added Lolotea.

"It feels like they grow faster than flowers after a late springtime rain," said Bodaway.

"Yes, they do grow like the wild things grow."

"How's your daughter like being a mother?" asked Henrietta.

"She's good at it," said Lolotea. "A real natural."

"That's good. With Zeb back as sheriff and all the shenanigans around town I don't suppose he's going to have a lot of time to help her out," said Henrietta.

"It's a mother's duty to raise her children. Zeb will help out as much as he can. He's got a big job to do."

Bodaway grunted out his beliefs with a certainty that the women would dare not argue with him. He was definitely old school. In his view of the world, it was a woman's job to raise the children and a man's duty to work and support the family financially and to set its order. He believed this despite the fact his wife had served by his side and done exactly the same kind of work that he had done in the United States Marine Corps.

The women, out of courtesy, changed the subject if only ever so slightly.

"We've been hearing lots of things about Sheriff Black Bear," said Lana.

"What've you heard?" asked Bodaway.

"He was killed."

"Everybody knows that," said Bodaway.

"He was killed by an Apache because he was a Lakota," said Henrietta. "Is that true?"

"How would I know?" murmured Bodaway.

"Because you're an Apache," replied Henrietta.

"Because you're an Indian," added Lana.

Her response brought about simultaneous ululations from Bodaway and Lolotea. The high-pitched auditory howl had Henrietta and Lana instantly covering their ears.

"What the hell was that craziness all about?" asked Henrietta.

"It was about your ignorance," replied Bodaway. "We were just letting Usen know that we are surrounded by those who are unfamiliar with true Apache ways."

"I'm not ignorant," said Henrietta. "I graduated high school and went to one whole year of massage college."

Henrietta pulled her hands away from Bodaway, a clear sign that she might no longer feel obliged to work on him. Bodaway looked over at this Luminox 8880 Black Ops watch that was sitting on a nearby chair. He pointed his thumb firmly towards his back.

"I've still got a half an hour to go on my massage. I've been keeping an eye on the clock," said Bodaway.

His voice was stern and commanding.

"Then take back that ignorant remark. I ain't ignorant."

"Yes, Bodaway, you should apologize," said Lolotea. "That is no way to talk. You know that a person must always show respect."

"I didn't mean you were stupid. I meant if you knew anything about Apaches or Indians you wouldn't have said what you said. If you did understand our culture, you'd know we don't all know the same things, have the same beliefs nor act in the same ways. Just because you heard that one Apache killed a man because he was Lakota doesn't mean all Apaches hate the Lakota. It doesn't mean anything like that at all."

"Well, Apaches do hate Lakotas, don't they?" asked Lana.

"The only Lakota I ever knew besides Black Bear was a tinhorn supply sergeant in the Marines. Can't say as I cared about either him or Black Bear one way or the other," said Bodaway. "I most certainly never gave killing either one of them a moment's thought."

"You don't think an Apache killed Black Bear?" asked Henrietta.

"No. I don't."

"Why not?"

Bodaway answered the question in a purposefully devious sounding way.

"If an Apache had reason enough to kill Black Bear, no one would have ever found his body."

The rough tone was nothing these women weren't used to hearing.

"I heard Black Bear was sliced into pieces," said Lana. "Like a loaf of store-bought bread."

"Who said that?" asked Lolotea.

"Don't remember exactly who said it first. But I can tell you this much, I heard it more than once."

"It's not true," said Lolotea.

"Sheriff Zeb had better find out who did the killing," said Henrietta. "Or folks are going to say he had something to do with it. In fact, some are saying it already."

Lolotea felt her blood begin to boil. How dare Henrietta say anything bad about the father of her little grandbabies.

"Enough," said Bodaway. "We will speak no more of this."

Lana and Henrietta went right back to work as if nothing had been mentioned at all. There would be plenty of time for gossip once the Skysong's were finished with their treatments. Henrietta and Lana began to talk among themselves.

"Did Senator Russell get his appointment time squared away?" asked Lana.

"Yes, he's booked the entire spa for next Tuesday."

"What's he doing in town?" asked Bodaway. "Isn't the Senate in session?"

"I don't know about that," said Lana. "I'm not a political person. I ain't even registered to vote."

"But his secretary called, and believe it or not, he's got a man for a secretary..."

The mention of a male secretary lightened the mood as all four of them began to giggle. One thing they could agree on was that secretarial work was a peculiar way for a real man to earn his daily bread.

"His man Friday told us the Senator got sick on a recent trip overseas," said Henrietta.

"I heard on the talk radio station out of Phoenix that he was in Egypt and Turkey," said Bodaway. "They said it was a fact-finding mission. That usually means vacation."

"His man Friday..."

The second reference to the male secretary as Friday brought down the house.

"...told me Senator Russell picked up a bug. I guess he's been sick for the better part of the last three weeks. He's coming home to convalesce. He made appointments here for seven days in a row. He thinks the healing springs of Kachina can cure him of whatever ails him," said Henrietta. "He's been coming here since Grandma Sally ran the place."

"I think that man has more wrong with him than even this place can cure," said Lolotea.

"And we both are big believers that Kachina Springs and the expertise in both of your hands can cure most anything," added Lolotea.

"Well, you're right about that," replied Lana.

"He's a big tipper and a regular whenever he's in town. I'll be happy to let him think whatever he wants to think," said Henrietta.

"He probably tips with taxpayer money," said Lolotea.

"What do you expect from a politician? They spend everybody's money but their own."

No one put up a single word of argument.

"Did his gal, I mean man, Friday say what was wrong with him?" asked Bodaway.

"No. Just that he was weak and taking some medications. He asked if I could work around some fresh scars. Seems he had to have something drained from his insides. Must've had an infection. A bad one."

"Maybe they drained some of the nastiness out of him," said Lolotea.

The four of them had another good laugh over Lolotea's statement.

"Even though he's been coming here for decades, I don't trust him," said Henrieta. "He speaks with a forked tongue."

Lolotea and Bodaway looked at each other and shook their heads. Using such a trite expression that was out of old western movies and inferred that Indians talked strangely was totally out of place. Henrietta saw Lolotea and Bodaway's mutual reactions.

"I don't mean to speak poorly when I say forked tongue. I meant the man is a liar. I don't mean to compare that old expression to movie Indians, either. I'm not ignorant like that."

Once again Bodaway and Lolotea exchanged knowing glimpses and shook their heads.

Henrietta continued speaking with a great deal of pride in her voice.

"After all, like I told all y'all earlier, I graduated high school and went to practically a whole year of massage school."

"I think we can all agree on that," said Bodaway. "I mean that Senator Russell speaks with a forked tongue."

"The devil's pitchfork of a tongue," added Lolotea.

A trip in and out of the tub brought Lolotea and Bodaway to the sweat wrap. Both of them enjoyed that part the most. Another ten minutes in the hot spring water was followed by the foot reflexology treatment. All the while, Bodaway and Lolotea could tell that Lana and Henrietta were bursting at the seams to ask them something. Lolotea finally spoke up. The aromatic and magically healing sage smudge got them all talking freely.

"What is it that you are dying to ask us?"

"We've heard Zeb knows who killed Black Bear. Is that true?" asked Henrietta.

"He hasn't said a word to me about who killed Sheriff Black Bear," replied Lolotea. "Has he said anything to you, Bodaway?"

Bodaway grunted. He had to pass gas but was too much of a gentleman to do so in front of even these nosy women. Even if he had known, it was the sort of information he would never share with Henrietta and Lana. In fact, it was the sort of thing he would not share with anyone except Lolotea.

With the smudge complete, Bodaway and Lolotea rinsed off in the hot springs. After completing their rinses, they showered and scrubbed away the sage smudge.

When they were dressed and ready to go, Bodaway placed a pair of twenty-dollar bills on the counter. Henrietta handed them back to him.

"As much as I'd like to put these twenty spots in my pocket, your money is no good today. You've got an extremely generous daughter and son-in-law," she said.

Her words made the grandparents beam with pride. After the Skysongs departed, Henrietta and Lana carried on with their gossip.

"I don't think they know who killed Black Bear," said Henrietta.

"If they did, they sure as heck didn't let on," replied Lana.

"I mean, everyone knows Zeb killed Black Bear. You don't think for one minute those two are going to rat out their son-in-law, do you?"

"No, but I had to ask."

"You're pretty certain that Zeb killed Black Bear, aren't you?" said Henrieta.

"I am very sure of it. Zeb killed Black Bear to get his job back."

"Exactly."

"And out of vengeance. That Zeb Hanks has got a mean ol' temper deep inside of him. He's just like his dad."

"Mmm-hmm."

"I understand why Bodaway and Lolotea didn't want to say anything about it," replied Lana. "But they know. For sure they know."

"Of course they know, but it doesn't matter anyway. Sheriff Hanks gets away with whatever he chooses."

"Always has."

"Always will."

"It's just the way it goes around Graham County."

"I should say."

"Just who the hell does Zeb Hanks think he is, anyway?"

"Power is as power does. He believes because of who he is and where he really came from that no one can tell him how to do things. Zeb Hanks thinks that he is the law. And because he is the law, he believes he is above the law. One day he'll pay."

"What goes around, comes around. Everyone knows that to be the truth."

Henrietta and Lana continued cleaning up, smugly believing they knew better than anyone else exactly what happened to Black Bear and what role Sheriff Zeb Hanks played in it and, even more importantly, why.

19

DEATH FILE 666: AN EXPLANATION FROM DR. ZATA

Tom pulled back the chair for Shappa. He then sat down across from Dr. Zata who was seated in Doc Yackley's chair. Sheriff Zeb Hanks was standing just to the doctor's immediate right. Kate stood at close attention behind Shappa, wary of any move she might make. Doctor Zata reached into his briefcase. He removed four identical files. All of them were marked identically: SHERIFF SAWYER BLACK BEAR. CASE FILE 666

Doctor Zata briefly glanced through the files before looking across the desk at Shappa and Tom. His face presented itself with a neutral countenance. He glanced down at the case file while absentmindedly drumming his large fingers on the desk top. The Tucson pathologist stopped drumming when his eyes caught Shappa glaring at him. Zeb's eyes and mind shifted toward Mount Graham. The clarity of the mountaintop and the heaviness in the room clashed like late summer monsoon thunderheads.

This was clearly not going to be an easy interaction. Zeb had a decent read on Shappa. She, no doubt, would be trouble. Tom was a bit of a wild card. Zeb had no clue as to how he would react to what he was about to learn. Before he had a chance to say a word, Kate's cell phone buzzed. It was someone from the Department of the Interior who had been involved in the final report of the dredging of Riggs Lake. Kate pointed at her phone and mouthed softly to Zeb.

"It's the supervisor of the crew that dredged Riggs Lake," said Kate.

Zeb nodded, tipped his head toward the door and mouthed, "Take it."

Kate excused herself.

"What's in the file, Dr. Zata? Sheriff Hanks?" asked Tom. "It's far beyond time that we knew. Please tell us everything you know. Please let us know exactly what's in the file."

"Information," replied Dr. Zata. "Information that may be difficult for you to hear. Information that when you read it will make the reality of everything sink in even more deeply than it already has. There's a good chance what you read and hear will be distressing."

"My son is dead. How much worse can it get?" snapped Shappa.

Shappa reached across the desk in a vain attempt to snatch the top file. Dr. Zata was old but his reflexes were sharp. He quickly pulled the files back toward him.

"I would like to talk to the two of you about some of my conclusions before you actually see the file," said Zata. "It might make it easier for you to see how I determined my conclusions."

"Yes," added Zeb. "I agree with Dr. Zata."

"What are you hiding?"

Shappa's tone was that of a person making a demand as well as an accusation. Zata responded with his professional voice.

"No one is hiding anything from you. I just want to talk to you about the file first. I'm trying to help you. You're going to have to trust me."

Shappa snorted like an angry bull. Tom placed his hand on her back. It was clearly an attempt to calm the irate mother. From the look in her eyes, Zeb could see the indignation she carried in her heart was about to explode in a dangerous fashion. It was a feeling he was intimately familiar with. Tom was more diplomatic as he responded

"Say what you have to say, Dr. Zata. Sheriff Hanks, if you'd like to add your two cents worth, well, that is fine too. But when you've done all that, we expect to be satisfied."

"We demand to have a thorough and complete look at everything in the file," added Shappa.

Her indignation was anything but righteous.

"Fair enough," replied Zeb.

Dr. Zata opened the file, keeping his hands firmly pressing it against his table in case Shappa once again tried to prematurely yank it away.

"This is going to be difficult for you to hear."

Shappa jumped in with a caustic timbre in her voice.

"I'm assuming you're going to give us the gruesome details of Black Bear's murder."

Dr. Zata was direct and to the point. He was an expert at reading the emotional state of people under duress. He knew far better than most the appropriate way in which to respond to those who are grieving. In this case he could see quite clearly there was no sense in pulling any punches.

"Yes, you're aware that your son, Sawyer Black Bear, was murdered."

"I really can't imagine much worse news than that," said Shappa. "What is it that has you dragging your feet on telling us the entire story?"

"I'm going to give it to you straight," said Zata. "Since that's the way you seem to want it."

"A lie, even a half-truth, is always much worse than the whole truth," said Tom.

Zata continued, attempting to control the tenor of the conversation.

"The end of your son's life was tragic and horrible."

The room quieted. Shappa and Tom both exuded differing kinds of tension. While Tom soaked in what he heard, Shappa quickly reverted to her usual fury filled mannerisms.

"What do you mean by that?" snarled Shappa.

"He was killed with a single shot to the head," said Dr. Zata.

After the doctor spoke, he waited for the responses and reactions from Black Bear's parents. Both appeared to take the news with a great deal of resignation. Zeb, for his part, could not help but think of his little children. His mind wandered to a bad place as he considered how he would feel if something terrible happened to them.

"Did he die instantly?" asked Tom.

The experienced doctor, pathologist and coroner leaned forward. He wanted to make certain Shappa and Tom heard every world clearly.

"I have a theory on that," said Zata.

The veteran doctor hesitated before continuing. Zeb could tell that Dr. Zata, as skilled and capable as any man in his position, was searching for exactly the right words. What he was about to tell Black Bear's parents would be psychologically devastating. Most of all, what he was going to tell them could never be unheard. And, if they were half-way human, the chance of his words triggering permanent PTSD in both of them was almost a certainty.

"What happened, Doctor?" demanded Shappa. "Give it to us straight."

Zeb knew what was coming. As nasty as Shappa had been to him, he felt sorry for her. There would be zero chance at unhearing what she was about to hear. The next few sentences could never be forgotten.

Zata pulled a picture from the top file. The photo was that of Black Bear lying on the autopsy table with the back part of his head shaved. The picture clearly showed the entry wound at the base of the skull. Zeb looked at Shappa and Tom expecting to see tears flowing from their eyes. Instead, what he saw surprised him. Both the mother and the father of the dead man studied the picture with great intensity. The looks on their faces belied the fact that the dead man lying on the table in the photograph was their only son.

Dr. Zata waited for a short moment before continuing. He anticipated they would ask why there was no serious exit wound. What appeared to be the exit wound was small lump pushing from the inside of his skull outward. He concluded from the looks on their faces that they both assumed the steel plate in their son's head had blocked the bullet from creating a large exit wound.

"What can you tell us?" asked Tom.

"He was shot with a low caliber handgun, a .22 at close range. The bullet remained lodged in his brain near the third ventricle."

Tom, with eyes glued to the image of his dead son, asked Dr. Zata a direct, difficult question.

"In your opinion, based on your findings, do you believe our son was executed at close range?"

The casualness with which he spoke made Zeb wonder if Tom had anticipated this sort of thing might be his only child's ultimate fate.

"That is a conclusion I cannot prove with one hundred percent certainty. However, based on the evidence I found upon autopsy, he was shot at close range. I can neither prove nor disprove that it was an execution based on the evidence," said Zata.

Shappa was quite less sedate. She was also less accepting of the conclusion or lack of it. She directed her gaze at Zeb and drilled deeply into his eyes.

"Do you know who did this, Sheriff Hanks? Do you know who is responsible for executing my son?"

As Shappa screamed at Zeb, a tear formed in her eye. For the first time Shappa's reaction to her son's death seemed human. The rage was turning to something else, something Zeb did not instantly recognize. Zeb studied the sole tear departing Shappa's eye. He rapidly formed a single conclusion. What formed in her eye was nothing more than a crocodile tear. The woman was incapable of any sort of genuine reaction.

"It's at the very top of my list of crimes to solve. The killing of a Graham County Sheriff is a very serious crime," said Zeb. "A proper resolution of your son's death is absolutely necessary."

"How can we trust that you have our son's best interest in mind?" asked Shappa.

"It is my sworn duty as an officer of the law."

The rage once again flared like the malicious flames of an incendiary rising fire in Shappa's eyes.

"For decades it was also the sworn duty of the United States Calvary to execute as many Indians as they could," said Shappa. "That order came from people who carried much higher rank than you."

"That was more than one hundred-fifty years ago, and those orders were long ago rescinded," said Zeb. "This is an entirely different situation. It is my sworn duty, as I earlier stated, to find out who killed your son and, if possible, why."

"And to bring them to justice?" asked Tom.

"Most importantly, it is my duty to see that justice is served and that your son's killer pays the price for what he has done."

"Dr. Zata, please give us the details," said Tom.

"The specifics are quite gruesome. Are you sure you want to hear them now?"

Shappa stared at the doctor, saying nothing. Tom answered firmly and for both of them.

"Yes. We do. Of course, we do."

Zata handed a file to Shappa and another one to Tom. The parents of Black Bear began to page through the death dossier of their child. Tom sought facts. Shappa read each word, digging through them with a certainty that the truth was purposefully being hidden from her.

"Here is what we know for certain," said Dr. Zata. "I will be direct."

"It is precisely what we need to hear and how we want to hear it," said Tom.

Shappa remained oddly wordless. Zeb interrupted the doctor.

"Black Bear left the office roughly three weeks ago. He told Helen, the office manager, that he was going fishing in the Sea of Cortez down in old Mexico. Apparently, he never made it there. That is based on what we have learned so far. New facts may arise that could change our opinion of the time line. His body was found less than two weeks later in Riggs Lake near the top of Mount Graham."

"How did his body get there?" asked Tom.

"We haven't figured that out yet," replied Zeb. "But we are working on that specific detail."

"Somebody must have security cameras along the road up the mountain. After all, most of that is federal land. With the telescopes on top of Mount Graham somebody must be protecting and looking after the installation," said Tom. "I know for a fact that AIMGO spends a ton of money on security."

"Indeed. You are correct regarding AIMGO protecting its property. We have reviewed a lot of footage of vehicles going up and down the mountain in the timeframe we are looking into. We have found nothing to date that has brought us closer to his killer or killers. However, you should know that the cameras that are directed over Riggs Lake were all shut down during the approximate time period in which we believe the killer or killers disposed of Black Bears' body in Riggs Lake."

Shappa slammed her hand on the table. The room reverberated with an angry echo.

"That's outrageous! How could that have possibly even happened? It's just another goddamned evil White conspiracy against a Native American. If the dead man was White and important, you'd have this figured out by now. You'd probably have even used all the satellite imagery that I know the federal government uses to keep an eye on AIMGO property."

Zeb held his hands up and put a serene look on his face attempting to calm the upset Shappa.

"We're working on figuring out exactly what happened with the cameras. We are searching for the missing footage. We've got some very smart people working on it," said Zeb. "You are also correct when you say that it doesn't make sense. And, yes, it is outrageous. Someone must have had this thing planned right down to that specific detail. We will figure out who shut off those cameras."

"Who found the body?" asked Shappa.

"Federal environmental workers who were dredging the lake."

"Is that a common thing to do?"

"Is what a common thing to do?" asked Zeb.

"Dredge Riggs Lake?" asked Tom.

"I hate to tell you this, but I've lived here all my life, and this is the first time I've ever even heard of it being done," said Zeb.

"Who ordered it?" asked Tom.

"My staff and others are sifting through the paperwork right now. Federal record keeping is a nightmare. Their filing system is a mess, to put it politely. No one wants to take responsibility for anything. The Department of the Interior is ultimately responsible for the paperwork and where the data is stored. But there are so many bureaucrats and elected officials who have their fingers in this pie there is a distinct possibility we may never be able to sift through all the red tape in order to get the actual paperwork we're after."

"Do you think someone ordered the lake dredged in order to find the body of my son?" asked Tom.

"That exact question has crossed my mind. But if someone went to all the trouble to drive a body thirty-five miles up a narrow road and into a remote area, I doubt they would do it so that someone would find it later," said Zeb. "At this time, I'm reasonably certain Black Bear's body wasn't meant to be found."

Suddenly Shappa gasped. Zeb could see that she had the autopsy report in her hand. Tom looked over his estranged wife's shoulder and began reading the report.

"What the fuck?" exclaimed Tom.

"What does this, this thing about harvesting organs, mean?" demanded Shappa.

Dr. Zata took command of the conversation.

"I'll be direct and to the point. I believe your son was executed. His body may have been kept alive in a vegetative state so that his organs could be harvested. As you can see from the report, his eyes, heart and kidneys were surgically removed. We are operating under the assumption that someone crossmatched his blood type and several other genetic factors and found him to be a suitable donor for their needs. That is the operating theory at this time. I wish I could tell you more. There is just so much we don't know yet."

"And when will you know more?" asked Shappa. "More importantly, exactly what are you doing to find out the entire truth?"

Zeb couldn't help but notice the tone of her voice went from irate to almost polite. The only time he had ever witnessed such a dramatic shift in mood was in several people he knew who had been diagnosed with bipolar disorder. He was no doctor and certainly did not have the ability to diagnose such a difficult disease, but something about her behavior was extremely odd.

"We're working on it with as much expediency as is possible," replied Zata.

This time Tom was firm in his question.

"When? When will you know?"

Zata's response was apologetic.

"Soon, I hope."

"That's hardly much satisfaction for a grieving mother," said Shappa.

Once again tears flowed. Zeb could not trust that they were genuine, nor could he assume they were false.

"Trust me. The coroner's office and the sheriff's department are working together and doing everything humanly possible to find the answers you are looking for," said Dr. Zata.

Shappa harrumphed. It was becoming clear to Zeb she was either doing all she could to keep from falling apart or displaying one false sentiment after another. It was no stretch on Zeb's part to see that she held her own version of the truth. It was highly likely she didn't believe a word either Zeb or Dr. Zata was telling her. She stared directly into Zeb's eyes as she pointedly questioned him.

"How can I know for certain that you didn't kill my son, Sheriff Hanks? How can I know even something that basic beyond a reasonable doubt?"

She turned her hardened gaze to Dr. Zata.

"And how can you prove to me, Doctor Zata, that you aren't helping Zeb cover the whole mess up?"

There was no reasonable or accurate way for either Zeb or Dr. Zata to answer Shappa's questions in a manner that would satisfy her. Thankfully, Tom interjected himself into the conversation.

"Sheriff Hanks, what are your next steps in the process of finding out who killed my son?"

Zeb leaned forward and directed a genuinely compassionate gaze into the eyes of the parents of the deceased former sheriff.

"I have everyone on my staff working on it. Dr. Zata and our local coroner, Dr. Yackley, are helping us as well. We are looking at it from every possible angle. We are using every available resource. We need a break or two and we can find out who killed your son."

Shappa's heart suddenly seemed to change. Tears fell from her eyes like stars from the sky. This time they appeared real to Zeb.

"I've accepted the fact that my son is no longer with us. I apologize for my outbursts. I would like to see his killer, or killers as you say, get the justice they deserve. The most important matter for me at this moment is that I return my son's body to the reservation and give him a proper ceremony."

"We are all in agreement on that issue," said Zeb.

"I am also certain I will have many more questions in the days to come. I will be in touch with you. I would appreciate it if you would be in touch with me whenever you learn anything," said Shappa.

Zeb was of two minds when it came to Shappa's shift in moods. Either she was a genuinely grieving mother, or she was an absolute sociopath. He truly could not tell which.

"Most certainly that will be the case," said Zeb.

Zeb grabbed two of his business cards, turned them over and wrote his private cell phone number on the back. Dr. Nitis Zata wrote his name and number beneath Zeb's.

"You can call either of us anytime, day or night."

Tom reached across the table and shook both Dr. Zata's and Sheriff Hanks' hands. Shappa did not. Instead she had a single request.

"My son's body?"

Doctor Yackley's able bodied assistants, Pee-Wee and Duke, were signaled. They helped load the body of Black Bear into the rented vehicle. Five minutes later, with Shappa behind the wheel, the parents of Sawyer Black Bear Sawyer headed north on State Highway 70.

20

PINE RIDGE SHERIFF'S OFFICE

"Helen, could you get the name and number of the Sheriff of Oglala Lakota County in South Dakota for me?"

Helen stepped into Zeb's office. She handed him a piece of paper with the Sheriff of Oglala Lakota County's name and phone number on it.

"Who's this guy?" asked Helen.

"Sheriff up that way."

"I got that. What can he help you with?"

"I just want to ask him a few questions."

"About Black Bear?" asked Helen.

Zeb looked up at Helen. If he told her nothing, she would make assumptions and likely let loose something that might let the wrong person know he was digging around for background information on Black Bear, Shappa and Tom. If he told her too much, she might also disrupt his investigation. As always, it was a perpetual balancing act between Zeb and Helen.

"You're right, I need some information on Black Bear," said Zeb.

"While you've got him on the line, you should find out whatever you can about Shappa too," suggested Helen. "I've got a real bad feeling about her."

He found it odd she didn't mention Tom, Black Bear's father, with the same trepidation.

"Probably not a bad idea, but I kind of hate to dig too deeply into a grieving mother's background. It doesn't hardly seem like the right thing to do at this moment."

"You're right," replied Helen. "There's a time and a place for everything. Black Bear will still be dead once they perform the end of life ritual for him. I suppose it can wait."

Helen did a one-eighty, left the room, but as usual left the door slightly ajar. As he had a thousand other times, Zeb got out of his chair and discretely shut the door completely. Of course, Helen witnessed the whole thing just as she had the prior thousand times. Little, if anything, escaped her eyes and ears.

Zeb glanced at the piece of paper. The 605-area code was familiar. The name of Sheriff Mitch Lentz was not. He quickly pulled up the web page for Oglala Lakota County, South Dakota. In terms of square miles, it was half the size of Graham County. The county was entirely within the Pine Ridge Indian Reservation and contained part of Badlands National Park. This made Zeb wonder who ultimately had control over the county and if perhaps he was barking up the wrong tree. A county inside an Indian reservation that contained part of a federal national park had to present unique problems for law enforcement. He was glad those problems weren't his.

Zeb brought up Google maps on his computer. Shelly had shown him some neat tricks and he was able to glean a significant amount of potentially useful information. The lay of the land was often key when it came to understanding people from an area and the crimes they committed. When Zeb put all he had learned together, he immediately realized that Sheriff Lentz's job, due to the remoteness of the area and the heavily bifurcated cultural beliefs, was likely not an easy one. Zeb held out hope that Sheriff Lentz would be able to assist him with his doubts about Black Bear, Shappa and Tom. Whatever he could help with was still to be determined.

Zeb looked at the phone number one more time, memorizing it. He tapped out the numbers on his phone. A middle-aged woman answered. She sounded polite. Zeb smiled as he listened to her Midwestern accent with its long drawn out vowels.

"Sheriff Lentz's office. How may I help you?"

"This is Sheriff Zeb Hanks, Graham County, Arizona."

"Greetings, Sheriff Hanks."

"Thank you, ma'am."

"Oh, you can call me by my name, Roberta or just Berta. This is South Dakota, we're not that formal around here."

"Thank you, Roberta."

"Now what is it that I can do for you?" asked Roberta.

"I need some information from Sheriff Lentz. If things work up there the way they work down here, I suspect I might be able to get more information from you than I could from him."

Roberta giggled. A born multi-tasker, she immediately brought up the Graham County Sheriff Office's website on her computer. She saw the face of the man she was talking to. Roberta, a woman with a wandering eye thought that Zeb was sure damn good looking enough to be a sheriff.

"You might be right about that, Sheriff Hanks. You want to know something?"

"How's that?" asked Zeb.

"You ain't a bad lookin' cowpoke."

"Ma'am?" asked Zeb.

"Pulled your picture up on the Graham County website. Nice hat."

"Er, thanks."

"I passed through Graham County on vacation a few years back. I drove by your office. Who picked out the color of your building?"

The bizarre, unearthly shade of paint that covered the exterior of the sheriff's office had long been a local joke. It was often referred to as late summer pond scum green. A committee of self-appointed busy bodies had chosen the color, much to the dismay of all who worked in the building. Zeb chuckled at her remark.

"Just so you know, I had nothing to do with that."

"Gawd, I hope not. What do you want to know Sheriff Hanks? It's been a little slow around here this week. I could use someone to talk to."

"Are you familiar with Shappa Hówakȟaŋyaŋ?"

This time it was Roberta's turn to snicker.

"We've got a jail cell with her name hanging over the door. That ought to tell you all you need to know. It's a little joke we have around here. She's been arrested so many times that some call the jail the Hówakȟaŋyaŋ Hotel and her cell the Shappa Suite."

"You know her well, then?"

"Well enough to know she's down your way picking up the body of her boy, Black Bear."

"You knew Black Bear?"

"He used to work for us. Sheriff Lentz hired him. God only knows why, but I guess you already know all that, don't you good lookin'?"

Though he was more than a thousand miles away, Zeb blushed. He was loyal and true blue, but it never hurt to hear someone give you a straightforward compliment. Zeb sat up a little straighter as he looked at his reflection in the window.

"I do know that. I mean, I know he worked for Sheriff Lentz."

"Of course, you do. We called Black Bear the Dire Wolf."

"Dire Wolf?" asked Zeb.

"He hunted wild horses for the Feds. That's real nasty work. Hunting, trapping and killing wild horses, that is. Practically no one will do it, even though the pay is especially good. People up here like to see horses run free. I guess Black Bear must have needed the money. I never got around to asking him why he took on that kind of work."

"I didn't know that about him."

"I don't suppose he advertised it."

"Nope. He never said a word about it."

"He was the kind of man who was around when nasty things needed being done. Not only did he do them, but he was part and parcel to getting them done quickly and efficiently. That kind of stuff was his specialty if you ask me."

"How's that, Roberta?"

"How's what?"

"You said nasty things were his specialty."

"Black Bear had quite a reputation as a child and a teen."

"Yes?"

"He was cruel."

"Cruel? How so?"

"I suppose maybe I make too much of it. I'm proud to say that I'm an animal rights activist."

"Good for you," said Zeb. "Animals need protection."

"Being part of the animal advocacy movement isn't a thing that's really looked on with a lot of respect around these parts by most of the locals. However, most of the folks out this way love their animals, regardless. I'm just one of the radicals, I guess."

"Yes, ma'am. You were saying something about Black Bear and cruelty."

"That boy. I mean Black Bear when he was, oh, eight, nine, ten years old and even into his teens. Well, he used to torture small animals. I'd say, hell, I'm certain, he even enjoyed it. Enjoyed it a little too much if you ask me. I only saw him doing it once. It made me sick to my stomach. I grabbed the little shit by his ear and took him right to his mama who did exactly nothing."

"That's not good," replied Zeb.

"I heard he did it a lot. I told Sheriff Lentz not to hire him because of that very thing. But would he listen to me? No. Not a chance. Sheriff Lentz and Tom Sawyer, Black Bears' father, but you knew that, didn't you, are long-time friends. I think they've even had a business or two together. On the side. Nothing to do with Mitch being Sheriff, of course."

"Of course," replied Zeb.

As it turned out, Roberta didn't have a clue or proof of any actual business dealings between the two men, but upon further questioning by Zeb, she held her ground on believing it.

"Anything else you want to say about Black Bear or Shappa?"

"If you ask me, Black Bear learned his nasty ways from his mother. I wouldn't swear to that in court because she is well known, politically powerful and has some pretty tough friends in the community. She's what you'd call a sordid sort of character."

Just as Zeb was about to ask her exactly what she meant Roberta changed the subject.

"Are you the same Sheriff Hanks that Black Bear beat out in the Graham County Sheriff's election last year?"

"Yup. I am. One and the same."

"That was big news around here. I mean Black Bear winning an election over an incumbent White sheriff in Arizona. Seemed like a big deal to everyone, especially the Lakota tribe, since Black Bear is one of them. But you knew he was a Lakota, now didn't you?"

"I did."

"Well, he might not actually be a true Lakota. At least, according to rumors that circulate around."

Roberta was beginning to sound more and more like Helen.

"What kind of rumors are those?" asked Zeb.

"Tribal records being what they were back in the day aren't exactly what you'd call accurate."

"Agreed," replied Zeb.

"The rumor mill says that four generations back Shappa's family got chased out of the Navajo tribe. They were part of a branch of a northern Arizona tribe. I've heard them called the Tewa Navajo."

"Tewa?" asked Zeb.

"I guess Tewa describes where they lived, in the flat lands next to ravines. But don't quote me on that one."

"I won't. What does the rumor mill say about why they got chased out of the tribe?"

"Well, that's where the story gets fishy sounding to me."

"Tell me anyway," said Zeb.

"You ever heard of a thing called a Skinwalker?"

"I have," replied Zeb. "The rumor mill down this way says they still exist in our area."

"No fooling."

"Nope, no fooling. The traditional Navajo call the Skinwalkers yee naaldlooshii."

Roberta repeated the Navajo word out loud so Zeb could hear her and correct her. She committed the Navajo word for Skinwalker to her memory.

"What are the rumors about Shappa's family?"

"Well..." Roberta's voice got really quiet and she began to whisper into the phone. "Seems as though they got kicked out of the tribe because of the initiation."

"From what I've read and what I've heard, the initiation rites are quite violent," replied Zeb.

"What I've heard is that to become a Skinwalker you have to commit the evilest kind of deed—the killing of a close family member. If you can do that, you get supernatural powers. From what I've heard, it's passed down from generation to generation. A Skinwalker can be a shapeshifter too. You know what that is, right?"

"I do. Please go on."

"They can turn themselves into animals, like a wolf or a coyote or even a bear."

Roberta stopped talking. Zeb assumed she had listened to her own words and figured she had said too much or that maybe she was sounding a bit crazy. When she went silent, Zeb helped her out of the awkwardness.

"I've got a couple of other questions about Black Bear, personal stuff. Do you mind if I ask you just a few more things?" asked Zeb.

Zeb knew she was hot to gossip. He asked her if she wanted to continue talking, only out of politeness, as he knew she did.

"I don't want to cross any lines, but I'll answer what I can. Sheriff Lentz won't be back from coffee for another ten minutes or so. You've got my ear. Go ahead. Ask away, cowboy."

Zeb was hoping Roberta could give him inside dope that Sheriff Lentz might want to safeguard. If Roberta was anything like Helen, she would protect her own and getting the sort of information he was after would be a long shot. Still, he had to try.

"Can you tell me anything more about Black Bear's childhood?"

"Like I said earlier, I watched him grow up."

"Was he ever in trouble for what he did?"

"You mean the animal torture?"

"That and any other stuff."

"Not really. Shappa was political. She was powerful, both in the tribe and in the White community. To speak out against her child would mean you were speaking out against her. Not too many folks wanted to run the risk of being on her wrong side. But sure, Black Bear made some trouble. What kid doesn't?"

Zeb thought back on his own childhood. She hit a bullseye with her answer. He had her pegged as a truth teller.

"If you don't mind, could you give me a two-minute rundown of his early life."

"This is the Midwest, Sheriff Hanks, no one tells a two-minute story, unless someone is squeezing out their final breath. But, for you, I'll try and keep it brief."

Zeb figured it was the long winters that made for the never-ending story Midwesterners were famous for.

"Black Bear was maybe three or four years old when his folks split up. Shappa did most of the raising of the boy. Radicalized him with her politics, if you ask me. But, then again, we all know how tough it is when a boy is raised only by his mother."

Zeb's mind drifted back to his own upbringing. His mother did ninety percent of the heavy lifting when it came to him and his brother. Roberta's words brought a strange thought to Zeb's mind. Suddenly he had the realization that his father did little more than teach him how to mishandle his anger. He chose not to share his thoughts with Roberta and asked her to carry on.

"Right," said Zeb. "It's tough."

"You got kids, Sheriff?"

"Two. Little ones. Just about toddlers."

"Make your marriage work."

Her advice reminded him of something Helen would say.

"Yes, ma'am."

"It's Roberta or Berta. Your choice. I'm not fussy. Just don't call me late for supper."

Zeb chuckled at what must be a Midwestern farm expression.

"Roberta."

"Anyway, his father was FBI at the time. But you know that too, don't you?"

"Yes, ma'am. Roberta, I mean. I was aware of that fact."

"He was a stern sort of guy. Working all the time. Hardly had any time for the boy. Nevertheless, Black Bear loved and admired him. I guess that's what a boy does, admire his father. Absence makes the heart grow fonder and all that folderol."

Zeb certainly couldn't say the same about his own father.

"I'd say that other than Shappa dragging him to every political event in the five-state area, and the animal torture stuff he did, Black Bear had a fairly normal enough life. He fished, played ball, chased the girls, oh Lordy, was he a charmer when it came to the ladies. He must have four or five kids of his living on the Rez. All from different women. They say he wore out the zipper on every pair of pants he ever owned."

Caught a bit off guard by Roberta's somewhat salty expression, Zeb chuckled awkwardly.

However, the news about Black Bear's sexual prowess barely moved Zeb's barometer. From the moment he arrived in Safford, Black Bear was known as a poon-dog. Zeb didn't know of any local offspring, though.

"When he graduated high school, he became a Jackrabbit."

"Jackrabbit?"

"He went to college at South Dakota State College over in Brookings."

"I assume he majored in law enforcement?"

"He majored in girls, whiskey, drugs and craziness is the way I heard it said. Got involved with some real hardcore radicals over there in Brookings. Some pretty strange politics if you ask me."

"Strange? How so?"

"Cultish."

"Cultish? Meaning what?" asked Zeb.

"He got involved with some group that called themselves the

Guardians of the Golden Flame. Crazy bunch. I think they're disbanded now," said Roberta.

"What was their agenda?" asked Zeb.

Zeb heard some rustling in the background. He overheard Roberta greeting Sheriff Lentz. She gave him a quick rundown on who she was talking to and what they were talking about. Sheriff Lentz said he would take the call in his office.

"Sheriff's here," said Roberta. "He can tell you a whole lot more about the Golden Flamers than I can. He probably knows more about Black Bear than I do. He dated Shappa for quite a while. I'm transferring you to him now. Nice talking with you, Sheriff Hanks."

"Likewise, Roberta. Thank you. You've been most helpful."

"If I was, I don't know how. Barely got the conversation started," replied Roberta, switching the call to Sheriff Lentz's office.

21

SHERIFF LENTZ

"Sheriff Hanks, this is Sheriff Lentz. How goes your day?"

"Well, I just had a nice little chat with Roberta, if that tells you anything."

Sheriff Lentz chuckled.

"It means you're more up to speed than I am on what's going on around the county. As you could probably tell, she runs the place."

"I have an assistant who does the same for me," replied Zeb. "Be lost without her."

"Ditto. I guess that's a good thing."

This time it was Zeb's turn to chuckle.

"What can I help you with?" asked Sheriff Lentz. "I have to assume this is about Black Bear or Shappa."

"It is."

"Shoot."

"Shappa just left town, town being Safford, Arizona, with her son's body packed in dry ice. Her former husband, Tom, is traveling with her. They're bringing Black Bear's body back there to give him a proper ceremonial send off."

"Yeah?" replied Sheriff Lentz. "Sounds about right."

"Meaning what?"

"Meaning Shappa would drive cross country with Black Bear's body so she could have the proper Lakota ceremony that will take him on his journey from this world to the next."

"That all sounds normal to you?"

"Yes, it does. Why? Is something raising your hackles?"

"Yes and no."

"What's on your mind, Sheriff Hanks? You're better off speaking it than leaving me guessing."

Zeb liked Sheriff Lentz's style.

"I got the distinct feeling that there's more to the picture than meets the eye when it comes to Shappa's motives," said Zeb.

"What do you suspect?"

"The little man inside me thinks she is destroying or has destroyed evidence," said Zeb.

"Black Bear's body? I know it's been mutilated and that a major autopsy has been performed on it," replied Sheriff Lentz. "All of which you are distinctly aware of."

"You know about all that, huh?"

"I requested the autopsy report."

"Did you suspect something?" asked Zeb.

"Nah. I did it out of curiosity as much as anything," replied Sheriff Lentz.

"Curiosity?" asked Zeb.

"Black Bear ran in a lot of odd circles and had more than a few strange bedfellows in his day. And I'm not necessarily talking about women. I'm talking about the sort that ran among his inner circle," said Sheriff Lentz.

"I had him pegged during his time down here as more or less a loner. Can you enlighten me?"

"Only to a degree," replied Sheriff Lentz. "It's complicated and I, more or less, kept my nose out of it at Shappa's request."

"I understand you and Shappa dated for a while."

Sheriff Lentz was not at all surprised that Zeb had that little bit of information. It was exactly the kind of information that would slip loose from Roberta's tongue.

"I take it you didn't have to work too hard to get the county wag who runs this place to hand over that little tidbit?"

"She offered it freely, but offhandedly."

"I dated Shappa at several different points in her life. Once when Black Bear was a young boy, right after his father left the family. Black Bear resented the hell out of me."

"I get that," replied Sheriff Hanks. "Seems like a natural reaction from a young kid."

"It was, but it also showed me he had a very dark side. He cut me with a knife when he was about seven or eight years old. It was done totally out of anger. Though, I suppose he felt he was protecting his mother."

"Shit happens."

"It does, but it also could have been related to his head injury," said Lentz.

"I was going to ask you about that," said Zeb. "How did that happen?"

"Black Bear was an adventurous kid, a real risk taker. He fell out of a tree when he was seven or almost eight, seven, yes, he was seven years old when he fractured his skull. He smacked it on the sharp edge of a granite rock. He shattered it so badly the surgeons couldn't even patch up the pieces of bone that he destroyed in the fall. They had to put a metal plate in his head. He had headaches for years from that little incident. Or, so he claimed. He lost some hearing in his left ear. Eventually he quit bitching about the pain and led a pretty normal life. He even played football."

"Risky."

"Yeah, I suppose it was, but the Rez doc gave him the okay to play. If you ask me, the skull fracture made him a little bit loopy along with the meanness that was already part of his nature."

"Loopy?"

"Yeah, loopy. He never seemed to be concerned about the consequences of what he did. It was like the injury or maybe the surgery took away his conscience. Who knows? Maybe he would have been that way without the injury."

"That's something we'll never know," said Zeb.

"I guess not. There was one weird thing about all that. I don't even know what made me think of it," said Sheriff Lentz.

"Please, do tell. You never know what bearing it may have on my cases and Black Bear's death," replied Zeb.

"Like I said, this is a strange memory. When Black Bear was under sedation during surgery, he claimed his mother came to him to comfort him and actually kept him from dying."

"I've heard of things like that happening under sedation," interjected Zeb.

"Well, he said she came to him, only she was a ghost."

"A ghost? Like a spirit?"

"I don't know for sure. I was never let in on all the details. It was one of those secret things between mother and son. But from that day forward, whenever he really needed his mommy, he called her Chindi."

"Chindi?"

"Yeah. It's a word for ghost, but it ain't a Lakota word."

Zeb made a mental note only because it was an odd thing. It didn't feel relevant to Black Bear's death.

"I take it you stayed in Shappa's and Black Bear's lives?"

"I did. I thought I was in love with Shappa. I carried the torch for her for another decade. Years later I took up with her again. Foolishly so, I might add."

"More trouble with Black Bear?" asked Zeb.

"He was a man by that time. He was off at college on a combined baseball, academic and tribal scholarship. He played some football there, too. The kid was a hell of a ballplayer. Fast on his feet, great hands and eyes like an eagle. He got hurt his freshman year. When he could no longer play ball, he got totally into politics, booze, chicks, you know how that goes."

"Shit happens," said Zeb, again.

"He joined up with a group of crazies that went by the name of The Guardians of the Golden Flame."

"They didn't by any chance wear golden pinky rings, did they?" asked Zeb.

"As a matter of fact, they did. How would you know about that?"

"It's a long story. To be honest I was guessing. One and one sometimes adds up to three. This time it actually added up to two."

"Tell me more," said Lentz. "About how you Arizona folks do your addition."

"Right before Black Bear beat me in the election last year, there were a series of crimes in the county. Recently, since Black Bear's death to be precise, a golden pinky finger ring seems to have worked itself into the criminal equation."

"Did the golden ring help you solve the crimes?"

"Er, no. That is, not yet."

"An open case I take it?" asked Sheriff Lentz. "A problematic one?"

"It's the case, a series of cases to be exact, that got me booted out of office and got Black Bear elected Sheriff of Graham County," said Zeb. "And, yes, it's an open case."

"You sound like you think Black Bear may have been involved in those crimes?"

"He might have been. I can't prove it one way or the other," replied Zeb. "Maybe if you tell me a little more about this Golden Flame bunch?"

Sheriff Lentz excitedly shared what he knew.

"They were a profit and power-driven group. Gold was their currency. Greed was their motivation. They were ruthless when it came to wanting power. They allegedly had friends in high places in the government, the corporate world and even overseas. But who knows how much of it is true?"

"Did they operate out of South Dakota?"

"The Black Hills is legendary for the amount of gold that was mined here. You know how it is, gold is the stuff that legends are made of. There are all sorts of stories of lost gold mines, hidden caches of gold, even secret Indian spirit guides that for the right offering will lead you to the lost gold."

"The last part sounds kind of hokey, but the rest of it makes sense," said Zeb. "The Guardians of the Golden Flame, I take it, were primarily after gold."

"And the power of authority. Authority to change old government treaties between the Indians and the United States government," said Sheriff Lentz. "Even international treaties, if you believe all that you hear."

"Any treaty in particular?" asked Zeb.

"One in particular up our way, but all of the Indian-US government treaties in general."

"What treaty are you talking about?"

"The Fort Laramie Treaty of 1868. Are you familiar with it?"

"I've heard my wife mention it," said Zeb.

"Jesus, a bell just went off in my head. You're the guy married to the Apache woman with special powers," said Lentz.

"I don't know about that..."

"You don't have to say nothin'. The local medicine man and I go way, way back. He was telling me the sheriff who got beat by Black Bear in the Arizona election was married to an Apache woman who has direct links to what he called All the Nations of All the People. That's mighty big medicine the way I understand it."

"You may know more about my wife than I do," said Zeb.

Lentz let loose with an easy laugh.

"Let's just say this county has more gossip than it does people."

Zeb let it go. He did not want to confirm nor deny anything about Echo's knowledge. He, himself, had only become truly exposed to some of it on their honeymoon. Zeb returned to the original topic.

"You were saying about the Fort Laramie Treaty? I don't know a lot about it. Can you educate me a bit?" asked Zeb.

"The treaty was between the United States and the Sioux and Arapaho tribes. If you're from South Dakota, you'd refer to the Sioux separately as the Dakota, the Lakota and the Nakota. The treaty created the Great Sioux Reservation."

"Which is what exactly?"

"Good question. The Great Rez was a large area of numerous lands west of the Missouri River. The treaty also gave the designation as 'unceded Indian Territory' to the Black Hills. This land was intended forever and all time to be Indian land."

"I'll bet gold changed all that," offered Zeb.

"It most certainly did. The U.S. reneged on the treaty. If you believe the tribe's side of the story, it happens all the time. In any case, the U.S. government redrew the boundaries which it claimed it had the right by prior treaty to do."

"An early form of gerrymandering," said Zeb.

"Some things never change. The net result was that the Sioux and the Arapaho who were nomadic tribes lost their territory. They were essentially forced into becoming farmers, something they knew little to nothing about. For the last 150 years there has been a constant court battle between the tribes and the government. Eventually, the U.S. Supreme Court made a ruling," explained Lentz.

"I get the feeling it didn't go well for the Sioux."

"You got that half right. In 1980 the court awarded the Sioux just over one hundred million dollars."

"A reasonable sum of money," interjected Zeb. "Enough to go a long way in helping the tribe."

"You're thinking like a White man."

"You're not the first to accuse me of that."

"The Sioux refused the money outright. They said the land was never for sale and that it is still their land. Today that money, the original 102 million dollars, which is held in trust, is currently worth 1.3 billion dollars. Shappa still holds enough political sway to stop those who want to take the money and be done with it. Needless to say, it's a sore spot with the local tribal folks, especially the younger ones who don't have a sense of history."

"Whew."

"Exactly."

"As a little historical side note that might interest you, the Fort Laramie Treaty was adopted by Congress and put into law in 1868. A few years later in 1874 General George Armstrong Custer led an expedition into the Black Hills to search for gold. A year later eight hundred miners had flooded the plains and taken over the territory that was legally part of the Sioux Nation. Of course, the tribes felt threatened and reacted by attacking the prospectors in order to save their land."

"Makes perfect sense," said Zeb. "I'm sure they thought they were acting within their rights."

"This set up the famed Battle of Little Bighorn. If you know your history, you know that battle took place in 1876."

"Custer's Last Stand."

"Precisely. The Sioux Nations won their final victory and took Old Yellow Hair's life, but not his scalp, in the process. As you can imagine, this didn't set well with the American public or the United States government."

"I can only imagine the fever pitch that must have been going on at the time," added Zeb.

"Within a year Congress passed an act that redrew the boundaries set forth in the Fort Laramie Treaty. The treaty forced the tribes onto permanent reservations. And so, the battle carries on and on and on and on."

Zeb couldn't help but think of Mount Graham and how it had been stolen from the Apache Nation. That court battle was less than a half a century old but would likely still be fought a hundred years into the future. He also thought of the Spanish gold that was allegedly hidden in the nearby Galiuro Mountains. The coincidences were incredibly strong. A brief thought entered Zeb's mind. Had Black Bear, as part of the Guardians of the Golden Flame cult, come to Graham County seeking additional lost gold? A second thought followed. Had Senator Russell sent him there to do just that? His thinking ended in a troubling third thought. As the Knowledge Keeper, did Echo play a role in all of this? And finally, was she in danger because of all of it?

"Indeed, it does," sighed Zeb.

"To answer your original question, the Guardians of the Golden Flame provided tens of millions of dollars, before they formally disbanded, to keep the legal battle alive and moving forward."

"Where'd they get that kind of money?" asked Zeb.

"No one seems to know the answer to that question," replied Sheriff Lentz. "But that kind of money likely involves gold. Lots of it."

"I take it you believe Shappa and Black Bear are somehow involved in all of this?"

"I have no doubt that Shappa has her fingers stuck deeply into the pie. Black Bear, well, I have to believe he was likely somehow involved as well. Even Shappa's former husband, Tom Sawyer, may have a role in all of this. That being said, I can't prove anything. Nor do I have any reason to be sticking my nose into it."

"I'm beginning to think I might have to stick my nose into it," said Zeb.

"It's dangerous turf, Sheriff Hanks. Tread lightly and carefully if you do stick your schnozzola into that hornet's nest."

Zeb's head was spinning. Sheriff Lentz was practically confirming Zeb's earlier theory. The Guardians of the Golden Flame who sought gold and power couldn't help but bring to mind the legend of the lost Apache gold. The link between Congress, the treaty and power once again brought Senator Russell to mind and the sway he held over many of the committees that had a huge say in all activities related to Indian lands. His heart began to race. Something innate, something intuitive, was practically screaming at him. Something was telling him that beyond a shadow of a doubt this was all connected.

However, at this moment he didn't have a clue as to exactly how. The faster he thought the closer his mind became one with Echo's. He didn't know why, but for a dynamic but fleeting second, he was certain she held the keys of knowledge that could help him solve not only Black Bear's death but come to a greater understanding of the lines between the White and Indian worlds in general. He didn't know how long he had been silent until he heard Sheriff Lentz clearing his throat.

"Sorry, lost in thought," said Zeb.

"Not a problem. Been there myself when it comes to this stuff," said Sheriff Lentz. "I hope I was able to help you in some way."

"You did. A great deal, in fact. However, right now I am left with more questions than answers. Do you mind if I get back to you at some point if I have further questions?"

"I'm an easygoing guy," said Lentz. "Anytime you think I can help you solve a case, give me a shout."

"One more thing," said Zeb.

"Yes, of course."

"Shappa flew into Phoenix a few days ago and drove down to Safford."

"To pick up Black Bear's body. You already mentioned that," said Sheriff Lentz.

"Any idea if she was on the local Rez or up your way say ten days ago?"

"Currently, I don't really have a reason to keep track of her. But I can do you a favor and ask around."

"Can you do it on the down low?" asked Zeb.

"Sure. Why? What am I looking for?"

"Black Bear's house was burned to the ground around that time. I was putting together a connection in my head and..."

"You were wondering if Shappa torched his place down there like she did up here?"

"Yes," replied Zeb.

"What she did up here was on Indian land and is traditional among the Lakota. It's not considered a crime."

"It is down here," said Zeb.

"You're assuming she came down there, torched Black Bear's Safford residence and returned back to the Rez? And that she kept it all under the radar. Is that right?"

"Something along those lines," replied Zeb.

"You believe she did it to destroy evidence, I take it?"

"Yes, I do."

"I'll see what I can find out."

"Thanks."

"Oh, and one more thing," said Lentz.

"Yeah?"

"Shappa knows how to kill a man in a dozen different ways. Watch your back."

22

ARSON INVESTIGATION

Fire Chief Austin Leary had early on in his investigation determined the fire that destroyed Black Bear's house was an act of arson. Accelerants were found at four key areas of the fire. Whoever wanted Black Bear's home destroyed made little effort to hide the fact that total destruction was the desired result. They also were smart enough or experienced enough to know exactly where to start the fires so that they would do the most damage possible. He spent three full days sifting through the debris with one of his men and a pair of local volunteers. When they finished, Fire Chief Leary called Zeb.

"Zeb, Chief Leary."

"Chief, how are things going at Black Bear's house?"

"We've wrapped it up."

"What've you got?"

"As I suspected, arson."

"Okay."

"Almost certainly gasoline was used an accelerant. Pretty straight-forward stuff. Has anyone filed an insurance claim?"

"I checked with Williams at the State Farm office, that's where Black Bear had his home insured. No claim has been filed."

"Unless they've taken to underwriting arson, they're not going to have to pay out one red cent on this one."

Zeb laughed. Leary was an Irishman but not necessarily known for having a sense of humor. On the other hand, the mere idea of Shappa profiting from arson elevated his dander.

"I've got a bag of artifacts I'm fairly certain you'll be interested in," said the Chief.

"I'm headed down that way," replied Zeb. "See you in fifteen minutes?"

"Sounds good. I'd like to get this wrapped up, paperwork filed and off my desk."

Five minutes later Zeb grabbed his hat from the rack and headed toward the door past Helen's desk.

"Where you headed, Zeb?"

"Black Bear's house. Chief Leary has finished his investigation."

"Arson?"

"Looks like it," replied Zeb.

"Any ideas who did it?" asked Helen.

"No one for certain," replied Zeb. "But in my mind, I've got a few suspects."

"I've heard some of those northern Indian tribes believe in destroying every earthly possession of a dead man," said Helen.

"Where'd you hear that?' asked Zeb.

Helen turned away and grunted out a low harrumph. Zeb recognized her reaction. She had been snooping and did not want to admit to anything.

"I have my sources."

"Ladies Aid Society or the Quilting Club?"

Even as the words slipped off his tongue, Zeb regretted having said them.

"Maybe if you took the time to cultivate a broader variety of sources of information, you'd have solved a whole string of unresolved issues in our lovely county."

Zeb did a doubletake. Helen rarely spoke to him like that. He knew her well enough to know that something else was eating at her.

He made a mental note to soften her up with a sweet treat from the Town Talk on his way back.

"I'll work on it," said Zeb, tipping his hat.

"I'm sorry," implored Helen. "It's just that I talked with your mother today."

"Yes?"

"You haven't seen her lately, have you?"

"Just once since I got back from my honeymoon. She seemed tired, but fine," said Zeb.

"She's not fine."

"What's going on?"

"I think you should talk to her about that and do it soon."

"Soon? As in today?"

"That would be the right thing to do."

Helen was surprisingly cryptic, especially considering the subject was her sister, Zeb's mother.

"Why all the mystery?"

"I can't really say," replied Helen.

Zeb knew Helen better than he knew his own mother. Unlike his mother, Helen generally wore her heart on her sleeve.

"Can't or won't?" asked Zeb.

"You need to talk to her. Soon." said Helen.

"You make it sound important," replied Zeb.

"It is. She's not well."

Zeb pulled one of the wooden waiting room area chairs up to Helen's desk. He spun it around, plopped down in it, leaned his arms over the back of the chair and spoke pointedly to Helen. His frankness was out of concern.

"What do you mean she's not well?" asked Zeb.

"When I called her this morning, she sounded terribly tired. She told me she hadn't slept well. In fact, she said she hadn't been sleeping well at all lately. And you know your mother, she always sees to it that she gets her rest."

Even when Zeb was child, even when his parents fought like cats and dogs, his mother always made a point of getting enough sleep. It was a characteristic of hers that he envied.

"I'll drop by and see her today," replied Zeb. "Right after I talk with Chief Leary."

The drive to Black Bear's house was short. Chief Leary was standing in uniform amidst the remains of the burned-out house.

"Zeb."

"Austin. What've you got?"

"Outside of what you already know, that it was almost certainly arson, fueled by gasoline, I can tell you that three neighbors reported seeing yellow smoke, another sign of burning gasoline."

"Right," replied Zeb.

"And two of the same three neighbors heard breaking glass before they saw the fire," said Leary.

"Meaning what?"

"Somebody broke out the windows to increase the oxygen supply to make the fire burn faster and hotter. It's a trick used by professional arsonists, or at least experienced ones."

"That's all helpful. Anything that can help me figure out who the specific arsonist is?"

"Yes and no. Whoever did it knew what they were doing. But, as usual, no one does a perfect job. That's damn near impossible," said Leary.

"What else you got?" asked Zeb.

"Everything is pretty much ashes or useless pieces of wood and metal. I did see that the gas stove handles were turned to the on position. That's another common arsonist trick, but it's one that is used on every television cop show. Therefore, everyone who starts a destructive fire knows to do that."

"Television writers," grunted Zeb. "I wonder how many crimes they help create every year?"

"A lot of them. No doubt in my mind," replied Leary.

"Anything else?"

"Just some silverware and this."

Leary handed Zeb a bag. Inside was a ring, a small gold ring. It was just the size that would fit a woman's hand or the pinky finger on a man.

"Found it under a piece of Nomex."

"Nomex?"

"It's a material that won't burn until the temperature gets to roughly 1200 degrees. It's used in safe boxes where people keep valuables that they want to survive a fire."

"Anything else in the box?" asked Zeb.

"The box pretty much melted and crushed. Inside were this ring and some gold coins that melted together. The ring must have been situated just right because it hardly looks damaged at all. Looks like an old family ring or something. Thought you might want it. Actually, I thought the family might want it back."

Zeb fondled the ring in his hand. He immediately noticed the dragon's tail. There was no reason to explain it to Leary. With the ring in his hand Zeb felt one small step closer to proving Black Bear was indeed part of something that was plaguing Graham County. He wished the gold coins were less damaged and might have been able to tell him something more. He was out of luck on that account.

"I'll see if his parents want it," said Zeb. "I might also have a forensic coin specialist see if he can tell me anything about the damaged coins."

"You should have a jeweler look at that ring. It seems old and the markings on it seem like they might mean something to someone," said Leary. "I'm no ring expert but I've never seen one like it."

Their conversation was interrupted by an ambulance call that popped on Zeb's two-way radio. He recognized the address. He looked at Leary, thanked him and ran to his truck. He didn't mention the address he had overheard was that of his childhood home.

Zeb flipped on his flashing lights and drove immediately to his mother's house. As he arrived, medics were already moving his mother to the ambulance. Zeb hopped out of his truck and raced to the scene. Zeb didn't recognize the men and women on the first responder crew. He pushed the panic that had risen to his throat back down into his gut. Zeb was barely able to squeak out his question.

"What's going on?" he asked.

"She contacted us seven minutes ago using her First Alert button. It's a good thing she had one. We found her on the floor. She's breathing, but she can't talk," said the attendant. "We're taking her to the ER."

Zeb walked beside his mother who was being transported on a gurney. She was alive, but not alert. Zeb reached over and clasped her hand in his. It was cold and clammy. Her face looked ashen and pale. He pushed bad thoughts out of his head, reminding himself that he was no doctor or even a first responder.

"Is she okay?" asked Zeb.

The first responders gently placed her in the back of their vehicle. Their response was methodical and professional, but not full of hope.

"She's alive. That's a good thing."

Zeb followed the ambulance to the ER. Doc Yackley was waiting at the entrance. He watched as they wheeled Zeb's mother past him and to the acute care room.

"Zeb."

Stunned, in a state of near shock at seeing his mother in the state she was in and feeling helpless, he didn't hear his name being called out. Doc grabbed him by the shoulder.

"Zeb. You can't do her any good. You can sit in the waiting area if you want. I'll get hold of you the minute I know anything."

Doc went into the hospital emergency room. Zeb followed him in and went into the waiting area where he immediately began pacing back and forth manically. He was beside himself. How could he leave? What good would it do to stay? Obligation and experience had placed him in the waiting area. He felt two things, hopelessness and fear. As he grabbed his cellphone and was about to call Echo, it buzzed. In his state of mind, he nearly dropped the phone as he fumbled to answer it.

"Yes?"

It was Helen.

"How's your mother?"

"I don't know."

"Did you see her?"

"Yes. She's alive, but unconscious."

"Are you waiting in the ER?"

"I am."

"Did you lock up her house?"

"No."

"You should. The local gangs monitor all emergency calls. While you were not sheriff, they hit a half dozen houses when incidents like this happened. Go lock it up. It'll take you five minutes."

"Can you go do it, Helen?"

"I've got people to call about your mother. People need to know. Go. Just do it. It will take you three minutes. Nothing is going to happen to your mother in that time."

Zeb knew Helen was right. Reluctantly he followed her advice. When he arrived at his mother's house, all the doors were open as well as some windows. He quickly locked things up. As he was leaving, he saw a stack of what appeared to be legal documents on the kitchen table. An attached note from Zeb's mother to herself indicated they should be returned to the safe deposit box.

On top of the stack was an envelope with Zeb's name neatly printed on it. It was not sealed. Zeb took a peek. Inside was a handwritten letter. His curiosity got the better of him. He unfolded the letter. Immediately upon reading the first few words a tingle shot up his spine and the base of his skull went numb.

23

THE LETTER

My Dearest Zebulon,

I love you. I need you to know that above all other things. My love for you is as true and constant as God's love is for all of his children. My love for you has been the same since the day you were born and will remain that way until the day I die. If there is a God in heaven my love for you will last for all time and eternity.

Zeb wiped away tears that began to flow involuntarily. A heavy sigh escaped his lips. His hands began to tremble. An invisible force pressed a heaviness against his chest. He had heard about how some people, when they knew they were dying, wrote letters to their loved ones. With the thought of his mother lying in the emergency room, his fear redoubled. Tears now fell uncontrollably from his eyes practically in tune with the beat of his pained heart. He pulled the letter away from his face so the escaping tears would not smear the ink of her beautifully handwritten letter.

There are things, many things, I have shared with you in your life. Good things and bad things. What I am about to tell you, well, I don't really know how you are going to take it. I hope you may come to see some good in my words of explanation. But, knowing you as I do, as the woman who raised you in both the Church of Jesus Christ of Latter-Day Saints and by means of Revivalist Religion, I believe you may even hate me after you finish reading this letter. I hope that the truth does not make you despise me. I feel that you must know the truth about yourself. No matter how angry this letter may make you feel, please, please, do not tear it to shreds. I beg of you to finish the entire letter before you pass judgement on me.

Zeb set the letter down and got himself a glass of water to calm his spinning brain. He felt faint. Blood seemed to be draining away from his head. His heart ached with an unrecognizable pain. He finished the water, grabbed the letter and took a seat, the one he always sat in as a child, at the kitchen table. In some mysterious way this letter was taking him back to his youth. He half expected to look up and see a box of Lucky Charms. He wondered what she meant by passing judgement as he continued reading the handwritten letter from his mother.

Zebulon, when I lost your brother, I truly believed my well of tears had run dry. Now, as I write this letter to you, they have returned in torrents. What I always wanted for you was simple and straightforward. I wanted more than anything that you find your own way in the world. I tried, God knows I tried, to make up for my earthly sins. When I had doubts, all I had to do was look at you and all that you have accomplished as Sheriff of Graham County and as a loving husband and father. Seeing those things renews my faith that I wasn't entirely a terrible person.

The last two words on the first page, terrible person, had Zeb shaking from head to toe. His mother was a saint. No matter what anyone thought or said, she was not a terrible person. What on earth could she possibly be talking about? He thought of the Reverend Willright, the Pentecostal preacher's words, *When God divided the deep blue sea, when He halved the sky overhead with the land on which we stand, he mixed together all that is good with all that is bad.*

Had his mother been a bad person? If so, he had never seen it. Zeb hesitantly turned to the second page of his mother's letter. His mind was trapped in a dense fog. He had not a clue as to what she might have written next. It could be just about anything.

Zebulon, dearest son of mine, please, please, I beg of you do not let what I am about to say create a hatred in your heart that cannot be mended. If that happened, I could never forgive myself for telling you the truth, a truth that you deserve and need to hear. Your life has turned out well even though it has been couched in a monstrously huge lie.

Zeb's neck tightened. His veins bulged. His mouth became dry. His heart fluttered out of rhythm. The skin on his head tingled with pulsating electricity. His mother had lied to him for his entire life about something important. How could she have done that? How could he have not known? He wiped away tears with his shirt sleeve. Through blurry, burning eyes he continued reading.

The man who raised you as his son, the man who died in prison, the man who provided for a roof over your head, was not your biological father.

The letter Zeb held in his hands slipped through his fingers and dropped onto the kitchen table. A breeze rushing through the open kitchen door blew it to the floor. Zeb, elbows on the kitchen table, placed his hands over his ears, as if not hearing might make take away the reality of what he had just read. He was at a loss for words. His thoughts were so jumbled as to be incomprehensible even to himself. Mindlessly at first, then shifting between confusion, frustration and anger, he eyed the letter on the floor. Did he even want to know how it ended? Did it matter? His mind turned to Echo and his children. A thousand what-ifs, all of them seemingly insane, ran through his mind. As one thought bled into the next, he knew his thinking was pointless. There was but one truth and it was written in his mother's handwriting and sitting on a piece of paper on the kitchen floor of his childhood home. He leaned over to pick up the letter, hitting his head on the corner of the table. A multitude of stars flashed in his eyes. Through the pain he noticed how spotlessly clean the floor was. His mother liked it that way. It was a strange thought, even he recognized that.

The relationship between my husband and me was tumultuous at best. Since he has passed, there is no reason to besmirch his name. However, it is my name that is tainted.

Zeb stopped. What on earth did she mean? How was her name tainted? Did he even want to know? Did he want to know why she would write such a thing? He stood and began to pace in a small circle. His world had just gone crazy. He was at a loss for what to think. Eventually he took his childhood seat once more and picked up the letter and continued reading.

Yes, Zebulon, your mother was/is a fallen woman. In my weakness I sought solace in the arms of another man. That man is Senator Clinton Jefferson Russell. He is your biological father.

Stunned and in disbelief, Zeb jumped to his feet, looked at the last two sentences, screamed aloud and began pacing back and forth like a lunatic. He closed his fist and punched a hole in the kitchen wall. Why had his mother written this obvious lie? How could any part of this be true? His spinning mind began to ask and answer questions faster than the speed of thought. As quickly he drew conclusions. Russell had seduced his mother in her time of weakness and taken advantage of her. Yes, that was it. His mother was a saint. Senator Russell was the devil. The devil was deceptive and strong enough to have fooled his mother. The devil had been fooling the world since the beginning of time. It simply couldn't be true that his beautiful mother had given herself to Senator Russell willingly. But, why would she lie? His mind kept spinning faster and faster. Maybe Russell had raped her? Yes, of course. Senator Russell was capable of such a horrifying act. But what would that make Zeb? He was nause-ated to the point of vomiting at the mere thought of it. He grabbed the letter and re-read it from start to finish. He stomped. He cried out in anger. He leaned his back against the wall, slid to the floor and wept uncontrollably.

When his body took a break from the frenzied tears, Zeb called out to God and demanded He let him punish the man who had done this to his sainted mother. Zeb plotted. He would put a bullet through Senator Russell's head. As he lay there slowly dying, Zeb would fire another bullet through his groin. No, he would torture him slowly for what he had done. Then he would cut him into a thousand pieces and litter the desert floor with the fragments of Russell's body. Zeb stopped when something this horrific came to his mind. Were these gruesome thoughts his true inheritance from Senator Russell? They were not what he had learned from his mother. His eyes fell on the last lines of the letter through tears of anger.

Zebulon, my son, I am truly sorry for the pain this will cause you. But know that I love you and that you are my beloved son. Think of your children before you take out any anger you may have on Senator Russell.

All my love,

Mom

PS - Zebulon, if you are reading this, I am probably dead. How strange it is to write such a statement. Please take my heartfelt advice seriously. One last time...I love you with all my heart.

Zeb set the letter down as he scanned the house he had grown up in. An infinite number of memories rushed in. His thoughts spun looking upon the family pictures on the wall, the framed pictures of him and his brother on their sports teams, school pictures, vacation pictures, images of a life lived...falsely. Zeb began to weep irrepressibly. Was he crying for his mother or himself? He did not know. It was a question that seemed to have no answer.

Jumbled in with his tears was an ever-growing desire to balance the score with Senator Russell. As his hatred for Russell rose, the thought of his mother popped into his head. He ran to his car and sped to the emergency room where he ran into a freshly scrubbed and dour looking Doc Yackley. The old doc's words were more than sobering, they were life changing. He placed his hand on Zeb's shoulder as he spoke.

"I'm sorry. I did all I could, but your mother didn't make it."

"What? What happened?"

"She had a massive stroke. She didn't suffer. God rest her lovely, beautiful soul," said Doc.

Zeb's knees buckled at the same moment Echo appeared behind him and grabbed him, preventing him from falling to the floor. Her strength was superhuman.

"Oh, Zeb. Sweetheart."

Her words filtered through a hollow tunnel that seemed to be coming from a million miles away.

"I'm here for you."

He knew she spoke the divine truth. Still, the Sheriff of Graham County had never felt more alone or lost.

"Zeb, I will help you through this."

Echo's words were straight from her heart. Zeb felt the slightest twinge of hope rising from his confusion.

"Zeb, I love you."

"Echo, I need you. I'm lost."

24

SENATOR RUSSELL - A SHORT NUMBER OF WEEKS AGO

S enator Russell and his top aide, Derrick David Pmensk, a former medical student, made the limousine trip to Johns Hopkins kidney transplant center late on a Friday afternoon.

Dr. Ankrit Kaviraj, understanding that he was meeting a high-ranking government official, agreed to see him after hours at the very end of the day. Owing to the seriousness of his condition, Senator Russell wanted to make certain no one knew he was being examined for a life-threatening illness of his kidneys. Russell knew all too well the influence structure in D.C. If as much as a hint of his potential demise were to become known, numerous power seekers would swoop in and take advantage of all that Senator Russell had spent the last thirty-plus years building. Even if he were to die, he wanted to have the final say in who took over the reins of his empire. But now, today, he was thinking about the possibility of a miracle as Doctor Kaviraj entered the treatment room.

"Senator Russell."

"Doctor Kaviraj."

The men shook hands and the doctor's gaze shifted to Derrick.

"He is my aide. He's a former medical student."

Doctor Kaviraj nodded politely but did not speak directly to the senator's underling.

"Senator Russell, I have both good news and bad news for you regarding the kidney transplant you require."

A ray of hope rose up as Senator Russell heard there was at least some good news.

"Yes?"

"Your genetic testing was very informative. The good news is it told us exactly the specifications of your requirements to have a successful transplant. Now we have some very specific parameters to deal within."

A smattering of hope swelled in Russell's chest. For a brief second he dared to believe that death was just a little less imminent.

"Good," replied Russell. "That's great news."

"Yes. The trouble here is that the specific parameters limit the number of people with whom you are compatible. I see that you list no living children or first or second cousins."

"That is correct."

Russell's mind went directly to Zeb and maybe, a one chance in a million maybe, to another man. For the moment he would keep the fact that he had one living son, and possibly two, a secret.

"You possess a rare gene that is non-compatible with over 97% of all the billions of people who are currently alive."

Doctor Kaviraj read the puzzled look on Senator Russell's face.

"Do you know your family history?"

"Of course."

"Are you aware that you are 3% Native American? It appears that you possess a rare gene that is found only in Navajo lineage."

Except for his great-great grandfather's days in the South Dakota Black Hills gold rush, no family member had lived outside of Arizona or married outside the White race. Old family photographs showed his great-great grandfather with a darker skinned woman whom the family always referred to as his maid.

"No, I am not," replied Senator Russell. "I have to assume with a finding as rare as that you doublechecked the test results?"

"Of course, we did, Senator Russell. With extremely rare findings, and this would fall into that category, we run a significant number of verifications tests."

"And you're one hundred percent certain of the results?" asked Senator Russell.

"This specific type of scientific testing is, for all intents and purposes, infallible," said Doctor Kaviraj.

"Well, if the testing says I am 3% Native American, most likely Navajo, then I must be," said Senator Russell.

"You most definitely are. In the absence of biological children, you need to find a compatible donor with this list of characteristics,"

Doctor Kaviraj handed the aide a piece of paper.

"Will that be difficult?" asked Senator Russell.

"There is currently no one in the national data bank who meets all of these specific criteria. Even if you did find someone, there is the distinct possibility that there are people who have been waiting for quite some time for a transplant also compatible with these benchmarks. In fact, only fifty percent of those in need of a single kidney find a donor within five years. Senator Russell, your case is complicated by the fact that both of your kidneys are failing rapidly."

If the senator had had a heart, it would have sunk. But he was not built like that. He immediately began thinking from whom and exactly how he could obtain the required kidneys or kidney, if only one could be obtained.

"How long do I have?"

"It is impossible to tell exactly," replied the doctor.

"Roughly. Give or take. How long? I won't hold your feet to the flames. I merely want some parameters."

"I am only guessing here, but based on similar cases, your age, your general health, etcetera, I would say you could live with the native kidneys for as long as six months without a transplant. But you must lead a healthy, stress-free lifestyle, eat properly..."

"Yeah, yeah. I got it."

"We can set you up for dialysis if it comes to that," said Dr. Kaviraj.

The senator growled beneath his breath. Two close friends had undergone dialysis with devastating side effects. In his mind dialysis was not in the realm of possibility. Senator Russell stormed out of the doctor's office. His aide, used to the senator's abrupt and rude behavior, stopped and thanked Dr. Kaviraj profusely. Derrick Pmensk quickly followed his boss out of the door where he found him impatiently waiting for an elevator to arrive.

"I have to get back to D.C. I've got work to do," snapped Senator Russell. "You heard the doctor. I'm operating on a very short leash."

"Stress free," said Derrick. "Remember what the doctor said."

"Fuck him. I'll find my own kidneys. You find an Uber back to D.C. I'll meet you there."

Derrick David Pmensk was flummoxed. He had seen Senator Russell's aggressive, erratic behavior before, but it had never been taken out on him directly. He walked the senator to his awaiting limo, held the door for him and pressed the Uber app on his cellphone. Senator Russell lowered the window before he ordered the driver to head back to the nation's capital.

"Derrick, the paper."

"What?" asked the aide.

"The paper with the required genetic characteristics. The one Dr. Kaviraj gave you."

Derrick pulled the piece of paper from his briefcase.

Inside the limo Senator Russell sealed the partition that divided him from the driver. He knew his hope for life lay in a single phone call to Dr. Stanislaus Steinman, the arbiter of all thing medically illegal. As the limo headed through the streets of Baltimore, Senator Russell was on the phone with Dr. Steinman.

"Dr. Steinman. This is Senator Russell."

"Yes, Senator, how may I help you?"

"Are you alone?"

"Yes."

"Are you on a burner phone?"

"No."

"Get on one and call me on mine. You have my number. Call me right back. Do it now."

Senator Russell's burner phone rang an instant later.

"Dr. Steinman this is in regard to the Guardians of the Golden Flame."

With that phrase, Guardians of the Golden Flame, everything changed. Dr. Steinman snapped to absolute attention. His mind swept itself into perfect clarity. He was, after all, speaking to the Ghost King of the Guardians of the Golden Flame, the absolute leader of the secretive sect.

"This is strictly confidential."

"Yes, of course."

"Should you tell anyone what I am about to tell you, your life and that of your family will be erased from the history books."

"Yes, sir. I understand."

"I'm going to be dead of kidney disease in a very short time unless I can find a set of kidneys that have the following criteria."

Senator Russell read Dr. Kaviraj's notes to Dr. Steinman. In addition, he told him everything the kidney specialist had shared with him. On top of that, Russell had secretly recorded the entire conversation with Dr. Kaviraj and transferred that as well to Steinman's burner phone.

"Got it," said Dr. Steinman.

"Do you think you can find me a pair of kidneys in thirty days or less?"

When ten seconds later the doctor had not replied, a very irritated senator reiterated his question.

"Hold on," replied Dr. Steinman. "I think lady luck is shining her brightest of beams directly on you, sir. I'm going to put you on speaker. I'm setting my phone down."

Senator Russell listened to the clicking of keyboard keys. Hope and horror huddled together tightly in his brain. Death had always been his greatest fear. Russell believed in hell and knew it was where his life's journey into the afterlife would culminate. The only thing that he had was hope for just a little more time before the fires of eternal damnation would be licking at his heels and ultimately searing his flesh for all time.

"Dr. Steinman, what've you got?"

"A perfect match."

The fires of hell abated at least for the moment.

"Who? Do I know the person? Am I related to them?"

Dr. Steinman answered in four freeing words.

"Sheriff Sawyer Black Bear."

The one in a million shot came arcing through the heavens like a summer rainbow.

"I can make it happen," said Senator Russell. "How soon can you put a team together for me?"

"Three days."

"Do it. I literally have no time to waste."

Dr. Steinman knew he need not bother reminding Senator Russell of dialysis or a single kidney. The mere mention of either possibility would throw Senator Russell into an apoplectic fit. Dr. Steinman spared himself any desire to know the details of how such an act would be accomplished. He knew beyond a shadow of a doubt the Guardians of the Golden Flame would be brought into play. He further spared himself any thought of how that might occur. The instant he finished his phone call with Senator Russell, Dr. Steinman began forming his team. Time was of the essence. He shook with fear at the thought of failing Senator Russell, the Ghost King of the Guardians of the Golden Flame. Failure was truly not an option.

25

ZEB AND ECHO

Elan and Onawa, even though they had been alive for less than a single year and had no formal means of communication, seemed to know not only what each other was thinking but what Zeb and Echo had in their minds as well.

Zeb and Echo watched as they lay on the living room floor on the same elk rug Echo had played on as a child. Echo's grandmother had claimed the magical powers of the elk had given strength and knowledge to multiple generations of Skysongs. Echo knew it to be true. She had witnessed it in many family members. She also knew the rug was hers and Zeb's only until the next child was born into her extended family. Jokingly, her father had referred to it as 'the roving rug'.

"Zeb, we need to talk about the letter."

Echo was right. Zeb knew they had to discuss what his mother had written. Still, he was hesitant. His mother had died the day he found the letter. Now, with the funeral over, Echo knew the time was right to talk about what Zeb had discovered. Also, he and Echo needed to figure out what to do with the belongings of a lifetime that were his mother's. Zeb was tough, but also aware it might be too soon to have the discussion Echo was suggesting.

"I know we need to do this, but can't it wait?" asked Zeb.

Echo, as the Knowledge Keeper, had certain insights unique to her position. Death, she had learned from the ancient glyph writings in the Galiuro Mountains, was so similar to life. To not compare the two could easily push a person into false thinking.

"It can wait," replied Echo. "But it is best dealt with right now."

Zeb looked at the playful Elan and Onawa who had suddenly stopped to study their parents. The quizzical expressions on their faces made it seem as though they were listening to their parents' conversation with more than a little interest if not a great deal of understanding.

"What needs to be said?" asked Zeb.

"You need to tell me the truth about what you feel and what you intend to do."

Zeb had given the specific topic about what to do regarding Senator Russell more than just a little thought. In fact, it had been continuously on his mind. At first, he had no doubt that the death of Senator Russell by some means of extreme torture was the only reasonable and appropriate answer. With time and as his anger mellowed, Zeb decided the torture to be extraneous. It was only Senator Russell's death that really mattered. He was by and large stuck right there. The death of Senator Russell for what he did to his mother was the only logical conclusion.

"You want him dead, don't you?" asked Echo.

Zeb nodded. Elan and Onawa intensified their gaze towards their father. Their intense expression did not go unnoticed. Zeb made a funny face at the twins, one that usually made them laugh. This time they remained impassive to his actions.

"Tell me exactly why you want him dead?"

"Because of what he did to my mother."

Zeb's response was rooted in an anger so dark it caused Elan, Onawa and even Echo to draw back. Their collective movements caught Zeb somewhat unaware. A feeling that his actions were being vetoed by a 3-1 vote was quite apparent.

"What did he do to your mother?"

"I don't know that he didn't rape her."

"You don't know that he did," replied Echo.

"My mother would never have had an affair with such a vicious, cruel and evil man."

"Think of what your mother wrote in the letter, Zeb. Everything she wrote indicates she was a willing participant in everything that happened between them."

Thoughts of the man whom Zeb had believed to be his biological father, the man who had helped his mother raise him, crossed his mind. He too, was cold, cruel, vicious and evil. When the thought of his mother's inability to choose good men as partners passed through his brain, he pushed it aside. There were certain places he simply could not allow himself to go. One of those was that his mother had a consensual affair with Russell and that he was the product of their love, not rape. Even though his mother's final letter said exactly that, he refused to believe it.

As Echo was about to speak, the doorbell rang. It was a clearly nervous Helen Nazelrod, Zeb's aunt and his mother's sister. Echo made her a cup of tea while she played with the children and made small talk with Zeb. Fifteen minutes passed.

"It is so nice of you to stop by and see our children," said Echo.

Helen was holding both Elan and Onawa in her arms, passing kisses between them as she spoke.

"I must admit, I have an ulterior motive."

"Yes?" inquired Zeb.

She handed Elan to Echo and Onawa to Zeb. Then, she took a chair across from the Zeb and Echo Hanks family. Seated with her legs crossed and her arms in her lap, she let loose a truth that could well determine the fate of those she was speaking to.

"Please listen to me. Let me speak my peace before you ask any questions," began Helen.

Zeb, Echo, even Elan and Onawa merely kept their eyes trained on Helen. Helen, in turn, remained strong and solid, not looking away for even a second.

"I have held this secret in my heart for decades, since before you were born, Zeb."

Outside the open windows it seemed the entire world had turned quiet and was tuning into Helen's every word.

"Your mother and Jonas had a horrible relationship. The man you thought was your biological father beat your mother and shamed her at every opportunity. It was no wonder she turned away from her Mormon faith to the Pentecostal religion."

"You knew about that?"

"Of course. Your mother and I shared everything."

Zeb gulped. Echo breathed a sigh of relief. Onawa began to squirm. Elan smiled.

"Therefore, what I am about to tell you is part of your life story that you need to know. I'm referring to what was written in the letter you found on your mother's kitchen table on the day she was taken to the hospital, on the day she died."

Zeb nodded, remembering Helen had talked with him that day when he was waiting at the emergency room. She was the one who insisted he go back to his mother's house and lock it up in case gang members were listening in on distress calls to the EMT phone center.

"The letter was in my possession. I knew you would be at the ER. I went to your mother's and put the letter on her kitchen table. I then called you to go back to the house, knowing you would find the letter."

Zeb opened his mouth to speak but Helen gave him the look that told him to remain quiet. He did as he was silently directed.

"I helped your mother write that letter. We wrote and rewrote it many, many times over the years. She wanted you to know everything. She felt it was her obligation to tell you the whole truth about her life and about your life. In some odd way she thought it might help you better understand who you are."

"Why didn't she tell me herself?"

Zeb sounded like a lost little boy as he posed the question to his aunt.

"Shame, I suppose. She didn't want you going through life thinking bad things about her. I suppose you could say she was self-ishly protecting herself, but I think she really was protecting you."

Helen took a sip of tea, cleared her throat and continued.

"I have known since your mother was pregnant with you who your real father is. Believe me, it was no small task keeping my mouth shut."

Her words broke the tension, if ever so slightly. Zeb could not come close to imagining Helen keeping a secret for a day or a week, much less decades.

"Your mother was in love with Jeffey. Yes, that's what she called Senator Clinton Jefferson Russell. It was her pet name for him. Personally, I never cared for the man, but your mother believed in her heart she was in love with him. Maybe she was. Who am I to say? Who are any of us to judge her feelings? And being stuck in a horrible marriage made everything terribly complicated. You're prob-ably not surprised by this and likely didn't know it, but your parents were separated at the time of her affair with Mr. Russell. You see, Zeb, your mother's heart was seeking someone to love and to be loved by. Clinton Jefferson Russell was a state representative back then. Your mother saw his potential. He was single. Your mother thought him to be ruggedly handsome as well as extremely intelligent. She fell head over heels in love with the man. Because of how she felt towards him and how he felt towards her, she gave herself freely and completely to him."

Zeb seethed at the thought but held it all in. He wanted to see the relationship from his mother's point of view but was finding it nearly impossible to do.

"For a short time, they had a deep and, what your mother believed to be, highly romantic love affair. Her whole world revolved around him. Then as quickly as you can say Jack Robinson, he turned on her. He found another woman. The other woman was someone he worked with and could see every day. Just like that he was gone like so much dust in the wind. Your mother, being who she was and bearing in mind that she still was in love with him, forgave him his every fault. Her heart was like that. You might say she had a foolish heart, but it was her way."

A tear formed in Zeb's eye as he thought of his mother's ability to love regardless of the circumstance. He thought of how many times he must have disappointed her and yet she never stopped loving him with all her heart.

"About the same time, Jonas temporarily straightened out his life. He begged forgiveness from your mother. He swore he would change. He promised the world to her. Your mother, not knowing she was pregnant and being the kind of person she was, forgave him. She decided the right thing to do was to give her marriage another chance. She did it, I believe, for what she felt were good and proper reasons. When she found out she was pregnant, Jonas had no reason to believe the child wasn't his. At first, your mother wasn't absolutely certain either as it all happened so quickly."

Zeb raised his hand timidly. Helen responded like a strict schoolmarm.

"Yes?"

Zeb had a resurgence of hope that Senator Russell was not his father.

"How did she find out who my father was?" asked Zeb.

"In those days it was no easy task. There was nothing around like *23 and Me* or *Ancestry dot com*. We had to use a process called hair analysis. We even had to send the hair samples from Jonas, your mother and Clinton Russell to a lab in New York. It was all very conclusive. Clinton Jefferson Russell is your father."

Zeb sighed. Echo took it all in. The kids went back to play, and the earth continued to spin around the sun.

"Most of all, Zebulon Hanks, other than her unbounded love for you, your mother wanted you to know that her greatest wish was that no harm come to Senator Russell from your hands."

Zeb's head hung low. Elan and Onawa watched intently as Echo rubbed his back. He felt shame for thinking the only answer to his problems was to kill Senator Russell, his own flesh and blood.

Echo whispered in his ear.

"Don't fret. An answer will come to you. The Creator of all things, living and dead, of all things seen and unseen, will guide you."

26

THE SET UP—A SHORT NUMBER OF WEEKS EARLIER

D r. Stanislaus Steinman knew it was not an option to fail Senator Russell. If he did, he and his entire family would closely follow Sawyer Black Bear into the hereafter. After hanging up from his phone call with Senator Russell, Dr. Steinman locked his office door, took a concealed key from a secret place and opened a hidden vault that contained a false drawer. Inside the revealed coffer was a small, golden book with the coded names and coded numbers of Dr. Stanislaus' contacts within the Guardians of the Golden Flame.

Each Guardian member was given twenty-five, and twenty-five only, names of other members. The Ghost King and Ghost Queen were the only people who knew all two hundred fifty members of the secret society. Most of the twenty-five names in Stanislaus golden book was linked to his specialty as a physician. A few others had 'special skills' he might need. He knew exactly who and what he was looking for, an assassin he could work with and who had experience in killing in a very specific manner. He had two names that fit the bill. Stanislaus himself would surgically remove Black Bear's organs. A transplant specialist would surgically place the new set of kidneys into Senator Russell, the Ghost King.

Stanislaus drew an imaginary line with his pointer finger under the first name. He whispered her name. There was a potential problem with his first choice.

He opened Black Bear's medical file. His heart ticked up a beat or two as his eyes danced from her name to Black Bear's file and back again. Stanislaus wrote down her contact information and set it aside. He ran his finger over the second name, Abel Benz. This name he knew well. They had worked together in the past. Abel was competent, discreet and incorruptible. Above all he was a man who could be relied on under any and all circumstances. He would do no damage to the organs of the person who was to be killed. Stanislaus wrote down Abel's coded contact information. He then reversed the processes he had undergone in obtaining the golden book. When he was finished, he kept the door to his office locked. The phone call would be made in private and on a special phone with unique features created for one-time only use.

The man known to Stanislaus as Abel Benz did not pick up his phone. Although Stanislaus was not a superstitious man, he considered this to be a bad omen. However, he had prepared for exactly this circumstance. He left a coded message. It was six words. Abel would know exactly what it meant. If he didn't hear back from Abel in ten minutes, the message would self-destruct.

"Movement across the horizon is imminent."

The message was simple. Movement meant services were needed. Across was Stanislaus' code name. Horizon meant a killing was in the offing. Imminent meant within 24-48 hours. Two minutes later Stanislaus phone rang. It was Abel Benz.

"Movement is impossible soon. Call me."

Call me meant Abel could talk clearly on an open line. Stanislaus rang his regular number.

"Dr. Stanislaus, good to hear from you. You're just the man I want to talk to."

"Yes, of course, Mr. Benz, what may I do for you?"

"Call in a prescription for a laxative for me. If you would be so kind."

"Of course, Mr. Benz. Are you constipated?"

"I had back surgery three days ago. The narcotics have me plugged up tighter than a drum."

Suddenly everything made sense. Able Benz had turned down the job for legitimate reasons. He was recovering from back surgery. In addition, the pain reducing narcotics had slowed his bowels. His needs were purely medical. His reason for not taking the job was legitimate.

"I'll call in a prescription for a stool softener right now. Heal quickly my friend."

"I will." Then he spoke words that he shouldn't have. "Sorry to leave you in the lurch."

If someone, somehow were recording the conversation, a sharp FBI agent could backtrack all of this and maybe even make sense out of it. That is, if they knew the connection between Benz and Stanislaus via the Guardians of the Golden Flame. It was extremely unlikely, but when it came to taking a man's life, the highest of precautionary measures were required. Stanislaus knew he had to say something that was highly innocuous.

"It's fine. We can do lunch when you feel better."

He hung up, cursed Abel's potential mistake and looked at the name of the second person he had written down. He tapped his pointer finger repeatedly on the name. In his mind he rechecked the list he had already hidden away. Indeed, the second name was the only option. He pondered if it could mean trouble. No matter, what had to be done had to be done. He was not the top of the food chain. There was no option when it came to following orders. He punched in the second number.

"Yes," came the reply. "How may I help you?"

Stanislaus spoke in code that directed her to use a secret burner phone. Within a minute a second burner phone rang. It was impossible for the call to be traced. He gave precisely the same coded message.

"Movement across the is horizon imminent."

"I am available. Where?"

"Arizona."

"When?"

"Less than 48 hours."

"Who is the target?"

Stanislaus had practiced in his head what he was going to say. He feared that if he hesitated so would the woman.

"Sheriff Sawyer Black Bear."

He perceived what he believed to be the slightest of hesitant exhalations on the other end of the line.

"Purpose of the action?"

"Organ donation."

"Where will I meet the rest of my team?"

"They will find you."

"Are you on the team?"

"Yes."

"The order is from royalty, isn't it?"

Stanislaus non-answer was an absolute rejoinder. Indeed, the command was directly from the top of the royalty chain, the Ghost King himself.

"Is the organ donation for the Ghost King?"

Once again, a non-answer was a directly reply.

"As the Ghost Queen, I demand an answer."

Stanislaus hesitated, but only for a brief second. He was well aware that if the Ghost King died, the Ghost Queen would be all-powerful. He did not want to make an enemy of her. Being on the wrong side of royalty was tantamount to a death penalty.

"You are correct in your assumption," replied Stanislaus.

"I'm in."

"How many others?"

"Myself, two assistants and you. That's the entire team."

"I'll be there in the morning. Let's get it done by noon. I don't want to be gone too long for anyone to question why I am not where I am assumed to be."

27

BLACK BEAR'S MURDER

B lack Bear was surprised by his visitor. A knock on the door before seven a.m. was always a surprise, even to a sheriff. He opened the door and immediately reached out and embraced his visitor. He called her by the pet name he had given her decades earlier, Chindi. Chindi was the English translation of Ch'įįdii, the Navajo term for ghost. Depending on your point of view, it was either an inside joke between the two of them or a sign of the deepest connection possible. Either way, it carried great relevancy.

"What are you doing here? What happened to your finger?"

He noticed a tightly wound, fresh bandage that was leaking a tiny bit of fresh blood on the first finger of Chindi's hand.

"One question at a time please."

Chindi needed a moment to come up with a reasonable lie about what happened to her hand. She had good reason for not telling him the truth, that she had blown the fingertip off when she was loading an unfamiliar weapon.

"First of all, a last-minute consulting gig is the thing that brought me to the area."

Lies slipped off her tongue with the ease and grace of stalking mountain lion at night.

"I thought since I had a little extra time, I'd drop by and say hello."

"Okay. Great. Lucky me. How much time do you have?"

"Time is short. I only have half a day. I thought we'd quickly run over to Tucson for brunch and catch up on things."

"We do have some catching up to do. Now what happened to your finger?"

"It was a stupid thing. I was cutting some meat and the knife slipped. I accidentally sliced off the tip of my finger."

"Did you go to the ER?"

"Yes, of course I did. They stitched it up. It'll be fine. I've cut myself before. It's no big deal."

"You're sure of that?"

"As sure as I am of anything."

Chindi and Black Bear smiled at each other. Chindi was full of confidence and always certain of everything. Black Bear figured she must be all right.

"I am about to take off on a fishing trip to Puerto Peñasco, Mexico. I have time for lunch. Your timing is excellent. It could not be better."

"Where are you staying in Puerto Peñasco? I know people who have beautiful homes there."

"I'm staying on a boat called *The Long Goodbye*. It was once owned by a movie star, Elliot somebody. Arrangements have already been made."

Chindi remembered a movie starring Elliot Gould as Philip Marlowe. It was based on a on a book by Raymond Chandler. It was called *The Long Goodbye*. In the movie Marlowe helps a friend out of a jam then gets implicated in a murder. It all seemed touchingly apropos.

"Good. Let's get headed to Tucson for that brunch you promised me."

"I'll drive," said Black Bear.

"No, no, let me drive," insisted Chindi.

Black Bear looked at his watch.

"It's about an hour and three-quarters there and the same back," said Black Bear. "That'll give us a couple of hours to eat, have a nice talk and generally bring each other up to date on our lives. Let's roll, mama."

State Route 191 was practically devoid of traffic. When they hopped on the I10 freeway, the pair had covered more than one old memory in vivid detail. With each passing minute Black Bear and Chindi felt closer in spirit. A few miles down the road Route 191 appeared again, this time heading south to Cochise.

"Wait, I've got a great idea," said Chindi. "I read about an Apache-owned diner in Cochise. The review says it serves the best corn-squash cakes with a side of breakfast antelope you'll ever eat."

Black Bear laughed out loud. The Lakota practically lived off antelope meat and organs. Black Bear knew it was one of Chindi's favorite meals. He readily agreed and was even vaguely familiar with the diner.

"You can take the girl out of Dakota but not the Lakota out of the girl."

Chindi smiled. Black Bear noticed the normal radiance that beamed from her face was somehow unusual.

"Something wrong?" he asked.

The question caught Chindi off guard. Had she inadvertently exposed herself?

"Er, no. Just thinking, that's all."

"Thinking about what?"

"Oh, about the hell you used to raise when you were a boy and about that time you and your cousin went fishing."

Chindi was purposefully distracting Black Bear. Black Bear did not want to hear about that incident. He didn't even want to think about it. For the last twenty years he had blocked it from his memory and placed it in a remote corner of his mind.

Back in the day, he and his cousin had fought viciously while fishing from a small watercraft. In a twist of fate, his much larger and stronger cousin had drowned. Many family members believed Black Bear, who was at the height of his bad temperament, killed his cousin. The truth was never discovered. It was not the only incident from his youth in which someone tightly bound to Black Bear ended up dying.

"Let's not talk about it," said Black Bear. "It is not important. Death never is. It is merely a transition we all must pass through. Isn't that what you taught me, Chindi?"

Now it was Black Bear who was doing the taunting. It was well known to him that Chindi could kill without conscience. She murdered people, regardless of age or ability to defend themselves, who got in her way. She had taught Black Bear to do exactly the same. The subject touched lightly on a raw nerve in both of them. The conversation ended abruptly, and a momentary, uneasy silence ensued.

The town of Cochise amounted to little more than an old hotel, a couple of run-down stores and a refurbished old building called Bimbo's Restaurant.

"Pull around behind," said Black Bear. "Let's go in the back door."

The gods were on her side. Outside the little abandoned building next to Bimbo's, two men in white waiter's jackets stood smoking cigarettes next to an old oil drum that was currently being used as a burning barrel. They looked up at the car but barely budged.

Chindi got out of the car and walked to the door of the abandoned building. Black Bear laughed as he shouted out, "Wrong door."

"Let's take a peek inside. I'm curious," said Chindi. "I love to look into abandoned buildings. You never know what hidden jewels you may find."

She turned to the smoking men. "Is it okay if we peek inside?"

Both shrugged their shoulders, maintaining a high level of disinterest as they inhaled deeply on their cigarettes. One of the men tossed some garbage into the smoking burn barrel,

Black Bear glanced at his watch. The fees for his fishing boat began precisely at 4 p.m. If they dilly-dallied, he would be late and end up paying for something he wasn't using.

"Oh, I suppose we can have a quick look," said Black Bear.

Chindi opened the door. It was exactly as she had expected. She stepped through the entrance. Black Bear was close on her heels. His jaw dropped when the steely cleanliness of a surgical operating room fell on his eyes. He stepped past Chindi, mouth agape. She held something deadly in the palm of her hand, something Black Bear did not see.

"What is this?" he asked.

Just as he was about to say the word place, he felt what seemed like a desert insect land on the base of his skull against his thick hair. He reached back to brush it away. His hand never reached its destination.

As Chindi pressed the barrel of the .22 Derringer against the Black Bear's skull, a single thought slowly entered her mind. It was a strange reflection on her part. In a single thought she recalled every kill shot she had ever performed. Her mind slowed and one sole thought dominated all else. She never once considered what would happen if her aim were not true and that it might cause great suffering. She only wondered if her victim would hear the sound of the bullet entering his brain. The dark side of her mind went so far as to imagine the feel like a bee sting and sound like a stick striking open skin. Legend says you never hear the one that kills you. But how would anyone ever know?

The single shot to his brain was somewhat muffled by the closeness of the gun barrel to hair, bone and flesh. The bullet piercing Black Bear's skull sent a splattering of blood that landed on her lower lip. Instinctively, she removed the fresh blood with her tongue. The taste did not register as anything particularly recognizable other than fresh blood.

Black Bear crumpled in slow motion, or so it appeared to Chindi's eyes. Within a second or two of the shot being fired, the pair of men in the white waiter's jackets who had been outside having a cigarette magically appeared. Wordlessly working as unit, they picked up the body and placed it on an aluminum table. Chindi noticed it was on wheels but did not budge when Black Bear's body was placed atop it. Another strange thought entered her mind. The wheels were locked in place. Would the placement of Black Bear's body on the gurney create skid marks?

Out of the corner of her left eye a shadow of a man appeared. The silhouette belonged to Dr. Stanislaus Steinman. Without the necessity of speaking a single word, the men went immediately to work. The keenness of their skills and the lack of words spoken between them indicated this was not their first rodeo.

The kidneys for the Ghost King were removed first. The heart, a highly expensive prize, went next. Several wealthy and highly connected men were in a bidding war for that organ. It would bring a handsome profit for the Guardians of the Golden Flame. The corneas would bring in enough money to pay for incidentals, like jet fuel.

Less than four hours later with the organs properly stored, what remained of Black Bear's human carcass was wrapped in plastic and placed in the trunk of a black Lincoln Town car. It was headed to Riggs Lake, by direct order from the Ghost King, for disposal. The organs on the other hand were headed to a private air strip in a remote part of the nearby desert. A Lear jet would take the kidneys directly to a small landing strip outside of Washington, D.C. In nearby Burke, Virginia, Senator Clinton Jefferson Russell was being prepped for surgery. The heart would be dropped off an hour later, eventually making its way to New York City where it would end up in the chest of the highest bidder. Chindi pondered the price it would secure. If all went according to plan, she would soon hold that knowledge.

Chindi put on a pair of gloves before thoroughly cleaning the gun of all fingerprints using 91% alcohol wipes. Five minutes later when the alcohol had undoubtedly dried, she burned the alcohol wipes and gloves. She departed the temporary surgical suite and the town of Cochise without so much as looking back. Her mind was moving in one direction, forward.

Along the route, when she could see for miles in all directions, she tossed the .22 out the window into an arroyo. She was literally in the middle of nowhere. Only an act of a cruel god would lead someone to the killing weapon. Chindi felt smugly secure.

She made her way in the rented vehicle to a second landing strip that was not only in the middle of nowhere but also secreted from the overhead eyes of drones, satellites or low flying planes. Her departure plane was ready to go. An Indian woman who closely resembled Chindi took the car keys from her hand, got behind the wheel and headed to a cash only rental car return in Phoenix.

28

SHELLY DIGS DEEPLY

S helly's computer was burning red hot with information. She had been awake for nearly fifty-four hours straight when Zeb, returning to the office to pick up Elan's Nuk, found her still hard at it. Zeb tapped on her office door when he saw the light was on.

"I thought I told you to go home and get some rest."

"Justice never sleeps," replied Shelly.

"That's supposed to be my line," retorted Zeb. "Seriously, what are you working on that can't wait until you get some rest? You were here when I arrived at work two days ago and you're here now. I know from talking to Helen that you've never left."

"I took a couple of cat naps."

From the dark circles under her eyes, they had done little good.

"Yeah, right."

"Maybe they were just kitty naps."

Zeb laughed along with his exhausted employee

"So, want to tell me what's going on?"

"You want to figure out who killed Black Bear, don't you?"

"Of course. No single crime has been on my mind as much as his death. In fact, all the crimes of Graham County rolled into one haven't eaten up as much of my time as Black Bear's death. Do you have something?"

"I might have a lot of stuff. I can't confirm it just yet, but the information I've got tells me I'm onto something."

Zeb pulled up a chair. He placed the Nuk he came for on the edge of Shelly's desk.

"Blue," said Shelly nodding toward the Nuk. "It must be Elan's."

"He won't take his nap or sleep at night without it. I want to break him of the habit, but Echo says he'll break himself from it in his own good time."

"I agree with her."

"I had a feeling you might," replied Zeb.

"I don't mean to stick my nose into family business," said Shelly.

"But the facts would tell me something else."

Zeb's tone was firm enough to make Shelly look up from her computer. She knew exactly what he meant, and it had nothing to do with Elan's Nuk. Echo had told him that they had been talking about Senator Russell being Zeb's father. That meant Zeb had all the facts. Shelly cleared her throat, stalling as she thought about what to say next. She didn't have to. Zeb said it for her.

"It's okay. I understand Echo needed to run it by someone before she talked with me about Senator Russell and my mother. I don't blame you in any way whatsoever. You were being a friend and a good listener," explained Zeb. "What I am surprised about was that Helen was able to keep a secret like that for all these years."

The wry smile on Zeb's face told Shelly he had come to some sort of peace about the whole situation.

"I suspect she was protecting your mother," said Shelly. "It was the right thing to do."

"Don't know that I'll ever fully understand women," said Zeb.

"Don't worry," replied Shelly. "You won't."

"It makes me wonder what else I don't know that I should," said Zeb.

"Excellent question. I may have some answers for you."

Shelly's response meant Elan was going to have to wait for his Nuk. Zeb took off his hat and set it on her desk.

"About that hat? One quick question before we start."

"Yeah?"

"What's the story behind it?" asked Shelly.

"That's an odd question that doesn't seem to have anything to do with Black Bear's death," replied Zeb.

"It doesn't. It's just that I've heard stories about your hat that make it seem almost mystical. Would you mind sharing?"

Zeb handed her his hat and insisted she try it on. She did. He noticed she looked surprisingly good in the beat-up, sweat-stained, old cowboy hat.

"It's not that big of a deal," said Zeb. "It's the link that binds Jake, Song Bird and me."

"There must be a story there," said Shelly.

"There is. Long story short, on the day the man I thought was my biological father died in prison Jake gave me the hat. Song Bird had originally won the hat in a shooting contest and had given it to Jake. It was, in retrospect, a rite of passage that has strongly linked me to Jake and Song Bird. At the same time, they took me under their wings."

"Aw, that's a beautifully sweet story," said Shelly. "I always wondered what the cement was that bonded the three of you so closely."

"Now you know."

Shelly took the hat off her head, flicked some dust off the brim and handed it back to Zeb who set it on the edge of her desk.

"Thanks for letting me wear it. I feel like I'm part of some secret club."

Zeb gave her a soft smile.

"What have you dug up that's got you working so late and so long?" asked Zeb.

"You told me you talked to Sheriff Lentz up on the Pine Ridge Reservation in Oglala Lakota County. You mentioned the Native

American tradition regarding the burning down the house of a dead person."

"Yes, I also told you that I suspected Shappa or one of her confederates had burned down Black Bear's house. As you also know, Chief Leary has confirmed that it was arson."

"Okay."

"I also chatted with Sheriff Lentz of Oglala Lakota County in South Dakota. Shappa burned down Black Bear's house up there. Since his house was on the Rez, there is no law against it."

"You saw a link?" asked Shelly.

"I did. I wanted to know if Sheriff Lentz knew if Shappa had been out of his jurisdiction, possibly here in Graham County, when the arson occurred."

"Perfect. My thinking exactly. I might have something for you."

Zeb leaned in.

"Yeah?"

"I think, and I mean think as I can't prove it yet, but I am fairly certain that Shappa was in Graham County at almost the exact time anyone last saw Black Bear alive and at the time his house was burned to the ground."

Zeb breathed in deeply and exhaled heavily.

"What exactly are you saying? What exactly do you know?"

"Nothing for certain and I could always be wrong. But here's what I do know. When I describe it to you, you'll understand that it doesn't make total sense. You will also understand my uncertainty."

Zeb grabbed Elan's Nuk and pensively flipped it around and around on his pointer finger. After about the twentieth trip around his finger, Shelly spoke up.

"That's annoying."

"Sorry. Bad habit. I use it to entertain the twins. It seems to fascinate them."

Shelly continued exactly where she had left off.

"I just might be able to prove that Shappa was in Graham County, or at least near Tucson, on the day Black Bear took off on his so-called fishing trip to Mexico."

"Show me what you've got?"

Shelly pulled up the picture of a Lear jet sitting on a runway. Next to the jet was a pickup truck, a GMC Sierra 3500. Although the sun was low in the background, the scene was clear and well-lit by what remained of the burning daylight. She pointed at the image without touching her screen. Specifically, she pointed to the tail of the jet.

"See that?"

Zeb ran to his desk, grabbed a pair of cheaters and was back next to Shelly in ten seconds flat.

"Yes. It says HB MT 100. What does that translate to?"

"It's nonsense."

"Nonsense?"

"Complete and total nonsense."

"How so?"

"The HB that you see on the tail is a country code."

"For what country?"

"Switzerland."

"Hmm."

"Hmm is right because the MT is code for Minot, North Dakota."

"Unless they picked up North Dakota and moved it to another continent, it seems someone made a mistake when they painted the tail code on the plane."

"Or someone is hiding something. Or, and this is where it suddenly becomes a big deal..."

Zeb stared hard at the screen and the numbers on the Lear jet as if they might begin talking to him.

"...the 100 indicates it is a military jet."

"What the?"

"I know. It doesn't make sense at all."

"I should say it doesn't."

"Exactly," replied Shelly. "So, I tracked down the license plates on the GMC Sierra 3500. Guess what I came up with?"

"What?"

"It is registered to Shappa Hówakȟaŋyaŋ."

"Were you able to get the flight plans for the plane or the passenger manifest?"

"Flight plans, yes. Passenger manifest, no. There is no requirement for a passenger manifest on planes like this," replied Shelly.

"So, we can't say for sure if Shappa was on the plane, but we do know where the Lear jet went. Is that correct?" asked Zeb.

"Half correct. I do know the plane landed at a remote private base near Cheyenne, Wyoming after it left Minot, North Dakota. After that it landed outside of Tucson. It landed on a remote, privately owned airstrip called Club Mex. It's just outside of Tucson."

"Club Mex? I assume it's known for illegal entry flights from Mexico?" asked Zeb.

"Once again, you're half right. It's called Club Mex because it has a Mexican restaurant. And, yes, it is a hot spot for illegal flights entering from Mexico."

"If you know that, the feds must know it. Why haven't they shut it down?" asked Zeb.

"Tom Sawyer has somehow seen to that. His fingerprints are all over official documents related to the place. I'd further venture a guess that Senator Russell is also involved," explained Shelly. "Once again, I can't prove it beyond a reasonable doubt."

"But you're certain. I can tell by the look in your bloodshot eyes."

Shelly nodded.

"Coincidentally, the Lear jet landed only a few hours before Black Bear departed on his fishing vacation and less than twenty-four hours before his house in Safford was burned to the ground."

"Coincidence? Or do we have something here?"

Shelly brought up a second screen. It was from the private airport just outside of Tucson.

"I can't prove Shappa got on the plane. However, I can prove she got off it," said Shelly.

She enlarged the image on the screen of the Lear jet at Club Mex near Tucson.

"The private landing strip is identifiable by the flags and..."

Shelly maximized the entry to the building. Over the main door it read Club Mex.

Zeb ran his finger across the Club Mex sign and chuckled.

"They keep the flags up at night, so they have to light them."

"Yeah, these people wouldn't want to break any federal laws," joked Zeb.

"The three flags are…"

"I recognize the American flag and the State of Arizona flag, but I've never seen the third one."

"Simply a matter of looking up private airport insignias and matching the insignia with the location and, *voila*, there you have it. I also found out that private airports are real stinkers about security. Because of their paranoia, perhaps legitimate paranoia, they have too many cameras for their own good. It took all of about five minutes to estimate the flying time for the Lear jet from Cheyenne to Tucson, another few seconds to match the tail codes and about ten minutes of going through old video footage to find this."

Once again Shelly pointed to the screen. There, in living color, was Shappa Hówakȟaŋyaŋ standing on the runway next to the Lear jet with the tail code identification that matched the one where Shappa's truck was parked. The footage was date and time stamped.

"Therefore, we, I mean you, are certain Shappa was just outside of Tucson on the day Black Bear was scheduled to leave on his fishing trip to Mexico," said Zeb.

"And I've got this. For some reason Black Bear had his own security camera…"

"That seems reasonable," said Zeb.

"Yes, of course. But he didn't just have a copy stored on his home computer. A backup was sent to his office computer."

"Whomever burned his house down, probably knew he had security footage stored there and wanted it destroyed. Makes sense," said Zeb. "A damn good reason for burning his house to the ground."

"Right. But what they weren't counting on, for some odd reason, was a backup on his office computer. I guess they figured he wouldn't want to bring personal stuff that could incriminate him in any way to his workplace."

"How did you even know to look on his office computer?" asked Zeb.

Shelly had the look on her face of a kid who had been caught with their hand in the cookie jar.

"Well, er, I set it up for him."

"The way you're hemming and hawing, I suspect he didn't know about the office computer backup and that it was linked to his home computer?"

"Well, I never trusted him after we dated. Call it woman's intuition. I suspected he was up to something really, really bad."

"What you did was against the law. You know that, right?"

"Not necessarily when you consider the fact that I had been granted access to everything he had access to. In fact, you could even say he tacitly gave me permission to have a back up to his system," explained Shelly. "After all, he hired me."

"You charged him?" asked Zeb.

"Had to keep it all above board. I gave him a twenty percent discount."

Zeb rolled his eyes. He often skirted the edges of the law, but he was the sheriff. There was a big difference between what he did and what Shelly did. He listened as she explained herself away.

"Black Bear was concerned that he might miss something, something small, something not very obvious. He routinely asked me to review his tapes. I suggested he give me a copy of all his tapes."

"And he agreed to that?"

"He did. It didn't really matter because I had access to everything anyway."

"I don't know that I would call that woman's intuition. I think I'd call it espionage," said Zeb.

"Call it what you will but take one look at this."

She brought up images of a stealthily moving person with their face covered and wearing a hoodie. He or she was carrying two large cans marked gasoline. At one point they set down the gas cans and smashed a window, allowing entry into Black Bear's house.

"Okay, we know someone used an accelerant. Chief Leary told us that. I find it no surprise they covered their face."

Shelly split the screen. On the right was the person breaking and entering into Black Bear's property carrying the gasoline cans. On the left was Shappa. Shelly zoomed in on the pants and boots of the arsonist on the right and Shappa on the left. The pants, with their broadened bootcut and embroidery, were clearly identical.

"Both people, women, are wearing Rock and Roll Cowgirl women's basic pocket applique denim jeans. Boot Barn is the only place that sells them."

Shelly stopped, reached into a file and pulled out a copy of Shappa's credit card billings. Listed was a charge at Boot Barn for $228.98. Shelly had already gone online and compared the U.P.C. barcodes from the pants and boots with the ones on Shappa's credit card billing. Everything matched.

"The arsonist is almost certainly Shappa," said Shelly.

"Good work," said Zeb. "Obviously she wanted to destroy something that was in the house, probably the security tapes and whatever linked Black Bear to the other crimes in Graham County that remain unsolved."

Zeb snapped his fingers. Without saying a word, he spun on his bootheels and went to his office. A minute later he placed a plastic bag in front of Shelly. In it was the gold ring that had miraculously been left undamaged by the extensive fire at Black Bear's residence.

"You think this is something else she was trying to destroy?" asked Shelly. "Why?"

"There is a link between this type of ring and everything else that has happened in Graham County. It is the common thread that ties everything together."

"You think Black Bear was in on all the crimes?" asked Shelly.

"Either he was, or his cohorts were."

"This may sound stupid, but what exactly were they after?"

From talking with Sheriff Lentz in Oglala Lakota County near where the legends of lost Black Hills gold were common and adding to that what he had learned about the legend of the lost gold in the Galiuro Mountains from Echo, there could be only one answer.

"Gold. Possibly tons upon tons of it. Enough to make a king's ransom many times over. Enough to make someone or some group wealthy beyond imagination. With that wealth would come incredible power," explained Zeb.

"Do you believe Black Bear was killed because he knew where the gold was?"

"It certainly could be that. However, my gut tells me no, the gold was not the primary reason. My instinct and history as sheriff lead me to believe something larger, maybe even something highly personal is at play. If I were a betting man, I'd say it was very personal."

"Okay. I can buy into that. Speaking of personal, there is one more thing you ought to know."

"Yes?"

"I found out quite by accident that Helen's first cousin, Henry…"

"I know Henry. He's from up Boise, Idaho way. He's had four or five heart attacks and coronary bypass surgery. But last I heard he was doing fine."

"What do you know about his and Helen's relationship?" asked Shelly.

"They were close in a strange way, but for good reason. He saved Helen's life when she was a child. He pulled her out of a lake when she was going down for the last time and very likely would have drowned if he hadn't been there to save her. She always said she owed him a life," said Zeb.

"Well, this is probably all just a coincidence, but Henry's life currently needs saving."

"How so? I haven't heard anything about that," said Zeb.

"I found what I am about to tell you quite by accident. I heard Helen on the phone talking to someone, Barbara Jean was her name."

"That's Henry's wife."

"I sort of figured it was either his wife or his daughter from the way they communicated," said Shelly.

"What were they saying?"

"This was two, maybe three months ago when I overheard the

conversation. I could tell Helen was concerned so I asked her about it. She was a tad reticent in discussing it."

Zeb chuckled. "That's not like Helen. Normally she loves to spill the beans."

"Henry, after numerous heart attacks and bypass surgeries, was no longer able to undergo any further stent procedures. His future was either an imminent transplant or death would come a knocking at his door. He was on a waiting list. However, his chances of getting a matching heart donor anytime soon were slim to none."

Zeb's heart practically stopped at the inference that Helen, although she didn't care for Black Bear, would have him killed in order to save Henry's life. Such a complex procedure would require all kinds of knowledge that Helen couldn't possibly have access to. Or could she have? The state required current medical records be kept, albeit without access by any employees, on all county sheriffs. The law was designed for reasons of mental health but, in typical bureaucratic fashion, had spread to all records. The reason behind the law was the Posse Comitatus ruling of 1878 under President Rutherford B. Hayes. The purpose of the act was to limit the powers of the federal government and put them in the hands of local authorities. It only made sense that you keep an eye on the mental status of people whom you were placing in positions of significant power. Helen could have sneaked into the records and matched up Henry's blood type, body size for ability to fit the heart inside the rib cage and she could easily determine with a phone call to Barbara Jean if Henry was sick with a serious infection. Shelly could see the wheels spinning inside Zeb's head.

"I don't believe for one minute that Helen would have Black Bear killed." Then she paused for an abnormally long second. "Do you?"

Without answering Zeb picked up the plastic baggie with the gold ring in it and headed for his office.

Shelly had but a single thought dancing in her head as Zeb walked out the door. Helen did owe Henry a life. Her own. What price would someone put on their own life?

29

THE RING

Z eb fondled the golden ring that seemed, at least peripherally, to be a link to all things involved in Black Bear's death. At the same time, he pondered his Aunt Helen. Like all of us, she had a hidden side that no one, or hardly anyone, ever saw. The more he thought about it the more it seemed, knowing her ethics and love for family, that she might have a dark enough side to kill Black Bear or have him killed out of some strange combination of duty, loyalty and obligation. After all, she herself had said she owed her cousin Henry a life because he saved hers. Zeb knew Helen well enough, or so he thought, that if she were guilty, she would eventually give herself away.

Zeb sat back, put his boots up on his desk and stared off toward the upper reaches of Mount Graham. Golden sunlight reflected off the telescopes that were directly in his line of vision. The dazzling beams radiating from the Vatican Advanced Technology Telescope, the Heinrich Hertz Submillimeter Telescope and the Large Binocular Telescope, one of the world's most powerful optical telescopes, practically hypnotized him. Mesmerized, he found himself thinking with an incredible amount of clarity as his mind drifted to those directly or peripherally connected to the ring.

He grasped the golden ring that had been found by Chief Leary in the ashy ruins of Black Bear's house. It set off a bad taste in his mouth. He put it back down on his desk and studied it. Randomly potential connections popped into his head.

First of all, Helen. Everyone had a breaking point. Helen had known for decades about the relationship between Zeb's mother and Senator Russell. Maybe some strange connection between Senator Russell and Black Bear had finally pushed her over the edge, and she took her longstanding, intense dislike of Russell out on Black Bear. The more he thought about that the more of a longshot it seemed to be. But, killing Black Bear for his heart that her cousin Henry so desperately needed and to whom she owed her life, well that was another can of worms altogether. But if she needed a heart and needed it transplanted, where would she get the money? Why would she choose Black Bear when someone else would be a much easier target? He breathed a sigh of relief as he crossed Helen off the list by drawing a single, but very light line through her name. She was off the short list of suspects for the time being.

Coming next to mind, of course, was Shappa. Zeb was certain she had burned down Black Bear's house based on the evidence Shelly had found. He was becoming more and more certain that she wanted to destroy evidence of some kind, likely of all kinds. If she knew about the ring and if it was at all connected to the crimes in Graham County, she would want to protect her son. At least that's how it appeared at first glance. She was tough for Zeb to figure out. Based on her history, her politics and her needs, Shappa's motives could be just about anything or anywhere on the map. He made a note to never trust anything Shappa said and to always doublecheck her motives.

The more he thought about it the odder he found it that she showed up just as Black Bear was leaving town for his vacation. Something in his mind told him that whole scene didn't add up. But what it didn't add up to was vastly unclear. Who, really, was Shappa Hówakȟaŋyaŋ? What motivated her?

Was it even remotely possible that the ring found in the ashes of Black Bear's destroyed house had been on his finger when someone harassed the ladies at the nursing home or despoiled the water supply in Safford? Could he have been hiding behind either the Nixon or Obama masks at Swigs? Obviously, the ring found at the school wasn't his. That didn't mean he wasn't in on that caper, though.

As sheriff, Black Bear had made enemies. It came with the territory. The Mexican cartels, local gang bangers, enemies of his father's or even human traffickers could have good enough reasons to go after Black Bear. The more Zeb thought about it, the longer the list became.

Finally, Zeb's mind drifted to Senator Russell. He frightened himself a bit when he felt the depth of his own rage toward the man he now knew to be his biological father. Zeb had no doubt he could look Senator Russell directly in the eye and kill him without feeling the least bit of remorse. He walked to the water cooler, poured himself a large glass of ice-cold water and guzzled it. It gave him a headache, but at least something other than Russell was on his mind, if ever so momentarily.

Sitting back into his chair, Zeb once again shifted his attention to Mount Graham. So peaceful in stature, it highly juxtaposed his own emotions. Fantasy after fantasy of exactly how to kill Senator Russell ran though his mind. He tried to push them away and out of his mind, but he could not. He fantasized everything from the fast kill of a bullet to the brain to a slow, tortuous death by a well-honed knife blade. He tingled as he considered the possible look on the Senator's face when he saw death come hurtling at him. Each and every possible murderous thought led quickly into the next one. But they always ended when he considered the possibility of losing Echo and his children. His thoughts were interrupted by a knock on his office door.

"Come in."

It was Helen. She looked angelic, solid, religious, like an older woman of virtue looks. How could he have ever supposed her to be the killer of Black Bear?

"It's awfully quiet in here. Something going through your head?" she asked.

"Just thinking about Black Bear's death," replied Zeb. "What brings you back in? I thought you were done for the day with that church thing you've got going on this afternoon?"

Helen placed a couple of work documents in Zeb's in box.

"I accidentally took some papers home with me. I'm in town for a Ladies Aid Bazaar Meeting at the church. I thought I'd drop them off in case you needed them."

"Thanks," replied Zeb. "It could have waited 'til morning."

"I read them when I checked them for typos. They seemed important."

Helen, more interested in Zeb's thoughts than her work, quickly bounced back to their original topic of conversation.

"Got it figured out yet?"

"Got what figured out?"

"Black Bear's killer."

The curtness of the question as it passed through Helen's lips made Zeb chuckle. She mistook his laughter for cynicism. It almost felt as though she were taunting him. The guilty, especially the single crime types, usually wanted to get caught. Helen fit that mold.

"What's so funny, Zebulon Hanks?"

"If I had an idea who killed him, I would guess that you would already know what I was thinking and who I thought the killer was."

This time it was Helen's turn to laugh.

"Who knows? Maybe I did it."

Zeb did a double take. Helen spun around and left the room, shutting the door tightly, without another word escaping through her lips. Two seconds later Shelly tapped on his door.

"Come in."

"Zeb, I've got something that will interest you."

Before she continued, Shelly picked up the ring from Zeb's desk and put it under a lighted magnifying glass. She handed the ring and magnifier to Zeb.

"Take a close look at the inside of the ring."

Zeb examined it thoroughly and saw nothing.

"I don't know what I'm looking for," said Zeb.

Shelly tilted the ring and pointed with a pen to a small carving on the inside of the ring.

"It looks like smoke," said Zeb.

"It's the sign of the Ghost Queen."

"What?"

"The Guardians of the Golden Flame have both a male and a female leader. The man is called the Ghost King and the woman, appropriately enough, the Ghost Queen."

"What would Black Bear be doing with the Ghost Queen's ring?" asked Zeb.

Zeb sat back in his chair. What felt like a credible theory was taking root in his brain. His thoughts were interrupted by a phone call from Echo. She had a request. The way she stated what she had to say indicated it was really more of a demand than a request.

30

ECHO AND ZEB

"My mom and dad scheduled us for this afternoon," explained Echo.

"Can we go tomorrow?" asked Zeb.

"If we don't take the gift as they have given it, we will have insulted them. Zeb, honey, they're old school. We've got to do this. Besides a massage and a spa will do us both good."

"Okay, I'll meet you there in twenty minutes. Who's watching the kids?" asked Zeb.

"Take a wild guess."

"Your mother?"

"Right. I think this gift is also a setup to allow her some alone time with the twins."

Twenty minutes later Zeb and Echo walked into the Kachina Springs Mineral Bath and Spa.

"No need to sign in, Sheriff. We know who you are. Anyway, the place was booked up solid by Senator Russell for the day. He's already come and gone. The place is all yours," said Henrietta.

They hopped in the hot springs for fifteen minutes until Henrietta called them to their respective, neighboring massage tables. Henrietta wasted no time in starting the gossip line.

"He looks terrible if you ask me," added Lana.

"Who looks terrible?" asked Echo.

"Why Senator Russell, of course," replied Henrietta.

"Like death warmed over."

"Like death eating a cracker," added Lana

"Really?" inquired Zeb. "I don't believe I have heard that expression before. What does it mean?"

"He's all dried up. He looks terrible, like death warmed over. You get it now?" said Henrietta.

"Yeah, I get it. He looks like shit," said Zeb.

"I know you don't like the man," said Echo. "But there's no need to use curse words against a sick man," said Echo.

Zeb agreed. Still, he hated the man. Henrietta, however, wasn't done with the subject.

"If you ask me, those scars on his belly aren't from any fluid being drained out of him. They're from something much bigger than that."

"Surgery is what I say," added Lana.

"Cancer maybe?" suggested Henrietta.

"Maybe what they call exploratory surgery. I've seen that a bunch of times," added Lana.

"Has to be something like," said Henrietta. "We've seen those kinds of scars before. Lots of times."

"Where are the scars? On whom did you see them?" asked Zeb.

Before Henrietta could answer, Lana lifted her shirt to the bottom of her bra line. She pointed to areas just below her lowest rib on each side and drew a finger toward the middle of her belly.

"It looked like he had zippers sewn right into him. Here and here," said Lana.

Once again Lana pointed to the area by the lowest part of her rib cage.

"Senator Russell is who you're talking about, right?" asked Zeb.

"Sure enough am," replied Lana. "You want me to draw you a picture? I took an art class online. Just one more way I like to get educated."

Zeb sat up, keeping his towel properly in place.

"Yes, please draw me a picture," said Zeb.

"Honey just take a chill pill," said Echo. "You're off duty for the next hour."

Lana took an exam form, the kind that people filled out to show where their aches and pains were located. It had an image of the front and back of a human body. She quickly etched in the places where Senator Russell had scars. Zeb examined it closely.

"Can I keep this?" he asked.

"Sure. You're the first person that ever wanted one of my drawings. Do you want me to sign it?"

"Sure, why not?" replied Zeb. "Please date it, too."

Lana was more than happy to comply.

"Old Senator Russell has aged a dozen years since we saw him last," said Henrietta. "Pardon my French, but he looks like he's going to hell in a bucket. Hey, you two have been to France, haven't you? Why don't you tell us a little about what Paris is like?"

For the next hour Henrietta and Lana listened and asked a multitude of questions as Echo, and periodically Zeb, told them what Paris was like. They were particularly interested in the underground catacombs and the bones of the dead.

When they were done getting massaged, Zeb tipped them each twenty-five dollars.

Zeb and Echo hopped back into the spa, cleaned up, got dressed and Zeb excused himself.

"Tell your parents thank you."

"Where are you going?"

"To see Doc."

"What about?" asked Echo.

Zeb held up the picture of the human body Lana had drawn of Senator Russell. He ran a finger directly over the scars. Their location meant something. He was unsure of exactly what.

31

DOC AND ZEB CHAT

Zeb ran into Doc Yackley in the parking lot of the hospital.

"Doc, you got a minute?"

Doc Yackley leaned up against the side of his Cadillac Sedan de Ville and lightly ran a finger along a very long scratch.

"What happened to your Caddy, Doc?" asked Zeb.

"Someone keyed it and flattened a tire to boot."

"When was this?"

"The day I did the autopsy on Black Bear."

"You didn't report it," said Zeb.

Doc rolled his eyes.

"No, yeah, right. With all the crime in Graham County, I know you don't have time for petty mischief like this. Besides, I think I know who did it."

"Who?" asked Zeb.

"Tribal Police Chief Burries."

"Why would she do that?" asked Zeb.

"She's an asshole," replied Doc.

"No shortage of assholes around these days."

"Bad actors pop up in cycles."

"Yeah, I guess you're right about that."

"When you've been around as long as I have, you notice these things."

"Right. Any guesses as to why Chief Burries wanted to vandalize your car?"

"I guess I rubbed her the wrong way."

"You? Rub an authority figure the wrong way? I find that shocking."

Zeb's sarcasm was duly noted by a strange curling of Doc's lips.

"You want me to look into it?" asked Zeb.

"No, I've got insurance."

"Your insurance company will probably want to know you filed a report with me," said Zeb.

"Send it over. I'll fill it out. More damned paperwork. What the hell is life coming to when the pencil pushers call the shots?"

Zeb shook his head. Doc was right about that. But Doc also knew that it was all done on computer and the day of the pencil pusher was long gone.

"Vandalism by adults gets right under my craw and festers like an infection. Vandalism by someone in authority is downright outrageous, outlandish and sickening."

"Zeb, it's over and done. My boys might try and even the score."

Zeb stuck in his fingers in his ears, pretending he had not heard what Doc Yackley had just said.

"If you want my help, if you want me to question her, just say the word."

"If it comes down to that, I will. What do you need?" asked Doc.

Zeb handed Doc the drawing from Lana at Kachina Springs. After he explained what it was, Doc gave it a quick once over and handed it back to Zeb.

"What do you think?" asked Zeb.

"She'd better stick to her job as a masseuse."

"No, I mean what do you think about the location of the scars?"

Doc took back the drawing from Zeb.

"Whose body is it supposed to be?" asked Doc.

"One of your patients," replied Zeb.

"Why be so cryptic? I'm too damn old for guessing games."

"I'm just trying to verify a theory," said Zeb.

"On whom?"

Zeb spit out the name of Senator Russell.

"Patient confidentiality is a real thing, Zeb. I must respect my patient's rights. It's the law of the land."

"It may involve a crime," replied Zeb.

"You have a court order that compels me to give you Senator Russell's records?" asked Doc.

"No, Doc. I'm asking as a favor."

"Sorry. I swore an oath. I'm too old to lose my license."

"Can you tell me anything?" asked Zeb.

"Not really other than anyone with scars like that is likely quite ill," said Doc. "Does that help you out?"

"Kind of, sort of…"

"From looking at the drawing, I most certainly don't have enough details, even if I could talk to you about whoever this is. I can say this much, I do have a patient, and this happens occasionally, who was vague on the health history no matter how I questioned him. I can't say that all my medical histories are totally complete. Sometimes when that happens, I have to do extra testing procedures. Most of the time some extra bloodwork will help me figure out exactly what is going on."

"What are you looking for?" asked Zeb.

"You're pushing the confidentiality thing to its limits, Zeb."

"What would you be looking for, theoretically speaking?" asked Zeb.

"You're still pushing the envelope."

"Can you tell me anything?" asked Zeb.

"I'm looking to see why this patient is so sick. Is that good enough for your inquiring mind?"

"Shouldn't the surgeon, being that those are definitely surgical scars, be handling all of that?" asked Zeb.

"The surgeon practices elsewhere. The patient signed a special release, a legal document, so he can have all the test results given directly to the surgeon and only to him. Because of who he is, he's got some sort of special rights through the Affordable Health Care Act that allows him to prevent me from seeing the results. Don't know why he'd want to do that."

"Seems like he's protecting the surgeon for some reason."

"Yup."

"I smell a rat."

"Then, I'd say your schnozzola is working just fine. It's all within his rights as a patient. You're just going to have to be satisfied with that."

Doc was getting testy. Zeb decided it was best not to push him. Still, he had learned something. Senator Russell was ill, quite ill. Zeb turned to leave.

"One more thing, Doc."

"Who do you think you are, Columbo?"

Zeb knew Doc well enough to know that meant he best shut his pie hole soon.

"Any chance if something unusual shows up in your patient you'd tell me? Out of respect for my late mother?"

Zeb had just placed the old doctor in a corner. Doc gave Zeb a compassionate gaze. In his heart of hearts, Doc knew Senator Russell was Zeb's father. That being said, Zeb did have some minimal rights to knowledge that might affect his own health. However, the circumstance wasn't strong enough or proven enough for Doc to give up anything.

"I'll think on it, but don't ask me again. I'll make up my own mind. Got that? And, don't worry, there is little chance I'll forget your request."

Zeb tipped his hat and sauntered away. He had plans to meet Echo at home.

Doc knew that Zeb knew the patient was indeed Senator Russell. Zeb knew that Doc was drawing far inside the lines, something he didn't always do. He wondered if it was possible that Russell had something on Doc Yackley.

Finding the truth was not getting any easier.

32

DECISION TIME

Z eb was torn. One part of him wanted to destroy Senator Russell regardless of his mother's request. Another part of him, from reading Doc Yackley's body language, told him that Russell would soon enough be dead of his own accord. Deep inside he knew he had to exercise caution as he now had a family to look after.

Somehow, by the grace of God, Zeb was able to contain his rage, if not permanently at least for the moment. Evil, he truly believed, needed to be destroyed. As hard as he tried to remove the thought of killing Senator Russell from his mind, he could not help but continue to plot out the Senator's demise.

His plans would have to be thoughtful. Senator Russell was always surrounded by people. Zeb would have to watch him for days to figure out when the senator would be alone. A single shot from up close would be ideal. A long shot with a rifle might end up being an attempted assassination and make him a heroic figure. In Zeb's fantasy world there was a two-week window. If he was going to kill Senator Russell, it needed to be done and over within that time frame. Fifteen minutes of hard thinking gave him enough ground-work for a decent plan. His mind was stuck on murdering Russell as

Echo arrived in her truck. A single look at Zeb and she knew what he was thinking. His eyes and a dozen other emanations gave him away. She chose not to pull her punches.

"You can't murder a standing United States Senator without the full weight of the United States government coming down on you like a bunker buster bomb," said Echo.

Zeb nodded. She was right. Even amidst his passionate hatred, he knew what he was up against. But, if done correctly, it could all be hidden. He had unlicensed, unregistered weapons and plenty of homemade ammunition that couldn't be traced if he destroyed the flux, molds and other gear he kept in an abandoned shed a few miles out of town on some old family property. His extreme quiet told Echo all she needed to know.

"You've never been in combat. You have no idea how to make a murder look like something else altogether. It's tricky and it takes special skills. It requires talents that you don't possess," said Echo.

Once again, Zeb nodded quietly. She was right. His ego, anger and lack of experience could get him caught.

"I can't let you do this," pleaded Echo. "Think of Elan and Onawa."

Zeb's mind jolted to the note he had found in their kitchen upon their return from Paris. It was a note that warned him to consider Elan and Onawa before taking any action. He had yet to show the note to, or even discuss it, with Echo. For some reason now seemed like the time to do so. He pulled out his billfold and reached into a secret compartment where he had hidden the note.

"What's that?" asked Echo.

Zeb's mouth turned dry as dust.

"Something, er, something that I should have shown you when we got back from Paris."

Echo reached for the folded piece of paper and asked what it was.

"Please don't be mad at me."

"Why would I be mad at you?"

He handed over the folded note. Echo read it carefully. Then she read it aloud,

"DON'T RUN FOR SHERIFF! THINK ABOUT ELAN AND ONAWA."

Zeb was embarrassed and ashamed. He knew that this note should have been shared with Echo the day he found it. To his surprise she remained steadfastly calm.

"Was there anything else?"

"Yes. A picture of Carmelita shortly after she was killed."

Echo did not hesitate one second before answering.

"You were thinking that you were protecting me, weren't you? I know you well enough to think that if you figured out who wrote this, there would be no need to show it to me. You should know by now that I understand what you're thinking."

Zeb breathed a sigh of relief. He felt he was off the hook for his mistake.

"But, I'm a big girl. You have to trust me enough to share these kinds of things with me. Don't you agree?"

"I do. It's just..."

Echo interrupted.

"No excuses. No explanations needed. It's beyond that. Let's just move forward."

She examined the note under a bright light.

"Any idea where or who this came from?"

"No. I found it on the floor near the kitchen table on the day we returned from Paris."

"On the floor?" asked Echo.

"Yes, next to the kitchen table. I assumed someone slid it under the door when we were gone."

"How could it have gotten all the way to the kitchen table? That's at least twenty feet."

A new thought entered Zeb's mind, one he had not previously considered. But it happened to be the first thought that came to Echo.

"I'd bet dollars to donuts it was sitting on the table, and when you opened the door, the change in air pressure or the wind blew it to the floor," said Echo.

"That would mean someone broke into our house."

"Did you check to see if anything was missing?" inquired Echo.

Zeb's face flushed. Yes, he had looked, but only superficially. In his haste, he had been foolish and incomplete.

"Your secret stash of money? Is any of it missing?"

Zeb, since inheriting so much money from Doreen, always kept a ready supply of cash, just in case. Just in case he might need it for some undefined, unknown purpose.

"You don't know, do you?"

Once again Zeb's cheeks turned red. It wasn't the money he was concerned about.

"Let's have a look," ordered Echo.

Thankfully, Zeb had systematically placed the ten grand in ten stacks of ten one hundred-dollar bills each. Fortunately, they were all present and accounted for.

"What else might someone steal?" pondered Echo.

"My weapons."

"Of course," replied Echo. "Have you checked them?"

"I've been in the gun safe. I don't recall noticing that anything was missing."

"You have a list of all your weapons and ammunition that is up to date, right?"

"Er, uh, not really. But I know what I've got."

Zeb stopped dead in his tracks.

"What?" asked Echo.

Zeb moved quickly to the garage workbench. He had forgotten to check on the .22 he had talked with Jake about. He had been called to the office in the middle of cleaning the gun and stuffed it behind some things. He meant to check on it but had somehow spaced it out.

Echo stood in the door between the house and the garage. She watched as Zeb hurriedly moved things about.

"What are you doing?"

"Looking for something."

"What?"

"A .22 I was cleaning and hid back here on this shelf. I was on automatic pilot. When I was looking before, I just assumed I had returned it to the safe. Now, I'm not so certain I ever put it back in the gun safe."

"Then let's open the safe and have a look at your arsenal," said Echo. "We can see if you put it away or not."

Zeb feared he had left it in the garage but had not properly put it away. He raced through the combination nervously. The first time it failed him.

"That one is on me. I hurried," said Zeb.

"Take your time. No one is going to break in now."

The second attempt was a success. In a glance that took less than a single second, Zeb could see what was missing. He said nothing at first, but his Sharps 4-Barrel .22 Rimfire Derringer was not where he always kept it. Also missing was a box of Remington .22 short shells. Zeb ran through his mind when he had last shot the gun. It had been a year or more. He had cleaned it maybe six or eight months ago. But he had a distinct memory of replacing it on the top shelf of the safe as it was one of his private collector's items. Echo read the concern on his face.

"What's the matter?"

Zeb carefully moved a few things around inside the gun locker. He had the location of all his weapons and ammunition memorized.

"Is the .22 missing?" asked Echo.

Zeb checked through his arsenal one more time.

"I'm afraid so."

"What kind of .22?"

"An old .22 Sharps Derringer pistol. The box of ammo that went with it is also missing. It was originally my uncle's. I inherited it when I was a kid. I've kept it in perfect working order for all these years."

"Don't you find it a bit odd that with all this heavy weaponry someone would steal a .22 caliber pistol, an old one at that? Did it have value as a rarity?"

"No. It was an inexpensive, but well-maintained gun. It has some value, but not a lot. I can't imagine why someone would steal it. For that matter I can't figure out how someone got into my gun safe. It doesn't make any sense."

"You suspect you know what happened with the .22. You left it in the garage. Now it's gone."

"I only clean that gun once or twice a year. I generally shoot it just one time a year. Other than that, it never leaves the gun case."

"What about the shells?"

"Echo, honestly, I have no idea. I have no recollection of touching them when I was cleaning the .22. Nor would I have had any reason to move them?"

"Who knows that there might have been a .22 in here?"

"No one that I know of. Well, I might have mentioned it to Jake and Song Bird in passing."

"You're going to have to find that gun."

Echo's voice was urgent and full of angst.

"Black Bear was shot in the head with a .22 pistol. If someone stole your gun and killed him with it, you're going to take the fall."

"But I didn't kill him."

"I know that. But what if the bullet they found in his brain matches one shot from your .22?"

"Shit."

"Exactly," replied Echo.

"Who would have the skill to break into our house and this safe?" asked Echo.

"Any decent locksmith or a professional thief, I guess. The house door is a piece of cake. By the time Elan and Onawa can walk, I'll be able to teach them to jimmy the backdoor lock. As to the safe, it's not that complicated."

Zeb's explanation got him thinking. He snapped his fingers.

"I think I might know where to start looking. I have a long shot guess on who pulled the trigger," said Zeb.

"Well, you'd better get to work. If this comes back to you, it could create a world of hurt."

Zeb kissed Echo and was out the door.

33

A LITTLE LUCK TRAVELS A LONG DISTANCE

Zeb put a phone call in to Shelly.

"Shelly, I need your help and I need it now."

"Interesting coincidence. I was just about to call you. What's up?"

"Do you have something for me?" asked Zeb.

"I do."

"Well? What is it?"

"I know precisely when and where Shappa took off from in the Lear jet when she headed back to South Dakota from outside of Tucson. Our suspicions are correct. It was Club Mex."

"I think I'll go have a look there right now. Can you send me the GPS coordinates?"

Shelly's nimble fingers flew across the digits on her phone.

"Done. Now what did you need from me?"

"Two things. First, is there any chance you can get any security camera footage anywhere near my house from when I was gone? Someone broke into my house when I was in Paris."

"Not a problem. There aren't any security cameras real close to your place. You should have one or two or three put in."

"You sound like my wife. I'll get it done," said Zeb.

"The good news is there are cameras that cover all the streets that lead to your house. Can you pin down the timeframe for me at all?"

"My guess is, and it is only a guess, that it happened very close to the time I left town."

Zeb quickly gave her those details.

"Got it. I'll start there. They take anything?"

"Maybe."

"Maybe? What do you mean, maybe?"

"I'm missing a .22 handgun from my gun safe and some shells that go with it."

It took Shelly about a half of a second to put one and one together.

"That's not good."

"Nope, especially as it points a finger of guilt directly at me when it comes to Black Bear."

"Did the intruders take anything else? Are any other guns missing? Any other ammunition? Clues of any kind?" asked Shelly.

"They left me a message on a piece of paper and a picture."

"That's something. It shows intent."

"A copy of the letter is in my upper right-hand drawer. It's short and says DON'T RUN FOR SHERIFF! THINK ABOUT ELAN AND ONAWA!"

"Short and not too sweet."

"Two things really get to me. First, that they mention my family. Second, the picture of Carmelita, well, whoever left it knew it would haunt me."

"Think. Are you sure it's not an official picture taken by the department? There must be back-ups on file. Have you checked on that?"

"Yes. Quite thoroughly. Nothing on our file matches the exact angle of that picture. I have no idea where it originally came from or who took the photo. All I know is that someone is using it to taunt me or try and break me down."

"Agreed. There is some really bad blood behind this."

"Since we're dealing with someone who would kill a sheriff, I suppose harming my children wouldn't be off the table," replied Zeb.

Shelly held back a gasp.

"I think whoever left the picture of Carmelita was counting on someone other than me finding it."

"Why would they leave that picture of Carmelita?"

"Good question. To raise doubt about me, perhaps. To twist my mind, maybe. I don't know for certain. It could be almost anything."

"I'd hate to think someone was setting you up as the perpetrator of a major crime spree."

That thought had crossed Zeb's mind. If his gun matched the one that killed Black Bear and was maybe tied to other crimes, maybe even other murders, he would be in deep shit. His mind went to the ATF fiasco involving the cartels and the ATF border gun problems that popped up under the Obama administration. The implications were wide and far-reaching.

"I don't even know with absolute certainty that I am being set up."

"Any ideas at all as to who it might have been that left the picture there?"

"Shappa is my best guess."

"That's ballsy on her part. But how could you possibly tie her to it?"

"I can't, but I think she's a professional at playing the criminal game," replied Zeb.

"Then, if she does have her fingerprints on this, she probably covered her tracks pretty well."

"Everyone makes mistakes."

"One more thing."

"Fire away."

"The bullet that Doc took out of Black Bear's brain is in Box 6 in the evidence locker. See if you can match it with any crimes committed in Graham County, say in the in the last twelve months."

"Any hints you can give me that might point me in some direction?" asked Shelly.

"It's a Remington .22 short rifle Golden bullet."

"That's the kind you use, isn't it, Zeb?"

"It is. I know Diamond Gun and Ammo carry them. That's a good starting point on figuring out who buys them locally."

"Okay. I'll check that out. It's a long shot, but Josh keeps great records. It'll take just a phone call to figure out who buys Remington .22 short rifle Golden bullets."

"I'm looking at the GPS coordinates now," said Zeb. "Seems like the private landing strip is between Cochise and Tucson. I'm headed out that way. I'll take the back roads so I might not have cellphone service for part of the trip. Contact me on the two-way if you find something of value."

Zeb stopped at the QT and grabbed a couple of waters, a Diet Coke and a juniper flavored Doctor Pepper for the trip. He also grabbed two soft shell tacos at Taco Jose's. Once he crossed the city limits of Safford, he took off his hat, set it on the seat next to him and downed the 20-ounce Diet Coke in one long swig. He ate one taco quickly and belched deeply before cracking open the juniper Doctor Pepper. He drank it more slowly and chewed the second taco slower as well, thinking of how Echo was often reminding him to slow down when he ate.

The season was particularly green. A few cacti still were blooming and the ride enjoyable as Zeb realized this was the first instance when he had time to himself in what seemed like ages. He thought about Echo and the kids, about Helen, about his extraordinary hatred of Senator Russell. Mostly he thought of his late mother. He had a good cry as he remembered the thousands of little things she had done for him over the course of his life. He felt just how much she loved him and how strong his love for her really had been. When the tears wouldn't stop, he ordered his mind to get a grip. The tears seemed to have their own opinion on the subject.

An hour into the trip the cola began triggering his bladder. Though he could stop anywhere as there was no one around for miles, he waited for just the right spot. It was akin to a game he and the man he had believed was his biological father often played when they traversed the back roads heading to a fishing creek or some hunting grounds. They would find a dried-up creek bed, and while urinating in it, pretend they were making it flow like a river. He stopped at a little spot known as Dead Bunny Creek. It was dry as a bone which made it perfect for playing the stupid little game he and his father had made up so many years earlier.

Zeb parked, stepped out of the truck, unzipped his pants and let fly. The sun beating on his face warmed him. He felt like a kid again as he arced the force of his urination as high as possible using the full force of his bladder. He chuckled as he realized the power of his bladder pressure was not what it used to be. When he dribbled out the last drop, shook himself dry and put his equipment away, something caught his eye. About twenty feet away something glistened. He cursed the fool who tossed what looked like a beer bottle into the otherwise pristine area.

"Goddamnit all. Why does anyone litter such a beautiful place as this?"

There was no one to hear him and no one who would likely ever see the remnants of the broken bottle. Still, he stepped off the road and walked down a small slanted runoff. As he approached what he thought was a broken bottle, he noticed it was something else entirely. It was a handgun, a Sharps 4-Barrel .22 Rimfire Derringer. He bent down and picked it up, but something told him to stop. He walked back to his vehicle and put on a pair of gloves. He returned to the scene, picked up the gun and examined it. Shock raced through his system when he realized it was the gun that had been stolen from his safe. He released the hammer and the barrel flipped open. One bullet had been fired and three remained. Zeb put the gun on half-cock and closed it.

Zeb looked around as if he might actually find another clue of some kind. Of course, he didn't, but his luck was phenomenal. A minute later his two-way buzzed. It was Shelly.

"You're the only person who has bought .22 short rifle Golden Remington bullets at Gun and Ammo in the last year. In fact, you bought the last box. He doesn't even sell them anymore."

"I found my gun," replied Zeb.

"You what?"

"That's right. I found my gun out here in the middle of the desert."

"What are the odds of that?"

"A million to one, at best."

"I wouldn't bet the farm on that kind of thing ever happening again. Congratulations."

"Another odd request coming at you."

"Yes?"

"I've got a bagful of spent bullets in the bottom right drawer of my file cabinet. Don't even ask why I saved them. It's a weird, old habit of mine."

"I guess we all have those kinds of things," replied Shelly. "Weird habits, that is."

"Grab a couple of them and have Jake run a test match against the bullet found in Black Bear's brain."

"What?"

"Yes, you heard me right. Compare the two."

"I'll see that it gets done today."

"Call me when you know something, anything."

"You can't truly believe lightning is going to strike in the same place twice and the bullets are going to match, do you?"

"Let's just say I've got a feeling and it won't go away."

"I'll hit you back ASAP."

"Thanks."

"Just doing my job."

"Right."

"Zeb?"

"Yeah?

"You didn't shoot Black Bear, did you?"

"Not that I can recall."

When Shelly didn't respond with laughter, Zeb added, "Just kidding. I didn't shoot the son of a bitch."

Zeb ended the call and headed down the road to the remote landing strip. When he arrived, he realized he would need the manpower of an FBI search to find anything. He left disgruntled and disheartened. On the road back as he reached the top of a hill his cellphone rang. It was Senator Russell.

"Zeb, I need to talk to you and Echo."

"Something in particular on your mind?" asked Zeb.

"Yes. Something very specific. When can you be here?"

Zeb had not said he would come. Senator Russell was hardly on his list of favorite people or even people he wanted to visit. What made Russell think Zeb would jump when he ordered him to? Zeb thought about it for a minute. Perhaps there was something to be gained.

"Two, maybe three hours," replied Zeb.

"Great. See you and Echo then."

34

STRANGE MEETING

Zeb, with Echo at his side, pulled into the half-mile-long cement driveway that led to Senator Russell's recently built mansion in Safford.

Zeb had played cowboys and Indians on this acreage and ridden his banana seat bicycle on this land as a child, hunted it for deer and rabbits and ridden his four-wheeler as a teenager on it all long before Russell had snatched it up in a dubious bankruptcy proceeding. Now this ten-thousand-acre parcel held the senator's house, his outbuildings, a dozen prize horses and various other exotic farm animals. Mostly it was pure, virgin desert.

"What do you think he wants?" asked Echo. "Why would he want to talk to both of us right now?"

"I have no idea. All he said was that it was urgent," replied Zeb.

Halfway up the long drive, Zeb stopped the car and pulled to the side of the road. He pointed to a small, hidden crag. It was a spot he knew well from his youth. It also provided the perfect location for a kill shot from a sharpshooter.

"That's the position I thought we would use if one of us was going to shoot Russell."

Echo took out her field glasses. She scanned the area with an intensity that took the rest of the world out of her mind. She spoke to Zeb in a whisper as though the whole world could hear her every word.

"It's perfect, but we've made the decision not to do it, right?"

Echo knew it was the right decision not to kill Russell. She was merely doublechecking to make certain Zeb still believed they had made the right choice.

"Right. I'm glad it didn't come down to putting him underground," said Zeb.

Echo looked thoughtfully at Zeb. If Zeb would have killed Russell, it would have been out of hatred and, therefore, immoral. That would have made it wrong. If she had chosen to kill the senator, had the circumstances dictated it so, she would have killed for a proper reason. He had threatened the life of her family. The difference in her mind was clear. She felt the need to explain her thinking to Zeb.

"I would have been ready, willing and able," replied Echo, reaching over and touching Zeb's cheek. "And the only one who could do this for the right reasons. If it had come down to that, which it won't."

Zeb nodded in the affirmative. Little did Echo know of Zeb's plan to usurp her had the assassination become necessary. The two of them had spent days scoping out Senator Russell's daily routine. He was nothing if not a creature of habit. Every night as the sun was setting, fifteen minutes precisely before it began to sink below the horizon, he would exit his house. In one hand he always carried Rémy Martin cognac in a tulip snifter. In the other a Gurkha Black Dragon cigar. Feeling the power of expensive alcohol and rich tobacco, Russell would watch the descending sun fall behind a canyon wall. In the coming darkness he would wait five minutes, rise from his chair, more clumsily each day, and return through a pair of monstrous glass doors to his living room. He would plop down in front of a television so large that when they spied on him, they didn't even need binoculars to tell what was on the screen. Oddly, he was a junk TV fan, often watching Mexican telenovelas. The course of his events each evening never varied. His lack of shaking up his routine made him neither a soldier nor a hunter.

Pointing out the hidden crag from this angle was merely a ruse on Zeb's part. Although he had agreed to let Echo take the death shot, that was never within the realm of possibility. Had the killing of Senator Russell come to fruition, Zeb would have done the deed a full twenty-four hours ahead of the well plotted plan the two of them had hatched. Zeb could live with murder on his conscience especially the assassination of the man whom he believed, in his heart of hearts, had raped his mother. Zeb was one hundred percent certain that Echo, even though she may have killed others in combat, could not live with such a matter as this on her conscience. And, under no circumstances, would he allow her to end up in prison.

Zeb put the truck back in gear and the pair slowly finished the drive to the front door of the palatial estate. A white-gloved gentleman opened the door before they could knock or ring the bell.

"Sheriff Hanks, Mrs. Hanks, Senator Russell is anticipating your arrival. He is at leisure in the study. Please follow me."

The butler, or whatever he was, probably a secret service agent or private security, walked semi-briskly across the open three-story foyer, down a long hallway. Making a left turn he headed down a second longer hallway. He stopped in front of a set of double doors that looked like they had been refurbished from a Mexican hacienda. He knocked gently on the door, not waiting for a response before opening it. When the split double doors opened, he announced the expected visitors.

"Sheriff Zebulon Hanks and Mrs. Echo Skysong Hanks."

After his quite proper announcement, the butler stepped inside the study and held the door for Zeb and Echo. Very shortly after they passed by him, he reversed his steps, shutting the door so quietly that Zeb looked over his shoulder to make certain he had departed.

As they entered the study, they saw only the back of Senator Russell's head. He was seated in an oversized, red, high-back, leather chair. He silently motioned them to his side with a small wave of the hand. Echo immediately noticed his arm was pale and heavily dotted with red, white and brown aging spots. His arm, in short, looked ill, frail and old. But it was when they saw his face up close, both immediately knew they were looking at a man who was not long for the planet.

The pale hand of the dying man made a second weak gesture. Directly across from him were two plush chairs. Between them was a wooden table with a bottle of **Rémy** Martin Louis XIII Grande Champagne Très Vieille Age Inconnu cognac and two tulip cognac snifters filled roughly one-third of the way.

Echo emitted a slight gasp that did not go unnoticed by their host. Russell, a hardened man in all things, bothered not to wonder what Echo was gasping at. In fact, her breath had been taken away when she saw the bottle. In France they had seen a decanter of this specific cognac. She remembered converting the cost in her head. The cognac liqueur was worth over fifty thousand U.S. dollars.

"A drop of water has been added to each of your drinks," explained Senator Russell.

His voice was weak but his eyes keen. He easily read the inquisitive looks on their faces.

"A drop of water reveals a more fruity, floral and spicy aroma. It makes the tasting experience smoother and, I believe, more genuine. I have learned the hard way that authenticity is always of the utmost importance."

Senator Russell lifted his snifter and waited for Echo and Zeb to raise theirs.

"To you, Zeb, your lovely wife, Echo, and especially to your darling children, Elan and Onawa."

Zeb felt a gnawing in the pit of his stomach as the names of his children slithered from the mouth of his nemesis and progenitor. Properly sipping the outrageously expensive cognac, Echo executed a quick study of the senator. Using her military training and the expertise she had learned as the Knowledge Keeper allowed her to draw accurate conclusions with rapid precision. The senator was not only dying, he was suffering significantly. From her point of view his distress was far more than mere physical pain. Experience had taught her bodily pain only went so deep.

"I was surprised to hear from you, Senator Russell," said Zeb.

"A curious thing to say to your host," replied Russell.

"Why would you want to see me? To see us?" asked Zeb.

Slowly the dying old man drew the tulip glass to his lips and sipped a taste so small as to be almost imperceptible. It was obvious the liquor soothed him.

"Zeb, you know we have unfinished business between us," said Russell. "I do believe it is important to address certain issues that we both know exist."

How could Russell have known that Zeb knew he was his biological father? It was the only important secret between the men. Why had Russell chosen this moment to speak?

"Your mother..."

It took everything Zeb had not to rise up out of his chair and attack the senator at the mere mention of his mother.

"...what was between us is not what you think."

Zeb was growing increasingly irate with each word that passed through Russell's lips.

"How can you possibly pretend to know what I think?" barked Zeb.

"I am a dying man as you have likely already presumed. I will share a little secret with you. A dying man must speak his mind. If he does not speak the truth, it will chase him into his grave and never be known to the world."

"What so-called truth do you think you have to share with me?"

Zeb's mind continued speaking silently. You raped my mother, and I am the result of that heinous act? You made me little more than a bastard child, Zeb thought.

Echo reached across the small wooden table and placed her smooth, loving and powerful hand on Zeb's forearm. Momentarily a sense of calm overcame his hatred and loathing.

"Let Senator Russell speak his piece," said Echo.

Zeb knew the voice she was speaking through by its tone. It was that of the Knowledge Keeper. He had become familiar with the subtle quality that arose whenever Echo drifted intentionally into her ancient, spiritual other self.

"I had a hand in you finding the letter from your mother," said Senator Russell. "Perhaps you might have even recognized that already?"

They had not.

Both Zeb and Echo were stunned into silence as they shared an identical and immediate question. Was Helen in cahoots with Senator Russell? Zeb shuddered at the notion of it as it meant the possibility of her obtaining Black Bear's heart for her first cousin, Henry, was real. After all, Helen was the one who had sent Zeb back to the family house when his mother had suffered the stroke. She was the one who had placed the letter on the kitchen table. If Russell had helped write the letter, it was almost a certainty Helen was aware of that fact.

"How?" asked Echo.

"It doesn't matter. But Helen was not a willing participant. I duped her into placing the letter there for you to find, Zeb. She's a good woman. She has not a single bad bone in her body. The woman is an earthly saint."

Zeb, though his head was still spinning about Helen, could not argue with the senator's words. His eyes locked on those of Senator Russell as he asked a question. The dying man did not waver upon hearing Zeb's words.

"So, you know that I know that you are my biological father?"

"Of course, I know. And I know what else you are thinking. You believe I forced myself onto your mother, don't you?"

Zeb slammed his fist on the table. In the process he shattered the wood as well as nearly fracturing his hand. He screamed his answer at the ever-weakening old man.

"YES! GODDAMNIT. YES!"

Echo sunk her fingers into Zeb's forearm with the strength of a dozen battle-hardened soldiers. For all she knew Zeb might kill Russell right on the spot.

"Zeb, my son..."

Zeb's face turned black. His head thundered like exploding dynamite.

"Don't you dare call me your son. You're a sperm donor at best. At worst you're a lying rapist."

Senator Russell, in the heat of it all, remained at ease and spoke with the composure of a man who wholly believed every word that came out of his mouth.

"I'm sorry. That was selfish of me. I only wanted to hear myself say that you were my son for my own benefit. I was thinking only of myself. Now that I've said it, I am filled with shame. My ego got the best of me. I shall never utter that phrase in your presence again. Please accept my apology."

Zeb's glare of hatred softened, if only by a miniscule amount.

Russell cleared his throat with another taste of the cognac before continuing.

"I've watched you from afar for all these years. I am proud of you and your accomplishments. I even protected you when I could."

Zeb rose to his feet, pointed a finger at his nemesis and shouted angrily.

"Liar. Goddamned liar. You can go directly to hell."

"I know this is almost impossible for you to understand, but I loved your mother. I loved her with all my heart."

In a voice that ranged from alto to guttural, Zeb shouted "Liar." This time he rose and moved a step closer to Russell. It took every bit of power in Echo's body to pull him back. Zeb's face was flushed crimson with hatred. A full frenzied storm of uncontrollable craziness, far beyond anything he had ever before experienced, clamored throughout every cell of his body. The force of it all rushed through his head with the ferocious power of thunder and the unconstrained speed of lightning. He found it impossible to believe that speaking so calmly at him was the man who defiled his sainted and recently departed mother.

"Please listen to what I have to say," begged Russell. "Then act in whatever manner you must. I know you well enough to know that you might very well kill me when I am done speaking. I accept that. If death by your hands in the next few moments is to be my fate, I fully accept that as my ultimate destiny. It is not your punishment that I might be fearful of, rather the unknown that might follow it."

Zeb trembled bodily as he half-sat and was half-pulled by Echo down into the chair. Feeling her husband's pain, Echo forced herself to hold back what would have been an onslaught of painful tears, tears for what Zeb must be feeling. Even with the power of the mind of the Knowledge Keeper working at maximum capacity, she had no idea of what might happen next. So rare was it that she had so little control over a situation that it took all she had to fight off the fear of what might happen in the next instant.

Senator Russell reached into his pocket. Zeb placed his hand on his gun. Russell pulled out no weapon, rather it was a key that appeared in his hand. He made a vain attempt to present it to Zeb. Zeb froze. His hatred of Russell did not allow any reaction. Instead, Zeb merely glanced at the key while keeping a cold, hard stare at Russell. Echo reached across the small table. She appropriated the key from Senator Russell's open palm and examined it closely. There was no doubt in her mind it was for a lock box.

"What does this key open?" she asked.

Russell kept his gaze on Zeb as he answered Echo's question.

"It's the key to the secret treasure chest that Marta and I shared."

"What in the name of God are you talking about?" demanded Zeb.

"You are aware of the crawl space underneath the steps that lead to the basement in your mother's house?"

"Of course, I am. But what in hell does this key have to do with that space?"

Zeb pointed to the key that Echo now held in her open and upturned hand.

"Your mother installed a secret safe in that area. She did it long after you moved out of the house. Inside the safe is a lockbox. It is a large one."

"Just what the hell is this all about?" demanded Zeb.

"The love between your mother and I never ended. Each week for decades we wrote each other a letter. Your mother, being the sentimentalist that she is, saved each and every piece of correspondence. Since they were private, I suggested to her long ago that she install a safe and put the letters in a lockbox inside the safe so no one could find them. I'm giving you the key so you can open the safe and read the letters. The combination is your birthdate. They, the many letters, will tell you without a doubt what the whole truth is between your late mother and me."

Zeb's mind was spinning like a top that had lost its axis and gone off kilter. He had absolutely no idea what to think or how to process the thoughts he was having. Was Senator Russell lying to him? If he wasn't, what was his endgame? Why tell Zeb about the letters at all? If they were as personal as Russell intimated, what business did Zeb have reading them at all? None of it made the least bit of sense. He simply couldn't believe what Russell was telling him and took none of what he said at face value.

"It seems there is an easy way to tell if Senator Russell is telling the truth," said Echo. "All we have to do is go open the box and read the letters for ourselves."

The senator pointed to a small closet directly behind Zeb.

"You don't even need to go to her house to find out the truth. Simply walk to that closet and you will find over a thousand letters your mother wrote to me. In them you will find the truth of what went on between us and how she felt about me, about you, about your brother, about Echo, about the man you thought was your father and just about everything else in her life. We had no secrets between us. I am willing to share all of this with you. I do not want to go to my grave with you hating me."

Zeb was quite literally frozen in his chair. All he had to do was walk a few feet, open the box and read a few letters in order to possibly know the truth. He didn't know, even if Senator Russell was telling the truth, if it even mattered at this point. Senator Russell was nothing if not a sneaky, devious man. All of this could simply be a set-up, a con of some sort. Zeb had zero trust in the dying man who claimed to be his father. He may have written fictitious letters that feigned proof of love for his mother in order to trap Zeb. Such a ploy would fit perfectly into what Zeb assumed he knew about Russell.

Echo, on the other hand, was eager to know the facts. She got up from her chair, walked to the closet. It took but a few moments to grab a dozen or so letters out of a box that was right where Senator Russell said it would be. As Echo silently read the first letter she came upon, both Russell and Zeb remained in a literal stare down, sipped their cognac slowly and with significant intent. As Echo read each letter, Zeb stared coldly at the man who claimed to be his biological father. The senator, on his part, washed down a pair of 40 mg OxyContin tablets with his next, somewhat larger taste of cognac.

Echo read four or five letters over a ten-minute period before uttering a single word. Russell and Zeb continued to stare each other down in silence. Zeb was certain that Echo was going to expose Russell for the fraud he was. When she finally spoke, Zeb's jaw dropped.

"From what I can tell," said Echo softly, "he is telling the truth."

"Take the letters with you and compare them with those in your mother's safe," insisted Senator Russell. "They are all dated. You can cross-reference my letters with your mother's. When you consider I am knocking on death's door, why would I choose to lie about anything? That sort of action would be pointless."

Zeb and Echo could not disagree with his argument.

Russell pulled a hanky from his pocket. Taking a short, distressed breath, he coughed weakly but with the maximum amount of strength he had in his chest. Zeb and Echo could see he had hacked up a significant amount of blood.

"Are you okay?" inquired Echo.

Zeb could have cared less if Senator Russell choked to death on his own blood. He was hoping the senator would say no.

"It's part of my illness. A rather disgusting symptom, I must say. I apologize for the uncouthness of it all."

"No need to do that," replied Echo.

The senator moved his fingers to the cellphone that was sitting on the arm of his chair. He tapped lightly on the screen. Fifteen seconds later the butler quietly entered through the door.

"Please call Doctor Yackley at once for me."

"Yes, sir."

The butler spun on his heels and departed the room.

"Can we continue our conversation at a later time?"

Senator Russell's voice was becoming weaker with each word.

As Zeb was about to state that he didn't see the point in any further conversation, Echo interjected her thoughts on the matter.

"Yes, Senator. Whenever it is convenient for you. We are at your service."

"Thank you my dear. You are a radiant beam of sunshine in Zebulon's life. He has chosen wisely. I wish you and your family brilliant futures. May you have a long and lustrous loving life together. May Elan and Onawa grow up to be good people like their grandmother was."

Once again, the senator tapped his phone and the butler appeared. He opened the door and silently motioned Zeb and Echo to follow him.

As they got in their truck and headed down the long driveway back towards town, a plethora of thoughts passed through both of their minds. Doctor Yackley's Cadillac Sedan DeVille, with the convertible top down, passed them at the end of the driveway. He honked twice and waved. Both noticed he had a rather un-Doc Yackley like serious look on his face.

35

PHONE CALL

There was too much to think about. Zeb and Echo were caught between strange hope and the deepest of doubt. Was the key Echo held in her hand going to reveal a strange and possibly horrifying truth? Were there actually true love letters in the box inside the safe under the stairs at Zeb's mother's house? Or was this all part of some devious ruse that Russell had cooked up? Zeb knew the truth was never close to Senator Russell's tongue and landed on it even less rarely. But something told him this might be different. He battled his own thoughts.

On one hand he hoped Russell was lying. If Russell were scamming him and Echo, it would justify the bullet that Zeb had shined to a golden glow for the sole purpose of ending Russell's life. On the other hand was the what if of his mother and Russell being long time lovers. Within that realm lived the distinct possibility of Russell actually being his father.

Echo rolled the key to the box at Zeb's mother's house between her fingers. Zeb's true fate lay in the ink of a thousand letters that allegedly were stored there.

"Let's go have a look," she said.

"Now?"

"Yes, now. Why wait? The truth is inevitable. We need to know what the truth is."

"I don't..."

"Do you not want to know all the facts?" asked Echo.

"It's just..."

"Just what?"

Zeb pulled his truck to the curb. He took off his hat and set it between himself and Echo. He flecked away a stray hair that was sitting on the brim. Echo could clearly see for the first time ever the frightened child that lived inside Zeb.

"I don't know if I am ready for all of this," explained Zeb. "I don't know if I ever will be."

Echo stood firm. As the Knowledge Keeper of all the People, as a mother, a wife and an Apache warrior, she knew what had to be done.

"And waiting will give you what?"

Zeb sighed. Of course, she was right. If the truth could be known, what was the point in waiting? The truth was not going to change. Zeb donned his hat, put the truck in gear and headed toward his mother's house.

Zeb had only been in the house a few times since she died. The first time was odd with the realization that she would never again be greeting him with her warm and beautiful smile. The other times he had been dealing with the details of his mother's life, paying the bills, picking up the house, checking the water, putting out the garbage— those mundane things that were necessary, somewhat emotional, yet somehow surreal.

The time from pulling into the driveway until he found himself standing in front of the hidden safe proved otherworldly. A pile of fresh laundry still sat on top of the dryer. Zeb picked it up and buried his nose in it. Even these many days after her death it smelled fresh. It smelled like his mother when he hugged her. He struggled to choke back tears.

Zeb opened the safe using his birthdate as the combination. The tinny sound of it clicking open startled Zeb.

"You okay?" asked Echo.

Then another startle. Zeb's phone rang. He glanced at the screen name that popped up. It was Doc Yackley. Zeb wondered what he could possibly need to tell him. It rang three times. Zeb was frozen until Echo suggested he answer. He clicked the phone on speaker.

"Zeb?"

"Yeah, Doc. What's up?"

"Senator Russell has just entered the onramp to his eternal reward or everlasting damnation."

Zeb and Echo merely looked at each other as though what they had just heard was inevitable and expected.

"Thanks, Doc. Appreciate the call."

"Yup."

With that Doc hung up his end of the call.

"What now?" murmured Zeb.

Inside the rather large safe was the box that Russell had described. It was big enough for the thousand or so letters that Russell had said would be there.

"I guess we take a look," said Echo. "You have something else in mind?"

Zeb wished the whole thing would just go away. He suspected the truth was not going to be palatable. His response was hangdog and sheepish.

"No."

Echo pulled a half dozen letters from the handmade leather bag she carried which doubled as her purse. In a matter of minutes, because Zeb's mother had organized the letters so efficiently, she crossmatched letters between Senator Russell and Zeb's mom.

Echo quickly read through them. After doing so she handed each to Zeb. In a matter of minutes, they discovered that the late Senator Russell had indeed been telling the truth.

36

SENATOR RUSSELL'S WASHINGTON, D.C. FUNERAL

Senator Russell's body was on a plane to Washington D.C. within the hour. Once there it was immediately embalmed for the viewing. For some reason, the details of which were explained to no one, Zeb and Echo were asked to accompany the body to its destination. Helen was simply informed by Zeb that the Secret Service had made the request and that he and Echo were going to honor it. The Secret Service had also asked Helen to say nothing to anyone about Zeb potentially being the late senator's illegitimate son. Helen honored their request. Deputy Kate Steele Diamond was left in charge of Graham County. Echo's parents took care of Elan and Onawa.

Senator Russell's body was formally viewed by tens of thousands of people while it lay in state in the Capitol Rotunda. Being a military hero and powerful six-term member of the United States Senate, his official funeral was held at the National Cathedral in Washington, D.C.

Zeb and Echo were invited to sit in the front row of the cathedral. Back in Safford, Shelly watched the proceedings on a closed-circuit feed that CSPAN offered. She also made a copy of the funeral for later viewing.

"They're giving him quite a send-off," whispered Echo. "I guess that's a good thing since he was a military hero and elected a half-dozen times to the U.S. Senate. I suppose a man in his position actually did a lot of good along the way."

Due to Zeb's long history with Senator Russell and his recent findings regarding his mother, the senator and his own lineage, Zeb's reaction was appropriately muted. While Zeb did not make it a habit of wishing anyone dead, he was relieved that Russell was no longer upright and among the living. The late senator, had he chosen to, could have seen that Zeb spent the rest of his days behind bars, or worse, in a Mexican jail.

But the real trouble was two-fold for Zeb. First of all, the fact that he was the product of a relationship between the late senator and his mother was almost unbearable in its truth. Secondly, Senator Russell's passing stirred up long-buried thoughts of Doreen's death and Zeb's murderous retribution of Carmelita Montouyez. Mental images of Doreen, dead in their bedroom, like all treacherous PTSD sights could not be unseen. Further complicating his emotions were his twins and the love in his heart for Echo. Sitting in the front row of the National Cathedral, Zeb was certain life could never be the same again.

Staring into Senator Russell's open casket triggered strange reflections in Zeb's mind. The bad contemplations stuck like glue. All that went into the death of Doreen and Zeb's subsequent murder of Carmelita was front and center. The sensation that had passed through his hands as he thrust the death sword through Carmelita's still beating, anxiety-filled heart was as fresh as the moment in which it happened. These thoughts, these horrific memories, as well as the sweet taste of revenge that accompanied Carmelita's death, were something he likely never would, nor could share with Echo.

As Zeb watched the funeral, he was laden with guilt, fear and deeply rooted anxiety. There was also a strange relief that Russell could not reach him from beyond the grave and create trouble for him regarding Carmelita, something the senator had known all about. His angst, while rooted in the murder of Carmelita, could be dealt with or temporarily buried when it rose up into his brain. Rather, his torment was from holding back such a monstrous truth from the woman he loved. In short, he was hiding a full-blown PTSD episode from Echo and would have to for the rest of his life. Or so he thought. Obviously, with Echo being the Knowledge Keeper in possession of second sight and having seen PTSD in so many of her fellow veterans, the truth lay elsewhere.

What was tied to those incidents was the ever-unsettling idea of his mother and the senator making love and doing so over time. The fact that they were truly in love, based on their correspondences, further complicated the situation. Zeb's mind bounced between all these thoughts like a ping pong ball hopped up on a combination of methamphetamines and crack cocaine.

Outside the National Cathedral Zeb and Echo stepped into a specially arranged limousine. Zeb asked the driver to take them to their hotel then. He shut the privacy window so he could speak confidentially to Echo.

"What's bothering you, Zeb?" asked Echo. "You're acting strangely."

"No, I'm not. It's just being here that's weird for both of us."

"Please tell me the truth."

Zeb lied.

"I was thinking about my mother."

An immediate reaction ripped through his mind. He couldn't shake the doom and gloom feeling that Echo knew everything. He sensed that reading his lies was no more difficult for her than slipping a hot knife through soft butter. The mere idea that his darkest private thoughts were not his alone brought a unique heaviness to his heart.

"What makes you ask?"

Echo pointed her finger at Zeb's face.

"Your nose gets all scrunchy when something is bugging you," replied Echo. "And your earlobes indent in the oddest way."

Zeb touched softly around his nose and lips. With thumb and first finger he caressed his ear lobe. These were 'tells' he was unaware of before Echo pointed them out. He attempted to make light of them.

"Hmm. I didn't know those things about myself. Having such obvious giveaways makes it incredibly difficult to keep secrets from you or even have a private thought, for that matter."

Zeb spoke with a forced chuckle. Echo did not think he was funny. Zeb felt her eyes searching him, stripping away the veneer of his lies. Quite possibly Echo was able to see to the depths of his soul. It was a frightening thought.

"I thought we agreed a long time ago to never keep secrets from each other," said Echo.

Her words landed on his ears like they could only come from someone who knew the exact truth. Echo, he knew, not only held his heart in her hands, but his ultimate fate was linked directly to her.

"I didn't mean I was keeping secrets from you. I only meant that it would be hard to do. That is, if I tried. I guess that works out for both of us. It keeps us honest."

"What else is on your mind?" asked Echo.

"I was thinking about Senator Russell."

"Good thoughts or bad thoughts?"

Echo knew the answer to her question but wanted to give Zeb the benefit of the doubt.

Zeb turned to his wife, the mother of his children, his partner for life, and allowed a little white lie to slip through his lips. He had long lived under a belief that little white lies hurt no one and therefore did not fall under the category of being actual, harmful lies. This was a lesson he had learned over and over from Pentecostal preachers. He had also inferred part of his white lies belief system from his Mormon upbringing. Truth be known, his mind was flooded with a sea of thoughts. He was thinking about Doreen, of both her life and her death. He was thinking about Carmelita and all that she had taught him, what she had taken from him and the life he ultimately took from her. He was thinking how Senator Russell was intricately wound into his past and wondering how his death might snake its way into his future. He shuddered at the almost infinite possibilities contained therein. But, that's not what he told Echo. Instead he chose the path of the little white lie.

"I was thinking about his death and Black Bear's death and what it means," replied Zeb. "I was also considering if those deaths were at all connected."

Echo knew instantly he was not speaking the entire truth. As a descendant of the great female warrior, Lozen, and as the Knowledge Keeper of all the First People, she carried a multitude of ancient skills. Intuition was near the top of her innate skill set.

"And?"

"And what?" asked Zeb.

"And what is your conclusion about his death and Black Bear's death and what it means."

Echo was holding Zeb's feet to the proverbial fire while giving him every leeway to tell her his entire truth.

"And...I'm uncertain as to what any of it means. Senator Russell was a powerful man. I do believe he had it in him to rid himself of anyone who might stand in his way," replied Zeb.

"Do you think Black Bear was standing in his way?"

Zeb paused. Black Bear was intricately linked to Senator Russell. That much Zeb was one hundred percent certain of. Could Black Bear have been enough of a threat in some way to Senator Russell that he had him killed? It was not out of the realm of possibility.

"I suspect he was," said Zeb. "Can I prove it? That's a horse of a different color."

"In your theory, because Black Bear was trouble for Senator Russell, he had him killed?"

"Not necessarily. I was standing in his way. He didn't kill me."

"But he made damn sure you didn't win the election," replied Echo.

"He could have killed me, or had me killed, if he had wanted to."

"But he didn't. If he absolutely needed you out of the picture so badly, why didn't he just have you accidentally killed?"

Echo used air quotes as she spoke the word, 'accidentally'.

"I think we both know the answer to that. He wouldn't have his own flesh and blood killed."

"I'd think twice about that. I don't think it would have mattered one iota that you were his son. The man knew no conscience."

"I never really got in his way. I am assuming that Black Bear must have."

"Maybe Black Bear had something he needed?" posed Echo.

"Perhaps."

"How deeply do you think the cartel was in bed with Russell?"

"About as deep as you can get. Why not? It stands to reason that the cartel and Russell mussed up the same sheets. Money and power often create odd and powerful alliances," replied Zeb.

"Why do I get the feeling you aren't telling me exactly what you think happened?" asked Echo.

Zeb slowly blinked his eyes as he looked down and to the right. It was yet another 'tell' that Echo recognized. He didn't want to tell her that he was almost certain that whatever this was, it was much bigger than just a U.S. Senator and a Mexican cartel. His delay in showing Echo the threatening letter and telling her about the picture of Carmelita taken immediately after her death made him look and feel less than forthcoming. It was obvious someone held the threat of exposure over Zeb's head. The unsigned note contained a mere nine words. DON'T RUN FOR SHERIFF! THINK ABOUT ELAN AND ONAWA. Clearly, someone was threatening him. But who? And exactly why? What was the end game? Echo, trained in human behavior and psychology and having practiced it at length during her time in Afghanistan, did not miss a single one of Zeb's body signals.

"Hmm?" asked Echo.

Zeb, lost in thought, did not reply, didn't even hear her say, 'hmm'. He knew Black Bear had made a fatal mistake by choosing to deal with the people he dealt with. It cost him his life. Whatever the gambit was, Graham County and Senator Russell were somehow linked to all of it. Zeb did not know exactly what to tell Echo. He didn't really have enough information to figure out who killed Black Bear, either.

Echo continued to watch Zeb. She would be patient. She knew the situation and the process weaving itself through Zeb's brain and mind was complex. She would allow Zeb time to let the truth bubble to the surface in a form that would be palatable enough to share with her. After all, what is love if not patient? Echo's mind slid into a memorized bible verse from her confirmation days when the Methodist Church had a strong presence on the Rez.

Love is patient, love is kind. It does not envy, it does not boast, it is not proud. It does not dishonor others, it is not self-seeking, it is not easily angered, it keeps no record of wrongs. Love does not delight in evil but rejoices with the truth. It always protects, always trusts, always hopes, always perseveres. Love never fails.

"I love you, Zeb."

Zeb looked up and into the eyes of the woman he cherished as much as life itself.

"I love you, too."

37

TOWN TALK

S ong Bird and Jake sipped coffee at the Town Talk. A wall
mounted television played and replayed the story of the dead
senator's life. Both men listened with half an ear.

"I guess we're all gonna die someday," said Jake.

"Yes," replied Song Bird. "Our bodies won't last forever. I trust our
spirits will."

Song Bird's statement was followed by a long and thoughtful
silence as both men momentarily pondered their mortality. Eventually Song Bird broke the quietness.

"That Senator Russell's demise happened in Safford was
somehow fitting. It was also somewhat ironic."

"How so?" asked Jake.

"His kidneys were failing," said Song Bird.

"Just about everyone knew that. I've heard he was also on the
short list for a kidney transplant."

"Funny that a man with his power couldn't bump himself up the
list and get at least one kidney donated to him."

No sooner had the words come out of Song Bird's mouth than
Maxine Miller, proprietor of the Town Talk, appeared at their table

with a carafe of coffee. She addressed Song Bird's comment as she poured the extra black java into his cup.

"He had a double transplant."

She spoke as though it were common knowledge. Maxine continued speaking as if Russell's double kidney transplant was anything but news.

"Did you fellas see Zeb and Echo sitting in the front row of the National Cathedral at the funeral?"

"No," said Song Bird. "We weren't watching all that closely."

"Whatever do you mean about the double transplant?" asked Jake.

"Yes," said Song Bird. "We've heard he was on a waiting list when he died."

"Well, according to Henrietta and Lana over at the spa, Senator Russell had been coming in for post-surgical massages for well over a month," explained Maxine.

"How did they know that?" asked Song Bird.

Maxine set down the Bunn coffee carafe on the table. With the first finger of each hand she drew imaginary lines just at the bottom of each side of her rib cage.

"Henrietta said he had big scars on both sides right where they do kidney surgery. She said if she's seen it once she's seen it a dozen times," replied Maxine.

"Did the late Senator Russell ever tell them that's what the scars were from? Did he tell them they were from kidney transplants?" asked Jake.

Maxine shrugged her shoulders.

"Well, now, I suppose he did. Why wouldn't he?"

"They told you he told them that he had kidney transplant surgery?" asked Song Bird.

"Well, no, not exactly. But they didn't have to. I just assumed that's what it was."

Jake and Song Bird looked at each other, half nodding and half shaking their heads. It seemed natural that Russell would have said something to them. Then again, he was a politician.

"Have you been listening to the news all morning?" asked Jake.

"Sure enough have," replied Maxine.

"Did they give any other details on Russell's death?"

"Depends on what station you listen to," replied Maxine.

"What did the conservative news station have to offer?" asked Jake.

"Conspiracy theories for the most part. They say he was purposefully given a cancerous kidney. They say that's what actually killed him," said Maxine. "It's hard to tell if stuff like that is fake news, or if it's the truth."

"Did they say what their source of that information was?" asked Jake.

"One person said the source was anonymous. Another source said it was some nurse who was in on the surgery. The story has been told both ways in the last few hours," replied Maxine.

"Odds are pretty good that you and I will never know the truth," said Jake.

"What did the liberal news station have to say?" asked Song Bird.

"According to them, and they hated him because of his stand on gun rights..."

"Right," interjected Jake.

"...they said they couldn't prove it, but the rumors were that he had surgical scars on his chest from a surgery after he had a heart attack."

"Did they say who their source on that was?"

Maxine blushed beet red. She bent forward and whispered like she was exposing some kind of secret.

"They said he had a heart attack a few months back."

"A heart attack? I didn't hear anything about that."

"Senator Russell's office kept it all hush-hush."

"Why would they do that?" asked Jake.

Maxine lowered her voice even further and spoke in a barely audible whisper.

"He was caught in bed with a lady of the night."

"A hooker?" asked Jake.

Maxine looked around to see if anyone had heard Jake's words. She was relieved when it appeared there was no one close enough to listen in.

"They called her both a lady of the night and a call girl. They said his heart exploded from all that Viagra he was taking. They said it was a fake kind of Viagra, like the kind they sell at gas stations. The TV guy said it was probably made in China and you could almost bet it had poison in it."

"Really?" said Song Bird.

"I guess you could say he died of a broken heart," interjected Jake.

"I'd say it was broke, but not broken," added Song Bird.

"Touché."

"The lady of the night was only twenty-five years old. Senator Russell is in his seventies. I suppose that accounts for something," added Maxine.

"He was too old to be messing around with a woman that young," said Song Bird.

"The blood that flowed through his heart was as bitter as cactus juice," said Jake. "That it exploded doesn't surprise me one bit. That rotten old blood of his probably ate right through the vessels of his heart."

"Russell was truly a son of a bitch," added Song Bird.

"I guess that made him an old son of a bitch."

"He should have known better than to have sex with a woman one-third his age," said Jake.

"He should have been more age appropriate," added Song Bird. "It might have saved his life. I know some old Indian gals that can still wiggle their hips pretty good. I think any one of them could give me a heart attack, given the chance."

Jake smiled and chuckled lightly. Maxine blushed but listened closely. Both men knew the pilot light that drove their sexuality was barely a flicker of a flame and for the most part merely a memory.

But what hung on their minds was the cruelty Senator Russell had performed over a lifetime, a lifetime punctuated by numerous, nefarious, evil deeds. His death, coming however it did, when it did, could have been much worse. If it was a heart attack and he had been driving, he might have taken others with him. If he had accidentally received a cancerous kidney, better him than some innocent person.

"Gone," said Jake. "But a long way from forgotten."

Both men lifted their coffee mugs to their lips. Though they were older men, their hands did not tremble in the least. Also, because of their age, Russell's death neither fazed nor delighted them. They had simply outlived an enemy. That in and of itself was but a small victory. Both men were acutely aware that Father Time and Brother Death would never be deterred. Song Bird raised his coffee mug to Jake.

"To Mother Earth."

"To renewal," replied Jake.

As though the universe itself were listening in on the men, Maxine turned off the TV and turned on KUAZ radio, the local NPR affiliate out of Tucson. They were doing a show on the late Ralph Stanley and his band, The Clinch Mountain Boys. Their final hit song, the haunting ballad, *Oh Death*, opened the program.

"I suppose there are worse ways to die," said Jake.

"In the end, it's all probably just about the same," said Song Bird.

"Yup, dead is dead. That's for sure."

"It's what happens after death that's the big surprise," said Song Bird.

Once again, the men toasted coffee mugs. This time to their own deaths and the big surprise that followed.

As Song Bird and Jake sat in silent remembrance of a man they cared little for, they had a surprise visitor, Shappa. At her side was Rambler Braing. She was looking for Zeb who had not yet returned from Senator Russell's funeral. Song Bird and Jake stood to greet her.

"Shappa, I trust Black Bear's Lakota end of life ceremony went well," said the medicine man.

"Thank you, Song Bird. He has entered another realm and is at peace," replied Shappa.

Song Bird bowed his head gracefully. Shappa returned the gesture, only she did not bow her head as low as Song Bird had.

"Can I help you with something?" asked Jake. "With Zeb out of town until tomorrow, Kate's in charge. But if I can, I'll help you."

"I have something I want you to pass onto Zeb," said Shappa.

"Have a seat," offered Song Bird.

Shappa chose to remain standing.

"This will only take a second," replied Shappa.

"What do you want me to tell Zeb?" asked Jake.

"The words are directly from my son. They are not my words," replied Shappa.

Song Bird tuned in tightly. Maxine, receiving a harsh look from Shappa, walked away from the private conversation.

"Yes?"

"It's important that you tell Zeb these words are from Black Bear."

"I got it," replied Jake.

"Black Bear wanted Zeb to know that Senator Russell was the money behind Black Bear's campaign for Sheriff of Graham County."

"I think Zeb is well aware of that fact," replied Jake. "Black Bear indirectly implied on numerous occasions that the senator wanted him as sheriff. Your son was also aware that Russell wanted Zeb out of the picture. I suppose now that Senator Russell is dead, it doesn't really matter who backed your son."

Shappa let out an incongruous bit of laughter. Even though it was highly likely no one at the café cared for or would miss Russell, Shappa's reaction seemed strange.

"I heard on the radio a young woman stole the heart right from his chest," said Shappa.

The crudeness of her words carried a dark implication to Jake. Anyone who would use such off-putting words about the recently deceased must have some sort of dog in the hunt. Jake's mind immediately went to a place that suggested it was Shappa's belief that Senator Russell was linked to the death of her son, Black Bear. Song Bird heard it differently. Shappa's sharpness implied to him that she had woven a web of deceit. About what and regarding whom, he could only guess.

The detective inside Jake rose to the surface. None of what

Shappa was saying made sense. Why would Black Bear have prepared before his death to send a message to Zeb, especially since what he was passing on was old information? Jake was immediately convinced Shappa had something up her sleeve. Whatever it was, Jake had no doubt Zeb would be on the receiving end of something bad that would be coming directly from Shappa.

"Senator Russell has a home here. It's a few miles outside of Safford. The family, some shirttail relatives, third and fourth cousins are having an open casket funeral service at the church day after tomorrow. I've heard they plan on dispersing the ashes at some future point. Since the Senator was so close with Black Bear, I am certain they would be honored if you would be in attendance." said Jake.

When Shappa answered without a fraction of a second's hesitation, something growled in Jakes guts.

"Of course. I would love to honor the man who helped my son rise to a position of prominence," said Shappa.

The sarcasm in her voice was unmistakable.

"In case you need to know, Zeb will be back late tomorrow night," said Jake.

"I have one other bit of information for Zeb. This one's from me, not Black Bear. Will you pass it onto him as well?" asked Shappa.

"Of course."

"Tell him I have information on where he might locate the gun that killed my son."

Jake was stunned.

"You can give me the information," said Jake.

Shappa smiled wryly.

"Oh, I don't think that would be such a smart idea," replied Shappa.

"What do you mean?"

"You know exactly what I mean."

"I'm afraid I don't," replied Jake.

"Let me just say that if this information ends up in the wrong hands, the gun might never be found."

With that Shappa walked out the door.

"What the hell is she talking about?" asked Song Bird.

"No idea," replied Jake. "But it felt like she was implying I was involved or that you or I might dispose of the gun if we got our hands on it."

Jake felt his chest tighten and his left arm becoming numb. A bout of dizziness and lightheadedness suddenly overcame him. He turned pale.

"You feeling okay?" asked Song Bird.

"Not so hot. I'm headed home."

"Do you want a ride?"

Jake coughed hard and slammed his fist against his chest over his heart.

"No. I'm fine to drive."

38

SENATOR RUSSELL'S SAFFORD FUNERAL

S enator Russell's people insisted Zeb and Echo ride on the private jet that carried the body back to Safford. Zeb was hesitant, but, ultimately, he and Echo accepted the invitation at Echo's insistence.

The Safford branch of the Church of Jesus Christ of Latter-day Saints was packed to overflowing for the review of Senator Russell's body. Practically everyone from town and half the folks from the reservation were in attendance. Noticeably absent was Deputy Jake Dablo.

While waiting for the funeral service that followed the viewing, Shappa slid into the seat next to Zeb and Echo. Zeb, feeling a tad awkward sitting between the women, fielded questions from Shappa.

"Why are they called Latter-Day Saints?" she asked.

The huge crowd made it possible to chat quietly without being disruptive.

"The name is a restoration for modern times of the original Church of Jesus Christ which was lost in the Dark Ages."

Zeb's answer was word for word from his studies as a teen in the church's Mutual Improvement Association classes.

"Why isn't there a cross or a crucifix in this church?"

"It is not permitted. Latter-Day Saints believe in the bodily resurrection of Christ," replied Zeb. "Basically, for that reason, the cross is not a necessity. It reflects Christ's death while the Latter-Day Saints choose to focus on the living Christ."

Once again Zeb was being quite literal to his studies as a youth.

"Is there always an open casket?"

"That is a personal choice of the deceased or their family."

A dozen questions later, Shappa simply folded her gloved hands in her lap and stared straight ahead. Zeb couldn't help but notice each finger of both hands had rings on them. Without staring he glanced sideways at her pinky fingers. Both, like all of her fingers, were ringed. He could not tell if the rings on the small fingers were identical. The ring on her left hand seemed to tail off and curve to the left at the bottom. Zeb wanted more than anything for her to remove the glove so he could have a better look at the ring.

Shappa, after sitting quietly for a few minutes, excused herself to make a trip to the ladies' room. She politely asked Echo if she wanted to join her. When Echo declined, Zeb waited until Shappa exited the pew to say anything. He spoke to Echo with great urgency.

"Follow her into the bathroom. When she takes off her gloves to wash her hands, try and get a look at the rings on her pinky fingers. I'm particularly interested in the one on her left hand."

"Did you see a ring that might match or at least be similar to the others you've been looking for?" asked Echo.

"I don't know for certain. Maybe. But please try and get a close look."

Echo discretely departed for the ladies' room. She was touching up her makeup as Shappa came out of the toilet stall. Shappa acted as though she didn't see Echo and went to the farthest sink to wash her hands. It took only a few seconds for her to discretely remove her gloves and wash her hands. From that position, the view of Shappa's left hand was blocked by her body. But Echo's keen eye caught sight of the ring on the small finger of her left hand in the reflection of the mirror. At the part nearest the knuckle it tailed off to the left, which was the right side in the mirror image, like the tail of an animal.

Secondly, she noticed a tightly wound band-aid on the first finger of Shappa's right hand. Dexterously, she removed it, tossed it away and replaced it with a thin, clear band-aid that she deftly removed from her small purse. She moved with such coordinated skill that the whole process took less than a half of a minute.

When her hands were once again gloved, Shappa noticed Echo and struck up brief, inane small talk. Echo excused herself, saying she had to check her lipstick and watched closely as Shappa departed the ladies' room. Standing in front of the same sink Shappa had used, Echo removed a tube of lipstick from her purse and checked the door to make certain Shappa did not return to the ladies' room. Using a pair of tweezers that she grabbed from her purse, Echo snatched the discarded band-aid. She placed it in a Kleenex and placed the slightly bloodied band-aid into her purse before returning to the pew.

When she arrived back at the pew, Zeb was gone. Catching Shappa out of the corner of her eye, Echo noticed she was looking up toward the open casket. Both women noticed Zeb had returned to the line to have one more look at the remains of the late Senator Russell.

"It looks like he's making it a long goodbye," said Shappa.

"He's funny that way. At his mother's funeral Zeb made a dozen return trips to have one last look. Unusual, if you ask me," said Echo.

Shappa gave a compassionate reply.

"We all mourn in our own way. Zeb has to do what he must. This can't be easy on him. It must be terribly difficult to find out a man is your father and have him die the same day."

Echo did not let the look on her face betray the thoughts behind her eyes. How could Shappa possibly have that tidbit of information? How could she have known Russell was Zeb's father on the same day the senator passed?

Echo sneaked a peek at the ring on the little finger of Shappa's left hand, memorizing it. This time she noticed the gloves were extremely tight fitting, almost form fitting exactly to Shappa's finger size. An idea popped into her head. She reached over and lightly held Shappa's left hand. As she rested her thumb against the side of Shappa's little finger, Echo slowly ran her first finger up, down and across the ring, memorizing all she touched. Enhanced tactility was yet another of the Knowledge Keeper's unique skills. Shappa didn't so much as draw back her hand as Echo spoke while she simultaneously examined the surface of the pinky ring.

"Yes. You are correct about how we grieve. Having just lost your son, it is likely you have an enhanced intuition about such things."

Shappa, a woman with a unique skill set all her own, sensed Echo was delicately fingering her ring. She reached over and placed her hand on top of Echo's, stopping the examination of the ring's surface.

"Thank you, my dear."

Shappa gently patted the exploratory hand, removed it from her own and placed it on Echo's leg.

Echo had discovered one piece of vital information. Not only did the ring tail off to one side, but it had two elevated letters. They felt like a G, as in Grand and a M, as in Master. The trouble was she had no way of being absolutely certain. Being close was not good enough. Being wrong could be misleading or deadly.

Zeb returned to the pew and whispered to Echo.

"I wanted to have one last look."

"We noticed how intensely you were looking into the casket," said Shappa. "Looking at something in particular?"

Indeed, he had been. But what he was looking for was none of Shappa's business. He responded with a blatant lie.

"No, I was just having one final private goodbye with a man who evidently had more to do with my life that I will ever know or understand."

In fact, he had noticed something. It was something he should have caught earlier. At the body review during the funeral in the National Cathedral Senator Russell had a ring on the little finger of his left hand. The way things were set up at the National Cathedral in D.C., no one could get close to the body.

At that time all Zeb could see was the presence of a gold ring on the little finger of Senator Russell's left hand. Here, in Safford, Zeb could get a much closer look. It took no time at all for Zeb to realize the senator had no ring on the little finger of his left hand. If it was in one of his pockets, it would be melted at the crematorium and ultimately given to the next of kin in a small jar. If it were melted, a piece of solid evidence directly linking Senator Russell to the Guardians of the Golden Flame would be eradicated. Zeb needed to know if the ring existed, where it was and precisely what it looked like. Crucial evidence lost at this point might make all else moot.

After the funeral ceremony, Zeb and Echo made small talk with Shappa who seemed in a hurry to leave. After Shappa was out of their line of sight, Echo opened her purse. She pointed at the band-aid that was resting atop the Kleenex.

"What've you got there?" asked Zeb.

"A sample of Shappa's blood."

Zeb caressed her back, leaned over and whispered in Echo's ear.

"Well done."

39

THE RING

S helly had spent hours manipulating the CSPAN footage of Senator Russell's funeral. Fortunately, she had set her television to record two hours before all the proceedings began. For the most part the first two hours told the history of the late senator's life. However, they did spend a few short minutes showing the funeral home that was handling the arrangements in D.C., arriving with the casket, opening it and setting up the front of the church for public viewing. It was then she discovered something no one else probably had seen.

Shelly honed-in on the late senator's body. She magnified and used her unique skill set to make the footage of interest sharp and distinct. When she had it as clear as she could possibly make it, Shelly buzzed Zeb's office.

"Yup?"

"Zeb, do you have a minute?"

"I do."

"Could you spend that minute in my office now?" asked Shelly.

"Be there in two shakes of a lamb's tail."

Shelly found some of Zeb's idioms to be nonsensical and

outdated, yet somehow a tad endearing. A minute later he walked through her door.

"What do you have for me?"

Shelly pointed to her oversized computer screen. She placed her finger on the image of Senator Russell at repose in the casket. Both the cap panel and the foot panel of the casket cover were wide open, presenting a clear and unobstructed view of the late Senator Russell's body.

"That."

Zeb leaned in. She was pointing to his hands which were at his side as opposed to being crossed on his chest.

"The little finger of the left hand."

Zeb put on his glasses and focused closely on what Shelly had observed. On the small finger of his left hand was a beautifully designed gold ring. The first thing he noticed was that as it neared the knuckle it curved off to the left, like it had a tail. What he saw excited him.

"It looks like a dragon's tail."

"I believe it is exactly that," replied Shelly.

She brought up another screen. It was an image that matched the ring.

"Look at this," said Shelly.

She pointed to two letters on the band of the ring, a capital G and a capital M.

"They stand for Grand Master. He was the Grand Master of the Guardians of the Golden Flame."

"That puts a twist into everything. I always assumed he was linked to the cult, but I had no inkling he was the Grand Master of the Guardians of the Golden Flame."

Shelly took out her camera. She dexterously plugged a mini USB end of a cable into the camera panel and the other end into the USB port on her computer.

"Now look at this."

During the body review in Safford, Shelly had surreptitiously taken photos of the inside of the late senator's casket by reaching into the casket with her cellphone. She had purposely focused in on the late senator's left hand. What she found was something that wasn't there, the ring of the Grand Master.

"No ring," replied Zeb.

Shelly flipped back over to a computer page she had lifted from a public FBI file that described the inner workings of the cult.

"The ring that is missing is hundreds of years old. It can only be worn by the Grand Master of the Guardians of the Golden Flame, according to research done by an FBI agent who infiltrated the group some years ago."

"I take it you've read through all of the available material?" asked Zeb.

"I have."

"Anything else of value jump out at you? I mean anything we can use?" asked Zeb.

"Lots," said Shelly. "But most interesting, at least to me, is the fact that the Grand Master can be either a man or a woman."

"Hmm..."

Zeb was puzzled by what conclusion Shelly might be drawing.

"My guess..."

"Is that after the viewing and before the body arrived in Safford someone was able to steal the ring," interjected Zeb.

"Right."

"And you're thinking it could now be on the little finger of either a man or a woman," added Zeb.

"Right again."

"Whoever has the ring is the new Grand Master. That person has access to all the information and power that goes along with being the leader of the group," said Zeb.

"Which, according to the FBI file, is control of hundreds, maybe thousands of people, hundreds of millions of dollars in gold and the ability to organize a whole lot of criminal activity," said Shelly.

"But the first step is to figure out who took the ring, when they took it, where it went and where it is now," said Zeb.

"Absolutely," replied Shelly.

"There were plenty of opportunities for that to happen. From the time the last of the viewers had left the National Cathedral to the time when the casket was being moved by hearse from the Cathedral to the airplane. Even in the airplane I noticed several people going in and out of the part of the plane that held the casket. Someone inside the cult could have had access numerous times."

"Or just a common thief could have taken it."

"Right," said Zeb. "At many times there could have been a thief around."

Zeb turned his attention to the onscreen page that described the cult in detail. Shelly had already highlighted what she felt were the most important facts for him.

"I'd be willing to bet if we find the ring, we have a direct connection to Black Bear's murder and likely all the shenanigans that have been going on in and around Graham County," said Zeb.

"That's a pretty good bet," replied Shelly.

Zeb, paused, deep in thought.

"What are you thinking?" asked Shelly.

"Whoever is currently wearing that ring could possibly be the key to everything."

"Sounds logical," replied Shelly. "Wait a sec, what do you mean everything?"

"Black Bear's death, Senator Russell's death, the school shooting, the robbery at Swig's..."

"Faux robbery," interjected Shelly.

"Whatever, the faux stabbings at the Desert Rose and the tampering with the city water supply. Everything has been a setup so one power hungry person could hold the reins as the Grand Master of the Guardians of the Golden Flame."

"To gain such a position must mean everything to them," said Shelly.

"According to the web page, maybe as much as a half billion dollars in gold is involved. It notes there are also jewels, property, ancient knowledge and all sorts of other things related to power of leadership."

"I read that," said Shelly. "Do you really think it's all true?"

"I don't know for certain, but I have no doubt it could be true."

"How can you be so certain?"

"I've got a lot of reasons..."

Zeb could not share the secrets Echo, as the Knowledge Keeper, had revealed to him. The hieroglyphs in the Galiuro Mountains spoke at length about numerous longstanding cults including the Guardians of the Golden Flame. Echo had told him only parts of what she had learned. One thing she did make abundantly clear was that the Grand Master of the Guardians had never used the power for good. Throughout history it had been used only for evil.

"...but I can't share what I know with you. I wish I could because I know it would help you find other leads, but I can't."

Shelly immediately knew his secrecy in the matter had to do with Echo. She didn't press the issue.

"Makes sense."

"Now I need to find out who had access to the body between D.C. and here," said Zeb. "Like I said earlier, I'll have a look into the people at the funeral home, the people on the plane that carried the body, etcetera, etcetera. I could use your help."

"I'm on it," said Shelly.

Kate knocked on the edge of the open door and walked in.

"Anybody seen Jake?"

"No," replied Zeb. "I left a couple of messages for him. He hasn't gotten back to me yet. That's not like him. He's probably busy with something."

"I've been trying to get hold of him since late yesterday," said Kate. "He hasn't answered me either. He's never, ever done that to me before. I don't believe he's ignoring me. It just feels strange that he's been absent with all that's going on."

"He wasn't at the viewing. That surprised me. It is very un-Jake like to miss something so important. He's been a stickler his whole career about criminals and funerals. You know, the old adage that criminals show up at funerals to have one last look at the results of their crime," said Zeb.

"You're right," said Kate. "He taught me early on that post-crime scene evaluations and funerals often are hotbeds of information."

"Who's on rural patrol today?"

"I am," replied Kate.

"Start out by Jake's place. See if he's around. Ask him to get hold of me."

"Will do. I'm headed out right now. Do you need me for anything else?"

"No. Just let me know what's up with Jake. Just from us talking about him, I've got a bad feeling welling up inside of me."

"Probably just the vibe from the funeral and being around Shappa," replied Kate.

Zeb shrugged his shoulders. He wished it were that straightforward, but he knew it was something more than that.

Kate scooted out of the office and to the rural patrol truck. She was as concerned as everyone was about Jake. It wasn't just because of his absence at the funeral. He had been seemingly out of sorts as of late.

"I'll give Shepner's Funeral Home a call and see if Jimmy Shepner knows anything about the ring," said Shelly. "I've done some computer work for him, so I know he'll talk to me. Is it okay if I tell him it's a request directly from you, Zeb?"

"Of course. Do it right away," ordered Zeb.

Zeb headed to his office and rang up Jake once more. No one answered either his land line or his cellphone. Ten minutes later Shelly knocked on Zeb's office door.

"What'd you find out from Jimmy Shepner?"

"I had a nice chat with Jimmy at the funeral home. The casket was sealed when it arrived on the plane. That is a standard protocol. He told me he had to unseal it when it arrived. He was also certain the seal had not been tampered with. He explained it was also standard protocol to check for tampering."

"That pretty much rules out anything happening while Senator Russell's body was on the plane," said Zeb. "We can assume the ring had to have been taken while the body was being handled in D.C. or after Shepner's worked on it and took it to the church."

"Can you get a peek at the footage of Senator Russell's body while it was being set up for the reviewal at the church here in town?" asked Zeb.

"I'll get right on it. The local LDS church has up-to-date equipment. I also got some footage of the casket while it was still at the National Cathedral but the reviewal was over. I'll have a tight look at that as well."

"Good. Let me know when you get something, anything."

Shelly likely didn't hear him as she was already out his door and headed to her computer.

Zeb's stomach growled. A lightbulb went on in his head. How could he have forgotten? Was his memory correct? He grabbed his cellphone and called Echo.

"Hey, Zeb. What's up?"

"I have a question. I'm asking you because I know you have a greater eye for detail than I do," said Zeb.

"For a man, yours is pretty darn good. What can I help you with?"

"Close your eyes."

Echo smiled sweetly. Zeb was using a debriefing trick she had taught him. It was something a head intelligence officer had taught her in Afghanistan. God, how she loved Zeb.

"When we were leaving the memorial service in D.C...."

"Yes, I'm there in my mind. After it was over, right?"

"Right. Use your mind to scan what you saw."

Echo was silent for well over a minute.

"I've got it. The woman in the blonde wig."

Zeb breathed a sigh of relief. It was exactly who he had in mind. He remembered her because she seemed too dark skinned to have platinum blonde hair. And, there was something funny about her hands.

"Her hands," cried Echo. "She had a golden ring on her pinky finger."

"YES! Do you see anything else?"

"Nicely dressed in a dark blue dress. Wait. Wait. She had an ankle tattoo. I remember how odd I thought it was for her to have a tattoo on her ankle. Not that it's a bad thing. She just didn't seem the type."

"Any idea or memory of what the ankle tattoo was?"

Another long minute of silence led into a second minute. Echo was deeply into a state of meditative reflection. Zeb could sense, even over the phone, that she was transfixed. He heard the babies fussing in the background. He knew they might break her concentration. Echo may have been the Knowledge Keeper and blessed with extraordinary powers, but she was first and foremost a mother.

"Sorry, Zeb. That's all I have."

"It's good enough. I've got a second source. I'll get on that. I love you."

"Love you too, Zeb. But I got to run. The kids are hungry."

Zeb set his cellphone down and rang up Shelly. When she answered, Zeb could tell she was eating something.

"Yah?" asked Shelly.

"I know exactly where you need to look and what you need to look for."

"Let me have it."

Zeb described the crucial time as just after the memorial ended and most people had departed.

"A woman walking toward the casket before it was closed. She wore a classy, dark blue dress and had platinum hair. The color of her skin didn't seem to match the lightness of her hair. There was a tattoo on her left ankle."

"Any idea of what the tattoo was?"

"No, sorry. That's all I have."

"Hold on, let me pull up the footage." Zeb only had to wait about fifteen seconds. "Found her. Platinum hair must be a wig. She's dark skinned, alright."

"Can you see who she's with?"

"She's walking ahead of people who look like officials handling the casket. The officials are probably from the local funeral home or Secret Service. All men and all dressed in black suits. Several have wrist communication devices. If I had to venture a guess, I'd say they're Secret Service."

"How far ahead of them is she?"

Shelly noted the digital timer on her computer screen and watched the seconds tick by as the woman walked solo to the casket with the officials behind her.

"Ten seconds. Nine point eight three seconds to be precise. The Secret Service agents seem to be patiently waiting for the church to empty. From what I can see when I scan in closely on them, they are paying little, if any, attention to her."

Shelly went into a play-by-play that reminded Zeb of a soft-spoken announcer at golf tournament.

"She kneels by the open casket. Her back is to the camera. From the looks of it she reaches inside the casket at or very near its center. She is quick, remarkably deft with her actions. Every move seems calculated. She remains kneeling. Eleven-point two seconds pass. She rises up and off the kneeler. Slowly and deliberately she walks away. She departs right in front of the men I have presumed to be Secret Service agents. She nods slightly at one man. I've seen him giving orders to the other men. I assume he is the one in charge of the others. Exactly four seconds later she walks out of the camera view. I know from the layout of the cathedral she is walking toward one of the exit doors of the church building."

"What are the odds of getting a facial ID on her?" asked Zeb.

"Based on the camera angles, I'd say fifty-fifty at best. Then I'd have to say I'd be guessing some. I don't think I can tell you beyond a shadow of a doubt who she is."

"Do what you can. Put it on the top of your to do list."

"I'm on it."

Things were getting hot. Zeb was moving in on either the killer or someone close to the killer. For the first time in days, his hope outweighed his doubt.

40

GOODBYE JAKE

The first thing Kate noticed as she pulled into Jake's driveway was that his car was not parked under the carport. The second thing she eyeballed was Jake's driver's door. It was not completely shut. It was the type of detail that Jake found annoying in others. He considered such an action to fall under the category of carelessness. Therefore, it was unlikely he would have made that kind of mistake.

An odd feeling, strange enough to make Kate shiver, ran up and down her arms as she called out, "Jake?"

No response.

Maybe he had been robbed? Maybe someone had shot him? Maybe he was in the trailer injured or dead? She loosened her holster and removed her weapon. There was no need to check to see if she had a bullet in the chamber. That was an automatic way of doing things as both Zeb and her husband, Josh, had taught her. She moved stealthily toward the trailer.

"Jake. You in there? You awake? You decent?"

The second question was absurd as Jake was an early riser. Everyone knew that. The third question was a hopeful joke.

She stepped on the stoop of the porch. Moving her head slowly, she stopped and peeked through the curtained front window. It was semi-dark inside. Nothing unusual appeared in her line of sight. No movement was apparent. Her eyes drifted to the front door. The door was ajar. That too was an indicator that something was wrong. She tightened the grip on her weapon. Kate knocked on the door, softly at first, then loudly. The lack of an answer increased her heart rate, heightened her senses and enhanced her overall alert level. Maybe he was in the shower? She pressed an ear against the outdoor screen. Again, nothing.

"Jake? It's Kate. You home?"

Something was wrong. She mumbled "fuck" under her breath and gently, quietly opened the door. One tiny step at a time she slipped through the threshold. Inside no one was moving about. Out of the quiet the sound of a clock radio playing old-timey country and western music came into earshot. She knew the radio station. It was Jake's favorite. A quick conclusion was that Jake's morning alarm had gone off, but he had not turned it down or shut it off. That too was strange. She hoped against hope that he was out for a morning walk. What were the odds of that? Practically nil. Once again, she cussed under her breath. This time she whispered, "Jake?" Once again, no response.

A quick perusal of the living room and kitchen, the front half of Jake's trailer, told her nothing, other than that Jake kept a neat house. The bathroom door was half-opened. She nudged it gently with her shoulder, keeping her weapon at the ready. Nothing. She glanced down the hall toward the two bedrooms. She knew the one at the end of the hall was Jake's. She headed down the short hallway as noiselessly as possible. Kate stuck her head in the spare bedroom. It was neat as a pin. It looked as if no one had been in there for days, maybe even weeks.

The door to Jake's bedroom was three-quarters shut. Kate opened it by pushing with the toe of her right foot. The hinges must have been recently oiled as even in this old trailer they did not creak. Her eyes naturally went immediately to Jake's bed. Her heart sunk. There lay Jake, unmoving and ashen. She had seen it before. He had the classic look of a dead man.

Kate placed her weapon into her holster and walked directly to the body. Jake's eyes were partially open. He looked peaceful, serene. Her hand went immediately to his wrist. Not even the slightest of pulsations bumped up against her fingers. She touched Jake on the neck, checking for a carotid pulse. Nothing. He was cold to the touch. Some early signs of rigor mortis had already begun to set in. Tears dropped, landing on the sheets by Jake's hand.

Memories began trickling in. Jake had mentored Kate. He had encouraged her at every turn and given her confidence in a job that before her had been only held by men in Graham County. He was the first to accept her skills and abilities. Jake had truly changed her life for the better. She sat in the chair, rested her hand on Jake's shoulder as she offered up a silent prayer. She said 'amen' aloud before pulling out her cellphone.

"Zeb."

"You sound terrible. What's going on, Kate?" asked Zeb.

"It's Jake."

Zeb's mouth immediately dried up as his heart rate zoomed.

"He's dead."

When he sent Kate to check on Jake, Zeb had been overcome with a bad feeling. But death, although it was within the broader spectrum of possibilities on his mind, was not what Zeb had believed would happen.

"I'll be right out. I'll also call Shepner's to pick up the body. Any reason to expect foul play from what you're looking at?"

"Nothing that is readily apparent. It appears as though he barely made it out of his truck and into the house where he plopped onto the bed and died."

"I hope he went quickly and without pain. Jake was a damn good man."

"He was one of the best."

"He changed my life."

"Mine too."

"Give the house and his truck a once over. See if you spot anything unusual."

"Yes, Zeb. I will do that."

"I'll be there in fifteen minutes or less."

Their mutual pain from of the loss of a man they both loved evoked an atmospheric heaviness. At the moment there was really nothing more to say.

While Kate waited for Zeb and Shepner's, she checked out Jake's truck, eyeballed the perimeter of the property and began detailing out the inside of Jake's trailer. Only one thing struck her as strange. On top of Jake's gun safe was a box of .22 caliber short bullets. Five bullets were missing from the box. No .22 pistol was in sight. Automatically, Kate gloved up and had a look.

Jake's key ring lay on the bed next to his dead fingers. He must have carried it into the house and kept it in his hand when he found his way to the bed. On it was the key to his gun safe. Kate removed it and opened the safe. There was no .22 caliber rifle, handgun or pistol.

Kate went to her vehicle and grabbed several evidence bags. In one she placed Jake's keys. In the other, she put the partially used box of .22 caliber short shells. She stopped in the middle of her task. This was about Jake Dablo, yet she was following basic protocol. She felt wholly inadequate. Guilt overcame her at the thought of merely following proper procedures and protocol. What she was feeling and what she was doing didn't seem to be enough. All of that would soon change.

She heard Zeb pull into the driveway, slam his door shut and walk across the gravel and dirt to the trailer door. In the quiet of an otherwise perfectly peaceful day, her hearing was significantly amplified.

"Kate?"

"Back here in the bedroom," responded Kate.

Zeb stopped in his tracks as his eyes fell on his longtime friend and professional mentor's dead body."

He reached over and automatically checked for a pulse. The ugliest kind of cold and darkness ran through his fingertips.

"Shit."

"I know."

"Strange, isn't it, how you hope against hope? In my mind and in my heart I was hoping it was all a bad dream, a mistake, that maybe you had missed his pulse and he still had some life in him."

"I know."

Zeb noticed the evidence-bagged .22 caliber pistol shells.

"Jake and I must be the last two old timers who still use .22 Remington shorts."

As the words left his mouth, Zeb realized he had just made himself a prime suspect in the case of Sheriff Sawyer Black Bear. The look Kate shot in his direction verified his thinking.

"I didn't shoot Black Bear," said Zeb.

The way he said it made him sound guilty as hell. Kate continued slowly working the scene, gathering anything of value that might tell her anything about either Jake's untimely demise or Black Bear's death.

"No one is suggesting you did. I'm just following fundamental protocol."

Zeb gloved up and took a closer look at the .22 shell box. He looked at it then at Kate.

"What?" asked Kate.

"I don't want to put a noose around my own neck, but these are my shells," said Zeb.

"What are these doing here?"

"Beats the hell out of me."

"How do you know they're yours? Don't all Remington .22 boxes look exactly alike?"

Zeb flipped the box upside down. He pointed to some barely visible printing.

"I always mark the date I bought the shells on the bottom of the box. I don't like shooting old shells. I remember this date and distinctly remembering buying them."

"Maybe you lent Jake a box?"

"Nope. Never did. I wouldn't. He didn't even own a .22. I know that for a fact."

"Then how did they get here? And what are they doing here?"

Zeb took off his hat and wiped the sweat from his brow with the shirtsleeve on his forearm before replacing the hat on his head.

"Kate are you comfortable with me helping you?" asked Zeb.

Being that he was potentially a suspect in the death of Black Bear, Zeb was uncertain if being part of detailing the scene of Jake's death might foul the chain of evidence.

"Hell, yes," said Kate. "But if anything seems at all like it could be linked to Black Bear's death, let me handle it."

"Okay."

"Give Jake's body a close once over," ordered Kate.

Zeb looked over at the dead man who had spent a lifetime mentoring him. He suddenly felt like the lost little boy whom Jake had saved from a life of despondency. It was one of those rare moments in a person's life when one's mind is both maximally saturated with thought while being simultaneously devoid of the ability to think clearly. Handling Jake's dead body was the last thing he wanted to do but it was also the least he could do. He gulped.

"I can do that."

"What do you think about a box of bullets with five missing shells?" asked Kate.

Zeb realized he had not told Kate he had found the gun.

"This is going to sound strange, but I have the gun," said Zeb.

Kate's response was barely masked by the shock in her voice.

"You do? How did you end up with it?"

"I found it in Dead Bunny Creek."

Kate's eyes widened as her gaze took in every part of Zeb's essence. His story was unfathomable for many reasons. Dead Bunny Creek was in the middle of nowhere. What was he doing out that way to being with? How on earth would Zeb have found a gun in a dry creek bed? Zeb easily read the level of doubt in Kate's eyes.

"It's a long story. Essentially, I was tracking down a lead on Black Bear's murder when I stopped to take a leak. The gun was just lying there in the middle of nowhere in Dead Bunny Creek. That is the long and short of it. Honest to God, I know it sounds unbelievable."

"Jesus, Zeb, I hope this doesn't end up in court. If you testify to that, who in their right mind is going to believe you?"

"I know. I know. But I swear to God Almighty that is the absolute truth."

"I'll need you to put it all in writing."

"I will."

"I also need the gun."

Zeb took a step toward the doorway when Kate stopped him.

"Where is it? In your car? Better let me bag it."

"It's sitting on the front seat."

"I'll be right back. Please don't touch anything while you are not in my presence," said Kate.

Zeb knew Kate was merely following the appropriate procedures. Still, it felt wrong and made him feel guilty of something he had no part of. Less than a minute later Kate returned with the .22 Sharps Rimfire Derringer bagged as evidence.

"Could this possibly have Jake's fingerprints on it?" asked Kate.

"It could."

"Your fingerprints?"

"I was cleaning the gun. I always do that with gloves on. It may or may not have my prints on it."

"Okay."

"Come on. Let's get to work. We are going to be scrutinized like crazy on this. Everything has to be done to the letter of the law. Kate, think hard. When you first started looking at the scene did anything seem out of place or wrong."

"No. Yes. It struck me as odd that the bullets weren't in the safe. It looks as though he barely made it from his truck to his bed. I doubt he would have carried the .22 shell box in with him when he came home and placed it on top of the safe before he laid down."

Zeb listened. He was having more than a little trouble concentrating. He knew Kate was probably correct as she described a man who was likely having a heart attack taking the time to grab a box of shells.

"You're certain Jake didn't borrow your .22?"

"One hundred percent certain," replied Zeb.

"Did he have a key to your house?"

"He did."

"Did he know the combination to your gun safe?" asked Kate.

"Affirmative," replied Zeb.

"Maybe he wanted to borrow your gun when you were in Paris and helped himself?" said Kate.

"Doubtful. I don't know why he would have done that. It doesn't make any sense for him to do something like that. He would have mentioned it to me by now anyway," replied Zeb.

"I checked the chambers and noticed one bullet had been fired. Or at least one chamber was empty and the other three were full," said Kate.

"You're lucky you didn't blow a finger off," said Zeb.

"I know my way around this gun," said Kate. "Believe me, when you live with someone who owns a gun shop, you learn more than your fair share of details concerning weapons. I know how easily the Sharps .22 can misfire because the firing pin is extended from the hammer and it has to be loaded while the gun is half-cocked."

Kate placed the bagged Sharps .22 next to the bagged box of bullets. Zeb watched as she stared at the evidence. She shook her head.

"I wonder why Jake had your partially used box of .22 short shells to begin with. I mean, he didn't own a .22. It just strikes me as odd."

"I've been shooting with him for decades. Even though he didn't own a .22, I know for a fact he enjoyed shooting them. I also know he always used long rifle .22 shells," said Zeb.

Zeb pulled out his cellphone and called Diamond Gun and Ammo. Josh Diamond answered on the third ring. He put the phone on speaker.

"Diamond Gun and Ammo, Josh speaking."

"Josh, Zeb. I've got you on speaker. Kate is with me."

"Hey, honey. How's the love of my life?"

"Zeb needs to talk to you," replied Kate.

The sternness in the tone of her voice told Josh this was serious business.

"Okay. Sheriff, what can I do you for?"

"I have a quick question about .22 shorts. But first I have some bad news."

"Yeah?"

"Kate and I are at Jake's trailer with Jake's body. It appears he has died of natural causes."

"I'm so sorry to hear that. I know how close the two of you were. I also know he meant the world to Kate. How are you guys doing?"

Zeb and Kate answered in unison.

"We're okay."

"When did this happen?"

"Based on what I can tell, and bear in mind I'm not an expert, I'd say within the last thirty-six hours."

"Jesus, that's too bad. Sorry, man."

"Yeah, thanks. We go way back. Way, way back. So does Kate. Kate found him."

A short silence followed. A black cloud, loaded with gloom and doom, hung over all of them. Finally, Josh spoke.

"As to your question about .22 shorts, I quit carrying them a while back. Zeb, as I'm sure you already know, Jake didn't even own a .22. However, he liked to shoot one for target practice. For that, he always purchased .22 long rifle shells."

"Thanks for letting me know that detail. It might be very helpful."

"You say you found a gun to go along with the bullets?"

"Yup," replied Zeb.

He chose not to go into any of the details of how he had found the weapon or that it was his.

"Anything else I can help you with?"

"Nope."

"Okay, later, and good luck."

"Later."

Outside, Shepner's hearse pulled into Jake's driveway.

"Shepner's is here."

"Okay."

"Zeb, we need to get an independent analysis verifying that the .22 bullet found in Black Bear's brain matches the one fired from your gun," said Kate.

"Good idea. Yes, we've got to do that." Zeb paused, thinking. "Shit."

"What?" asked Kate.

"That evidence is tainted."

"What do you mean?" asked Kate.

"Jake did the testing. With the shells being found at his place, things he said that were overheard, me, his boss and best friend finding the weapon in the middle of nowhere..."

"It's not going to add up to most people," said Kate.

"It sure as hell won't."

"What exactly do you mean about Jake saying things that were overheard?" asked Kate.

"Jake was speaking his mind to Song Bird in the Town Talk. Jake said he was surprised someone hadn't put Black Bear down like a sick dog. He also implied it wouldn't have bothered him to do exactly that. I'm certain he said it loud enough for others to hear."

"Jake said a lot of things he didn't really mean. It was just his way of doing business," replied Kate. Besides, if Jake did kill Black Bear, why would he have kept the box of bullets and gotten rid of the gun? It doesn't make sense," said Kate.

"I know it doesn't. But we knew Jake. Not everyone will have the same opinion when they hear the facts," replied Zeb.

"People might even think he was planning on sneaking the bullets back into your safe but never got around to it," said Kate.

"That doesn't make sense because that would mean he was setting me up. He'd never do anything like that."

"It would take you off the hook because the killing happened while you were in Paris," said Kate.

"The exact timing doesn't exactly rule me out. Black Bear was most likely killed same day I left for the airport," said Zeb.

"Still, it seems odd that your bullets were taken and that they

show up at Jake's place. How could they have gotten here? We've got
to figure that out. I don't think Jake did it. However, we do have to rule
it out. Don't you agree?" asked Kate. "After all, you said from the
beginning that we must leave no stone unturned."

"What if we make Jake appear guilty of murder?" asked Zeb. "He
has no way to defend himself."

"Doesn't matter," said Kate. "We've got to do the right thing when
it comes to the police work. We have to check out every possibility."

"You're right. You'd better run the weapon and bullets over to
Tucson. We need to have results that are totally independent and
nonbiased. I don't want it looking like we are influencing the results."

"I'll leave right now."

"For God's sake, I hope this doesn't blow up in our faces."

"Ditto," replied Kate. "Being a murderer would be a terrible way
for Jake to be remembered."

Kate began the drive to Tucson. In her mind she had not ruled
out Zeb as a prime suspect. She had also not ruled out Jake as a
candidate for murder of Black Bear. As troublesome as it all felt, Kate
kept telling herself that she had to do her job.

41

BALLISTICS

Zeb called a friend, Angel Jiminez, at the ballistics lab of the Tucson Police Department. He and Angel were friends from Zeb's days on the Tucson force. Angel was also the leading expert on ballistics in Arizona. After a few minutes of chit chat, they got down to business.

"Angel, I've got a huge favor to ask of you," said Zeb.

"Let me guess. You've got an important case that needs to go to the head of the line, and you need the results yesterday," said Angel.

Zeb cleared his throat. Obviously, he wasn't breaking new ground.

"Yeah, that's about the size of it."

"Who's the victim?"

"Sheriff Sawyer Black Bear," replied Zeb.

"I read about that. I heard all about it on the news, too. You already have the bullet that killed him. I know that much. Do you have the gun?"

"I'm almost one hundred percent certain I do. However, there are some complicating factors. That's why I need your expertise."

"That's what everyone needs me for," replied Angel.

"The weapon belongs to me."

"You? Hmm?"

"Yeah."

"That complicates things."

"It most certainly does."

"Maybe you should let the Feds handle this one?" suggested Angel.

"You know exactly how well I trust those bastards," said Zeb. "I'm not going to put myself in their line of fire. They'll fuck with me just to make their own lives easier."

"Okay. Okay. I hear you. Still, being that we're old friends, I don't want that to muddy the waters."

"You won't."

"Still..."

Angel's hesitancy was not only reasonable but easy to understand.

"How about if I invoke the name of Max Munoz?"

Zeb was digging deep. The three of them, Angel, Max and Zeb had gone through training together for the Tucson department back in the day. Although they rarely socialized, the trio remained as thick as thieves professionally speaking.

Angel quietly reminisced before answering. The three of them all came from similar backgrounds, lower income, small town boys who excelled in athletics and not necessarily in academics. All three were avid outdoorsmen. Most of all they all shared a love for the law and all that it could do.

"You got it. I'll help you out."

"Thanks."

"You do know that the federal boys and girls will end up with a copy of my report in their file."

"About that...."

"Yes?"

"I need you to do me a little favor."

"Put the report on the slow boat to China?" asked Angel. "Maybe even temporarily bury it?"

"Something like that. At least, don't rush it over to them."

"I don't want to end up with my balls on the chopping block. But, okay. Just this once. So, please don't ask for any other special favors in the near future."

"Gotcha," replied Zeb. "No more favors on this case."

Are you bringing the gun over yourself?"

"No. I'm sending my deputy, Kate Steele Diamond."

"She cute?"

"Beautiful. She's also married to a good friend of mine."

"Just checking. You never know."

"She's a top-notch cop."

"I assume she's on her way here at this very moment?"

"She is. She'll be there in ninety minutes or less."

"That's good timing. I'm just finishing something up. I'll get right on your case the minute she gets here. It shouldn't take me long. I assume you sent similar bullets so I can run an accurate test?"

"When we found the gun, there were still three chambered bullets. I left those in the gun for you. You can use those. By the way, the gun is a four shot .22 Sharps Rimfire Derringer."

"Collector's item, eh? Not a gun with a lot of oomph. Dangerous gun to handle because it misfires so easily."

"Right on all accounts."

"Okay."

"I am operating under the theoretical assumption that the shell that was found in Black Bear's brain is the fourth one that was chambered. I hope I'm wrong."

"If it matches, is from the same gun and the gun and bullets were yours, well, it won't be hard to make a case against you."

Angel was not telling Zeb anything he did not already know.

"Well, there's another hiccup in the case," said Zeb.

"Give it to me."

"The box of shells, which are mine, were found in the possession of my deputy, Jake Dablo. He was sheriff before me and had been my deputy."

"Had been?"

"We found his body at the same time we found the box of shells at his trailer. It appears he died of a heart attack in the last day or so."

"No matter how you cut it, you've got some serious complications on your hands."

"I know."

"How'd he get the box of your shells?"

"I don't know."

"Really?"

"Please don't doubt me on this one. I'm telling you the total truth," said Zeb.

"Okay. I take you at your word."

"One other thing. The gun wasn't in his possession. It was found away from any crime scene," explained Zeb.

"You're not making this an easy case, are you?"

"No. Absolutely not. That's why I'm only dealing with the best people. It's why I called you."

"No need to blow hot air up my skirt," said Angel.

"I wasn't," replied Zeb.

"Somebody, and I assume you don't know who, tossed it?"

"Right."

"Do you suspect your recently deceased deputy dumped the gun?"

"I doubt it, but I don't know. I don't know that he ever had it in his possession."

"Jesus, Zeb. You didn't check the gun for fingerprints personally did you?"

"No."

"Thank God for small favors."

"Were there any fingerprints found on the weapon?"

"I don't know for certain. No one has officially checked it yet. I eyeballed it and appeared to me that someone wiped it clean."

"Nothing about this case is straightforward, is it?" asked Angel.

"That's why I need you."

"If we have a match, it doesn't prove who pulled the trigger."

"I realize it just proves the weapon is the one that fired the bullet that killed Black Bear."

"Or not," replied Angel.

"Or not. Right now, I need to know if my gun is the murder weapon."

"Okay. Just the facts are what you will get."

"I owe you one."

"Let's see how this unfolds first," said Angel. "You might not like the outcome."

"I'll cross that bridge when I come to it."

Less than two hours later Kate arrived. An hour after that Angel had proven with a 99.9% chance of accuracy that the bullet found in Black Bear's brain had been shot from the gun Kate had brought to his lab. The .22 had a rare fingerprint on both the bullet and the casing due to a small manufacturing defect in the gun barrel. Kate thanked Angel and headed back to Safford.

"I'll call Zeb," she said.

"It's your case," replied Angel. "Good luck."

Kate rang Zeb's cellphone as she headed back to Safford.

"Zeb."

"Kate. What did you find out?"

"Almost a 100% chance that the gun you found, your gun, was the weapon that killed Black Bear."

"Shit. Shit. Shit. Goddamnit all."

"Doesn't make either you or Jake guilty."

"Doesn't make us innocent either."

"A good lawyer could make the case that you both probably had cause to see him dead."

"Let's not even go there," said Zeb.

"Okay. Then let's run the case like we would on any murder case," said Kate. "Let's get all the facts and make no assumptions."

"We've got to keep it out of the press for as long as possible," said Zeb.

"Agreed. For now, we keep everything in-house. But we also need to be aware of how that will look when it does come out to the public," said Kate. "The TV stations and newspapers will have a heyday."

"It's a risk I'm willing to take and it's on me. I'll call a meeting for later today and let everyone else know the plan."

"Zeb, I know how close you were to Jake and what he meant to you. It's going to be important, either way, that you remain impartial."

Zeb hung up his cellphone without commenting back to Kate. It was going to be next to impossible to remain impartial. After all, Jake Dablo meant as much to him as anyone in the world. He didn't want his mentor's legacy to be that of a sheriff killer. Nor did Zeb want to be accused of a crime he didn't commit.

42

STRANGE NEWS

Helen didn't bother with the phone. Instead she simply shouted through Zeb's open office door. Zeb tipped his head to the side so he could see her.

"Zeb, Doc Yackley on line one."

"Did he say what he wants?" asked Zeb.

Helen shook her head. Zeb knew that Doc would have said what he wanted if that was the way he was going to do things. Sometimes Helen figured Zeb was clueless, so she played along and asked Doc.

"Zeb wants to know what you want."

"I want to talk to him. Good gracious, but he can be as thick as a brick."

Helen laughed.

"He wants to talk to you, Zeb. Line one."

"Thanks," replied Zeb.

Helen chose to listen in on the conversation. She figured if Doc wasn't willing to send the information through her to Zeb, it must be really important. She put her hand over the receiver and breathed as quietly as possible.

"What's up, Doc?"

"Zeb, I got some information that I know you're going to want."

"Yeah? What is it?"

"Doc Zata and I have been doing a little bit of investigatory work on the side on Black Bear's case," explained Doc.

On one hand Zeb was fine with it as Doc might dig up something useful. On the other hand, he may have opened a pathway down a dead-end road. Either way, he was creating more work for the sheriff's department.

"Yeah? And?"

"Are you sitting down?"

"Doc, I'm not a child."

"Okay. Here's the long and short of it. We did some genetic and other tests on both Senator Russell and Black Bear."

"Yeah?"

"We've got enough evidence to prove that the cancerous kidneys in Senator Russell's body were from Black Bear."

Zeb's jaw dropped halfway to the floor.

"Yeah?"

"You realize the implication, don't you?"

"I'm afraid I do. Someone, maybe Senator Russell himself, had Black Bear killed in order to get his kidneys. Jesus H. Keerist."

"Exactly. But that's only part of it," said Doc.

"Yeah?"

"We did deep enough genetic testing to prove that there is a 94% chance that Senator Russell was Black Bear's father."

Zeb went quiet, like he'd never gone quiet before. His world came to complete and utter standstill. The implications were not only obvious but ominously surreal.

"Zeb, you still on the line?"

"I am."

"Now you're sitting down, aren't you?"

"I am."

"You know what that means."

"I do."

Zeb could barely speak. His voice was little more than a hollow squeak.

"It means Black Bear and I are half-brothers."

"That's right," replied Doc.

"Oh, my Lord. That's a twist I didn't see coming."

"There's no way you could have," said Doc.

Helen, still listening in on the conversation, dropped the phone.

"Thanks, Doc...I think. Any other news for me?"

"That about covers it. Seems like it ought to be enough."

"It sure as hell is."

Zeb walked out of his office. Helen was sitting at her desk. She appeared to be in shock. She heard Zeb walking toward her desk.

"Some days," she said. "I wish I wasn't such a busybody. Some things I'd just rather not know."

"Well, you do know them. I have to ask you to keep it all under your hat for the sake of the investigation. If any of this becomes general information, I won't have a chance at solving Black Bear's murder."

"What are you going to do, Zeb?"

"My job. And, if I'm lucky, figure this mess out ASAP."

First, he called Echo and explained he just discovered that he and Black Bear were half-brothers. Sensing the stress in his voice she said, "I'll be right there." Before he could protest, she hung up.

43

EVIDENCE, A FRESH LOOK

Zeb placed the box of .22 Golden Remington short shells in the middle of his desk. Next to it he placed the Sharps 4-Barrel Rimfire Derringer that had been stolen from his safe and found at Jake's trailer. He poked at them both with a pencil. Then, he put on gloves, lifted the objects one at a time and examined them with an eagle eye.

As he cocked the hammer and opened the barrel, something caught his eye. Since he had already checked the gun not once, but twice, he kicked himself for having missed something so obvious. He turned on the flashlight on his cellphone. As he examined the open gun, he spoke to himself.

"Well, I'll be damned."

His door was open. Zeb called out to Kate who was passing by his office door.

"Kate, come here."

"What's up?"

"Glove up. I want you to doublecheck my work."

"Okay."

Kate, from living with Josh, an expert in all things regarding guns, knew her stuff.

"How well do you know this particular Sharps .22?"

Her giggling response had Zeb shaking his head.

"Well, I asked Josh about it last night. Prior to that, I didn't know a whole lot. He gave me the encyclopedic version of its history, the cook's tour, if you will, of everything about it."

"Great. Cock the hammer and open the barrel."

Kate had no idea where this was headed. She did as Zeb instructed. Zeb handed her the cellphone with the light still on.

"Here. Tell me what you see," said Zeb.

"You sound like my husband. Is this some sort of a quiz?"

"Kind of. Sort of. I want to know if you see what I see. It's something I missed the first two times I examined the gun."

Now her interest was piqued.

"I can see the gun has been cleaned. I would expect that since it's your gun. I can also see you missed something. These marks."

Using a pen, Kate pointed to some gunpowder marks near the firing pin and chambers.

"This gun has been recently misfired. I can tell by the marks here and here. Josh told me they misfire often because of a firing pin problem."

"Well done."

"What exactly does that tell you?" asked Kate.

"You need a special cleaning agent to remove the marks that are left by a misfire. Whoever cleaned the gun must've not had it."

"Or they had to clean it in a hurry."

"Whoever shot Black Bear with this gun didn't know this gun. It misfired in their hand."

"Therefore, whoever killed Black Bear probably has a hand injury," said Kate. "Probably on their trigger finger would be my guess."

"Right on the money."

"We know someone who has an injured trigger finger."

Zeb had previously explained to Kate about Shappa's band-aid that Echo had dug out of the trash at the body review of Senator Russell.

"Do you think Shappa killed her own son?"

"She sure as hell just jumped to the top of my list of suspects."

"Why would she? Kill him, I mean?"

"Motive is another issue we've got to figure out," replied Zeb. "But I suspect Shappa could have one. Something about her isn't right. I can't put my finger on it. Echo thinks Shappa is disturbed in a way that happens only in the truly irrational mind."

"Hmmm. I need to think about that one. I don't know Shappa well enough to make such a statement. I suspect she is a dangerous woman. But to kill her own son? That takes everything to a whole different level."

"It does. Indeed, it does."

Zeb's mind lit up.

"Kate, I want you to run the gun and bullets over to Dr. Zata in Tucson. I think he will be able to do some testing procedures that the police lab doesn't do. He's kind of a nut. He and Doc think they're the reincarnations of Sherlock Holmes and Doctor Watson."

"I've heard about that," said Kate. "I think it gives the old friends a hobby and makes them feel young again."

"I know you're right," replied Zeb.

"But I don't have to make the trip to Tucson."

"Why not?"

"This is your lucky day. Dr. Zata is in town visiting Doc Yackley at this very moment. And, believe it or not, he carries a traveling laboratory with him. From what I heard Dr. Zata and Doc are doing some kind of an experiment they cooked up."

"How do you know that?"

"Helen was talking to Doc's secretary as I walked by her desk. I was practicing being Helen by listening in."

"Never thought I'd live to see the day when someone out-snooped Helen."

"Well, it was more or less accidental."

"We need to put together what we know," said Zeb.

"I could use a good brainstorming session," replied Kate.

Kate discretely shut the door to Zeb's office. Helen was still prattling away with Doc Yackley's secretary and didn't seem to notice.

While Kate was closing the door, Zeb, with gloved hands, moved the murder weapon and box of shells to a desk that sat in the corner of his office. He pulled it away from the wall. Kate and Zeb sat on opposite sides of the table with the evidence between them.

"I've had Deputy Kerkhoff detail the box of shells for fingerprints. Twice," explained Zeb. "She couldn't find any fingerprints on the box that weren't mine."

"None? Not even Josh's?"

"No, but I know why his weren't on the box."

"Do tell."

"I remember when I bought them. It was taken from a fresh carton of shells, a small carton that held twenty-four boxes as I recall. I cut it open with my knife and took out the box myself. I carried it to the register and paid Josh in cash. I told him I didn't need him to package it up as I was going to take it home right away. He never touched it."

"Well that explains the lack of fingerprints. But you'd have thought someone at the plant would have touched it when they were packaging it," said Kate.

"I have to assume everything is done by automation. Efficiency is the buzz word at manufacturing plants."

"I guess it must be."

"Deputy Kerkhoff even did some chemical testing on the box and came up with exactly nothing. Not even a hint of latex residue. It doesn't appear at all like the shell box was cleaned by any chemical, cloth or paper."

"Odd. I assume your theory is that someone just reached in and took out the shells?"

"Exactly."

"But they moved the box of shells from your safe to Jake's trailer."

"I know. I can't figure how they did that without leaving a trace of something behind."

Kate touched the shell box. It was quite rigid. She closed her eyes and ran her gloved first finger across the top and bottom of the box. Nothing was out of the ordinary. Running her finger ever so lightly on the sides of the box, she stopped and opened her eyes.

"Turn off the lights, Zeb. Pull the curtains tight. Make the room as dark as possible."

Zeb had no idea what she was up to but followed her directive to a tee. He watched in the dimly lit room as she ever so carefully and with the lightest of touch ran the first finger of her right hand over the sides of the box. She abruptly stopped and placed the first finger of her left hand directly across from where she was holding her right hand.

"I've got it."

Kate's voice was at once triumphant and relieved.

"Got what?"

She turned on her phone light, tipped the cardboard box that held the shells and pointed the light at an obtuse angle. She pointed to one side, then to the side directly opposite.

"Here." Kate gently rested her fingertip against the box. "And here."

Zeb held the box between his finger and thumb. He saw what she was talking about. There were slight, arced indentations in the box.

"I think whoever stole them was well prepared. They brought a set of tongs or some small grabbing instrument and used that to pick up the box when they broke into the safe. The only thing that was left behind were these small indentations," added Kate.

"Excellent deductive reasoning," said Zeb.

"My only question would be why didn't you send it to the crime lab in Tucson?" asked Kate.

"I still want to keep this in house as much as possible. I don't know who to trust and who not to trust. I figured it would be safer that way."

Kate nodded but considered the chain of evidence. If this went to court, a sharp attorney would rip Zeb's move to shreds. But the deed was already done.

"We've got to figure out who pulled the trigger," said Zeb.

"We do. No doubt. But something is still puzzling me."

"What?" asked Zeb.

"The gun. How can it be possible to leave no trace of evidence on an odd little gun like that? It's full of nooks and crannies. It has all kinds of places for evidence to hide."

"I wanted Doc's friend, Dr. Zata, the pathology guy, to look at it. He's got access to all the equipment in the world..."

"...and, like you said, he's got a crime solving hobby."

Kate keenly eyed the gun, moving it into several different positions.

"I see that."

"It was tested as thoroughly as this office is capable of," said Zeb. "Deputy Kerkhoff was extremely detailed in her approach. Like I said, she didn't find a single thing."

There was a knock on Zeb's door. Outside Helen could be heard saying, "Echo, just go on in. Kate is in there talking to Zeb about Black Bear's murder and the evidence they've got."

Zeb walked over and opened the door. He gave Echo a kiss and shut the door.

"You doing okay?" asked Echo.

"Yes."

"Do you need to talk about it?"

"We can. Later. We've got other issues right now," said Zeb.

"Do you need me to leave the room so you two can talk?" asked Kate.

"No," replied Zeb. "You're going to hear it soon enough anyway, so I might as well tell you."

"Tell me what?"

"Black Bear and I were, er are, half-brothers," said Zeb.

Kate was stunned. Truly that was something that had not shown up on her radar. Echo took it all in stride. Based on her reaction, or lack of it, Zeb had the feeling she already had a suspicion about Black Bear being his half-brother.

"What? Did I hear you right? You and Black Bear are half-brothers?" asked Kate.

"I just found out myself. It seems Senator Russell spread his seed far and wide."

"I'm sorry," was all that Kate could think to say.

"It's all right. I haven't processed it yet. So, I don't know what to say about it myself. It all seems very weird and, to be honest, unreal. I mean really not real."

The silence that filled Zeb's office gave everyone a fresh moment to consider the situation. Finally, Echo spoke.

"What are you two working on?"

Zeb picked up his phone and hit the speed dial number of Doc Yackley. From the conversation it was obvious Zeb wanted Doc and Dr. Zata to come by the office as soon as they could.

"I need you to check out a gun. Black Bear's murder weapon," explained Zeb.

Doc Yackley mumbled something to Dr. Zata and put the phone on speaker.

"I would like to work in a sterile environment," said Dr. Zata. "Can the two of you come over to the morgue?"

"Three of us," said Zeb. "Echo is with us too. We'll be there in five minutes."

44

TESTING

Zeb handed the evidence over to Doc Yackley who promptly set it on a sterile table. Doc Yackley and Doctor Zata stood back, crossed their arms, rested their chins on their fists and observed the evidence with scientific eyes. Both were seemingly deep in thought, planning and plotting their course of action.

Zata made the first move. He bent forward and observed the gun and box of shells up close. He moved his hands behind his back, interlocking his fingers. He uttered one word. "Hmm."

Doc Yackley, wearing a white lab coat stood to Zata's right. He nodded in agreement with something left unsaid. Zata then pointed at the gun and spoke to no one in particular.

"Tiny little thing, isn't it?"

"Just right for doing the job it did," added Doc.

"Yes, yes. Perfect. Someone had this well thought out."

"Yes."

"It's your gun, is it not, Sheriff Hanks?"

Zata's question embarrassed Zeb. After all, he was the sheriff, it was his gun and it was used in the commission of what Dr. Zata referred to as a 'malum in se' act.

"Pardon me, Doctor Zata, I am unfamiliar with the term you just used," said Zeb.

"Sorry, Sheriff Hanks. Thinking out loud is a bad habit of mine. Malum in se is an act which is evil within itself. Murder is wrong. It is evil by its very nature."

"I cannot disagree with that," replied Zeb. "Although there are extenuating circumstances at times."

Dr. Zata interrupted Zeb.

"In that case we would say it is a crime that involved extenuating circumstances. That may not necessarily fall into the category of malum in se."

Dr. Zata turned to Doc Yackley. The exchanged a few words and some exaggerated hand gestures. Yackley departed to a small room. When he returned, he was pushing a small wheeled table. On the table were a doctor's bag and numerous instruments. Dr. Zata grabbed a couple of tools. To the unknowledgeable they looked much like screwdrivers. Doc Yackley laid out a single piece of sterile paper, snapping it gently before resting it on the table.

The men placed the .22 Sharps Derringer and the box of .22 shells on the sterile paper. Slowly and with great precision they took the gun apart, one piece at a time. Each part was examined separately by the doctors. Periodically, one of the men would grunt or the other would point at something. Doc handed Zata a small surgical knife. With the utmost precision Zata scraped several parts of the gun and the side of the box over several glass slides. Doc dug into the bag and pulled out a mini microscope. Nothing close to a compete sentence was uttered while they worked. Eventually, Zata held out his hand and said, "KOH." Doc Yackley hand him a small brown bottle. Zata unscrewed the top and pulled out a liquid filled dropper. He put a minute amount of the potassium hydroxide on each slide. Doc produced a miniaturized black light from Zata's bag of tricks.

"Zeb, turn off the lights."

The room went dark. Both Doctors of Medicine began to chuckle.

"So simple. We should have seen it."

They continued to laugh. Stopped laughing. Then began again.

"How could we have not seen this? We overthink everything."

"What?" asked Zeb. "Are you talking about?"

"A tiny amount of Super Glue residue is on the trigger."

"Super Glue?"

"It was one of the first things my old school chum looked for," said Doc. "He's got a buddy in the Tucson police crime lab who keeps him up on fingerprint hiding schemes."

"Yes?" asked Zeb.

"A thin layer of Super Glue on the tip of the finger, at the spot containing a dozen points of reference for regular fingerprint identification, will cover up any remnants of fingerprints. He also advised me that most professionals use acid, sandpaper or a razor blade to scrape away the skin on their fingertips before applying the Super Glue to their fingertips. That way there is almost no chance of leaving any trace of a print whatsoever."

"The killer knew what they were doing," said Zeb.

Doctor Zata, who obviously had taken a shine to Echo, called her to his side.

"Did you take science class in high school or college?"

"Yes," replied Echo. "I loved biology the most. Histology also."

"Then you're familiar with a microscope and how it works?" asked Zata.

"Yes."

Zata pointed toward his set-up.

"Have a look."

A beaming smile came across Echo's face. Oddly, she recognized the organism from histology class. Echo and Zata exchanged a knowing glance.

"You're very blessed that Doc Yackley knows Dr. Zata," said Echo.

"Yes? What are you referring to?" asked Zeb.

"Dr. Zata found something else on the box that you missed," said Echo.

Zeb's faced showed not only defeat but additional embarrassment. What could he have forgotten or missed?

"What?" asked Zeb

"Ringworm," replied Echo.

"Ringworm?"

"It is something you wouldn't have been on the lookout for," said Doc Yackley.

"It's a fungal infection. More correctly stated, *tinea pedis*. Very specifically one would designate it as *Trichophyton rubrum*," explained Dr. Zata.

"I'm sorry, but I'm just not tracking you on this one," said Zeb.

"Dr. Zata has a lot of weird hobbies, fungus not being among the least of them. When he swabbed down the box and parts of the gun, he found *trichophyton rubrum* in multiple places."

"Doesn't ringworm grow on the toes?" asked Kate.

"It does, but someone touching their feet can easily transfer it to their fingers where it can live for quite a while."

"What's quite a while?" asked Zeb.

"Two days easily, months if the conditions are right."

"So, there's a chance whoever handled the box had ringworm. If we can find someone with ringworm, we can narrow down our list of suspects," said Zeb. "That's a hell of a shot in the dark."

"Yes, but maybe not. Dr. Zata already had Doc Yackley check Jake's body for ringworm."

"I take he didn't find any on Jake."

"None."

"That doesn't rule Jake out as the murderer. However, it sure as hell cuts down the odds of it being him," said Zeb.

"I've got an idea. It's a long shot," said Echo.

"At this time, I'll take any shot. What do you have in mind?" asked Zeb.

"How far is Sheriff Lentz willing to go for you?"

Zeb stared blankly at Echo. He had no clue as to what she was talking about.

"Think he'd break into Shappa's house and steal a pair of her dirty socks for you?"

"The real question is would I do it for him?"

"That answer better be yes," said Echo. "One hand washes the other. We all know that."

45

SHERIFF LENTZ AND DIRTY SOCKS

Z eb found Sheriff Lentz's number on the recent call list on his phone. He took a deep breath and punched his number. What he was about to ask was nothing short of crazy, not to mention illegal. He was banking on the brotherhood of the badge to pull him through this little escapade.

"Sheriff Lentz's office, this is Roberta."

"Roberta, this is Sheriff Zeb Hanks from..."

"Sheriff Hanks, so good to hear from you. I truly enjoyed our little conversation last time we talked. What can I do you for?"

"I need to talk with Sheriff Lentz."

"Well you just happen to be in luck. He's in his office sipping some tea."

"What kind?" asked Zeb.

"Chamomile. He's got a bad gut. Goes with the turf."

"I hear ya'. Can you put me through to him?"

"Yes, sir, Sheriff Hanks. My pleasure."

Zeb heard Roberta set the phone down and shout out, "Mitch, it's Zeb Hanks, that Arizona sheriff that knows Shappa and Black Bear for ya'."

"Thanks. I got it."

"Sheriff Hanks, to what do I owe the pleasure of a call from you?"

Zeb had been hoping for some banal chit chat before jumping off the cliff and asking Sheriff Lentz, whom he barely knew, to commit the crime of breaking and entering for him.

"How's the weather up Dakota way?"

"Windy, like always. But I doubt you called for a weather report."

"Um, er…"

"Must have to do with Shappa or Black Bear. Am I right?"

"Bingo," replied Zeb.

Zeb broke into a hard sweat on his face and under his arms. The odor from his armpits wafted to his nose. What he was doing was clearly wrong. Plus, he didn't have a legal leg to stand on when it came to direct facts. But his gut told him he was on the right track, or at least some kind of a track that just might lead him to where he needed to be.

"What do you want? Or should I be asking, what do you need?"

"This is going to sound a little odd," said Zeb.

"Yeah?"

"I need a pair of Shappa's socks."

"What the hell?"

"I said it was going to be odd."

"You weren't kidding."

"I wasn't."

"I hope you're not some kind of foot fetish pervert."

"You're funny. Rest assured that I'm not. It's business."

"You need Shappa's socks for part of an investigation?"

"And I have certain parameters that I need met," explained Zeb.

"Really? Now I'm wondering just how strange your request is going to be."

"I need them to have been worn and to be unwashed. If they had blood on them, that would be even better."

"Let me break this down. You want a pair of Shappa's dirty socks, knowing full well they aren't something I can just ask her for? You want her blood as well?"

"Right."

"She must be a suspect in your case. She is, isn't she?"

Zeb knew there was no option but trusting Sheriff Lentz. However, in the back of Zeb's mind was a concern that Lentz still carried a torch for Shappa.

"That leaves me one option...breaking and entering followed by theft."

"Yes, that more or less sums it up," replied Zeb.

"I've traveled down some strange roads in my day, but this is among the weirdest maps I've ever been requested to follow," said Lentz.

Zeb nodded as though Lentz could see him through the ether of a phone call.

"Might I ask what you are hoping to find on her socks?" asked Lentz.

"The fungus that causes ringworm. I suggest you use gloves."

Zeb's response caused Lentz to break out into uproarious laughter. When he stopped laughing and paused to catch his breath, he started laughing again.

"Is ringworm some kind of a joke in your neck of the woods?" asked Zeb.

"No. It's just that last time I had a serious relationship with Shappa she gave me ringworm. She's been fighting it for years. She still has trouble with it as far as I know."

"That's good to know, but I need proof, recent proof, that she is, in fact, infected."

"Lucky for you I never returned the key to her place when we last broke it off. Not that she's one to lock doors. I guess it wouldn't be much trouble to sneak in and grab some socks. Sort of makes me sound like a degenerate. I mean breaking into someone's house, going through their dirty laundry and taking a pair of socks crosses the border of bizarre."

"I know. Sorry to ask, I truly am."

"I can help you out with her blood type. It's O negative. She is a universal donor. There was a story in the local paper when she got her two-gallon pin."

"I guess she does have her good side," said Zeb.

"She does. But, as you know, the woman has a very dark side as well. If I'm going to do this rather nefarious deed, I am going to have to trust that it's in the name of justice. If I can help you put the finger on the killer of Black Bear, it'll be worth it."

"It might do precisely that," replied Zeb.

"Want to run how that all works by me?" asked Lentz.

"I've got the gun that fired the bullet that ended up in Black Bear's brain."

"How'd you come across that?"

"Long story short..."

"Not something we're used to in Dakota. I'm all ears and I've got time. Give me all the information you want to."

"Long story short, the gun with the box of shells, one of which was fired from the gun that killed Black Bear, was found in my deputy's trailer. The box of shells had five missing. The .22 is a Sharps 4-Barrel Rimfire Derringer."

"AKA the rat killer. No double entendre intended."

"Rat killer just might be appropriate in more ways than one. Anyway, the gun had one empty chamber and three full ones. The brand of the bullets in the box matches the bullets in the weapon."

"Okay. That works fine. About the fungus? I'm a little lost there."

"A pathology forensics expert coincidentally happens to be best pals with the local doctor who did the original autopsy on Black Bear. They worked together on the case. Actually, they are still working on it."

"Give me some names so I can understand who we are talking about," said Lentz.

"The local doctor is Doc Yackley. His pal, Dr. Zata, is the pathology forensics expert by way of both professional training and long-time hobby."

"Interesting. A double expert with a personal fascination regarding crime solving," said Lentz. "That kind of person can be either helpful or dangerous or both."

"This time a lucky star was shining on us. He was helpful. I have no reason to believe he's some sort of nut job. Dr. Zata took the murder weapon apart. When he did that, he found no fingerprints, not even a partial."

"If this Dr. Zata didn't get as much as a partial print, what did he find?"

"This is interesting. I think you might be able to use this information in the future on your own cases. When he didn't find anything, he went hunting."

"It's so odd not to find anything," said Lentz.

"Right. Here's his hypothesis. The shooter likely used acid or a razor blade to scrape away the surface of their fingertips. Dr. Zata believes they concentrated the destruction on the reference area points, the papillary ridges of the fingertips."

"Makes sense."

"Zata's theory is that the shooter also applied a thin layer of Super Glue to the tips of their fingers before handling the weapon. A combination of acid, scraping and Super Glue makes it an almost absolute certainty of complete eradication of fingerprints."

"How does all of this lead me directly to Shappa's dirty laundry?"

"When Zata took the gun apart he found...wait, let me go back one step. Look at your trigger finger."

Lentz did as Zeb suggested.

"You see where the tip of your finger bends?"

"Yes."

"On the underside of the finger the skin is smooth until it comes to a crease. See that?"

"I do."

"The bone at the tip of the finger is called the distal phalanx. There are three long bones in the finger. The name of the other two don't matter. In fact, I don't remember the names offhand. Anyway, if you look at the distal phalanx, the tip of the finger and bend your finger ever so slightly, you'll see a line across the surface of the skin."

"That's easy to see."

"Good. That's called the distal interphalangeal joint. According to Dr. Zata, that joint tends to naturally be the perfect breeding ground for fungus, bacteria and viruses. A person under a lot of stress would have some sweat on their hands. That would make it an even better place for the fungus to survive."

"Is there going to be a quiz on this later?"

Both men laughed loudly.

"Right where that crease is, the finger touches the trigger when you fire the gun. If there is any small amount of the ringworm fungus, it will be left on the trigger..."

"If the shooter was such a god-awful pro, why wouldn't they have wiped down the trigger?" asked Lentz.

"A chemical evaluation by Dr. Zata showed they did exactly that," said Zeb.

"Then where did the fungus come from?"

"Whoever pulled the trigger, and in this case I have a fairly strong suspicion it was Shappa, when they pulled the trigger, their finger was resting toward the top of the trigger mechanism. The jarring action of the shot forced some of the fungus to migrate up inside the gun. The way Dr. Zata has it figured the shooter also possibly picked up the fungus from the box of shells. He found some there as well. Dr. Zata thinks that when the shooter was transferring shells from the box to the gun they ended up with fungus on their hand."

"Doesn't ringworm grow on the toes?" asked Lentz.

"It does, but someone touching their feet can easily transfer it to their fingers where it can live for quite a while."

"Your friend, Dr. Zata, is one thorough guy."

"He and the local doc went to school together. They have fantasies about being a modern-day Sherlock Holmes and Doctor Watson."

Once again, the men roared heartily. They had both seen many times when the public carried out such imaginative fancies, usually to no good end.

"I take it if you can match exactly the same type of fungus on Shappa's socks with what was on the gun, you have an absolute result?"

"It's not quite that direct. Here's what the doctor told me. I have this written down so I may not be pronouncing everything correctly," said Zeb.

"You could fool me," replied Lentz.

"Tinea manuum is found on the hands. *Tinea pedis* is found on the feet. Tinea unguium is found in the toenails."

"You just said a mouthful."

"Speaking of mouthful, I trust Shappa didn't and you don't have a foot fetish," joked Zeb.

"No problem there. I'm no toe sucker. Never have been, either. Never tried it, even in my youth."

"That's fortunate for you. In any case tinea manuum, the type of fungal ringworm found on the hands, is identical to tinea pedis, which is found on the feet. If Dr. Zata can, using a microscope and other techniques that I don't really understand, match scientific details of the fungus found on the gun with the fungus found in Shappa's socks, we have a pretty good case."

"Pretty easy to see how someone could transfer the fungus from their feet to their hand, just by rubbing their feet."

"That's what I'm surmising happened," said Zeb.

"Can you put Shappa at the scene of the crime?" asked Lentz.

"We can place her in the vicinity of where Black Bear likely was on the last day of his life," said Zeb.

"It's all sounds pretty circumstantial," said Lentz.

"I'm hoping that if I have enough evidence, even if it's circumstantial, I can somehow break Shappa down and get her to make a mistake," said Zeb.

"I've lived with her twice. I've dealt with her through a lot of different situations and events. I wouldn't hold my breath on breaking her. She's as tough as nails and as hard as granite. You're going to need some luck and a break or two."

"I know. I might just have one."

"You found blood on the weapon. That's why you asked me to find a bloody sock, right?"

"Exactly."

"Where did you find blood?"

"When Dr. Zata took the gun apart, he also found a miniscule amount of blood had also migrated from near the trigger into the weapon. It was intermingled with the fungus."

"Is the blood O-negative?"

"It is."

"Once again, circumstantial at best. Millions of people have O-negative blood."

"But if we can match other factors..."

"Meaning what, exactly?"

Zeb looked at the notes he had taken when Dr. Zata and Doc Yackley laid out the details for him.

"The good doctors explained it to me this way. There is something called genotype. O negative blood has a genotype called OO. It also lacks something known as A and B antigens. It's technical and above my pay grade, but my personal Sherlock Holmes and Doctor Watson understand it like we understand the law," explained Zeb.

"Whew. You're damn lucky to have a couple of experts so interested in the case," said Lentz.

"I tell you beyond a shadow of a doubt that with these guys it's an addictive hobby. They would like nothing better than to personally crack or help crack a big case. Funny thing is, I think in their minds it would slap an exclamation point on their already stellar careers."

"I'll bet. As we're talking, a couple of things came to mind. I think we can agree that Black Bear was Shappa's weak spot. And, from what you're saying, you believe she killed him," said Lentz.

"That's correct," replied Zeb.

"If she was willing to kill the one person she loved the most in this world, I don't know how you're going to find a weak spot."

"I know, or should I say I highly suspect, she's power hungry and greedy. I'm going to try to appeal to that part of her nature. Trick her somehow."

"Good luck with that. I wish I had something solid to offer you in terms of all that, but unfortunately, I don't," said Lentz. "I can tell you one other thing you might not know about her. It may be of value to you."

"Yes?"

"Shappa has as bad of a case of gold fever as anyone I've ever known or ever heard about. Even back when I was with her, years ago, she had a stash of gold that would make her a millionaire a few times over. Even that amount of loot wasn't enough for her. She spent a lot of time seeking out supposed gold stashes, shuttered gold mines and the like. She even sought out nearly all the local fabled Indian links to gold. There are so many stories of lost and never found gold fortunes in these parts that you could write a dozen books on the subject."

"I may be able to exploit her weakness," said Zeb.

Lentz responded with great skepticism in his voice.

"How?"

"I do have one ace in the hole," said Zeb.

"What's that?"

Zeb hemmed and hawed. He didn't know Lentz, who had been extremely helpful, well enough to share what he knew about the so-called Galiuro Mountain treasure trove of gold that went back to the Spaniards and the Aztecs. He certainly couldn't say a word about Echo being the Knowledge Keeper of all the People. For all Zeb knew, Lentz might still be carrying deeply buried feelings for Shappa. After all, even though he and Lentz worked on the same side of the law, Shappa and Lentz had been lovers not once, but twice.

"If you don't mind, and I don't want to offend you, I'd rather not say."

Lentz chuckled.

"If I were in your shoes, I wouldn't tell me either. But I suspect you're thinking I might mention part or all of this to Shappa. Don't worry. I won't. That train has left the station for good. Best of luck to you."

"Thanks," replied Zeb, turning off his phone.

Zeb lifted his feet onto his desk and stared across the highest elevations of Mount Graham. His mind was spinning with hope.

46

ZEB AND ECHO DISCUSS SHAPPA

Helen greeted Echo with her usual cheerfulness.

"How are those two little rascals of yours doing?"

"Growing bigger and smarter by the minute," replied Echo.

"Count your blessings and enjoy every second. The days go by faster than you can imagine."

"I try to keep that in mind," said Echo. "Is Zeb available?"

Helen pointed to Zeb's closed office door.

"Just go in. Unless he's changing a lightbulb, he's not doing anything important. I just heard his boots hit the top of his desk."

Echo smiled, tapped on the door and did not wait for a reply before entering Zeb's office.

"Hey, honey," said Zeb, sliding his boots off his desk.

"Hey there, handsome man of mine."

"What brings you by?" asked Zeb. "Tea?"

"No, I'm good, but go ahead if you want some."

"Nah."

"You got a minute?" asked Echo.

"For you? I've got all the time I've got. You look serious. What's up?"

"I want to see the letter again," said Echo.

Zeb knew right away what Echo was referring to—the threatening letter he had found on the kitchen floor when they had returned from Paris. The letter he waited too long in telling Echo about.

"Why? You know exactly what it says," said Zeb. "You're only going to make yourself feel threatened if you read it again."

Echo gave Zeb the look that all husbands get from their wives when they are not going to take no for an answer. Zeb knew he was fighting a battle he could not win or, for that matter, even bring to a draw. He opened the drawer of his office desk, reached in and grabbed the letter. Echo took a seat in the oversized chair that sat across from Zeb's desk. She leaned forward and took the letter in her hands.

"Do you have a sample of Shappa's handwriting?" asked Echo.

"Yes. She had to sign for Black Bear's things. It's only her signature."

"That might work."

Zeb left his office. Echo could hear him asking Helen for the official papers Shappa had signed. A moment later he placed the letter with Shappa's signature on his desk. Echo took it and placed the threat letter next to the document.

"I don't pretend to be a handwriting expert, but it looks to me like Shappa's signature and the letter were written by the same hand."

Zeb put on his cheaters and examined them both for at least the tenth time.

"Maybe. Maybe not. Hard to tell. I'm no expert either."

"Last night you said you were going to talk with Sheriff Lentz regarding Shappa again," said Echo.

"I just now got off the phone with him. Not more than a minute ago as a matter of fact."

"What did you learn about Shappa?"

"She's got a long history of fungal infections," replied Zeb.

"Hmm. I won't ask how you figured that out," said Echo. "I suppose it is helpful, but hardly conclusive."

"Might be very valuable. As you know, Dr. Zata found fungus inside the gun. It's a theory, a long-shot theory, I'm working on. I don't have all the information I need to get to the answers I need just yet."

"Okay. Anything else?"

"The O-negative blood that Zata found when he took the gun apart. As you also already know it's the same type of blood that flows through Shappa's veins."

"Her veins as well as millions of others," said Echo.

"True. But at least it's something."

"Okay. I agree. Inconclusive in court, I'd bet."

"You're right about that."

"From the way you sound it's enough to keep you digging into her as a suspect."

"It sure is. She's also got a big-time covetousness for gold. To hear Lentz tell it, her desire for gold rises to the level of lust."

Echo smiled.

"What?" asked Zeb.

"She has a weak spot that is exploitable then," replied Echo.

"How?"

"Let me worry about that," said Echo.

"But, but…"

"Don't worry. I'll keep you looped in."

Zeb knew right away it had to do with Echo's skills as the Knowledge Keeper and what she had found out in the Galiuro Mountains.

Echo kissed Zeb and headed out the door. She stopped in Zeb's doorway and turned back toward him.

"Wash and dry your hands. I don't want you bringing home any fungal infections."

Zeb gave her a thumbs up. He had no idea that what Echo had in mind meant that it was do or die time.

In her truck Echo made one phone call. On the other end of the line Shappa Hówakȟaŋyaŋ answered.

"Shappa, this is Echo Skysong."

"Yes, Sheriff Hanks' lovely wife and the mother of his two beautiful children, Onawa and Elan," replied Shappa.

It was clear what message Shappa was intending to put forth. She knew who Echo was and about her family. Echo sensed a thinly veiled threat. Shappa's innuendo only redoubled Echo's belief in what she needed to do. Echo wasted no time in getting right to the point.

"We need to meet."

"Why?" asked Shappa.

"I have something that is of great value to you."

"Might I ask what you have that is of value to me? Do you know who killed my son?"

"If I did, it would make no difference in the matter at hand."

Shappa became acutely suspicious. Echo, as Zeb's wife, probably had access to any and all inside information regarding the investigation into Black Bear's murder. Why would Echo want to step outside the rules of protocol to offer her any information? Naturally distrustful, but instinctually needing to know what was on Echo's mind, Shappa was willing to play along. If the shit hit the fan, what was one more murder, even if it was the wife of Sheriff Zeb Hanks?

"What is it?"

"We need to talk."

"We're talking right now," replied Shappa.

"It would be better to talk face-to-face."

The hair on Shappa's arms stood on end. Curiosity was climbing quickly.

"I might be able to make that happen. I need more information than you're offering, though."

"Are you on a secure line?" asked Echo. "I don't want any of this being heard by Zeb or any of his cohorts."

The implication that Echo was sidestepping Zeb had Shappa not only listening with intent but lowering her guard.

"Yes, this line is safe. Go on."

Echo answered with a single word.

"Gold."

Every inch of Shappa's skin tingled in hopeful ecstasy.

"I'm all ears."

"I am in a unique situation. If you can do me a simple favor, I can supply you with one thousand pounds of gold. All of it in ten-pound bars."

Shappa did a quick calculation in her head. At current market value that came roughly to twenty-four million dollars. Shappa knew that with that kind of money came great risk.

"Where would you get a thousand pounds of gold?" asked Shappa.

"I don't need to get it. I have that amount...and more."

Shappa began to salivate at the thought of one thousand pounds of gold.

"Can you prove to me that you have the gold?"

"I will send you an email with me standing in front of the gold. I'll send it right now, if you promise to destroy it once you've seen it."

"Send it."

Two seconds later the selfie image of Echo standing in front of a pile of gold bars appeared on Shappa's phone. Shappa's heart began to thump wildly against the inside of her rib cage. She was mesmerized by the dream of a lifetime. Not only would she be the head of the Guardians of the Golden Flame, but she would be one of the wealthiest women anywhere. Her heart seized with greed.

"Pictures can be faked," said Shappa.

"I can show you the gold in person any time you want to see it. The sooner the better."

Not that what she would be required to do mattered, but Shappa asked.

"What do you want me to do for you?"

"Kill my husband."

"Why?"

"He is blocking my only path to true power and authority. Like you, I have great power. He is getting in my way. Unlike you, I am not a Skinwalker. My powers would be diminished significantly if I killed him myself."

Shappa smiled broadly. Echo's statement was something she understood at her very core.

"With delight."

"When can you be here in Safford?"

"I've got some deep commitments. I can be there in three days."

"Great," replied Echo.

Shappa paused. Echo sensed a question coming her way, so she pre-empted Shappa, thus dangling the bait directly in her face.

"What is it you want to know?"

"You're the Knowledge Keeper, aren't you?"

Echo could tell it was a wild guess on Shappa's part. Echo decided to lead her on.

"If I were the Knowledge Keeper, I could never divulge it to anyone."

Shappa took it all as code talk. She was certain Echo was confessing, if ever so obtusely, to being the Knowledge Keeper of all the People. If Echo were the Knowledge Keeper, Shappa could murder her and assume the highly important position by default. That would make her not only wealthy beyond her wildest dreams but nearly immortal. Strength ran through every sinew of Shappa's body as she considered the power and wealth that would soon be hers.

Then a shocking bit of truth came out of Shappa's mouth. Echo knew it to be the truth as it was written into the glyphs of the Galiuro Mountains.

"Before the 1878 Navajo Witch purge my grandmother was the Knowledge Keeper. She was killed by the blue coats because of her power."

47

ECHO: A PLAN, PRAYER AND PREPARATION

Echo's mother had agreed to keep Elan and Onawa for a week. If Shappa had killed Black Bear, killing Zeb, Elan, Onawa, her parents or even Echo would not be outside the realm of possibility. If Shappa were guilty and had killed Black Bear for gold or power, and likely it was both, she must have a plan in mind.

Echo headed to the hieroglyphs and petroglyphs in the Galiuro Mountains to pray for guidance. Once there she went to work. Getting everything necessary for the sweat lodge was first on her list. If she was going to be able to do what was necessary, she would need not only the help of the Creator but help from the women Knowledge Keepers who now resided in the realm of the spirit world.

As she gathered the necessary elements of fire, wood, water and stone, prayer was continually at the forefront of her mind and guiding her along a path of righteousness and honor.

Her first task was to build a specific lodge. Gathering fresh cut willow branches and shaping them into a one-woman lodge was an effortless task performed with the intent a Knowledge Keeper carried in her heart. Images of those who had preceded her in this area of expertise flashed through her mind. The spirit images of all the women radiated beauty, love, strength and endurance as she spread ancient animal hides across the willows. The spirits joyfully gave her their wisdom.

Since this was the rare individual ceremony, Echo was also the fire keeper. She built a fire inside the center of the lodge and covered it with rocks. In no time the inside of the structure was steaming like a sauna.

Echo exited the lodge and performed a special prayer to each of the directions. She then entered the sweat lodge, covering the opening behind her. Tilting forward at the waist, she made four circles around the interior of the lodge, praying all the while. When she had completed the circles, Echo blessed the fire with tobacco, sweetgrass and other fresh herbs she had harvested nearby.

Taking a seat at the eastern edge of the sweat lodge, she pulled a small, animal skin-covered drum into her hands. With a rounded, leather-covered stick she began to beat rhythmically. Her uniquely created song blended with the pounding of the drum and matched the beat of her heart. Soon Echo was spiritually with her sister ancestral Knowledge Keepers. Their presence enveloped her in love, carrying her to a previously unknown place that was at once familiar. Surrounded by the beauty of all that is possible, her prayers were answered. The blessing of guided direction was given to her.

Echo put the drum to her side and prayed. The spirit world became so powerful that the ancestral Knowledge Keepers seemed to have taken human form. Echo could hear their prayers as they sang to her with advice and guidance. Hours later, exhausted, Echo departed through the opening and moved around the lodge four times in a clockwise direction.

Once outside she lay on some tufts of grass that had grown near some trees. The sand, protected from the sun, was also cooling. Echo drifted back into the reality of this world with the knowledge of what needed to be done. She was at peace and grateful.

48

PHONE CALL FROM SHERIFF LENTZ

Z eb's personal cellphone buzzed. He was surprised to see the number was that of Sheriff Lentz.

"Mitch."

"Zeb. Be expecting a package today with a pair of socks, a bloody handkerchief and a band-aid with blood on it. All are from Shappa's house. I had it overnighted to you."

The excitement in Sheriff Lentz's voice was unambiguous.

"Thanks. Muchas gracias."

"Glad to help a brother officer."

"Glad for the help. You got it done quickly."

"I know little secrets about her comings and goings. She is a creature of habit about a lot of things."

"Notice anything odd when you were inside her place?" asked Zeb. "Anything that can help me?"

"Funny you should bring that up. I did notice a couple of things that I found odd."

"Yeah?"

"All of the images, pictures, what have you, of Black Bear were either turned around, lying face down, removed or covered."

"I guess she may have a little bit of a conscience after all."

"Could be, but I think it's more of a superstitious thing."

"How's that?" asked Zeb.

"A lot of folks around here, and not just the Native Americans, believe that the spirits of dead people can see you for a year after their death, especially if the death came suddenly and unexpectedly."

"We've got a lot of folks around here that follow that same kind of thinking," replied Zeb. "Must have some basis in lore..."

"Or fact," interrupted Lentz.

"Perhaps. As Hamlet put it, 'There are more things in heaven and earth, Horatio, than are dreamt of in your philosophy.'"

"First time I've heard a sheriff quote Shakespeare," said Lentz.

"Don't be too impressed. It's the only thing I remember from my entire junior year of English literature. I have no idea why that quote stuck with me, but it did."

"Cool."

"You said there were a couple of things you noticed. Anything else that is relevant to the case?"

"Maybe, maybe not. I don't know. But it did strike me that Shappa left some handwritten notes that I interpreted as being from a conversation she might have had with your wife."

"They talked?" replied Zeb.

"I don't want to interpret a few lines of handwritten scratches, but I get the feeling the two of them are cooking up some kind of strange brew."

"Any idea at all as to what they might be up to?" asked Zeb.

"No. It doesn't make sense. Seems to have to do with gold. A lot of gold from what I could tell."

"I'll keep that in mind," said Zeb. "Anything else?"

"No, but I would appreciate being kept on the inside of whatever it is you find via the blood and the dirty socks."

"Roger that," said Zeb. "And wash and dry your hands thoroughly. The fungus we're looking into can live a long time and is hard to get rid of once you have it. If you haven't done that already, clean up everything you've touched since you grabbed the socks, etcetera."

Lentz's mind raced through everything he touched since he grabbed the socks. His conclusion was pretty basic.

"Shit!"

Zeb laughed out loud.

"I wish you'd mentioned that before."

"I thought I had."

"Maybe you did. I know what a mess the fungal infection was for Shappa when I dated her. I got infected more than once from her and had a hell of time getting rid of it. I'd sort of blanked it out of my mind. Shit! Shit! Shit!"

"The local doc and one of his buddies told me you need to detoxify yourself. I'd suggest you talk to an expert who can tell you which herbs and medicines can help you get rid of it."

"Thanks. It sucks to have to work on something related to a former girlfriend."

"That's life sometimes," added Zeb.

"Well, I guess."

"I will get back to you as soon as I have anything conclusive from the doctors. They are deeply involved and heavily motivated. I suspect it won't take them too long to narrow the scope of our investigation and probably even offer up some new leads."

"Great. I'll be waiting with itchy fingers and bated breath. Later."

"Later."

Zeb called Doc Yackley. Dr. Zata was coming over for a gourmet meal Doc was going to prepare for him. Doc assured him they would be working on everything tonight as soon as the package arrived.

49

SOCKS AND BLOOD

"Wasn't Socks the nickname of President Clinton's cat?"

Doc Yackley, holding up Shappa's socks in gloved hands posed the question to his cohort.

"Yes it was. Socks was a stray cat that wandered onto the White House grounds when Bill Clinton was president."

Doc Yackley pointed at the socks, a bloody handkerchief and band-aid with blood on it that Sheriff Lentz had been sneaky enough to remove from Shappa's house.

"I hope Socks smelled better than these socks."

"Cats ritualistically keep themselves clean using their tongues and saliva. The tongue is covered with small barbed papillae that can remove dirt, fleas, loose hair, food particles and other debris," replied Dr. Zata.

"TMI. Too much information," replied Doc.

"You asked."

"Okay, let's get to work and see if we can match the blood on the handkerchief with Shappa's and the fungus on the socks with that on the gun," said Doc.

The two old doctors went to work, like always, diligently and in almost complete silence. Using a microscope, slides and some other handy tools of their trade, it took little time to come to a conclusion. Dr. Zata peered into the microscope.

"Well, I guess that's that."

Zata stepped aside and Doc peered down the scope. He pulled his head back and made a few notes.

"Do you want to write up the report or should I?" asked Zits.

"I got it covered," replied Doc. "I think this is going to make Zeb happy."

"Now he can prove Shappa had her finger on the trigger."

"How's he going to prove she shot Black Bear beyond a shadow of a doubt?"

"That's his job," replied Zits. "I'm sure he'll get it done."

"I hope so. I get a really bad vibe from Shappa."

"Anyone who would shoot their own child, well, I guess they would not be someone to be trifled with."

"Can we consider this case closed?"

Zata and Doc shook hands.

"As far as what we can do to prove Shappa's guilt, we are done."

"Coffee?"

"Hell yes. Let's head on over to the Town Talk and kick back awhile. We've worked hard enough for a couple of old farts."

The men drove to the café. When they got out of Doc's Cadillac, each noticed how the other walked stiffly and with a limp.

"We're getting old," said Zits. "And I don't like it."

"Old in body doesn't mean old in spirit. Let's enjoy each minute of each day. It's all we really have anyway."

The men high-fived each other and ambled into the Town Talk.

50

ECHO AND SHAPPA: THREE DAYS LATER

E cho was acutely aware of just how devious and evil Shappa truly was. If she were to enter into a secret alliance with such a woman, she would need not only foresight, but eyes in the back of her head. A woman who would kill her own son for gold would certainly kill someone she barely knew without likely batting an eye. However, with her family's lives very possibly on the line, along with god knew what else, she would have to be outlandishly precise and clever.

An incoming text set off the buzzer on Echo's phone while Zeb was still asleep. The message was direct and to the point. It read: 'Meet me in three hours on the west side of the Home Depot in Safford. I'll be driving a dark green Nissan Armada with California license plates.'

Echo erased the message and was putting down her phone when Zeb's voice made her jump.

"Who was texting you at this time of morning?"

Echo looked over at Zeb. His hair was tousled. His eyes were crusty and even from a few feet away a whiff of his morning breath fouled the air.

"We need to talk," said Echo.

"Now? Before breakfast?"

Echo hopped out of bed. Her firm buttocks, even at 6 a.m. and with a few wrinkle marks from the sheets, looked erotically beautiful to Zeb. Echo noticed him staring at her.

"Get your mind out of the gutter. Meet me downstairs. I'll make some tea."

Zeb yawned and stretched.

"Okay, but my mind was most certainly *not* in the gutter."

"And please brush your teeth so I can properly kiss you good morning."

Zeb ran his tongue over his teeth. Echo was right. It was best that he got right on top of brushing them.

Echo had the hot pot pre-set from the night before. By the time Zeb had his pants on, she had a cup of tea setting at his usual place at the table.

"Morning sunshine," said Zeb.

He walked over to Echo, wrapped his arms around her and gave her a hug and a good morning kiss.

"My breath okay?"

"We need to talk," said Echo again.

"I've heard. What's up?"

Zeb brought the cup of tea to his lips as Echo responded.

"I've put out a hit on you."

The freshly sipped hot tea blew up and out of his nose when Zeb heard the words. He wiped the remnants off with the back of his sleeve.

"What? What the hell are you talking about?"

"I hired out a hit on you. I can't put it any simpler than that."

"You put out a hit on me? What'd I do to piss you off that much?"

"It's not for real."

Zeb pretended to wipe sweat off his brow.

"Whew."

"I mean the hit woman thinks it's for real, but it's not. I certainly don't want you dead."

"I figured as much. Mind telling me what the hell is going on?" asked Zeb.

"Do you want the long version or the CliffsNotes version?"

"Let's start with the CliffsNotes."

"I'm going to get Shappa to confess to killing Black Bear and get it on tape."

"I don't know. You're heading into dangerous territory. The woman is filicidal. Any woman who would kill her own son wouldn't hesitate for one second to put a bullet in your brain, or mine or that of anyone we know for that matter," said Zeb.

Zeb stopped short of mentioning Onawa, Elan or even Echo's parents. It was a seed he did not want planted. Nevertheless, it stuck his mind. How could it not?

Echo, on the other hand, had learned from combat what she could safely keep in her mind and what needed to be put elsewhere.

"That's precisely why she needs to be stopped now."

"It's my job to nab her, not yours."

Echo's face turned deadly serious.

"She's a threat to everyone I love. That makes it my battle. It makes it our battle."

Zeb knew there was no arguing with Echo.

"What do you have in mind?"

"I'm meeting Shappa in three hours by the Home Depot. She just flew into Phoenix. She's on her way here in a dark, green Nissan Armada with California plates, right now."

"What's your plan?"

Echo knew she was walking a mighty fine line. She needed Zeb's help. In order to get it she would need to expose some of what she was privy to regarding the Aztec/Spanish/Apache gold that was in the hands of the Knowledge Keeper. She also knew it would be difficult to allow Shappa to walk away alive, even if they got her confession on tape. None of it was insurmountable, but it was going to be tricky.

"How can I help? We need to work together," said Zeb.

"Here."

Echo handed Zeb a detailed, hand-drawn map of the special

petroglyph/hieroglyph area of the Knowledge Keeper in the Galiuro Mountains. He immediately recognized exactly where it was located.

"I want you here."

Echo had placed a large X where she wanted Zeb to hide.

"Bring your .30.06," she said.

"You want me to kill Shappa? Just like that? Put a bullet in her?" asked Zeb.

"I am hoping it doesn't come to that. Mostly I want you to have it for your own protection."

"Okay. I had already assumed she would come armed."

Echo pointed to another spot where she had drawn XX.

"This is where I will be taking Shappa to talk with her. This is where I will show her what she wants and needs to see. Hopefully, I can deal with her directly and get this all over with."

"What are you going to show her?" asked Zeb.

"I'm going to show her what she thinks she wants to see," replied Echo.

"You think you can do it without anyone getting hurt?" asked Zeb.

"I want no human being to die out there today."

Zeb found Echo's choice of words particularly curious.

"I'm taking the Aravaipa Canyon Road. I want you to park behind that large group of pyramidal arborvitae trees near the first farm. It's about a half mile off the main highway on the canyon road."

"I know the spot. I know exactly where you are talking about. Why don't you want me to go ahead and get ready before you get there?" asked Zeb.

"Shappa has a great sense of trickery. She also has extraordinary powers. There is a real possibility she would either sense or notice if you were in the area ahead of us. Wait for about five minutes after my truck goes past you. Follow us once we get down the road a piece. I will be driving at an average speed of forty miles per hour. I plan on turning off one mile before the regular road ends. That way you will pass us by, come in from the back side, and there is no way she will be able to see your truck. I placed a red flag near where you're to hide your truck. Remove it when you get there. I have an accessible view to that spot. That way I will know you are set. Got it?"

"I do."

"Make sure your vehicle is well hidden. I've already cut a bunch of branches that you can cover your truck with."

She pointed to the X on the map, about a quarter mile short of her and Shappa's intended meeting place.

"This is the spot where you will hide. I've marked it with a dark blue flag. The flag is near the ground, so be looking down for it. Like with the car, remove the flag so I can be certain you're in place. Give yourself enough time to walk the mile. It's mostly uphill. Wear good shoes."

Zeb smiled. To be wearing good shoes was a saying she had brought home from the war. Her field commander said it before each potential combat engagement. Zeb took this as a strict warning that he be prepared for potential engagement with the enemy. In this case, that meant Shappa.

"I've got to eat breakfast and get a few things done at the office," explained Zeb. "We don't know if Shappa will be on time. Text me when you see her pulling into the Home Depot. I'll leave then. It will give me plenty of time to get hidden behind those arborvitaes."

Zeb pulled Echo in close and kissed her deeply.

"I'm glad you brushed your teeth," she said.

Zeb was amazed at how cool Echo remained under the onset of imminent danger. His anxious heart was already preparing itself for what lie ahead.

The first thought that entered his mind was the possibility of putting a kill shot on the mother of his half-brother. He knew there was a very high likelihood that Shappa had killing Echo on her mind. What if things did not go as planned? The possibility of Shappa killing them both was not out of the picture either. He cleared his mind and began intense mental preparation for what was surely going to be a difficult day.

51

FATE APPROACHES

The text from Echo was succinct. 'Shappa's truck is pulling into the parking lot right now. Get moving.'

Zeb grabbed his hat, slipped it on and headed out the office door. When he was halfway through the door, Helen shot a question in his direction.

"When can I expect you back?"

"Late this afternoon. I think."

"Where are you headed?"

"The Galiuros."

"Are you meeting Echo?"

"Yes. She wants to show me something."

"Do you want me to inform anyone of where you are?"

Zeb hesitated before answering.

"If I don't check in by the end of the day, send someone to check on me."

Helen did not care for the sounds of that.

"What is going on?"

"It's complicated, but we've got a tip that might help us solve the Black Bear mess...all of it."

Helen sized up Zeb's body language. She knew him well enough to know something serious was in the offing.

"I'd feel better if either Kate or Clarissa knew what was up. What if you need back up?"

"This isn't officially sheriff's business," replied Zeb.

Helen peered knowingly over the top of her glasses. Zeb knew Echo didn't want anyone other than him to know what she was doing out in the Galiuros. Giving his exact position to Helen to give to one of his deputies might blow up in his face. On the other hand, knowing roughly where he was seemed harmless. His reply weakly departed his lips. Helen knew better than to accept his words as all that should be said.

"I'm taking Aravaipa Canyon Road."

Zeb grabbed a map and pointed to a spot about three miles from where he would be hidden with his eyes directed on Echo's and Shappa's interaction. If someone fired a shot, its echo would ricochet down the canyon to that point. He drew a circle.

"If someone needs to look for me, this is where I'll be. This is where they should look."

Helen snatched the map and secreted it away in her top desk drawer.

"Thank you."

Zeb smiled, tipped his hat and headed out the door.

S happa pulled into the west end of the parking lot. Echo drove next to her. She spoke to Shappa through their open windows.

"Hop in. I'll drive."

"I'm catching the red-eye back to Dakota. I need to control my own time. I'll follow you," replied Shappa. "We've got each other's cellphone numbers. We can contact each other if we get separated."

"Not much of chance of that, at least for the first twenty miles," said Echo.

"Shouldn't be a problem then, should it?"

"Okay. Follow me."

Echo headed down the Aravaipa Canyon Road. With her plan speeding repeatedly through her mind, in seemingly no time they were at the turnoff to the old Klondyke store. She kept an eye on Shappa who trailed her by roughly a half mile. The rolling, sometimes flat road, was particularly dusty. Echo did her best to keep the kicked-up sandy dirt to a minimum. Turning towards the Galiuros, just when the road became distinctly hillier, Echo's cellphone rang. It was Shappa.

"Echo, something I ate on the plane upset my stomach. I'm going to pull off the road and use nature's facilities."

"It's about a mile to the turnoff. I'll wait there for you."

"Great," replied Shappa. "See you shortly."

Shappa looked back down the road and pulled out a pair of binoculars. As suspected, she was being followed by a sheriff's vehicle. The deception was totally anticipated. No doubt Sheriff Hanks himself was in the truck.

Shappa pinned herself to the ground calling on yee naaldlooshi, the power witch. Time, tradition, family lore and experience had taught her to push away the pain of transformation of becoming a she-wolf.

Zeb's truck moved at a steady pace down the road. In the distance sun glinting off glass distracted him. Then, without warning, a large animal, a wolf or maybe a very large coyote, suddenly leapt in front of Zeb's truck. He twisted the wheel fast and hard to the left to avoid the large black animal with the strange silver streak on its head. His actions caused him to drive his truck into the ditch. His right foot never reached the brake pedal. He drove over a large boulder, breaking his axle in half. His truck had barely slowed before crashing head on into a rock embankment. In the process Zeb was knocked unconscious. His truck was instantly useless.

The large animal sprinted to the disabled truck. With nostrils flared and nose elevated the scent of fresh blood excited the animal's instincts. Its yellow eyes spotted a thin trail of blood trickling from the bottom of the driver's door. Aroused, it jumped onto the hood of the truck and searched with widened yellow eyes. Zeb was immobile, slouched over the steering wheel. The female creature waited a full minute. There was no movement. Another minute passed. Zeb had not moved as much as a single muscle.

From her vantage point, Shappa the she-wolf, was certain Zeb was dead. Jumping off the hood of the truck, she scampered back to the Armada. A moment later Shappa was standing next to her rented truck. She took a moment to gaze upon Zeb's wrecked vehicle before getting back into her Armada. Backing up to Zeb's truck, she grabbed her cellphone and took pictures of the slumped over sheriff and the blood leaking from the truck. Satisfied that Zeb was going nowhere until his funeral, she settled in behind the wheel and made tracks toward the gold and Echo.

When he finally came to, Zeb was slumped over the wheel, surrounded by the smoke created by the detonation of the nylon airbags. He rubbed his knee, not knowing how much time had passed. Glancing at his watch, he determined less than five minutes had gone by. In his head Zeb quickly recreated what had happened. With ever-increasing conscious awareness, the pain in his leg became more severe. Zeb's eyes fell on his bloodied pant leg. Slowly, his vision went from blurry to clear. He shook his head, hoping to clear it. As he looked around the inside of the car, he got a grip on the reality of his situation. With an aching neck, he glanced up, over the airbags and down the road and up the mountainside in the direction of his destination.

A little more than a mile ahead Echo watched as Shappa's vehicle approached. She pulled in next to Echo. She immediately noticed Shappa's face had flushed and her eyes had widened. She looked powerful, not sick. Only excitement would create such manifestations.

"Are you doing okay?" asked Echo.

"I'm fine now."

"The road gets quite a bit rougher up ahead. You sure you don't want to hop in with me?"

"I'm good. Let's get to business."

"Okay."

As Echo pulled away, she caught the image of Shappa out of the corner of her eye. Only it was not Shappa that she envisioned. Instead Echo, if only fleetingly, saw the face of her grandmother. The superimposition of her grandmother's face upon Shappa's shook her to her core. Echo knew that one of the tricks of a Skinwalker was to steal the face of someone close to their intended victim in order to keep them off guard. Echo was now one hundred percent certain she was dealing with a Skinwalker. She reminded herself not to look Shappa directly in the eyes under any circumstances. Doing so would allow Shappa to steal her essence and greatly weaken her physically, should their meeting end up in hand to hand combat.

Echo headed into the mountains with Shappa hanging closely behind her. There were many tight corners on the winding mountain road where Shappa could have easily rammed into Echo's back bumper and pushed her into oblivion. However, Echo knew that would likely not happen as Shappa's greatest desire was gold. Without Echo leading her to gilded, prized elemental ore, Shappa's lust would never be satisfied.

In the distance Echo's eyes fell upon the hiding place where she expected to see Zeb. Her heart shifted when she saw no hint of him. Perhaps he had hidden himself so well that she simply could not see him. She had instructed him to leave some obvious sign of his presence. Either she missed the indicator, or he was not there yet. A troublesome thought landed with lightning speed in her brain. What if somehow Shappa had figured out what the plan was and had been able to do away with Zeb? Echo had spent hours preparing for this exact situation. War had taught her that in the first minute of combat all plans become little more than theory. She moved forward into Plan B. It could be carried out without Zeb's aid and assistance.

Glancing again in the rearview mirror, she caught sight of Shappa. The face of her enemy was hardened, like those warriors she had seen who spent months in the wilderness waiting to engage in a single act of killing. That type of person was beyond frightening for the simple reason they believed their mission mattered more than their own existence. She prayed that Shappa's greed held sway over all else. Shappa's gluttony for gold would buy Echo some time. The indulgence and desire for gold would also steal clarity from her mind.

The road ended. The last half mile would be traversed on foot. Echo took a few seconds to recheck her already checked gun and other hidden weapons. Shappa stepped out of her vehicle. She had donned a vest made of wolfskin. Attached to the outer part of the vest, near the left pocket, were several unusual items. The first one that caught Echo's eye was a braided band of hair. It was rather similar in color to Echo's hair. Next to it, sewn into her vest, was a miniature leather quiver. The color of the quiver matched the wolfskin, making it well camouflaged. Jutting out of the quiver were what appeared to be bones honed into knives. Each glistened with the appearance of fresh human bones. A leather pouch that appeared beautifully handmade dangled from Shappa's belt. When Shappa turned to close the door of her vehicle, what seemed to be a small dart gun jutted out of her right rear pocket.

Whatever all these things were, they carried a dark aura and vibrated ominously to Echo, the Knowledge Keeper.

52

FATE ARRIVES

During the short walk to where Echo had placed the gold neither woman spoke. Echo's ears picked up the subtle sound of Shappa's feet skimming so lightly across the desert floor as to be barely discernable from the wind. The noiseless movement meant only one thing. Shappa was already on the hunt. Echo once again glanced to the spot where Zeb was supposed to be hidden. If he was there, Echo did not see him.

When the gigantic black wolf with a silver streak on its head had surprised him by jumping in front of his truck causing Zeb to break his axle in the ditch, Zeb also had severely damaged his knee. It slammed against the undercarriage of the dashboard, gashing his leg. Swollen and bleeding, he began limping his way toward his destination. Three miles walking up and down hills in pain and on uneven ground seemed daunting. Zeb had taped a compression bandage over the bleeding wound. It helped slow the blood flow but did nothing for the pain. Each forward step with his left foot caused a stabbing sting of agony in his knee and upper leg. He glanced at his watch and looked up toward the sun. There was a good chance Echo and Shappa had already reached their destination. There was also a chance he was simply too late to help Echo. He forced himself not to go into panic mode. Freaking out would only make the pain worse and slow his pace. Yet, he needed a large amount of adrenaline to force himself forward. With every step he kept his ears perked for the sound of a gunshot.

W hen they turned the corner and the collection of one hundred ten-pound bars of gold came into view, Echo and Shappa's reactions were polar opposites.

Echo calmly turned to Shappa to observe her reactions. Shappa's pupils dilated with excitement as she saw the stack of bars shimmering in the sunshine. Instantly she felt the dreams of a lifetime rising to their potential. Shappa turned to Echo with a single thought in mind. How can I kill this bitch most efficiently? Then Shappa's greed grabbed her.

"There's more gold than what you're showing me, isn't there?"

Echo hesitated. There was more, so much more. Would it do any good to answer her question? A split-second decision was necessary. Echo was up to the task.

"Yes," replied Echo. "Of course there is."

"Where?" asked Shappa.

Echo pointed to the one hundred neatly stacked bars.

"We have a deal for this amount of gold and this amount of gold only."

Shappa mentally weighed her options. She could kill Echo right now and disappear with twenty-four million dollars-worth of gold. Or, she could bide her time and possibly end up with ten times as much. Maybe a hundred times as much gold, if the legends she had heard held true. Shappa lingered briefly upon an old adage she had heard many times. A bird in the hand is worth two in the bush. Somehow it did not seem applicable when so much more gold might be had for such little effort.

· · ·

*Z*eb trudged through a deep arroyo, twisting his bad knee. The pain zinged down his leg which he now had to drag. Forward movement felt no easier than slogging through quick mud. He cursed his injury, his aging body, his pain and his situation. His 30.06 felt clumsy, heavy in his hands. However, one thought of the distress Echo could possibly be in had him moving forward with a renewed burst of energy. Zeb calculated how long it would take him to cover the distance between himself and Echo. Twenty minutes seemed right. Maybe eighteen if he pushed himself with all he had. The thought of Elan and Onawa going through life without their mother had him digging deeply into a resilience he didn't know he had. The once painful movement of each step disappeared. There was only one thing to do—get there for Echo's sake and safety.

"How are we going to get all of this gold out of here?" asked Shappa.

"The gold is not going anywhere until you offer proof that Zeb is dead," replied Echo.

Shappa eyed Echo resting her hand on her sidearm.

"Proof?"

Shappa pulled out her cellphone and clicked on the photos app. Up popped a half-dozen pictures of Zeb leaning against the steering wheel and the blood that had leaked out the driver's door. Echo gulped. She silently and quickly sent a prayer to Usen that Zeb was still alive.

"You checked his pulse?" asked Echo.

"The door was jammed. I couldn't get it open. I've seen dead people many times. Zeb Hanks is dead. I promise you that."

Echo dared not believe it. She would have felt the universe fracture at the moment of his death. She had not sensed any such thing. She did not believe he was dead but was certain he was incapacitated. The Zeb she knew was not the kind of man to die easily.

"Why did you want him dead?"

Echo had already explained her reasoning to Shappa. She had anticipated Shappa would once again ask the question, perhaps trying to trick her. She created a lie that Shappa would have no choice but to believe as it fit her paradigm of life and death.

"He was robbing me of my power."

Shappa nodded. "Of course, he was. That's what men do to powerful women."

No further explanation was required. Shappa was satisfied with Echo's response.

"How are we going to get a thousand pounds of gold out of here?" asked Shappa.

"Follow me."

Echo led Shappa down a side trail. Hidden behind a big rock was a small ATV.

"Good planning," remarked Shappa.

"Planning is my area of expertise," replied Echo.

"Let's get to work," said Shappa.

Echo got behind the wheel and parked the ATV with great precision. With the utmost caution she exited the vehicle and made her way to the stack of gold bars. As she approached Shappa, she jingled the keys and made a show of putting them in her pocket.

E ach forward step was once again deeply pained as Zeb progressed up higher into the mountains to the designated spot. He was unaware that Echo had all but given up on him arriving to aid her. The blood on his pant leg was beginning to dry. The compression bandage was holding back new blood from dispersing. His breathing was labored as he climbed upwards over rocks and through arroyos. Fatigue was setting in. Adrenaline was fading. Sheer grit and the power of love were the only things still propelling him forward. He stopped for ten seconds to catch his breath. In the distance he heard a motor turning over with some difficulty. He instantly recognized the sound of the engine's starting pattern. It was Echo's ATV. What did it mean? Was Echo moving about? Had

Shappa overpowered her and discovered the ATV? Certainly, Echo would not have handed over the keys to the ATV without good reason. Then, the engine of the ATV abruptly stopped. He knew the engine. It did not run in idle. Echo had started it and shut it off. She was merely making certain it would start. By his best estimation, Zeb was roughly half of a mile from where he needed to be. He did not like the odds. Hearing the engine catch and rev up strongly, Zeb began to quicken his pace. The potential of what lay ahead carried a significant amount of fear.

S happa worked at twice the pace of Echo in loading the gold bars onto the back of the ATV.

"We're going to have to make two trips," said Echo.

"I think we can do it in one," said Shappa

"I know the load capacity of this vehicle," replied Echo. "Believe me, you don't want to break down and have to hand carry these bars one at a time to your vehicle."

Shappa, sweating profusely from excitement and work, took off her vest.

"How many do we have loaded?" asked Shappa.

Echo leaned in and began to count.

"Forty-eight. Let's load two more and take them to your Armada," said Echo.

The women each grabbed one last gold bar to complete the first load. Echo, with a nod of the head, allowed Shappa to deposit her brick first. As she stepped away from the back of the ATV, she reached into a hidden pants pocket. Echo, gold bar in hand, bent forward and placed it in the back. All the while she tightened every muscle in her body and braced for the inevitable. Fate now held all the cards.

. . .

Zeb heard the sickening thud come echoing down the canyon. He knew all too well the sound of a blackjack crashing against a skull. He prayed Shappa's blackjack was covered with thick leather as that might offer Echo a bit of protection. Zeb begged God that Shappa's end game was to elicit more information from Echo and that Echo had not been killed by the blow. He was less than two hundred yards away from the women. He listened for the sound of an engine starting. When it did not happen, Zeb realized there was no guessing what was going on. He took his 30.06 off safety and moved as quickly as he could through the rocks and underbrush.

With each step he covered a few more feet. By the time he reached a small knoll he dropped cautiously to his knees and began to crawl. Popping his head over the rim of dirt and sand covered rocks, he witnessed Shappa digging through Echo's pockets. He quickly concluded she was searching for the ATV key. It took little time at all for her to find it.

Zeb lifted his rifle to his shoulder and eyed through the scope. Resting his hand on the trigger, he slowed his breathing to prep for his shot. One breath in. One breath out. His eyes were focused. His heart was calm. Zeb's finger rested against the trigger as he waited for Shappa to turn slightly. He wanted a body shot, a shot to the heart. A head shot would be iffy in case Shappa, for some reason, moved her body suddenly. It was not a risk he wanted to take. He could take no chance that anything would go wrong. He watched as Shappa moved toward the remaining gold bars. In a surrealistic scene, she sat down on top of the gold bars, took out her cellphone and took a selfie. She checked it, holding her hands over her eyes to block out the sun. Apparently dissatisfied with the shot, she took another, then another, until she had the one she liked.

The rifle was getting heavy in his hands. Zeb rested it on top of the ridge line for a few seconds. Cold sweat trickled down his forehead. Patience was vitally important. Zeb once again raised the rifle to his eye. He was waiting for a straight on shot to Shappa's chest. He wanted a shot that would enter her body, pierce her heart and leave a gaping hole as it exited through her back.

Then something inconceivable, something unimaginable happened. Shappa, as she approached the ATV, turned to have one more look at the remaining gold bars. Her foot hit something and down she went. In the process an immense trap, a wolf trap came immediately to Zeb's mind, snared her leg. As she crumpled and hit the ground, her arms flew out in front of her and landed in a second wolf trap. This one clenched and closed around her neck. Bones cracked. Shappa's skull was crunched in half by the powerful jaws of the wolf trap. Blood spewed in every direction. It all happened instantly, yet in slow motion. Shappa never made a sound except for an oomph when her body fell to the ground after being snared by the first trap. Zeb could hardly believe what he witnessed with his own eyes.

Holding onto his gun, he moved as quickly as he could toward Echo. Shappa was clearly dead and of no danger to him. Echo let out a small, incomprehensible groan.

Zeb knelt next to her. Gently rolling her over and protecting her from the bright sunlight, he waited for Echo to open her eyes. Not knowing what else to do, he softly rubbed her face. Five minutes later she opened her eyes. Sounding bewildered she spoke to Zeb.

"Is Shappa dead?"

"She won't be bothering you in this lifetime," replied Zeb.

Echo exhaled a sigh of relief.

"And you're all right?"

"I've got a sore knee, but basically I'm fine."

"Good."

"Do you know who you're talking to?" he asked.

"Give me a kiss, then I'll tell you," replied Echo.

Zeb bent down and kissed Echo lovingly.

"Colonel Hanshoffer. Is that you?" said Echo.

They both began to laugh. Colonel Hanshoffer was Echo's war time commanding officer.

"Close enough," said Zeb, kissing her a second time.

"Pardon me if I don't feel romantic, but I've got one pounder of a headache," said Echo.

"Roger that."

"Oh. Be careful. I've got four wolf traps buried right around where I parked the ATV. I buried them like IED's."

Zeb quickly spotted the other two and had a pretty good idea how Echo had pre-planned for Shappa's demise. There would be plenty of time to talk about that later.

Echo stared off into the distance before closing her exhausted eyes for a moment's rest. Zeb gazed down on her lovingly before tracking his eyes up the side of the canyon wall in the direction Echo had stared before shutting her eyes. There, high on the canyon wall, in a place that would be impossible for anyone to reach, was an ancient petroglyph of an Indian trapping a wolf.

53

STENCH, DENT AND REVENGE

Doc Yackley and Dr. Zata finished the autopsy of Shappa Hówakȟaŋyaŋ. As they finished cleaning up, Zeb walked into the autopsy room with Tribal Chief Burries at his elbow. Zeb approached the men, reached out and shook their freshly washed hands. Chief Burries carried a scowl on her face and offered no greeting.

"Zeb," said Doc. "What can I do for you?"

"Chief Burries has been in contact with Sheriff Lentz up in Oglala Lakota County. He has requested she accompany the body of Shappa back to the Pine Ridge Reservation."

"Curious request."

Zeb glanced at Chief Burries. No doubt she was behind the request as some sort of power play. Not that it mattered, but it was just one more way for her to create a hassle, a small one, but a hassle, nevertheless.

"What do you have in mind, Chief Burries?" asked Zeb.

"Shappa's ex-husband and I are going to drive the body north first thing in the morning. Can you release the body to me immediately?"

Zeb looked to Doc Yackley and Dr. Zata for direction. They nodded in the affirmative.

"Take her away," said Doc. "Do you have a casket?"

"We don't need one. Tom is bringing a truck, a wooden crate and some blankets. He should be here any minute."

"If you don't mind, I'll supervise the loading of the body," said Zeb. "By law I have to witness the exchange of the body."

"More White man regulations," grunted Chief Burries. "Ridiculous."

"We've got the final paperwork to finish up to send to the state and feds," said Doc Zata. "Please excuse us."

"Thanks, Docs," said Zeb.

Once again, Chief Burries was thankless. Chief Burries and Sheriff Hanks stood silently waiting for Tom Sawyer, the crate, blankets and truck. Doc Yackley and Dr. Zata walked into Doc's office, shut the door, grabbed a few things and sneaked out the side door.

When the doctors arrived at Chief Burries truck, Pee Wee and Duke had already done their nefarious deed. A thousand dents from pellet guns peppered the sides and hood of Burries truck. Now it was the doctors' turn.

Doc Yackley, by no means a spring chicken, slid under the rear end of the truck near the exhaust system. Dr. Zata crouched nearby. They communicated in short bursts, not unlike surgeons in the middle of an operation.

"Automatic stinker."

Zata chuckled as he handed Doc the tricked out automatic air freshener. He had disabled the motion sensor so as not to have it constantly working and exchanged the liquid air freshener with weasel lure, a putrid smelling substance. Zata removed the peel tape from the Velcro backing that they had added.

"Cleaning rag."

Zata handed Doc a rag to clean the undercarriage of the truck where he was going to attach the homemade device. He cleaned the area and handed the rag back to Zata.

"Duct tape."

Zata handed Zeb a six-inch piece of duct tape. Doc attached the spray device with the Velcro, checking to make sure it stuck cleanly. He doubled his effort by adding the duct tape.

"Timer."

Dr. Zata had rigged up a battery run timer that ran on AAs. He made a plug-in device so the timer attached to the air freshener. On the back of the timer there was also a Velcro patch.

Doc attached the timer to the bottom of the truck in the area he had already cleaned with the rag. He pressed the Velcro against the bottom of the truck and checked that it was sticking well.

"Duct tape."

Zata handed Doc a second piece of duct tape. Doc placed it over the timer ensuring its stability. With a careful hand he connected the spray device and the timer.

"Duct tape."

Zata handed Doc the final piece of duct tape. It was short. Doc used it to press the wire up against the undercarriage of the truck to make sure if Burries ran over a stick or big rock it wouldn't accidentally get yanked on. With that their prank was all set. Chief Burries was going to not only be befuddled, but Doc would have his revenge.

Doc slid out from under the car. Just as they walked back into the building Tom Sawyer pulled up. Their timing was perfect.

"That ought to do it," said Doc.

"Yup. It ought to."

"How often did you set the timer to go off and spray the weasel lure?" asked Doc.

"Every four hours."

"Good."

"If she doesn't get under the truck and find it, there is enough weasel lure to last about one hundred twenty sprays."

"Three solid weeks of hell..."

"And confusion."

"Dirty deeds..."

"Done dirt cheap."

The cunning old doctors patted each other's backs. Both old men felt vital and young again.

"Revenge, as they say…"

"Is the best revenge."

They high-fived.

"Get your car fixed to your satisfaction?" asked Zata.

"Better than brand new," replied Doc. "Better than brand new."

54

TOWN TALK

T he Monday morning staff meeting at the Town Talk had brought everyone together in one spot for the first time since Echo had trapped Shappa. With what they found on her body and in her cellphone all the crimes had been resolved. Zeb felt like he owed the staff a complete explanation. Most everyone on the staff had a partial explanation. Some of the answers to the crimes might never be known. Maxine Miller filled everyone's cup with regular coffee except for Zeb who drank chamomile tea. Song Bird, though not part of the staff, was attending the meeting. He drank the mud from the bottom of the Bunn carafes.

Attending the meeting were Zeb, Echo, Kate, Clarissa, Rambler, Helen, Shelly, Song Bird, Josh Diamond (Kate's husband), Doc Yackley and Dr. Zata who happened to be in town visiting Doc. Noticeably absent were Jake and Black Bear. Zeb tapped the edge of his tea cup with a spoon.

"It is important that you all know how much your work on these cases means to me. Therefore, a thorough explanation of what happened is appropriate. You all know most of what happened but some of the details and inferences of how we got the problem solved might not be any clearer than Song Bird's coffee."

Laughter among the already elated group filled the private back room of the Town Talk.

"As you all know, the crimes committed at the school, the nursing home, the water plant and at Swig's were a ruse, a ruse to get me out of office and to lead us astray."

"It worked for a while, didn't it?" said Song Bird.

"It did indeed," replied Zeb. "But before I get into all that, I lift my cup to my mentor and long-time friend, Jake Dablo."

The room became quiet and still.

"Without his help we would never have solved this case. Without him I would not be the kind of sheriff I am today. May he rest in peace."

A murmuring of amens filled the room. Zeb allowed a few moments of quiet before continuing.

"Shappa Hówakȟaŋyaŋ was a power hungry and greedy woman. She, along with Senator Russell, were behind everything that happened. They sought power and gold through a cult, a secret society known as the Guardians of the Golden Flame. Senator Russell was the Grand Master. Shappa Hówakȟaŋyaŋ was second in command until Senator Russell's planned death. At that time, she became the Grand Master."

Confusion covered the faces of many of the attendees. They knew Senator Russell had died of kidney cancer. How could that have been planned?

"I see that topic is causing some confusion."

Rambler Braing spoke for the confused in the group.

"It certainly is."

"Shappa knew, we believe she got her information from Black Bear's doctor, that Black Bear had kidney cancer. She also knew Russell needed a kidney transplant or he would die. She preyed upon his desperation. She made a deal with the devil, killed her son and had his cancerous kidneys transplanted into Senator Russell, assuring his death. When that happened, she became the Grand Master of the Guardians of the Golden Flame."

As the entire group began to understand the unfolding of the crime and just how wicked it all was, a palpable tension drifted through the room. When it came to people like Shappa and Senator Russell, no one was truly safe.

"You should also know, if you don't already, that Senator Russell was my biological father. I guess my mother actually did love him."

Helen forcefully interjected her two cents worth on the subject.

"She did, and you are a product of that love."

"Russell was also Black Bear's biological father. Shappa used Senator Russell to get what she wanted. In the process they slept together. It's a long story and I don't have all the details, but it's a fact."

Clarissa and several others gasped at the implications of Black Bear and Zeb being half-brothers.

"Senator Russell bequeathed all of his property and money to me. I am going to set up a charitable foundation for the general welfare of the people of Graham County with the money. I am going to donate his property to the City of Safford for general use purposes. I am selling his other properties and adding those funds to the general fund of Graham County. In death, Senator Russell will actually be doing a lot of charitable things for everyone in the area."

The group applauded Zeb's gestures.

"One of our big breaks came when the rings kept popping up in everyone's memories. The rings were worn only by members of the Guardians of the Golden Flame. From what Shelly has discovered, the Guardians of the Golden Flame are still very wealthy and operating in numerous capacities. They may well come after us."

"Let 'em come," said Kate.

Her response brought a universal chuckle from the group. After all they had taken down the leadership and mucked up the works, albeit temporarily, of the evil collective.

Zeb hoisted his tea cup.

"I salute all of you who helped return normality and safety to Graham County. Long may we run."

Everyone chanted in unison.

"Here, here. Here, here. Here, here."

At that moment Lolotea and Bodaway came through the door with Elan and Onawa. Just learning to walk with assistance, they stumbled excitedly toward Zeb and Echo crying out, "Dada. Momma."

Smiles and hopefulness filled the back room of the Town Talk. The future could not have looked brighter.

THE END

ALSO BY MARK REPS

ZEB HANKS MYSTERY SERIES

NATIVE BLOOD

HOLES IN THE SKY

ADIÓS ÁNGEL

NATIVE JUSTICE

NATIVE BONES

NATIVE WARRIOR

NATIVE EARTH

NATIVE DESTINY

NATIVE TROUBLE

NATIVE FATE

NATIVE ROOTS (PREQUEL NOVELLA)

THE ZEB HANKS MYSTERY SERIES 1-3

AUDIOBOOK

NATIVE BLOOD

HOLES IN THE SKY

ADIÓS ÁNGEL

OTHER BOOKS

BUTTERFLY (WITH PUI CHOMNAK)

HEARTLAND HEROES

ABOUT THE AUTHOR

Mark Reps has been a writer and storyteller his whole life. Born in small-town southeastern Minnesota, he trained as a mathematician and chiropractor but never lost his love of telling or writing a good story. As an avid desert wilderness hiker, Mark spends a great deal of time roaming the desert and other terrains of southeastern Arizona. A chance meeting with an old time colorful sheriff led him to develop the Zeb Hanks character and the world that surrounds him.

To learn more, check out his website www.markreps.com, his AllAuthor profile, or any of the profiles below. To join his mailing list for new release information and more click here.

BB bookbub.com/authors/mark-reps
facebook.com/ZebHanks
twitter.com/markreps1

HEARTLAND HEROES - CHAPTER 1

KNOCK, KNOCK, KNOCK—KNOCK, KNOCK—KNOCK. I rapped out the clichéd three, two, one pattern on wooden frame of the front screen door of Charlie's house. The pine wood of the front door sang in response to my knuckles. I wasn't about to burn any more daylight than was absolutely necessary on the first day of summer vacation. It was time to get rolling. It was time to play ball.

Charlie had probably slept right through the chirp of baby robins, the rising warmth of the morning sun and even the wafting smell of coffee percolating on his parents' new Maytag gas stove. When he didn't shout down from his bedroom, I gave a second dramatic rap on the door. Sort of a bump-ba-da-dum-dum. Dum dum.

I imagined Charlie lying in bed, opening his grit-filled eyes to the peeling, yellowed wallpaper that drooped in the corner of his bedroom. I had done my best to wake him from a distance by roaring through the neighborhood on my Hiawatha Starfire bicycle. I used Topps baseball cards clamped tightly with clothespins through the tires' spokes to create the perfect noise. Corvette muffler meets rock and roll guitar is what Charlie called it. He accused me of having a serious ongoing fantasy about a buxom movie star, either Raquel

Welch or Marilyn Monroe, rolling into town and being so duly impressed by the sound that she'd beg me for a ride. I think it was more his fantasy than mine, but it worked for me too. I spent my days working on style and imagination. The old-timers around town called me a dreamer. I took it as a compliment.

Standing and waiting at the front door I could hear Charlie mumbling through his open bedroom window.

"Dog gone it all! Crap."

Charlie was being Charlie and if this day was like every other he was cursing himself for not having untied the ever-present knots in his shoelaces before having gone to bed. At night his shoes were dripping wet from dew that glistened from every blade of grass we traipsed through playing moonlight tag or capture the flag or some other night game. They were also most certainly caked with the ever-present reddish-brown iron ore dust that clung to everything in our hometown. Charlie's shoes always smelled like an infected dishrag that had been used to wipe up sour milk. Try as I may, I could never teach him about the importance of proper shoe maintenance.

"Hey, Charleston," I shouted. "Let's get going or we'll miss the big dance."

He caught my reference like it was an easy pop fly.

"Hold your horses. It's spring training, not the world get serious," he shouted through his bedroom window. "I'm trying to get my shoes on."

"Error's on you, hotshot. You should learn to untie 'em at night, dunderhead."

He pushed open the screen and cupped his hands around his mouth. He lowered his voice so his mother wouldn't hear his wise crack.

"Go lick the crack of a frog's butt and tell me if you hallucinate."

I rapidly stuck my tongue in and out of my mouth. I wiggled it just like a snake I'd seen on a National Geographic special.

"Okie dokie, dominokie. Find one and I will. But make it a girl frog, would you?"

"I'm gonna make you do it. My sister's got a pet toad in her room."

"Okie dokie, smokey. But a toad ain't a frog. By the way, do I get to kiss your sister too?"

"If you're dumb enough to do that, I sure as heck ain't going to try and stop you."

Charlie's mom must have heard the commotion. She came to the door with a smile on her face and a red and white plaid kitchen towel in her hands. Mrs. Scerbiak's life was like something right out of an ad in *Better Homes and Gardens* magazine. A hundred times I'd seen her dreamily waltz past her new kitchen dinette set, running a single finger across its Formica top as she performed the double duty of assuring herself of its existence while checking for cleanliness. Many times she had wishfully affirmed to anyone within earshot that a genuine Betty Crocker kitchen would be hers one day.

When I heard her coming, I turned and tossed a small stone toward a nearby streetlight. I missed by a mile.

"How's the arm, Maximillion? Is your aim true?"

She was the only person in the whole wide world who I liked calling me Maximillion. I had a soft spot in my heart for her, and she had one for me. It was an unspoken kinship that I understood but never spoke of with her or anyone else. We had both lived through a common, horrible experience. We had suffered the loss of a mother in childhood. Mrs. Scerbiak's mother had died in a regional flu epidemic in December of 1931 when Mrs. Scerbiak was only one year old. I knew the date because Charlie and I put flowers on her grave every year on her birth date. My mom passed on July 4, 1952. She died during childbirth...mine.

Mrs. Scerbiak was the only person on the planet who knew and somehow understood that a secret part of me felt responsible for my mother's death. Guilt is a strange and powerful animal. What else besides guilt do you know of that is invisible, has no substance or form yet can still weigh a ton?

"It's early in the baseball season, Mrs. Scerbiak. By the time the World Series rolls around in October I bet I'll be able to hit that pole nine times out of ten...with my eyes shut."

I fired one last shot at the light. I was hoping to impress my surrogate mother. I came no closer to hitting it than I did the first time. I missed it by the proverbial mile. She smiled and invited me in the house.

"Charlie's up in his bedroom. He's probably trying to get his shoes untied," she said with a knowing wink.

I scooted through the front door, politely removing my baseball cap as I passed under the threshold. Bounding up the stairs, three steps at a time, I landed on the upper stoop and made a high-speed right turn, practically a ballet-type pirouette, using the wooden handrail as a brace. From there it was a quick summersault across the crumpled sheets of Charlie's unmade bed. Doing an 'army man-in-training' dive to my final position, I landed in a kneeling, praying position on the opposite side of his bed.

"Smooth move, ex-lax."

"Sgt. Rock's got nothin' on me, Private."

"Right arm."

"Left off."

I nodded, pulled my baseball cap from my back pocket, handed Charlie a stick of fresh, dust-powdered baseball card gum and fanned out a brand-new set of player cards. He popped the gum in his mouth and scanned all thirty of them with a single glance.

"Look at that. How'd you ever get Eddie Mathews, Mickey Mantle, Hank Aaron, Stan "The Man" and Whitey Ford all in one short set?"

"I've got an in with the commissioner of baseball."

"And I'm a monkey's uncle."

"The monkey part I can believe, especially the way your arms hang to your knees, but you ain't nobody's uncle."

I snatched up the Eddie Matthews card. With a sidearm flick of my wrist, I sent it sailing in Charlie's direction.

"Then here you go, Cheetah. Send your thank you note to Baseball Commissioner Bill Eckert."

Charlie's nimble fingers deftly snared the falling card in mid-flight.

"Nice hands," I said.

"Thanks, man. I was born with both of 'em," said Charlie waving them in the air, slapping me with a double handed high five.

"You wouldn't be getting that card if he wasn't a Brave."

"I wouldn't take it for all the tea in China if it was a Yankee," Charlie replied.

Friendly banter, a perfect way to start the first day of summer. I think Charlie and I took opposing points of view on things just to practice our arguing skills. Mrs. Scerbiak said we might both make good lawyers someday. In reality we never really disagreed much on anything, but both of us always tried to get in the last word. Charlie said I always tried to make my point by talking louder but insisted that he was the master of logic. I balked at that, saying he argued with the emotion of a girl, whereas I always made certain of my facts.

We were both vigorously breaking in the baseball bubble gum and memorizing the statistics on the back of the new baseball cards when Charlie's dad poked his head into the room. He pounded his knuckles on the door and let out an 'ahem' to get our attention. We looked up for half a second, acknowledging his presence before returning to our business.

"What are you boys doing?" he asked. "Prayin' for rain?"

"Ha! Ha! Good one, Mr. Scerbiak," I said. "But what Charlie is praying for is that he doesn't strike out today like he did last week-end...with bases loaded...in the bottom of the ninth."

The mere reminder of his shortcoming in last week's game earned me a sharp knuckle rap to the shoulder.

"Max, did your dad say if he was joining us for coffee this morning?"

"It's the highlight of his week. He'll be there."

Charlie's dad smiled and headed outside to his rusting '55 Pontiac Star Chief. Lots of black coffee, a sweet roll and guy talk at the Hi-Way Café with his buddies was as much of a ritual as going to church on Sunday.

"C'mon, let's get movin'," I demanded.

Charlie glanced at the clock radio on his bedside table.

"Jeez, you're right. We'd better get some warmups in before game time."

A few moments of effortless, coordinated teamwork and the baseball cards were stashed away in the top dresser drawer. Charlie placed them next to some of Grandma Ptacek's prayer cards, an old family rosary, a salt lick and a couple of pieces of half burned incense. This was Charlie's special voodoo amalgam aimed at seeking good fortune in baseball and to a lesser extent life in general. The way he had it figured, maybe the Good Lord willing, this odd collection of artifacts would present him with the good fortune of becoming a professional ballplayer with the Braves. In our minds combining the magic of baseball with the faith of religion was as routine as eating crackers with soup.

"Mom, we're going to Nordich Field to play ball," yelled Charlie.

"Are you going to be home for lunch? Is Max coming with you?"

"We haven't decided yet."

"Well your mother needs to know so she can figure out how many cans of tuna to open for sandwiches. So what's it going to be? Shall I plan on the two of you or not?"

I pulled a pair of crumpled up one-dollar bills from the front pocket of my grass-stained pants. Charlie gave me the thumbs up.

"No, Mom. We'll grab something to eat at the Burger and Suds. See ya'."

"Be home for dinner then."

"Okay, all right. I'll be home for dinner," Charlie grumbled. "Gad, she treats me like I'm still a kid."

I told Charlie to quit bitching about all the rules his mom laid down for him.

"It's really nice your mother gets dinner for you every night," I said. "Now turn that frown upside down before it's seen all over town."

"And makes me look like a silly old clown. I know, I know. Oh, okay, I guess you're right."

"You're darn tootin' I'm right. I mean how many guys have a mother who has her own cooking column in a newspaper? Huh?"

"Gimme a break."

Racing down the stairs, we jumped over the bottom five steps and landed with a loud, echoing thud. Bolting through the screen door, we were mounting our bikes by the time the door banged shut. Charlie cringed, drawing his shoulders to his ears as the slamming sound of the door reached us. He had been warned a thousand times *not to slam the door*. An equal number of warnings had been issued when it came to running down the stairs. Some things were tougher than others for growing boys to remember.

I gave my bicycle a fake kick-start and revved the tasseled handlebar grips. Pulling back on the handlebars to lift the front tire in the air, I yelled over my shoulder in Charlie's direction.

"Listen for the sonic boom."

I loved speed. I had my entire future mapped around it. My plan was simple - high school, Air Force Academy, Air Force flight school, astronaut training, mission to Mars. My bike was christened Friendship Seven. My dog, Laika, was named after the first dog into space. I was going to be the next John Glenn.

"The only sonic boom you'll ever make is through your butt cheeks."

Charlie shot past me like I was standing still.

"Boom boom, hot shot," he shouted.

"Boom boom yourself."

Halfway down High Street, in front of a house owned by a new guy named Schumann, Charlie slammed on his brakes. I almost rear-ended him.

"Look at that," he said pointing to a NO TRESPASSING sign nailed to the new security fence. "Can you believe that kind of crap?"

"I saw it on the way over to your place. I stopped and sneaked a peek over the top of his fence," I explained. "He's got the biggest, ugliest black wolfhound I've ever seen back there. It trots back and forth like it's guarding some sort of Nazi prison camp. I wonder what the heck he's up to."

"I don't know. My dad says he heard Schumann put in a security system with an electronic eye. It's even got a camera."

"I'll betcha' anything it's one of those infrared jobbies that can film in the dark," I said.

"He's up to no good, that's for sure."

"One day, electronic eye and guard dog be danged," I said, "you and I are gonna to sneak up and have a peek into his house to see what he's hiding. Cuz I know he's up to no good."

"How do you know that?" asked Charlie.

"I got a sixth sense about it."

"I'm game for peeking into Schumann's house but only if he's not around," replied Charlie.

"Don't sweat the small stuff. I've already got a plan up my sleeve. When the time comes, we'll play it safe. He'll never even know we were there."

"Why do I get a bad feeling when you start yacking like that?" asked Charlie.

"Because you still need to be tucked in at night, that's why."

"Shut up!" he said slamming the front tire of his bike into my spokes.

"Listen, man, I've already been checking out *Mister Privacy Fence* with Uncle Herb," I said.

"What'd you find out?"

"Uncle Herb knows everything that goes on around town."

"That's a newspaper guy's job."

"Right. Besides, we've got every right to check him out for ourselves. It's practically the law."

"What law is that?" Charlie asked.

"Dummkopf, it's the law that says this is our turf. Anybody new who moves in on it we get to check out. It's a matter of respect and common sense. Just ask any of the old guys."

"I never thought about it like that, but I guess you're right."

"There's something else that's fishy about Schumann too," I said.

"What's that?"

"Schumann claims he grew up for most of his life right here in town."

"I never heard of no Schumann family around here before."

"Me neither. And think about it, that handlebar mustache of his?" I added. "Don't tell me that doesn't look a bit on the suspicious side."

"That scar on his face is a dead giveaway that he's no good. That thing has to be four inches long."

"It runs from his left ear right across his cheek. I'll betcha ten to one that it's closer to six inches. And how about that gold wristwatch he wears?" I implored. "It must weigh a ton. Plus he wears rings on three fingers and he's not even married."

"I tell you the thing that spooks me the most," said Charlie. "He always wears sunglasses, even when he's in the shade."

"How about the weird way he pulls a hanky from his pocket to wipe the ore dust off his boots? I never saw anybody else do that."

Our tongues burned hot with every rumor that passed through town with good reason. We had the two primo sources of gossip at our fingertips. The first was Ora Mae's Smiley's Nursing Home for Women and the second was the old men who idled away their days in the corner of town square known as Veterans Park.

READ HEARTLAND HEROES ON AMAZON NOW

Coming soon from Mark Reps, author of the ZEB HANKS series - THE GREATEST BASEBALL GAME EVER PLAYED...The time is 1939. The place is a baseball field on the top of the nearly completed Mount Rushmore monument. The game is the greatest one ever played.

Made in the USA
Middletown, DE
31 August 2024

60125362R00234